IN MEMORIAM

'*In Memoriam* is the story of a great tragedy, but it is also
a moving portrait of young love, and there is often a lightness
to the book, even humour. It's a difficult balancing act, but one
that Winn, who is erudite, fast talking and very funny, pulls off . . .
Winn was twenty-six years old when she began it, but *In
Memoriam* doesn't read like its author was still finding
her footing as a writer' *The New York Times*

'Alice Winn's devastating debut will smash your heart to
smithereens . . . as thousands of young men die in the most
horrific of ways, Gaunt and Ellwood attempt to survive
the slaughter and keep their love alive' *Daily Mail*

'First love, class, male camaraderie and the horrors of the
war are all explored in this quietly heartbreaking epic with
the unforgettable appeal of *Birdsong*' *Good Housekeeping*

'*In Memoriam* is both brutal and beautiful; the kind of
rich and atmospheric and devastating story that you
spend days recovering from. Anyone who loved
Sebastian Faulks' *Birdsong* or Ian McEwan's *Atonement* as
much as I did needs to read this book' Anna Bonet

'Winn's accomplished debut presents two indelible
characters – athletic Henry Gaunt and lyrical Sidney Ellwood,
English boarding school chums who both believe their love for
each other is unrequited. Whether they're posturing schoolboys
on the cusp of the First World War or enduring the visceral
shock and horrifying randomness of death in the trenches,
Gaunt and Ellwood are unceasingly drawn to each other,
each afraid to risk following his heart until it may
be too late' *Washington Post*

'Stunning . . . brutal and unflinching but also beautiful.
A triumph' Karen Angelico

'Winn offers a fresh look at a subject many of us believe
we know well. A tender story as much about love as it is
about war' Rowan Hisayo Buchanan

'A searing and harrowing novel about the love story
between two young men played out against a backdrop of
the horrors of the First World War. The writing was so
visceral and intense, I honestly felt as if I was in the
trenches with them, and I'm still thinking about the
book weeks after reading it. An incredible
debut' Nikki Smith

'*In Memoriam* is magnificent – dazzling and wrenching,
witty and wildly romantic, with echoes of *Brideshead
Revisited* and *Atonement*. I loved it' Lev Grossman,
author of *The Magicians*

'Extraordinary. A truly epic tale of love unspoken,
love shared and love lost. An instant and
unforgettable classic' A.J. West

'An astonishingly confident and impressive debut, this
love story set in the First World War is shocking,
brutal and memorable. It left me shaken – and
very impressed' Lucy Atkins

'Winn's superb debut chronicles a romance between
two English boarding school classmates during the First
World War . . . both men grapple with the realities of war,
which Winn vividly renders with descriptions of the wounded . . .
Amid the chaos, Winn stages excellent action scenes: a tense
scouting mission, as well as a tunnel-digging episode
involving an escape from a German prisoner-of-war camp.
The hunger the men feel, as well as their shell shock,
is palpable, but it is the men's love for each other
that resonates. This is a remarkable
achievement' *Publishers Weekly*

IN MEMORIAM

Alice Winn

PENGUIN BOOKS

PENGUIN BOOKS

UK | USA | Canada | Ireland | Australia
India | New Zealand | South Africa

Penguin Books is part of the Penguin Random House group of companies
whose addresses can be found at global.penguinrandomhouse.com.

Penguin
Random House
UK

First published in the United States of America by Alfred
A. Knopf, a division of Penguin Random House LLC 2023
First published in Great Britian by Viking 2023
Published in Penguin Books 2024

004

Printed and bound in Great Britain by Clays Ltd, Elcograf S.p.A.

The authorized representative in the EEA is Penguin Random House Ireland,
Morrison Chambers, 32 Nassau Street, Dublin D02 YH68

A CIP catalogue record for this book is available from the British Library

ISBN: 978-0-241-56783-8

www.greenpenguin.co.uk

To my parents

IN MEMORIAM

THE PRESHUTIAN

VOL. XLIX.—No. 739.   JUNE 27TH, 1914.   Price 3d.

Editorial.

O Jove! Save the editor from the editorial! But term has ended, and a marvellous one at that, so conclusions must be drawn for the hungry readers of the humble PRESHUTIAN. Another splendid year has passed, and those grand Upper Sixth men now leave us for the glories of Oxford, Cambridge and Sandhurst! We cherish a hope that they will remember us poor schoolboys from time to time, as they bounce from lectures to revels. May our futures be as bright as theirs!

—S. CUTHBERT-SMITH

Notes on News.

The Bishop of London preached on Sunday, June 14th.

"Would the person practising Bach's *Well-Tempered Clavier* six times a day on the piano near the Old Reading Room kindly learn a new piece? Sincerely, *A Musically Frustrated Gentleman.*"

The three audience members at the junior boys' performance of Aristophanes' lesser-known plays report the experience was "exactly what Aristophanes would have hoped for."

The debate next term will be "This House declines to believe in the existence of ghosts." Contact H. Weeding if willing to argue in favour of the occult.

Debating Society.

ON Monday, June 22nd, the Society met to discuss the motion that: "In the opinion of the House, war is a necessary evil."

Mr Ellwood proposed. After a few insolent remarks regarding the opposition's brass tie pin, he gave a rather colourful if inaccurate history of the Punic Wars. Mr Gaunt, arguing (in a most cowardly fashion) *("Can I keep that in?"—Author. "Only if you don't mind Gaunt's almost certainly violent revenge. He is a prize boxer, although a beastly pacifist."—Editor.)* against the motion, suggested that war destroys the soul. Those listeners who have fought Mr Gaunt in the ring were inclined to mutter mutinously, "What soul?" This in no way *(cont. pg. 5)*

Poetry.

EVENING AT PRESHUTE COLLEGE

The sky grows cold, and in the
  troubled west,
The sun sinks sleepily towards
  other worlds.
The dark of night soothes the
  troubled breast:
From Heaven have the Clouds of
  Dreams unfurled.

The Chapel's steeple stabs into the
  sky—

"It's too long again, Ellwood."—Editor.
"It's barely three stanzas!"—Author.
"That's too long, Ellwood."—Editor.

The London Gazette

Of TUESDAY, the 4th of AUGUST, 1914.

𝕻𝖚𝖇𝖑𝖎𝖘𝖍𝖊𝖉 𝖇𝖞 𝕬𝖚𝖙𝖍𝖔𝖗𝖎𝖙𝖞.

WEDNESDAY, 5 AUGUST, 1914.

A STATE OF WAR.

His Majesty's Government informed the German Government on August 4th, 1914, that, unless a satisfactory reply to the request of His Majesty's Government for an assurance that Germany would respect the neutrality of Belgium was received by midnight of that day, His Majesty's Government would feel bound to take all steps in their power to uphold that neutrality and the observance of a treaty to which Germany was as much a party as Great Britain.

The result of this communication having been that His Majesty's Ambassador at Berlin had to ask for his passports, His Majesty's Government have accordingly formally notified the German Government that a state of war exists between the two countries, as from 11 p.m. to-day.

Foreign Office,
August 4th, 1914.

THE PRESHUTIAN

VOL. XLIX.—No. 741.   OCTOBER 17TH, 1914.   Price 6d.

KILLED IN ACTION.

Beazley, Sec.-Lieut. L. S. W., Wiltshire Regt., Sept. 20th, aged 22.

Hickman, Lieut. M. E., Worcestershire Regt., aged 20.

Milling, Lieut. L., Gordon Highlanders, aged 23.

Roseveare, Sec.- Lieut. C. C., Royal Munster Fusiliers, Mons, August 27th, aged 22.

Scott-Moncrieff, Capt. M. M., King's (Liverpool) Regiment, Sept. 20th, aged 25.

Straker, Sec.- Lieut. H. A., Royal Munster Fusiliers, Mons, August 27th, aged 18.

DIED OF WOUNDS.

Conlon, Lieut. G. T., West Yorkshire Regt., aged 21.

Cuthbert-Smith, Lieut. S., Northumberland Fusiliers, Mons, August 24th, aged 18.

Hill, Lieut. A., 19th Lancers, Indian Army, aged 19.

WOUNDED.

Day, Lieut. H. J., Middlesex Regt.

Hattersley, Major F. K., Royal Field Artillery.

Le Hunte, Lieut. R. Royal Scots.

Matterson, Sec.-Lieut. A. R., Bedfordshire Regt.

Parsonage, Sec.-Lieut. D. K., Somerset Light Infantry.

In Memoriam.

Lieutenant S. Cuthbert-Smith

(Killed at Mons, August 24th, aged 18.)

Anyone reading THE PRESHUTIAN in the past two years will remember Cuthbert-Smith as the facetious editor of that publication. He had won a scholarship to Balliol College, Oxford, where he would have studied Classics. But Cuthbert-Smith could never have been a scholar. There was too much of the soldier in him. The following description of his death was written by his commanding officer:—"In a wild push to capture a German machine gun, Cuthbert-Smith was shot in the stomach. Due to enemy fire, we were unable to remove him to a local cave that was in use as a hospital until 5 a.m. the next morning. Brave chap only asked for a bit of morphia so that he wouldn't disturb the others. He died quite painlessly and weren't we sad to lose such a gallant fellow! It was a true soldier's death." We at Preshute can only regret his loss and envy his noble death, which any one of us would gladly suffer for our country.

S. A. Ward

Second Lieutenant C. C. Roseveare

(Killed at Mons, August 27th, aged 22.)

Preshute has suffered many blows since the outbreak of war, but none hit us harder than the death of Clarence Roseveare. He leaves behind two brothers in the Sixth Form, including our illustrious Head Boy. Clarence himself was Head Boy. But his death, like his life, was honourable and manly, coming close to touching perfection in its English gallantry.

Extract from a letter from his Commanding Officer:— "He came past me with a very cheerful face, and laughing, under a very hearty cross-fire from machine guns, and sang out to me, 'Shall I push on?' and I answered, 'Go on, laddie, as hard as you can.' Poor lad, he was shot through the heart shortly after. I placed him in a trench, hoping that the wound would not be fatal. The only words to me were, 'Don't mind me.' When I *(cont. pg. 3)*

I

ONE

ELLWOOD WAS A PREFECT, so his room that year was a splendid one, with a window that opened onto a strange outcrop of
roof. He was always scrambling around places he shouldn't. It
was Gaunt, however, who truly loved the roof perch. He liked watching boys dipping in and out of Fletcher Hall to pilfer biscuits, prefects
swanning across the grass in Court, the organ master coming out of
Chapel. It soothed him to see the school functioning without him, and
to know that he was above it.

Ellwood also liked to sit on the roof. He fashioned his hands into
guns and shot at the passers-by.

"Bloody Fritz! Got him in the eye! Take *that* home to the Kaiser!"

Gaunt, who had grown up summering in Munich, did not tend to
join in these soldier games.

Balancing *The Preshutian* on his knee as he turned the page, Gaunt
finished reading the last "In Memoriam." He had known seven of the
nine boys killed. The longest "In Memoriam" was for Clarence Roseveare, the older brother of one of Ellwood's friends. As to Gaunt's own
friend—and enemy—Cuthbert-Smith, a measly paragraph had suf-
ficed to sum him up. Both boys, *The Preshutian* assured him, had died
gallant deaths. Just like every other Preshute student who had been
killed so far in the War.

"Pow!" muttered Ellwood beside him. *"Auf Wiedersehen!"*

Gaunt took a long drag of his cigarette and folded up the paper.

"They've got rather more to say about Roseveare than about Cuthbert-Smith, haven't they?"

Ellwood's guns turned back to hands. Nimble, long-fingered, ink-stained.

"Yes," he said, patting his hair absentmindedly. It was dark and unruly. He kept it slicked back with wax, but lived in fear of a stray curl coming unfixed and drawing the wrong kind of attention to himself. "Yes, I thought that was a shame."

"Shot in the stomach!" Gaunt's hand went automatically to his own. He imagined it opened up by a streaking piece of metal. *Messy.*

"Roseveare's cut up about his brother," said Ellwood. "They were awfully close, the three Roseveare boys."

"He seemed all right in the dining hall."

"He's not one to make a fuss," said Ellwood, frowning. He took Gaunt's cigarette, scrupulously avoiding touching Gaunt's hand as he did so. Despite Ellwood's tactile relationship with his other friends, he rarely laid a finger on Gaunt unless they were play-fighting. Gaunt would have died rather than let Ellwood know how it bothered him.

Ellwood took a drag and handed the cigarette back to Gaunt.

"I wonder what my 'In Memoriam' would say," he mused.

" 'Vain boy dies in freak umbrella mishap. Investigations pending.' "

"No," said Ellwood. "No, I think something more like 'English literature today has lost its brightest star . . . !' " He grinned at Gaunt, but Gaunt did not smile back. He still had his hand on his stomach, as if his guts would spill out like Cuthbert-Smith's if he moved it. He saw Ellwood take this in.

"I'd write yours, you know," said Ellwood, quietly.

"All in verse, I suppose."

"Of course. As Tennyson did, for Arthur Hallam."

Ellwood frequently compared himself to Tennyson and Gaunt to Tennyson's closest friend. Mostly, Gaunt found it charming, except when he remembered that Arthur Hallam had died at the age of twenty-two and Tennyson had spent the next seventeen years writing grief poetry. Then Gaunt found it all a bit morbid, as if Ellwood *wanted* him to die, so that he would have something to write about.

Gaunt had kneed Cuthbert-Smith in the stomach, once. How different did a bullet feel from a blow?

"Your sister thought Cuthbert-Smith was rather good-looking," said Ellwood. "She told me at Lady Asquith's, last summer."

"Did she?" asked Gaunt, unenthusiastically. "Awfully nice of her to confide in you like that."

"Maud's A1," said Ellwood, standing abruptly. "Capital sort of girl." A bit of slate crumbled under his feet and fell to the ground, three stories below.

"Christ, Elly, don't do that!" said Gaunt, clutching the window ledge. Ellwood grinned and clambered back into the bedroom.

"Come on in, it's wet out there," he said.

Gaunt hurriedly took another breath of smoke and dropped his cigarette down a drainpipe. Ellwood was splayed out on the sofa, but when Gaunt sat on his legs, he curled them hastily out of the way.

"You loathed Cuthbert-Smith," said Ellwood.

"Yes. Well. I shall miss loathing him."

Ellwood laughed.

"You'll find someone new to hate. You always do."

"Undoubtedly," said Gaunt. But that wasn't the point. He had written nasty poems about Cuthbert-Smith, and Cuthbert-Smith (Gaunt was almost certain it was him) had scrawled, "Henry Gaunt is a German SPY" on the wall of the library cloakroom. Gaunt had punched him for that, but he would never have shot him in the stomach.

"I think I believe he'll be back next term, smug and full of tall tales from the front," said Ellwood, slowly.

"Maybe none of them will come back."

"That sort of defeatist attitude will lose us the War." Ellwood cocked his head. "Henry. Old Cuthbert-Smith was an idiot. He probably walked straight into a bullet for a lark. That's not what it will be like when we go."

"I'm not signing up."

Ellwood wrapped his arms around his knees, staring at Gaunt.

"Rot," he said.

"I'm not against all war," said Gaunt. "I'm just against *this* war. 'German militarism'—as if we didn't hold our empire through military might! Why should I get shot at because some Austrian archduke was killed by an angry Serb?"

"But Belgium—"

"Yes, yes, Belgian atrocities," said Gaunt. They had discussed all this before. They had even debated it, and Ellwood had beaten him, 596 votes to 4. Ellwood would have won any debate: the school loved him.

"But you have to enlist," said Ellwood. "If the War is even still on when we finish school."

"Why? Because you will?"

Ellwood clenched his jaw and looked away.

"You will fight, Gaunt," he said.

"Oh, yes?"

"You always fight. Everyone." Ellwood rubbed a small flat spot on his nose with one finger. He often did that. Gaunt wondered if Ellwood resented that he had punched it there. They had only fought once. It hadn't been Gaunt who started it.

"I don't fight you," he said.

"Γνῶθι σεαυτόν," said Ellwood.

"I *do* know myself!" said Gaunt, lunging at Ellwood to smother him with a pillow, and for a moment neither of them could talk, because Ellwood was squirming and shrieking with laughter while Gaunt tried to wrestle him off the sofa. Gaunt was strong, but Ellwood was quicker, and he slipped through Gaunt's arms and fell to the floor, helpless with laughter. Gaunt hung his head over the side, and they pressed their foreheads together.

"Fighting like this, you mean?" said Gaunt, when they had got their breath back. "*Wrestle* the Germans to death?"

Ellwood stopped laughing, but he didn't move his forehead. They were still for a moment, hard skull against hard skull, until Ellwood pulled away and leant his face into Gaunt's arm.

All of Gaunt's muscles tensed at the movement. Ellwood's breath was hot. It reminded Gaunt of his dog back home, Trooper. Perhaps that was why he ruffled Ellwood's hair, his fingers searching for strands the wax had missed. He hadn't stroked Ellwood's hair in years, not since they were thirteen-year-olds in their first year at Preshute and he would find Ellwood huddled in a heap of tears under his desk.

But they were in Upper Sixth now, their final year, and almost never touched each other.

Ellwood was very still.

"You're like my dog," said Gaunt, because the silence was heavy with something.

Ellwood tugged away.

"*Thanks.*"

"It's a good thing. I'm very fond of dogs."

"Right. Anything you'd like me to fetch? I'm starting to get the hang of newspapers, although my teeth still leave marks."

"Don't be daft."

Ellwood laughed a little unhappily.

"I'm sad about Roseveare and Cuthbert-Smith too, you know," he said.

"Oh, yes," said Gaunt. "And Straker. Remember how you two used to tie the younger boys to chairs and beat them all night?"

It had been years since Ellwood bullied anyone, but Gaunt knew he was still ashamed of the vein of ungovernable violence that burnt through him. Just last term, Gaunt had seen him cry tears of rage when he lost a cricket match. Gaunt hadn't cried since he was nine.

"Straker and I were much less rotten than the boys in the year above were to *us*," said Ellwood, his face red. "Charlie Pritchard shot us with *rifle blanks*."

Gaunt smirked, conscious that he was taunting Ellwood because he felt he had embarrassed himself by touching his hair. It was the sort of thing Ellwood did to other boys all the time, he reasoned with himself. *Yes,* a voice answered. *But never to <u>him</u>.*

"I wasn't close with Straker, anyway," said Ellwood. "He was a brute."

"All your friends are brutes, Ellwood."

"I'm tired of all this." Ellwood stood. "Let's go for a walk."

They were forbidden to leave their rooms during prep, so they had to slip quietly out of Cemetery House. They crept down the back stairs, past the study where their housemaster, Mr. Hammick, was berating a Shell boy for sneaking. (Preshute was a younger public school, and eagerly used the terminology of older, more prestigious institutions: Shell for first year, Remove for second, Hundreds for third, followed by Lower and Upper Sixth.)

"It is a low and dishonourable thing, Gosset. Do you wish to be low and dishonourable?"

"No, sir," whimpered the unfortunate Gosset.

"Poor chap," said Ellwood when they had shut the back door behind them. They walked down the gravel path into the graveyard that gave Cemetery House its name. "The Shell have been perfectly beastly to him, just because he told them all on his first day that he was a duke."

"Is he?" asked Gaunt, skimming the tops of tombstones with his fingertips as he walked.

"Yes, he is, but that's the sort of thing one ought to let people *discover*. It's rather like me introducing myself by saying, 'Hello, I'm Sidney Ellwood, I'm devastatingly attractive.' It's not for *me* to say."

"If you're waiting for me to confirm your vanity—"

"I wouldn't dream of it," said Ellwood with a cheery little skip. "I haven't had a compliment from you in about three months. I know, because I always write them down and put them in a drawer."

"Peacock."

"Well, the point is, Gosset has been thoroughly sat on by the rest of his form, and I feel awfully sorry for him."

They were coming to the crumbling Old Priory at the bottom of the graveyard. It was getting colder and wetter as night fell. The sky darkened to navy blue, and in the wind their tailcoats billowed. Gaunt hugged his arms around himself. There was something expectant about winter evenings at Preshute. It was the contrast, perhaps, between the hulking hills behind the school, the black forest, the windswept meadows, all so silent—and the crackling loudness of the boys when you returned to House. Walking through the empty fields, they might have been the only people left alive. Ellwood lived in a grand country estate in East Sussex, but Gaunt had grown up in London. Silence was distinctly magical.

"Listen," said Ellwood, closing his eyes and tilting up his face. "Can't you just imagine the Romans thrashing the Celts if you're quiet?"

They stopped.

Gaunt couldn't imagine anything through the silence.

"Do you believe in magic?" he asked. Ellwood paused for a while, so long that if he had been anyone else, Gaunt might have repeated the question.

"I believe in beauty," said Ellwood, finally.

"Yes," said Gaunt, fervently. "Me too." He wondered what it was like to be someone like Ellwood, who contributed to the beauty of a place, rather than blighting it.

"It's a form of magic, all this," said Ellwood, walking on. "Cricket and hunting and ices on the lawn on summer afternoons. England is magic."

Gaunt had a feeling he knew what Ellwood was going to say next.

"That's why we've got to fight for it."

Ellwood's England *was* magical, thought Gaunt, picking his way around nettles. But it wasn't England. Gaunt had been to the East End once, when his mother took him to give soup and bread to Irish weavers. There had been no cricket or hunting or ices, there. But Ellwood had never been interested in ugliness, whereas Gaunt—because of Maud, perhaps, because she read Bernard Shaw and Bertrand Russell and wrote mad things about the colonies in her letters—feared that ugliness was too important to ignore.

"Do you remember the Peloponnesian War?" said Gaunt.

Ellwood let out a breathy laugh. "Honestly, Gaunt, I don't know why I bother with you. We skipped prep so that we *wouldn't* have to think about Thucydides."

"Athens was the greatest power in Europe, perhaps even the world. They had democracy, art, splendid architecture. But Sparta was almost as powerful. Not quite, but close enough. And Sparta was militaristic."

"Is this a parable, Gaunt? Are you Christ?"

"And so the Athenians fought the Spartans."

"And they lost," said Ellwood, kicking at a rotting log.

"Yes."

Ellwood didn't answer for a long time.

"We won't lose," he said, finally. "We're the greatest empire that's ever been."

———

They were in Hundreds the first time they got drunk together. Gaunt was sixteen and Ellwood fifteen. Pritchard had somehow—"at *great* personal cost," he told them darkly—convinced his older brother to give him five bottles of cheap whisky. They locked themselves in the bathroom at the top of Cemetery House: Pritchard, West, Roseveare,

Ellwood, and Gaunt. Ellwood, Gaunt later discovered, had insisted on buying his bottle off Pritchard. Ellwood had a morbid fear of being perceived as miserly.

West spat his first mouthful of whisky into the sink. He was a big-eared, clumsy, disastrous sort of person: stupid at lessons, average at games, a cheerful failure.

"Christ alive! That's abominable stuff," he said. His tie was crooked. It always was, no matter how many times he was punished for sloppiness.

"Keep drinking," advised Roseveare, from his lazy position on the floor. Gaunt glanced at him and noticed with some irritation that, even dishevelled, he was immaculate. He was the youngest of three perfect Roseveare boys, each more exemplary than the last, and he was good-looking in a careless, gilded way that Gaunt resented.

"I quite like it," said Ellwood, turning his bottle to look at the label. "Perhaps I shall develop a *habit*. I think Byron had a *habit*."

"So do monks," said Gaunt.

"That was nearly funny, Gaunt," said Roseveare encouragingly. "You'll get there."

Gaunt took a swig of whisky. He didn't much like the taste, but it made him feel light, as if people weren't looking at him. Or, perhaps, it made him feel as if he shouldn't mind it if they did. He climbed into the bathtub and sank out of sight, clutching the bottle to his chest.

"Lord Byron was a sodomite," said West, with the air of someone imparting an important state secret.

Gaunt closed his eyes.

"My father told me," West continued. "Said he ought to have been shot."

"Your father thinks everyone ought to be shot," said Roseveare.

"Not everyone," protested West.

"Well, let's see," said Pritchard, counting on his fingers. He was on the cistern, his knees bracketing West, who sat on the toilet lid. "There are the homosexuals, the Catholics, the Irish, and anyone who doesn't like dogs."

Pritchard was a forgettable-looking person, and people *did* tend to forget him, because Charlie Pritchard was an athlete and Archie Pritchard was a scholar, whereas Bertie Pritchard—commonly known by the older boys as "Mini," which he hated—didn't know yet what he was good for. Nothing much, as far as Gaunt could see. But Ellwood liked him.

"You've forgotten the poor," said Ellwood, climbing into the bath with Gaunt. "The Great Unwashed." He settled himself between Gaunt's legs and sat facing him.

"Oh, and the Jews, of course," said Pritchard. "Can't leave them out. Bad luck, Ellwood."

"I'm Church of England," said Ellwood mildly.

"What do you say, West?" asked Pritchard. "Does conversion cut it with the Squire?"

"Look—" said West.

"Are you circumcised, Ellwood?" asked Pritchard.

Ellwood smiled easily, as if he weren't the least disturbed by the question of his Jewishness.

"Shall we have West's father check?" he asked.

He wasn't circumcised. Gaunt knew, had noticed before, in the showers. He stayed silent.

"He isn't," said Roseveare. "Not that it will matter, West's father is very definite. 'Fraid it's death for poor old Ellwood."

"Now—" said West.

"Alas," interrupted Ellwood, stretching back in the tub with a sad smile. "And there was so much I wanted to do! Still—what's that Euripides quotation I'm thinking of, Gaunt—about death?"

"Πᾶσιν ἡμῖν κατθανεῖν ὀφείλεται," said Gaunt.

"That's right. 'Death is a debt which every one of us must pay.' If I'm to die tragically young, I suppose it may as well be for West's father."

"All right, all right," said West. "I never said I *agreed* with him." He rested his chin on Pritchard's knee so that he could better see Ellwood in the bath.

"No, really, don't let me dissuade you," said Ellwood. "A bit of bloodletting is just what this country needs. I'm with your father. Slaughter everyone, why not?"

"Stop winding up poor West; he hasn't the brains for it," said Pritchard, in a lofty tone that suggested *Pritchard* was a known sage.

"I have plenty of brains!" protested West.

"By the way, Pritchard," said Ellwood, "just what did you have to do for your brother to procure us such excellent drink?"

"It's unspeakable," said Pritchard, shaking his head. "Suffice to say, you all owe me some tuck."

"Pritchard Major made him lick his shoes in front of the Upper Sixth," said West. Pritchard twisted his hair. "Ouch! Lay off!"

"I told you that in *confidence*!"

"Did you really lick his shoes? Which ones?" asked Ellwood.

"What do you mean, *which ones*? Why should that make a difference?"

"No, that's fair," said West. "I wouldn't mind nibbling on a shoelace if it was from someone's Sunday best."

"It's important to have standards," agreed Roseveare.

"Right. Give me back my whisky. I shall find more grateful recipients."

Ellwood pressed his leg against Gaunt's and grinned as Pritchard tried to wrestle West's bottle from him. Gaunt leant his cheek against the cool porcelain and smiled back.

Two hours later, Gaunt was still only tipsy, but Ellwood was absolutely sozzled. He turned around in the bathtub and leant his back against Gaunt's chest, one hand resting on Gaunt's thigh, the other clutching the bottle. Gaunt's entire brain focused on the heat of Ellwood's back against his chest, the graceful, haphazard hand on his thigh.

Gaunt shifted his groin minutely back. A protective measure.

"I had a second cousin on the *Titanic*," Roseveare was saying. It was 1913, and the *Titanic* was the subject of frequent and fascinated discussion. Roseveare and Pritchard lay on the floor. West had inelegantly wedged himself into the sink and was whistling "The Blue Danube." He had been whistling it for forty-five minutes.

Ellwood's head lolled back onto Gaunt's shoulder.

"What?" asked Gaunt.

"What do you mean, 'What'?"

"You just went all cloudy and glum."

Ellwood hesitated before speaking.

"It's Maitland," he said, in a low voice. "You know he's leaving at the end of the year."

Gaunt was glad Ellwood couldn't see his face, because he couldn't make up his mind as to what to do with it.

All the way through Shell and Remove, Ellwood was continually summoned to John Maitland's study "to discuss the lower-school teams." Maitland played outside right on the football First XI, and accordingly was worshipped by the whole school, from the loftiest master to the lowliest new boy. He could do as he pleased. Not that anyone would ever have said so explicitly—what boys did together in the dark was only acceptable if obscure. It was unspoken, invisible and, crucially: temporary. There was no doubt in Gaunt's mind that both Maitland and Ellwood would cast aside their immaturity and marry respectable young women when they left Oxford or Cambridge.

But for now, they were *particular friends.*

"I'm very fond of him," said Ellwood.

Pritchard and Roseveare were still discussing the *Titanic.*

"I should be ashamed to survive something like that," said Pritchard.

"It does seem unmanly," said Roseveare.

"Just . . ." continued Ellwood, ". . . not the way I'm fond of . . ." He trailed off.

"My sister?" offered Gaunt. Ellwood laughed rather unpleasantly.

"Yes, Gaunt, your sister," he said.

Roseveare sat up abruptly and peered at them in the tub.

"You two look awfully cosy."

Gaunt tried to push Ellwood off him, but Ellwood wouldn't budge.

"Don't embarrass him, Roseveare, or he won't be my cushion any more," he said.

Roseveare laughed.

"Only *you* would dare use Gaunt as a cushion."

"What's that supposed to mean?" asked Gaunt, automatically balling his hands into fists.

"Only that you'd punch the living daylights out of anyone else who tried it," said Roseveare.

"I'll punch *you* if you don't stop sticking your nose where it's not wanted," said Gaunt.

Ellwood hushed him, laughing a little, and Gaunt unclenched his hands.

"What are you two discussing, anyway?" asked Roseveare.

"Girls," said Ellwood.

"Hmm. Carry on," said Roseveare, dropping back to his elbows.

"Say you were on a sinking ship," said Pritchard, as if Roseveare had never left. "Wouldn't you rather drown than live, knowing you'd been a slimy little coward?"

"Oh, certainly," said Roseveare. "Anyone would."

"I wonder how the girls were, as the ship went down," said Pritchard.

"Quite desperate for comfort, I expect," said Roseveare. Pritchard gave a lecherous sort of laugh.

Gaunt leant into Ellwood's ear until his lips almost touched it, so that no one could hear him.

"I'm sure Maitland feels the same way," he said. "You're just passing the time until you can marry Maud, aren't you?"

Ellwood sighed. "Yes, I suppose so." He pressed his forehead into Gaunt's neck. Gaunt gripped the edges of the tub. "I'm sorry, I know it makes you uncomfortable when I talk about him."

It *did*. From everything Ellwood told Gaunt about Maitland, and from what Gaunt could see for himself, Maitland was only a step removed from a Renaissance prince. He was handsome and talented and brilliant, and yet Ellwood didn't want him. If *Maitland* wasn't capable of keeping Ellwood's affections . . . !

Ellwood gave easily of himself, always had, but to Gaunt it had never seemed like a true sign of his feelings. Ellwood just liked being loved.

"It doesn't make me uncomfortable," said Gaunt, uncomfortably.

"Yes, it does. I can feel how tense you've gone now," said Ellwood. He put one hand on Gaunt's neck. "Like you're waiting for me to hit you."

"I don't mind you making me uncomfortable, Elly," said Gaunt softly. Ellwood turned his head on Gaunt's shoulder to look at him. His lids were heavy with alcohol, but the irises were just the same as always. Luminously brown. Gaunt was struck by a drunk—or stupid—or brave impulse to tilt his face forward.

He didn't.

Ellwood's fingers curled on Gaunt's thigh, sending excruciating tingles up his leg. There were only a few inches of electric air between them. Gaunt was glad he had thought to edge himself away already. It would have been disastrous for Ellwood to feel what that curl of his fingers had done to him.

"I just want . . ." said Gaunt. Ellwood closed his eyes. ". . . to be your friend."

Ellwood turned his head forward.

"I've had too much to drink," he said.

"Bed?" asked Gaunt.

Ellwood gave a dry huff of laughter.

"Propositioning me, Gaunt?"

Gaunt felt himself flush.

"Obviously not," he said.

"Obviously not," repeated Ellwood. He climbed carefully out of the bath, nearly stepping on Pritchard in the process. "Cheero, boys, I've an appointment with some sleep I've been meaning to catch."

———

Gaunt's eighteenth birthday was in December of 1914, four months after war was declared. The boys crowded into his dorm, led by Ellwood, and wrapped him up in his blankets. They carried him, bundled up, into the high-ceilinged front hall, and then, grabbing the edges of the blanket, threw him high into the air eighteen times.

"And one for luck!" cried Ellwood, and Gaunt, grinning, tightened his dead-man, crossed-arm pose. The boys hoisted him low, shouted "Nineteen!" all at once, and threw him so high that he had to reach his hands out to stop himself hitting the ceiling.

Mr. Hammick smiled indulgently as they trooped back upstairs to the dormitories.

"Only a year till enlisting age, Gaunt!" he chirped. Gaunt flashed him an awkward smile.

"What do you keep under your nightclothes, Gaunto?" said West, wrapping an arm around him. "Felt like you were made of bricks."

"You really are a lumpy bastard," said Pritchard.

"Almost boxed his way into the floor above," said Roseveare.

"The next person who calls me lumpy is getting thumped," said Gaunt.

"Oooooh!" cried the boys in high, mocking voices.

"Happy birthday, old boy," said Ellwood quietly.

Gaunt's mother and sister arrived during lunch. He was telling Ellwood about an interesting passage he had found in Thucydides (Ellwood only pretended to hate lessons) when West flicked a forkful of peas at him. Or tried to—most of them hit Pritchard, who sighed and shook them from his hair with a look of martyred resignation.

"Sorry, sorry!" said West. "Isn't that your mother, Gaunt?"

Gaunt had not been expecting visitors. He was to have a school cake that evening, and he knew that Ellwood would give him a gift—that was quite enough for him. It was always strange to see parents in school, like spotting a fox in the city.

"Who's the girl? Have you been hiding away a sister?" asked West.

"A *twin* sister," said Ellwood, treacherously.

"She can't be your twin. She's pretty," said West. Gaunt knocked him lightly on the head and dashed out to Court, Ellwood following close behind.

"Henry!" said Maud, then, quieter, "Sidney."

Ellwood waited until Gaunt had hugged Maud to answer.

"Hallo, Maud," he said. "Have you shrunk?"

Maud laughed. Ellwood always made her laugh. When he came to stay in the holidays, he'd lounge in the garden, trying to provoke her into flirtation. He never succeeded—Maud wasn't the flirting type—but Gaunt could tell she liked it.

"He's very silly," she had said once, fondly.

"Do you think," said Gaunt, to whom this seemed a profound misinterpretation, like calling Napoleon *a bit of fun.*

"Of course, he doesn't care about anyone," said Maud, and Gaunt had been too devastated to answer. He never could, when she said things that were new and true and terrible.

"No, Sidney, I haven't shrunk," she said now. "You've grown, and you're hoping for a compliment."

"Won't you give me one?" asked Ellwood, with a grin. Maud laughed again and shook her head.

"Happy birthday, Heinrich," said Gaunt's mother. Several passing boys turned around at the sound of her German accent.

"Let's go inside, shall we?" said Gaunt. He didn't need to add fuel to the rumours that he was a German spy. It was bad enough that his middle name was Wilhelm.

"You're welcome to use my room," said Ellwood.

"Thanks," said Gaunt, who had intended to use Ellwood's room with or without Ellwood's permission.

He took his mother's arm. Maud and Ellwood walked ahead, not touching. Maud laughed at everything Ellwood said, and once, Ellwood did a self-satisfied little skip.

Ellwood walked them to Cemetery House, taking them through the grand front entrance that few boys ever used, and guided them to his room.

"How lovely," said Maud, looking at the paintings that Ellwood had bought in town.

"It's a capital room," said Ellwood. "I hate to think of someone else getting it next year. Do you like that painting, Maud? It's poorly done, but it made me think of the Battle of the Nile, so I had to buy it."

"I like it very much," said Maud. "I've always been fond of Nelson."

"Don't start Ellwood on Nelson," said Gaunt.

Ellwood threw himself against the wall, pressing his hands to an imaginary chest wound.

"Kiss, me, Hardy!" he cried.

"Don't laugh," Gaunt told Maud. "You'll only encourage him. Clear off, Elly, we don't want any entertainment."

"Oh, all right," said Ellwood. He bowed slightly to Gaunt's mother and smiled at Maud. "It was marvellous to see you both. Stay as long as you like, Henry; I'll be out for ages."

Gaunt nodded, and Ellwood left.

Gaunt's mother and sister settled down on the sofa, and Gaunt leant against the windowsill, facing them.

"How are you?"

His mother burst into tears. Gaunt fumbled in his suit pocket for a handkerchief and was very glad when Maud produced hers first. He had used his own to stem Pritchard's nosebleed that morning, after Master Larchmont threw a book at his face. (Pritchard had deserved it.)

He carried on pretending to search for his handkerchief until he heard the sounds of his mother's sobs slowing.

"Oh, Heinrich, it's dreadful, dreadful. . . . Your Uncle Leopold has been . . ." She was prevented from continuing by the onset of a fresh wave of sobs.

Gaunt examined his nails.

"Uncle Leopold has been accused of spying for the Germans," said Maud.

Gaunt looked up. Maud was watching him steadily, stroking Mother's back.

"*Has* he been spying for the Germans?" he asked, directing his question to Maud.

"Of course not!" said his mother, and Maud hushed her soothingly.

"Do stop crying, Mutter," said Gaunt. "It'll be all right."

"Father thinks it'll come to nothing, but there was a brick through the drawing-room window this morning," said Maud. "And half the servants have given their notice."

Gaunt's fingers itched for his cigarettes, but he wasn't going to insult his mother and sister by smoking in front of them.

"It'll pass," he said. "In three weeks no one will remember."

Maud looked at him disbelievingly, but his mother blew her nose and sat up.

"Your father's under scrutiny at the bank because of it. . . . You must enlist, Heinrich. If we have a son in the army, no one will dare say we are not patriotic."

Gaunt blinked, then regained control of his face.

"I'm not nineteen yet," he said, evenly.

"As if that matters! You're six foot two!"

"I'm going to Oxford to read Classics."

His mother stood. Gaunt straightened up away from the window.

"Do you want Maud to die an old maid?" she asked. Maud made a small, protesting sound from the sofa.

"The War will be over in a few months. By the time Maud is ready to marry, it will have been long forgotten."

"People never forget cowardice!" hissed his mother, so fiercely that Gaunt blinked again. He smiled.

"And you, Maud? Would you like me to die for your marriage prospects?"

Maud looked away from him. Guiltily, he thought.

They had been at a garden party together in London the day the War was announced. Several German aristocrats had hovered by the strawberries and cream.

"Have I a patriotic duty to stab one of them with my fork?" Ellwood had asked.

"*Don't*," Maud had said, furious, "don't be so *glib*, can't you see—"

She left before she could finish her sentence, and Ellwood whistled with a humorous look at Gaunt. But Gaunt hadn't found it funny.

"It's frightening to be hated," said Maud now.

Gaunt went back to the window. In Court, Ellwood was sitting on Roseveare's shoulders, Pritchard was sitting on West's, and they were attacking each other with long rulers held out like sabres on a cavalry charge.

> "*Theirs not to make reply,*
> *Theirs not to reason why,*
> *Theirs but to do and die.*
> *Into the valley of Death*
> *Rode the six hundred.*"

Like every English schoolboy, he knew Tennyson's "Charge of the Light Brigade" off by heart. Ellwood had a habit of reciting the whole poem in a sonorous voice when he was too tired to be interesting.

"It's a foolish war," said Gaunt.

"Father says it won't last long," said Maud. "It will probably be finished by the time you go to the front."

He wondered if she believed this. She read *The New Statesman*; he knew if it weren't for the atrocities in Belgium she might have been a conscientious objector.

"You must sign up before it's too late," said his mother. "If you enlist as the War is ending, people will say you did not intend to fight."

Gaunt balled his hands into fists and rattled them gently on the windowsill.

. . .

"I'd like to see *them* sign up!" ranted Gaunt, striding back and forth across Fox's Bridge. Ellwood sat cross-legged on the stone parapet.

"I would *die* if someone gave me a white feather," he said.

Gaunt had gone into town, planning on buying a nice new pair of boxing gloves with the crisp pound note he had in his pocket. He had stopped in front of the window of Wyndham & Bolt, and was deliberating on whether it might not be better to buy a smart hockey stick instead, when two young women approached him. They were elegant creatures, with new London hats. The prettier one spoke.

"Why aren't you at the front?" she asked.

Passers-by paused to hear his answer.

"I'm not nineteen."

The two women looked at each other.

"That's what they all say," said the less pretty woman, and she held out a white feather. Gaunt stared at it blankly.

"For a brave soldier," said the prettier woman, with a nasty laugh. Gaunt couldn't move. He was rooted to the ground, and his stomach was burning, his skin smarting with the derisive looks of the crowd around him. Seeing that he was not going to take it, the woman tucked the white feather into his buttonhole.

". . . a rotten shame," he heard someone mutter. "A strapping young lad like that . . . !"

"They should never have dared say that to you if they were men," said Ellwood. "You would have knocked their teeth out."

"I couldn't do a thing."

It was as if he had been turned into stone. He had been utterly paralysed by shame. It didn't matter that he thought the War would damage the empire, that he disagreed with it on principle. Faced with all those scornful, staring faces, he had wanted nothing more than to disappear. It was as if *he* was the enemy.

The brook flowed noisily beneath them, and they spoke over a cacophony of birdsong. It was difficult to imagine that in France, men were shooting machine guns at each other.

"I'm not a coward," he said. He had meant to sound forceful, but instead the words came out like a question.

Ellwood hopped down from the parapet.

"Henry."

Gaunt looked up, and Ellwood put a hand on his shoulder. He froze, instantly fighting the instinct to shrug away—but there was something grounding about being touched. He had felt so contagious in town. Ellwood's liquid brown eyes widened in surprise.

"Of course you aren't a coward."

"Perhaps I am," said Gaunt, with a small laugh. "It's only—Ernst and Otto."

Ellwood knew his Munich cousins. He had gone to visit in 1913. They had all got drunk together on monk-brewed beer and sung Bavarian songs. Gaunt sometimes wondered how much of his high-minded pacifism came from the simple fear of being ordered to kill his cousins. He imagined stabbing Ernst with a bayonet, lobbing a grenade at Otto.

"You're not afraid of dying, Henry. You're just opposed to killing. That isn't cowardice."

Gaunt nodded briskly. He had been drinking, and was having trouble focusing on anything but Ellwood's hand on his shoulder. They hadn't touched since the day Cuthbert-Smith died. Not that Gaunt kept track of these things.

He was having trouble tracking *anything*. He was only staring hungrily at Ellwood, noticing how his long black lashes fanned out slightly sideways, how the whites of his eyes were rather too white. Ellwood had the most absurd lips Gaunt had ever seen, a true cupid's bow, as if a woman had painted them on his face with lipstick.

Ellwood's other hand slowly, tentatively went to Gaunt's jaw. Gaunt resisted leaning into it, but his eyes fluttered shut.

"Henry," said Ellwood, so softly that Gaunt had to lean forward to hear him (that was why he leant forward: to hear him) and then Ellwood's nose was nudging his. Gaunt's lips were tingling. He couldn't seem to think. He tilted his mouth away from Ellwood's, and Ellwood pressed his lips against his cheekbone.

Gaunt wanted to scream. *The bridge should break in half under the weight of us,* he thought. *I'm cracking up.* He thought of the brick flying through the drawing-room window at home, of the words "Henry

Gaunt is a German SPY" still scrawled on the cloakroom wall, fresh as the markings on Cuthbert-Smith's grave. He thought of the way George Burgoyne spoke about Ellwood behind his back: "We all know what Ellwood gets up to when he calls boys in to look at the lower-school cricket teams. . . ."

Ellwood burnt through people. He didn't want them, once he'd had them.

He thought of Ellwood leaning against him, fully clothed in that empty bathtub.

"You're just passing the time until you can marry Maud, aren't you?"

"Yes, I suppose so."

The white feather was in his pocket, and Ellwood's hands were in his hair. He couldn't think. His skin was on fire, blazing with shame and something else, something he didn't want to recognise, and suddenly he couldn't stand it. He turned abruptly away from Ellwood and found his cigarette case.

Ellwood was flushed, bright-eyed.

"Everything all right?"

Gaunt nodded, sure that he had made an utter fool of himself.

"Cigarette?" he offered. His hands were trembling. Ellwood took one and leant forward so that Gaunt could light it. The match cast a flickering shadow on Ellwood's delicate face.

"Henry," he said, smoke tumbling out of his mouth in tendrils, "are you all right?"

"I'm fine."

"Yes, I know you're fine. But are you all right?"

"Christ, Ellwood, drop it already!" The words came out sharper and more scornful than he had intended. Ellwood tried to smile, but could not quite manage it. He drew his cigarette to his lips. Somehow it always looked very *French* when Ellwood smoked. It made Gaunt not want his own cigarette. He tossed it into the river and walked away. Ellwood raced to keep up.

"What's the hurry?"

Gaunt didn't answer.

"Listen, Henry—"

Gaunt stopped.

"Yes?" he said. Ellwood looked miserable. It felt good to make him look like that. Let *him* feel something for once. Gaunt was sick of feeling things.

"Did I . . ." Ellwood's eyes dropped away from Gaunt's burning look. "Did I offend?"

"Of course not," spat Gaunt.

"Wait for me," said Ellwood, because Gaunt was off again, striding past the pond full of bad-tempered swans.

"Look, I've got a lot of prep to do, all right?"

"Henry, I'm sorry, I shouldn't have done that."

In Munich, Gaunt had once pressed himself against Ellwood's leg and discovered that Ellwood was hard. Whatever Ellwood's usual standards, Gaunt knew that Ellwood was tempted, occasionally, by the ease of their friendship, by how convenient it would be to use each other. And perhaps Gaunt should have acted then—settled for a cold fumble in a Bavarian field, something to remember once they left school and put aside their abnormalities. He might have done it if he had thought Ellwood would have bothered remembering it. But Ellwood was never more callous than when speaking of boys he'd once seemed to love.

"Forget it," said Gaunt. "It doesn't matter."

"I didn't mean to insult you."

Gaunt stopped to look at Ellwood, who was chewing his mouth. He forced himself to smile. He was being irrational, and, more than that, he was being unkind.

"It was decent of you to try and cheer me up, Elly. I'm sorry I'm in such a rotten mood."

"Henry . . ."

"I need to be alone until I'm feeling less beastly, I think," said Gaunt, avoiding Ellwood's eyes. He was too drunk for them.

"All right," said Ellwood, unhappily.

Gaunt nodded at him and loped away, feeling Ellwood's gaze on the back of his head. He walked past the priory, through the graveyard, out the school gates, and into town.

It was late afternoon on a Saturday, but the Recruitment Office was still open. There was no one there but a uniformed man with a formidable Lord Kitchener moustache.

"I'd like to enlist," said Gaunt.

"Excellent! Just the sort of man we need! Schoolboy, are you? How old?"

What might he have done with an extra year? He and Ellwood wanted to walk the Canterbury Trail. They had planned the route already, the inns they would stay at, the places they would camp. A small tent that they would share.

"Nineteen," he said.

"Quite. If you sign right here, we'll get you sorted."

Gaunt did not hesitate before he signed, although he felt as if his name was being ripped from him. He was simmering with a restlessness like that he felt in the boxing ring; a determination to hurt and be hurt, an impulse towards disaster and destruction, and nothing else would have satisfied him. He would not be a pansy German pacifist. He could not help that he was German, and he could not seem to help whatever he felt when Ellwood pressed himself close.

But he could jolly well kill people.

TWO

GAUNT WAS LATE FOR SUPPER, which was eaten in House on Saturdays. Pritchard left a space next to him on the bench when he sat down.

"Where's Jaunty Gaunty?" he asked, grabbing Ellwood's bread roll.

"Give that back, you utter heathen."

Pritchard licked the roll and handed it back to Ellwood.

"I don't know, he's late," said Ellwood, carefully cutting off the part that Pritchard had licked.

West leant across the table, putting his elbow in the butter dish.

"Oh . . . ! Not again," he said, wiping disconsolately at his jacket with a dirty handkerchief.

"Late to supper?" asked Pritchard, dipping his own handkerchief in his water glass and passing it to West. "Our gluttonous giant? Is he sick?"

"Some girls in town gave him a white feather," said Ellwood. Pritchard and West exchanged glances.

"Poor beggar," said Pritchard.

"A white feather?" said Burgoyne loudly from down the table. As always when Burgoyne spoke, he sounded self-important and meddling.

"Shut up, Burgoyne," said Ellwood.

"It's about time someone gave Gaunt a feather. His opinions on the War are an absolute disgrace."

"Very brave of you to say all this, when he's not here to give you a bloody nose," said Pritchard.

"I'm not scared of that bully."

Trust Burgoyne to see Gaunt as a bully, thought Ellwood. Burgoyne was a spiteful snob, and Gaunt had taught him a lesson on more than one occasion.

"Is Burgoyne claiming we mistreat him again?" piped up Roseveare from another table. "Give it a rest, Georgie Porgie, or we'll show you some actual bullying."

Burgoyne looked outraged, and tried to respond, but West tipped his cup of tea into his lap.

"Ow! You've burnt me!" cried Burgoyne.

"Wet yourself, did you?" said Pritchard, looking concerned. "You'd better see the nurse, Georgie. This keeps happening."

"You're brutes, the lot of you," said Burgoyne, getting clumsily to his feet. "You're what's wrong with the public school system."

Ellwood leant his face into Pritchard's shoulder as they both convulsed with laughter.

"Oh, Lord!" said Pritchard, as Burgoyne stormed out of Hall. "He *does* take things seriously!"

"We ought to rip up his study again," said West. "I went in the other day to look for an Aeschylus crib sheet, and would you believe that he has several items of furniture *as yet unbroken*?"

"Ye gods! What an appalling state of affairs," said Ellwood.

"Poor fellow," said Pritchard, who was soft-hearted. "Let's leave him alone for a week. It's not his fault he's hopeless at games."

"It bloody well is," said West. "He doesn't even try!"

They ate their bread and butter and cocoa. Gaunt had still not appeared when Mr. Hammick stood.

"Boys, I had some excellent news this evening, which I know will make you all proud. Our very own Henry Gaunt has enlisted. He is to be an officer in the Royal Kennet Fusiliers, Third Battalion, and I can say with confidence that he will bring honour on Cemetery House!"

The room erupted into cheers.

"Good old Gaunt! What a dark horse!"

Mr. Hammick was grinning with pride.

"Why didn't you say something, Ellwood?" said West. "Fancy him signing up like that without telling anyone! What a hero."

"I didn't know," he said, smiling feebly. Pritchard cast him a sympathetic look.

"He probably wanted to surprise you."

"Yes," said Ellwood.

"He'll send you some A1 letters, I'll bet," said West.

"I wish *I* could join up," said Ellwood. "My mother made me promise I wouldn't until I finished school."

"Mine, too," said Pritchard. "Mothers just don't understand about war."

Ellwood's mouth was so dry that the last of his bread tasted like glue. He chewed in silence as Pritchard and West argued about the Royal Kennet Fusiliers.

"They were at Poitiers."

"Don't be absurd. They didn't have rifles in the Hundred Years' War."

"Yes, they did, towards the end!"

"No, they had *cannon,* they didn't have rifles."

"If you think I'm going to take your thick-headed word for it—"

"Listen, you dunce, the fusiliers can't possibly have been founded before the Renaissance, because the army was organised along feudal lines before that—"

"Right. That's it. We'll settle this like men. Meet you by the swans in ten minutes."

"The swans? Are you mad? They can break a man's arm!"

Of course Ellwood was proud of Gaunt. He recognised that bravery could only exist where there was fear, and so of all of them, only Gaunt was truly capable of heroism. Ellwood and the rest of the First XI were all so desperate to fight that there would be nothing courageous about their enlistment.

But he had always imagined them signing up together. Joining one of the public school regiments with all their friends, singing songs as they marched to war, gleaming rifles slung over their shoulders. Cavalry charges and sharp uniforms.

He longed to save Gaunt's life.

He rested his hand against his lips. Was that how Gaunt's skin had felt? No, it had been rougher. Years he had wanted to kiss those cheek-bones, and the moment had passed so quickly that he could scarcely believe it had happened.

He knew it was their hug on Fox's Bridge that had compelled Gaunt to enlist.

I should work for the Recruitment Office, he thought wryly. *The Amazing Pacifism Cure! One Embrace Will Send Conscientious Objectors Fleeing to the Front!*

He wasn't surprised. Gaunt always fled when their friendship threatened to tilt into something more complicated. It was an uncomfortable, unspoken thing between them. Ellwood was in love with Gaunt. Gaunt was thoroughly decent and conventional.

Never had this been clearer than after that unpleasantness with two older boys, Sandys and Caruthers. They were caught together. No one knew the details. No one asked. They disappeared onto the afternoon train with their trunks and night cases, never to be heard from again. They had committed the cardinal sin: they had been found out.

"You must be relieved," said Ellwood to Gaunt, although he wasn't at all sure about Gaunt's feelings. He never was.

Gaunt didn't look up from his Greek translation. A sweep of sandy hair had fallen into his eyes.

"Why?" he asked.

"You know why. Sandys was always ragging on you."

"What an idiot, to get caught like that. And just before he was due in the ring with Pritchard's brother!" said Cuthbert-Smith.

"I was looking forward to that match," said Gaunt, turning a page in his exercise book. "Sandys is a damned fool."

Yes, Gaunt thought Ellwood was a fool, all right. Although he *had* closed his eyes when Ellwood touched his face on Fox's Bridge; leant forward as if he wanted to be kissed . . . But Ellwood knew from experience how easy it was to convince himself that Gaunt was secretly pining for him, and it was a theory that didn't hold up. There had been too many missed opportunities. Too many moments when Ellwood had almost told him, and Gaunt had made some remark about women and marriage.

Well, they hadn't done anything that friends couldn't do. He had not entirely given himself away. Yes, the gentle cheekbone kiss had been intimate (he could feel his face get hot as he remembered it), but it was still within the realm of masculine affection. If Tennyson could get away with writing poetry about Arthur Hallam for seventeen years, Ellwood could certainly kiss his closest friend on the cheek to comfort him. Although Gaunt had obviously been repelled, since he had fled into the army.

Ellwood smiled and joked through the rest of dinner, hiding his self-reproach.

It was dark when they gathered outside to watch Pritchard and West fight, and the hostile swans quickly put an end to the affair. "Retreat! Retreat!" cried the boys when the swans charged at them, and they went into the woods and played at war instead.

———

Pritchard came to stay for a week during the Christmas hols. He was an inadequate substitute for Gaunt—his eyes glazed over when Ellwood talked about any poet but Kipling. Still, he was cheerful, and occasionally had moments of startling insight. Gaunt didn't approve of him, of course: thought he was stupid, and brutish towards West. But Ellwood knew that Pritchard never pushed West further than he could tolerate, knew how finely balanced their friendship was.

Thornycroft Manor was full of Ellwood's mother's guests: elegant women and the men who yearned for them. The women flirted gently with Pritchard and Ellwood at the dinner table.

"You're very close with your mother," said Pritchard one evening. It was too wet to go on the roof, really, but Ellwood had insisted. If Gaunt had been there (and Gaunt *should* have been there), they would have gone on the roof. Ellwood loved all rooftops, but he particularly liked the roof at Thornycroft. He went there in the mornings, sometimes, and gave himself to that strange country rapture, that deep, bone-warming feeling that England was his, and he was England's. He felt it as strongly as if his ancestors had been there a thousand years. Perhaps he felt it more strongly because they hadn't.

He and Pritchard sat uncomfortably on the slanted window ledge, shoes scraping against the slick wet tiles.

"She's a dear old thing," said Ellwood. It wasn't raining, but there was a thick, damp fog that made their cigarettes soggy.

"She's not very *motherly*."

"No," said Ellwood. "She's always said we're both twenty-five in our heads. That's why we're such good friends."

"I wish *my* mother invited dozens of society beauties to my house for Christmas," said Pritchard.

"I scarcely notice them," said Ellwood.

Pritchard cast him a sidelong glance. "Still no word from Gaunt, I take it?" he asked.

Ellwood gave up on his damp cigarette. "None," he said.

"You've had fights before," said Pritchard.

"We didn't fight, exactly."

"Gaunt's a puzzle," said Pritchard. "He'd be the most terrific rugby player if he tried at all."

"He hates rugger," said Ellwood.

"Hates everything," said Pritchard, "except for Greek, and you."

Ellwood laughed. He had never explicitly confessed to Pritchard, yet somewhere along the way, Pritchard had understood.

"I don't know, Bertie." Ellwood leant back against the window frame and sniffed the cold air. "I've an uncle who's a colonel. I'll worm Gaunt's address out of him, somehow."

"It'll sort itself out once you're at the front together," said Pritchard.

"Of course, you're right," said Ellwood. "It'll be much easier, then."

———

Wednesday 13th January, 1915
Cemetery House
Preshute College

Dear Gaunt,

I've only just managed to get hold of your address. How is training going? Several more boys have enlisted, including poor old Gosset. Mr Hammick was cross as anything. They had to call the army and retrieve him—he was already halfway to France! I can't believe they let him join, he looks about eight. Still, it's given him no end of credit with the younger boys, and he says he'll just keep signing up until he sees some action.

I'm sorry about Fox's Bridge.
Do write back and put me out of my misery.

Affectionately,
Ellwood

———

Tuesday 26th January, 1915
Randall's Farm,
Leatherhead

Dear Ellwood,
    Training is exhausting, but rather idyllic. The men are jolly
short. I'm told that the army height requirement is only five
foot three, and that in parts of London, half the men don't
make it. Makes me feel rather guilty, as if I've stolen six inches
off them by force. Perhaps I have. They are astonishingly kind
to one another. When one of them struggles, the others shout
encouragements—no bullying of any sort. A more different
attitude from that of the public school boy cannot be imagined.
    We are going to the front soon, not sure when. I'll write when
I know more.

With affection,
Gaunt

———

It was amazing how much less affectionate "With affection" sounded
than "Affectionately."

———

Monday 1st February, 1915
Cemetery House
Preshute College

Dear Gaunt,
    Cadet training has increased to five times a week, so there's
hardly any time for games, but no one minds one bit. We have

the most amazing trench-digging competitions. It's jolly good fun, although Burgoyne whinges that it's below his station.

We don't talk about the "In Memoriams," but I know we all simply dread having a dud one. Do you remember Dods? He was killed the other day, and this is what they wrote: "Lieut. Dods led us all the time, and was himself first where the battle was hottest. I can see him now, revolver in one hand, and sword in the other. He certainly accounted for six Germans on his own, and inspired us to the effort of our lives. He had only been six months in the service, was little more than a boy, but the British Army did not possess a more courageous officer."

Can you imagine anything so glorious? I wish the cavalry had more to do. I should have felt like Napoleon, charging at Fritz on a warhorse, "sabring the gunners there!"

But then there was poor old Clarke's "In Memoriam": "He was shot in the lung on his second day. We didn't know him well but he seemed a cheery chap." A cheery chap! Might as well have said, "He was dull as ditch-water and no one cared if he lived or died."

Do you suppose the Romantic poets would have had anything to write about if it hadn't been for the Napoleonic Wars? I can't tell you how glad I am to be alive and young when we are. A war is what we needed: an injection of passion into a century of peace. It will galvanise us into a twentieth-century Renaissance, says Master Larchmont, and he would know.

I've enclosed a poem I had published in *The Preshutian*. It's rousing stuff, about a brave young second lieutenant storming into the German wire. It's not my best, though. I can't wait to join you, Gaunto. Not just because I want fodder for my ART.

With Affection,
Ellwood

———

The summer of 1913, Ellwood had spent three blissful weeks in Munich with Gaunt, walking through the clean countryside and discussing poetry and mythology.

"I feel . . . as if I've woken up," said Gaunt one day, when they were alone in a field. (He and Gaunt were somehow always alone in fields.)

" 'We see into the life of things,' " quoted Ellwood.

"Wordsworth? 'Tintern Abbey'?"

Ellwood grinned.

"Sometimes I think you've read more than I have, Gaunt."

"Of course I have. I'm just less pretentious."

Ellwood smiled, although the words stabbed a little. Gaunt was the only person around whom Ellwood allowed himself to talk about things like *souls*.

"Take that back," he said.

"Shan't."

"I warn you. We poets are fierce when angered."

Gaunt laughed. "How very frightening! You may be better than me at cricket, Ellwood, but—"

Ellwood lunged at him, and, because he had taken him by surprise, succeeded in knocking Gaunt over. He seized Gaunt's hands and pinned them to the ground, kneeling over him. Gaunt was still laughing.

"How dare you?" he said. "I wasn't ready! You're a cheat, Sidney Ellwood!"

Ellwood's brain frizzled at the sound of his name in Gaunt's voice.

"Take it back! Say I'm not pretentious!"

"Oh, but you *are*. You're a cheat, and you're vain, and—" Gaunt effortlessly overpowered him, rolling him over onto his back. But where Ellwood had kept all his weight on his knees, Gaunt lay on top of him.

"—and you're *pretentious*," said Gaunt, but their faces were too close now. Much too close. Gaunt seemed to sense this. With a mischievous look, he nipped at Ellwood's nose with his sharp teeth.

"Ow! That hurt!"

"Can you 'see into the life' of this?" He bit Ellwood's ear.

"You're feral. You ought to be put down," said Ellwood.

" 'In this moment there is life and food / For future years'—"

He bit Ellwood's chin.

"Stop that, you mongrel! You don't deserve Wordsworth!"

" 'Sensations sweet, / Felt in the blood, and felt along the heart'—"

Gaunt's teeth bit at Ellwood's throat. Ellwood tilted his head back. He was shivering. Gaunt had a delicate scrap of his skin between his teeth, and Ellwood could not speak without revealing how desperate he was. *Queen Victoria,* he thought wildly. *Queen Victoria in her mourning clothes. The Jubilee.* Anything, anything at all, anything that wasn't Gaunt's mouth at his neck—for now Gaunt's lips were where his teeth had been, but it wasn't a kiss, it was—Ellwood didn't know what it was—all the Queen Victorias in the world couldn't have prevented him from growing hard just then, and he knew Gaunt would feel him, for their thighs were pressed against each other's—

Gaunt sat up.

"You're not pretentious," he said, dully. "You're just clever."

The sky was so blue. *In this moment there is life and food for future years.*

"Right," said Ellwood. "I— Good."

"We ought to get back."

"Yes. Yes."

Gaunt got to his feet, put his hands into his pockets and walked away without waiting for Ellwood to stand.

———

Tuesday 16th February, 1915
Somewhere in Belgium

Dear Ellwood,

We arrived in Belgium three days ago. It is difficult to describe.

I wrote that last sentence a full five minutes ago and have been hovering with my pen near paper, trying to think. I'm afraid I shall be a disappointing correspondent, Elly.

We landed in France and then boarded trains to Flanders. Everyone was in a jolly mood. It was nice to feel that something was finally happening after weeks and weeks of waiting. When we disembarked, you could hear the thunder of the guns, and I confess that even I found it thrilling. Children delight in being frightened of storms. It exercises some need within them. The guns had much the same effect on us. It was like fireworks gone mad. It made me feel I was at the centre of the universe.

We camped in a heavily bombed-out village for a night, and got our marching orders the next day.

A large battle has already been fought in these trenches. I cannot begin to describe the smell.

I agree with your assessment of your poem. It is not your best. They say you should write what you know.

You'll never guess who is here—your old friend John Maitland. He's dashing as ever and bounded over to ask about you. He is a captain already. He went with me on my first patrol, which he needn't have done.

I apologise for the poor quality of my handwriting. I haven't got my ear in yet; I still think every shell has my name on it. I gather that learning to decipher the various sounds they make and where they'll land is a bit like getting your sea legs. I hope to God I improve soon, because the old guard laugh each time I throw myself to the ground, and the mud is foul. It's not like mud, Elly, it's cursed. It's—

Like everything else, I can't explain.

Your friend,
Gaunt

———

Gaunt had spent so long quietly loathing John Maitland that it was strange to learn his hatred had been unwarranted.

"Did something happen?" asked Maitland, when Gaunt came back from patrol. Gaunt shook his head, annoyed that he had not better hidden his distress.

"All in order," he said, but he fumbled with his cigarette case. They were alone in the dugout.

"How were the snipers?" asked Maitland.

"On good form," said Gaunt. "Sniping away."

"Ah," said Maitland. "Whisky?"

"Please."

Maitland poured him a glass.

"There was—" said Gaunt, and Maitland glanced sharply up. "There was a fellow having a bath. He didn't know we could see him. The snipers didn't want—he was singing; not a care in the world."

Maitland lit a cigarette.

"You ordered them to shoot, of course?" he asked.

Gaunt nodded. He had ordered it, had cut off that rich German voice, just as surely as if he had sliced through it with a knife.

"That's good," said Maitland. "You did the right thing."

"I know," said Gaunt.

"It's always hard once they've done something human."

"He's the first Boche I've seen. They're usually tucked away."

"Their trenches are much deeper than ours," said Maitland. He nudged Gaunt's glass with one finger. "Drink up. You'll feel better."

"I feel fine." Gaunt took out a cigarette and plugged it into his mouth. "Damn. Where've my matches got to?"

"They're in your hand," said Maitland.

They were. Gaunt lit his cigarette, frowning.

"It's all right," said Maitland. "You should have seen what a state I was in, the first time I heard one of them laugh. It's hard to want to kill someone once you've heard that." Maitland paused. "I still hear him laugh, sometimes. That first man."

"I'm fine," said Gaunt.

Maitland smiled. "That's what Sidney used to say about you. That you were always fine."

There was nothing Gaunt wanted less than to talk to *Maitland* about Ellwood. He took a deep inhale of smoke and pulled a pile of letters to be censored towards him. As he scanned through them for place-names, he thought of the first time he was caught smoking at Preshute.

He had been fourteen, and was sentenced to clear out the back of the cricket nets, which were clogged with leaves and mud. It was one of those useless punishments, but it was preferable to caning. Ellwood insisted on helping, although the cricket fields were cloaked in a thick, penetrating dampness.

"They ought to take the nets down in September," said Gaunt. "It's sheer laziness."

"I say, Gaunt," said Ellwood, leaning on his shovel. "What did Fitzroy want to talk to you about, on Tuesday?"

Gaunt's hands stilled on the net.

"Wanted me to light a fire in his study," he said, when he had recovered his composure.

"What, for half an hour?" asked Ellwood.

Gaunt didn't answer.

"Look here, Henry, I won't tell anyone," said Ellwood. "I swear it."

"You know what Fitzroy's like," said Gaunt, not meeting Ellwood's eye. "What do you think he wanted me for? What does Maitland ever want *you* for?"

"Maitland and I just talk," said Ellwood.

Gaunt smiled rather tightly.

"Well, then," he said. "Fitzroy and I just talked."

It hadn't even occurred to him to say no to Fitzroy. Gaunt wasn't much good at sports, and he was a swot. He could not afford to make an enemy of anyone on the First XI.

But Gaunt had already been at school long enough to know you ought never, ever to *talk* about it. It was typical of Ellwood not to understand that yet.

Ellwood knocked a few muddy leaves out of the net.

"We ought to win the House Cup," he said. "What with Maitland and Fitzroy. We're awfully lucky to have them."

"Awfully lucky," agreed Gaunt.

Four years later, in a dugout on the front line, Maitland caught his eye and smiled.

———

Monday 1st March, 1915
Cemetery House
Preshute College

Dear Gaunt,

Maitland! Please send him my love. Careful of calling him dashing, you'll make me jealous.

It's funny thinking of you going to the front and complaining about mud, of all things. You always used to come back from football more covered in it than the rest of us put together. I hope you get used to the shells soon. We want you home in one piece, after all—or perhaps with a few choice scars that you can point out to your grandchildren—"These wounds I had on St Crispin's Day!"

Anyway, I have news myself. Something thrilling has finally happened—but I will start at the beginning.

I woke up this morning and saw that a note had been slipped into my room. Naturally, I assumed it was from Lantham. Lantham is my friend at the moment. He is fifteen, and has the most sensuous features, like a woman in a Rossetti painting. He's always sending me notes. So I lumber out of bed and unfold the paper—but it's not from Lantham! I don't recognise the handwriting.

"Hermit Cave. Midnight."

Well, you can imagine my curiosity.

At midnight, I sneak out of House and make my way to the Hermit Cave, which is always locked and barred. Except for tonight! The gates stand open, and the cavern is utterly dark and silent. I strike a match and enter. You know how the cavern seems quite small, like a shell-covered alcove? Well, it turns out that is a trompe-l'oeil. At the back, there is a sharp turning that leads to a shell-encrusted tunnel.

As I crept along, I noticed that the shells were increasingly accompanied by bones, until there were whole skulls embedded in the walls, grinning at me. Bones galore, you've never seen anything like it! Then I heard a sound.

"Who goes there?" said I, fearless in the face of the unknown.

"Les hommes en flammes," said a deep voice, and several figures stepped forward wearing the most hideous plaster masks.

"Sidney Ellwood, you have been nominated to join the Ardents," said the shortest among them, whose voice sounded an awful lot like Roseveare's. "Should you accept, you must swear never to speak a word of our ancient society to anyone for as long as you live."

(You may be wondering how it is that I am so faithless as to write all this to you. Well, firstly I am <u>writing</u> not <u>telling</u> you about it, and secondly, were you here, I should insist that you be inducted too. I don't care to be part of any group where you are not welcome.)

"I swear it," said I, solemn as anything, and they cut my palm with a gleaming silver dagger (it was a school bread knife, they'd stolen it from Fletcher Hall) and made me daub the walls with my blood. Then they took off their masks, revealing Roseveare, and two boys from Hill House, Grimsey and Finch. Of course it was Roseveare who'd nominated me. We all got thoroughly drunk and I was sick in a bush on my way back to House. It seems that even secret societies cannot improve on the joys of inebriation.

I had known for some time about the Ardents, but I never dreamt—well, it makes me feel as if I—belong, rather.

I've got a rotten headache now and am missing you terribly. I am torn between wanting the War to go on so that I can join you ("We few, we happy few, we band of brothers!"), and wanting it to end so that you can join the Ardents. Two such thrilling worlds! Aren't we lucky?

Your friend,
Ellwood

———

Thursday 11th March, 1915
Somewhere in Belgium

Dear Ellwood,

Your letter made me laugh, for which I am very grateful. It was a little like having you here. I have folded it up and put it in my inner breast pocket, you know, the pocket where people keep those miraculous Bibles that seem to stop so many bullets in *Daily Mail* articles. David told me that in his last battalion he had a captain who was so dead-set against bullet-stopping Bibles that he used them for target practice.

But perhaps I haven't told you about David yet. He is my first lieutenant and the most terrific fighter. He's what someone like Burgoyne would call a "temporary gentleman" (disgusting term), that is to say, he was a factory worker in Lewisham before the War. Maitland says that these working-class officers are better in the field than the public school boys, which I know will shock you. Certainly David finds it easier to relate to the men than I do, and I think they prefer taking orders from him than from us.

I was with Maitland when I first met him. We were splitting a bottle of rum and complaining about Rupert Brooke. Did you ever meet him? He was at Rugby. Anyway, in January he published a series of the most bone-chillingly soppy poems about the War, including one which I'm afraid to say reminded me a bit of that last one you sent me. It begins:

> If I should die, think only this of me:
> That there's some corner of a foreign field
> That is for ever England.

Then it ends with some claptrap about laughing under an English heaven. Maitland and I were joking that Brooke has inadvertently uncovered the government's plan for conquering Europe: cover each square inch of it with British corpses until it's all <u>forever England</u>. We were interrupted when David ducked in. We exchanged a few remarks about the weather, and then David stuck out his hand.

"I'm David Hayes, by the way." He has an accent so thick it reminds me of West's fake one he uses when he's drunk. His uniform is all wrong, too, his khaki is so light it's practically yellow, and his tailor appears to have been in some sort of crazed fever dream when he took his measurements. His sleeves end halfway up his arms. One can't help but admire a man who has risen above the crowds of sharply dressed Etonians despite looking like that.

"Gaunt," I said, shaking his hand.

"Do you public school boys even have first names?"

Maitland and I looked at each other.

"Of course we do," said Maitland, easily. "I'm John."

"Henry." I hated saying it aloud in that trembling dugout. Henry is the name I'm called by people who care for me: to bring it here is to collapse the world. But David doesn't see it that way. So Henry and David and John discuss casualties and censor the men's letters and write to their families when they die.

I would like very much to join the Ardents. Fancy the Hermit Cave going on like that! I'm not keen on bone walls, however. You're mistaken when you say I've never seen anything like it.

Be careful with poor old Lantham. I haven't forgotten those broken little poems Macready asked me to give you when you lost interest in his friendship.

Do write again soon, with lots of school news. In a fit of scholarly fervour, I only packed Thucydides, thinking I might write a book comparing wars, but really there is only so much discussion of hubris one can bear when the shells are bursting overhead. Your letters are a welcome respite. Hope you are well, don't drink too much. Ha! I can't talk.

Gaunt

———

In Lower Sixth, Gaunt and Ellwood had shared a study, which caused Gaunt exquisite new pain. It meant that he always stopped outside the door to listen, to check that Ellwood was alone before he entered. It meant hearing, one day, Ellwood's musical voice through the wooden door: " 'But since she prick'd thee out for women's pleasure / Mine be thy love and thy love's use their treasure!' "

And then Macready's pleased reply:

"I say, Sidney, that was awfully clever. Did you write that?"

Gaunt had gone to the gymnasium and stripped down and beaten his fists into a dangling punching bag until Cuthbert-Smith found him. Then Gaunt had fought with him instead, clean and neat and by the rules.

He knew the lines Ellwood had quoted. They were from Shakespeare's Sonnet 20. Ellwood had written them in pencil on the wall above Gaunt's bed, and Gaunt had hoped they meant something.

———

Wednesday 24th March, 1915
Cemetery House
Preshute College

Dear Gaunt,

I'm not sure how I feel about this David character. It seems awfully untoward to go about demanding people's Christian names like a child or an American.

You say my letter made you laugh. Well, your letters are quite the most popular in the school. Everyone is surprised that you are so poetic, but I knew all along.

I hope you won't mind this letter being rather less charming than the last. You see, something unsettling has happened. At first I thought it was nothing: I started losing things. My nice fountain pen went first. Then I misplaced a whole pound note. Not that I minded, of course; you know I don't care about money. But then my cricket bat went missing!

There was villainy afoot.

I told the Ardents about everything but the pound note, because I truly wasn't fussed about that, and we determined to find the culprit. (Things have been glorious with the Ardents. Every night we meet and roam the school like stray cats. We smoke long pipes on the roof of the Fletcher and Grimsey is teaching us to fence.) Unfortunately, Grimsey was a little hasty in accusing poor Lantham. He cornered him after Chapel, and said, "I know your dirty secret, and I should leave the school if I were you, for your life will be hell on earth if you don't." (Grimsey is as grim as his name.) Of course, poor Lantham was convinced that his "dirty secret" meant ME. He was so upset by it all that he made himself quite ill and ended up in the san. Meanwhile, I went to my room and found—

I'm so angry when I think of it that my hand shakes, can you see?—my notebook of poems in the fire. I tried to rescue them but it was too late. All twenty-two poems, burnt. Some had been published already, but most had not, and I had no copies. They were destroyed, the thoughts and hopes of years, the records of my growing soul, the truest version of me!

In all seriousness, it . . . it was a hard afternoon and I missed you more than ever. I know you would have understood. It's not just the poems. It's the fact that someone burnt them.

The boys have never had a problem with me and my eccentricities. Oh, I know Burgoyne has his opinions, but he hasn't voiced them in ages, not since Hundreds. Do you remember? You fight so many people I think it must be difficult for you to keep track. Maitland was leaving at the end of the year, and he wrote me a letter. It was a careful thing, affectionate in that sexless, Tennyson way. I was in the common room when Burgoyne began to read it out loud. I have no idea how he got it, I thought it was under my mattress. He read it in a cold, sneering voice, and everything Maitland had said suddenly seemed sordid and meaningless. I couldn't move a muscle, I just stared at him.

Everyone was still. I think even my closest friends were listening to see if there was anything in that letter that would destroy their good opinion of me.

Not you. You seemed to wake up. You grasped Burgoyne gently by the arms, and banged your head neatly into his, right into his nose, which broke with a crunch. It was different from when you broke my nose; much more efficient. You took the letter out of his hands and gave it to me.

You will say I am dramatising, but I wrote it all down. I write everything down.

I'm rambling, and you're in the trenches, probably about to go cut off someone's head or something, and this is all very self-indulgent. The point is, after that no one ever said another word. Now I wonder whether one of those silent boys who did not speak up for me waited till you were gone to sneak into my room and burn my poems.

This is a rubbish letter. I'm sorry.

Ellwood

———

They ought to have been too young the summer of 1914 to attend balls—they were only seventeen. But London was different that summer. It blazed with a sort of frantic revelry, dancing on the brink of disaster. Gaunt and Ellwood had three engagements a night. Dinner parties, opera outings, balls, garden luncheons, walks in Hyde Park, country-house weekends, balls, card nights, theatre premieres, evenings at the French ambassador's house, chatting idly in German with frazzled German diplomats, more balls, about a million coming-out parties in which Gaunt escorted blushing white-dressed girls down marble steps without remembering their faces or their names, balls, balls, balls, as if London were squeezing the last drops of prosperity out of the world before it ended.

Ellwood danced with all the prettiest girls. He was insufferably graceful, and knew how to put them at ease. He was rich and handsome. Too young to marry, but that didn't stop mothers from setting out their traps.

Ellwood stayed at Gaunt's house in London and was more than usually extravagant. When they went for drinks at the Hurlingham with Pritchard and West, it was always Ellwood who paid. He lent Roseveare vast sums of money so that he could buy a horse.

"Did Roseveare ever pay you back?" asked Gaunt a few weeks later.

Ellwood flushed. "I don't know," he said. "I don't notice that sort of thing."

They had been in London a few weeks when Gaunt came across a letter from Ellwood's mother. Ellwood had left it, unfolded, on the dresser in his room, where Gaunt found it when he went to borrow a pair of cuff links.

Thursday 30th July, 1914
Thornycroft Manor

Dearest Sidney,

I've asked Mr Utterson to give you another advance on your allowance, as you requested. I'm glad you're having such a nice time, but you have spent quite a lot of money, haven't you, darling? Of course, I wouldn't like you to do without, but I can't imagine how you've spent three hundred pounds in a month. One thinks of all sorts of dreadful scenarios, involving gambling and laudanum. You aren't gambling, are you, darling? Write back quickly and set my heart at ease.

Your ever loving
Mother

"You ought to pay Ellwood back," Gaunt told Roseveare, at Lady Asquith's ball. Ellwood was dancing with Maud. She had pink roses threaded through her hair, and beamed as Ellwood spun her across the floor.

"Has he said something about it?" asked Roseveare, sounding surprised.

"No," said Gaunt, "but he's burnt through his allowance. He'll have to dip into his capital if you don't pay up soon."

"Oh, Sidney's a good sport about money," said Roseveare. "He doesn't mind a bit. Anyway, his mother's family are rich as Croesus. Venetian Jews, you know, like something out of Shakespeare."

Gaunt happened to know that none of Ellwood's relatives had ever set foot in Venice. They had made their fortune in Baghdad in the 1790s, a fact that Gaunt knew Ellwood found depressing. Gaunt wondered when, exactly, Ellwood had put it about that his family was Venetian. Ellwood probably didn't consider it a falsehood—merely a romanticisation. He was so peculiar when it came to his mother's Jewish relatives.

Ellwood bent his head to Maud's with a conspiratorial look and spoke into her ear. Maud laughed, and Ellwood's face lit up in a smile.

"Well, *I* mind," Gaunt told Roseveare. "An Englishman ought to keep his word."

Roseveare was cold towards him for the rest of the evening, but a few days later, he ostentatiously handed Ellwood a check for ninety pounds. Ellwood didn't even look at it before putting it away, red-faced.

"Thanks," he said. "There was no rush."

———

Sunday 11th April, 1915
Somewhere in Belgium

Dear Elly,

It breaks my heart to think of your poems, truly, it does. I know how much you pour into them, even if I disagree with some of your more, shall we say, patriotic ones.

I do remember thumping Burgoyne. He jolly well deserved it, but I can't say that it changed him much for the better. Sometimes I wish we had tried a different tack with him. Perhaps if we'd been more patient, he wouldn't have got so twisted up.

I'm sorry about the time I broke your nose. I didn't want to hurt you.

It's hard for me to write. I think of you making jokes to distract yourself and the trenches seem to close over me. Maitland and David are some comfort. On quiet nights, David shouts puns at Fritz. "You know why they call them Lewis guns? Because you'll Lewis a limb if you come any closer!" Of course, the Germans haven't a clue what he's on about. They sing a lot, and if it's a song our men know, they'll join in. They are a Saxon regiment, which is a relief. I dread the day I have to shoot at Bavarians. My mother tells me Otto was badly injured at Neuve Chapelle, but Ernst is all right. I don't know if you care.

You mentioned that my letters are "the most popular in the school." Please, Ellwood, please tell me you haven't been publishing well-edited fragments of my writing in the ghastly "Letters from the Front" section of *The Preshutian*. I'm sure you haven't been. You know how I would hate it. Don't you?

David and I share letter-censoring duties, and it's much less fun than you would think. David in particular is very disappointed.

"I thought we'd find out that everyone was secretly a pervert or a murderer!" he said.

Murder. What a quaint idea.

Mostly the men talk about the mud and the rats and God. We have to censor the mud and the rats, but God is allowed to remain, which strikes me as ironic. It is a dull job, but less odious than the other: writing condolences. Over and over again, about men I know, or men I don't, about men who died valiantly, or men who died in ways I refuse to describe, men I liked and men I didn't, men too old to go to war, and boys too young. One runs out of ways to say, "Your son died painlessly and was a credit to the Empire." The worst is when you realise you are addressing the same poor woman twice: two letters to thank her for her two sons. I don't think they should allow brothers to join regiments together.

I'm sorry. This is not what I intended to say. What I meant to say is this: You'll write more poems. They are not lost. You are the poetry.

Yours,
Gaunt

———

Thursday 15th April, 1915
Cemetery House
Preshute College

Dear Gaunt,

I'm afraid to say I did publish the bit about the guns sounding like fireworks. It was so beautifully written I couldn't resist. I'm sorry, I see now that I should have asked.

It's funny, I never thought about who writes the condolences. I shouldn't like that job at all. Are you all right, Henry? I know you always are. Yet you seem a little . . . well, look after yourself, that's all. And of course I care about Ernst and Otto. They were absolute bricks, and when this is all over, I look forward to visiting them again with you. My God, did they know how to do breakfast! Remember those strange white sausages? And Mad King Ludwig's castles? And girls in dirndls?

Of course, they're still bloody Fritz and need to be taught a lesson. But there are the Boches, and then there are Germans.

Well, we must return to the Chronicles of Ellwood. Much has happened since I last wrote. First stop: Lantham.

When I found out what Grimsey had said to him, I called a meeting of the Ardents. I was nervous, because we are not to have any secrets from each other, yet I had not told about Lantham. We sat in a circle and began passing round the port I had nabbed from Mr Hammick's office and I told them about my poems being burnt.

Grimsey put his head in his hands.

"So it couldn't have been Lantham," he said.

"No. And it wouldn't have been Lantham anyway, because he's in love with me," I said.

They fell silent.

"He looks like a Nancy-boy," said Grimsey. "I'm not surprised." His tone was rather scornful, and I was glad I hadn't mentioned that I love Lantham back.

"You can't always tell, from looking," said Aldworth mildly. I haven't mentioned him before. He's a quiet chap, awfully popular, although he never says a word.

"All this is beside the point," I said, "which is that Lantham didn't do it."

Again, there was a long silence, where I tried to keep my hands from fidgeting by necking more of that horrid port.

"Well, you ought to have said," said Grimsey, finally. "I must have given that poor fairy quite a scare."

I laughed.

"Yes, I think you did."

No more was said about it. But when Roseveare and I walked back to House, he said, "Aldworth is inverted, you know."

Several interactions between myself and Aldworth suddenly took on new meanings.

"Is he?" I said. "Christ, I'm tired. Wasn't that port awful?"

Roseveare rolled his eyes at me and let the subject go.

Does it bother you when I speak about this sort of thing? You never act as if it does. But perhaps you are too polite.

The next day, at lunch, Aldworth brought me a package. I opened it with great commotion, and everyone stopped eating to watch. Inside was a diary.

"How marvellous! I shall be able to record all my innermost thoughts and feelings!" I exclaimed. After lunch, Roseveare hastily covered it with this clever trick ink he'd ordered from a catalogue. It's quite invisible until it gets on your hands. Then it's bright purple. We left the diary on the desk in my room.

Then we waited. It didn't take long. That evening, we were all in the common room watching West and Pritchard beat each other with cricket bats, which, by the way, is extremely dangerous and probably accounts for why Pritchard is so bad at sums, when Roseveare nudged me in the ribs.

"Look at Burgoyne's hands."

I know, I know: of course it was Burgoyne. I only didn't think of him to begin with because it was too obvious. But there he was, reading a novel, and peeking out from the sides of his palms was a purplish stain. Roseveare quietly locked the door, and I stood up on the sofa.

"It has come to my attention that one of you dislikes me," I said to the room, which instantly fell silent. "But instead of facing me like a man, he has decided to wage a cowardly war of subterfuge. So I give him a chance, now, to face me like an Englishman. I swear none of my friends will harm him, and we will fight with dignity."

No one came forward. Burgoyne studied his book.

"Right," barked Roseveare, and he explained about the ink. "Everyone show your hands."

Everyone did, except for Burgoyne, who kept his glued to his novel.

"Come on, Burgoyne," said Pritchard.

"I won't. This is childish, and I refuse to take part."

The boy next to him grabbed his book, and then of course we could all see that his hands were stained.

"It's quite all right for you to dislike me, Burgoyne," I said. "I don't mind at all. But you must be honourable about it."

At this, Burgoyne seemed to puff up, like those fish they eat in Japan.

"Honourable?" he said. "Honourable? My ancestors CONQUERED this country, Ellwood, centuries before yours crawled out of the mud! How dare you speak to me of honour?"

"You're a snob, Burgoyne," said Roseveare, coldly.

"Of course I am!" He looked quite mad. "We all are! Do you mean to tell me you would befriend one of the grammar school boys in town? Of course you wouldn't."

"That's different," said Roseveare.

"No, it isn't! The townies know their place, and we know ours. But Ellwood here seems to want the classes below to stay right where they are, while he clambers over my head. Well, I'm not having it. You don't belong in the Ardents, Ellwood."

"No one cares how honourable your ancestry is, Burgoyne," I said, "when you behave in such a sneaking manner—"

Burgoyne let out a high-pitched laugh.

"Me, sneaking! I'm not the one who's a Jew."

Mr Hammick says I was quite right to hit Burgoyne in the eye ("You can't help being a Jew," he said, in somewhat misguided sympathy), but that because Burgoyne's father is on the school board, he has to punish me. So I have detention every Saturday for the rest of term. I had my first one the other day. Mr Hammick made me a nice cup of tea and we talked about cricket.

Thanks awfully for saying all that stuff about my poetry. It made me grin like anything. Send my love to Maitland, won't you? And keep some for yourself, while you're at it.

Yours,
Elly

THREE

S ANDYS DIDN'T LET go of Gaunt as he locked and barricaded the door, and pulled the blinds.

It was the blinds that let Gaunt know what was going to happen.

"Gaunt! Gaunt—I'm fetching—reinforcements—" cried Ellwood, outside the door.

"What do you want, Sandys?" said Gaunt, straining to break his arms free. But Sandys was stronger, although Gaunt had better technique in the ring.

Sandys bent him over the desk and hissed into his ear.

"What do you *think* I want, Gaunt? Christ."

Gaunt's heart constricted. His summer growth spurt ought to have put him safely beyond the reach of older boys, yet here he was: trapped.

"Let's leave Christ out of it, shall we?" he said into the desk.

"Shut up." Sandys pulled Gaunt back, still twisting his arms. But when his hand snaked to the front of Gaunt's trousers, it moved slowly, hesitantly.

It wasn't as if Gaunt hadn't *thought* about sleeping with Sandys. It occurred to him often, when they boxed, in quick flashes of images as they wrestled each other to the ground. He had generally been able to punch the thoughts away, but he sometimes suspected Sandys knew what he was doing. They made too much eye contact in their fights.

"Let go of me, Sandys. Let's just get this over with."

Sandys dropped his arms. Gaunt stood straighter and rolled out his shoulders.

Sandys kissed his neck, gently, wrapping his arms around Gaunt's chest. *Good Lord, it felt good to be touched.*

"Don't be such a fucking *girl* about it, Sandys," he snapped.

Sandys dropped him instantly. Gaunt turned to face him and got to his knees.

"Wait—" interrupted Sandys.

"Oh, what *now*?"

"I don't want you to unless . . . unless you want to."

Gaunt rolled his eyes so hard he actually moved his head, and was about to explain what an unbelievably stupid thing that was to say, when Sandys dragged him to his feet and drew him close. Gaunt couldn't help it. He let out a small sound. Sandys' hand roamed over him, and it felt—wonderful—

"I don't want to do anything if you don't want to," whispered Sandys.

Ellwood would return soon, would try to break the door down to rescue him, but for now it was quiet.

"What do you say, Gaunt?" murmured Sandys. "Where do you want my hand to go next?"

Despite himself, Gaunt told him.

————

Thursday 11th March, 1915
Somewhere in Belgium

Dear Sandys,

Thanks for your scandalous postcard. I've stuck her up on the wall in the hopes that David and Maitland will think I'm a womaniser. Ha.

Got another letter from Ellwood today. He's still hooked on Maitland, ever so curious about everything I said about him. Seemed rather jealous of me, in fact, for getting to spend time

with him. Well, it's no surprise. I am rather hooked on Maitland.
(Not like that.) He was always kind to me, but I assumed that
was because of Ellwood's fierceness. Now I see him with the
men, and know that he is a true gentleman. Handsome, too,
which as you know is not my strong point. . . . I wrote back to
Elly right away, cool as you please, no mention of the man's face
I saw floating in a muddy trench this morning. It had detached
from the skull. The nose was all flat and it had no eyes. Just a
mask of skin. Ho-hum.

I told Ellwood about David Hayes. I'll admit I told him partly
because I knew it would make him jealous. It bothers Elly that
I never call him by his Christian name. (How could I? Call him
Sidney, as his wife will one day: I'd rather die.)

It's maddening that all this—that he—can still have my
attention, even at the front.

He's friends with Lantham now. Remember Lantham? Easily
startled. Long eyelashes like a girl. Apparently Lantham writes
him notes. I wish them every happiness.

Are you still in contact with Stephen Caruthers?

It's nice to have someone to write to honestly, Sandys.

Sincerely,
Gaunt

FEBRUARY 1913—Hundreds

When they were done, Sandys gave him a shy smile.

"Hit me," said Gaunt.

"Sorry?"

Gaunt shoved him.

"Hit me."

"I don't want to!"

"Christ, Sandys, at least make it *look* as if I put up a fight."

"Oh. Right," said Sandys. "Well—where would you like me to—"

"Oh, forget it," said Gaunt, and he slammed his head into the corner
of a desk.

"Gaunt!" cried Sandys in alarm, but Gaunt was already walking to the window and lifting the blinds.

"Did that do it?" he asked, turning his head to look at Sandys. "Will I have a bruise?"

"The size of China, I should think. Are you all right?"

His brain had shut down to prevent the impossible thoughts. Ellwood had returned some time before, had cried out his name as Sandys touched him, it had been . . . distracting. . . .

"I'm fine," he said, and unlocked the door.

————

Monday 22nd March, 1915
Somewhere in France

Dear Gaunt,

Things here have been rather unrelenting. I am so tired of it all. A friend of mine was blown up last week. I found him before anyone else. He was still alive, just about, but not in pain yet. I wanted to kill him. You wouldn't let a horse or a dog suffer like that. But I'm a gentleman, and gentlemen don't kill their friends. I hovered with my hand at my revolver, trying to force myself one way or the other. What is civilised in such circumstances? But then another officer arrived. He saw where my hand was and looked at me with revulsion. I felt a monster.

I called for the stretcher-bearers and they took him away. He lay whimpering in the clearing station, alight with pain. He couldn't form words through the wretched agony. His eyes— well, I don't need to describe them to you. You will have seen eyes like that, all the humanity scraped out of them. Days and days. No one could survive with so many pieces of them missing, but we had to save him, or else we wouldn't be civilised any more. He died this morning, thank God. If I am ever in his position, I hope there's no one civilised nearby, only a quick-moving angel of death with a bullet in his barrel.

Perhaps you think it ungrateful of me to complain about the War—I, who have so much to gain from it. I'm well aware that if I make captain, no one will remember why I wasn't able to go to Cambridge. Why I spent last year hiding in the country.

I am not surprised that you continue to worry about Ellwood even here. I am surprised that you are telling me about it. I always thought we reflected each other, Gaunt. Now I hope, for your sake, that we don't.

You asked about Caruthers. I received the telegram informing me of his death two days ago. Killed in action near Artois. No details. I was in the reserve line, and showed the telegram to a fellow officer, who read it with vague sympathy. I found I could not remember the sound of Stephen's voice. It was then that I realised all that the telegram really meant.

Yours,
Sandys

FEBRUARY 1913—Hundreds

Sandys cornered Gaunt the next day, pressed him against a wall.

"You've been looking at me."

"You're imagining things," said Gaunt.

"You enjoyed yourself yesterday. I know you did."

"I've forgotten about yesterday. So should you."

"Ellwood isn't interested in you."

"Ellwood has nothing to do with this," said Gaunt, drawing away.

"He has everything to do with it. And you're wasting your time; everyone knows he's mad for John Maitland."

"Look, I don't know what passionate *Troilus and Criseyde* tale you've been telling yourself is going on between us, but—"

"I'm not fucking *in love* with you, Gaunt!" Sandys had him against the wall again. Footsteps echoed down the hall. Sandys grabbed his wrists and twisted them above his head.

"Say 'mercy,'" he hissed, as a Remove boy walked by.

"No," said Gaunt, coolly. Sandys twisted his arms more. Gaunt did not struggle against him.

"I'll kill you," growled Sandys into his ear.

"I'd like to see you try." The boy passed them without stopping, keeping his head down. Sandys pressed himself aggressively into Gaunt. He was hard. They both were. The boy rounded the corner.

"You're awfully close friends with Stephen Caruthers," said Gaunt.

"Shut up," said Sandys, his words hissing into Gaunt's neck.

"Only he doesn't really go in for this sort of thing, does he?"

"You've made your point, Gaunt."

Sandys loosened his hold slightly. Gaunt could have slipped away. He didn't.

"Do you know where my room is?" asked Sandys, quietly.

Gaunt nodded.

"Meet there in five minutes."

Sandys let go of him and strode down the corridor. Gaunt knocked his head hard against the wall behind him, several times.

He never intended to go to Sandys' room, but somehow, throughout the Lent term, he kept finding himself there. They had quick, angry sex and never kissed. (Sandys tried once. "*What are you doing?*" Gaunt asked him in alarm. Sandys never attempted it again.) When they finished, Gaunt would leave without saying a word, and never think about what had happened until the next time Sandys cornered him. Except that he must have been thinking about it, because he found himself lurking in the same places, the places Sandys was likely to find him.

"Why is Sandys persecuting you?" asked Ellwood.

"He's not."

"I wish you wouldn't be so *brave* all the time."

"I'm not being brave. I'm fine."

"How does he keep managing to drag you into rooms and beat you?"

Whenever anyone spotted Gaunt and Sandys going into a room together, Gaunt made Sandys hit him in some noticeable place.

Gaunt shrugged, and answered all Ellwood's questions in monosyllables until Ellwood stopped asking them. This never took long, although he could feel Ellwood's eyes on the bruise on his jaw for the rest of the evening. Ellwood left him alone, but he always found some way to make it clear that he was unhappy about it.

———

Saturday 10th April, 1915
Somewhere in Belgium

Dear Sandys,
 I hadn't heard about Caruthers. I'm sorry. I wish I could be more articulate, but the English language fails me. It sometimes feels as if the only words that still have meaning are place names: Ypres, Mons, Artois. Nothing else expresses.
 I know all that Stephen was to you. I am sorry.
 Perhaps in the circumstances, it is cruel to tell you that I had another letter from Ellwood today. It is a cruelty I must give in to, for I haven't anyone else to tell. He was upset and earnest and each word splintered into me. You told me once I was wasting my time, and I am beginning to think you were right. Years and years I spent, loping down country lanes with Ellwood at my side, my hands in my pockets—what a coward I was! But I was frightened—that he would laugh at me, or that he would play at loving me as he did with Macready. God, he destroyed Macready. You should have read his poems. Awful dross, like weeping with ink.
 You were far braver than I was. I wonder if your bravery then sustains you now that you have lost him.
 Perhaps I would rather Ellwood had played at loving me, if only for a few weeks, than never to have had anything at all. (Ellwood would tell me there's a Tennyson quotation for that.) There's an empty space in my mind where those memories might have been.
 I hope you are keeping safe.

Sincerely,
Gaunt

MARCH 1913—Hundreds

Gaunt walked past Sandys' bedroom. (There was no reason for him to be in that part of the school. If anyone had asked him why he was there, he would have said he was going to the laundry room. He probably would have half-believed himself, too.) The door flew open and Sandys pulled him inside.

"What happened to *you*?" asked Gaunt. Sandys' face was distorted by puffing, bleeding bruises.

"Ellwood."

"You're twice his size."

"He had about a dozen friends. You've got a lot of allies, apparently."

Gaunt tried not to smile. "That's rather touching."

"No, it fucking wasn't."

"I can quite understand why *you* wouldn't see it that way."

"Just tell him we're friends!"

"We're not friends."

Sandys made an exasperated sound.

"Then *what are we*?"

Gaunt shrugged. "I haven't given it much thought."

"Look, will you stop acting as if I'm trying to . . . ensnare you into marriage or something—"

Gaunt's head jerked up.

"*Marriage*, Sandys?"

Sandys rubbed his eye and winced. "Just tell him we're friends," he said again.

Gaunt rapped his knuckles on the door frame. "Fine. But we're not. Friends. I'm not going to be writing you letters when you leave school, or anything like that."

"I don't want your letters, idiot."

"You've got pus leaking out of your eye."

Sandys rummaged for a handkerchief, but Gaunt found his first. It already had blood on it from when Sandys had hit him two days ago. Gaunt's handkerchiefs were always covered in blood.

"Thanks," said Sandys.

"I'm sorry about Ellwood. He can be . . . loyal."

"I thought he was carrying on with John Maitland. What's he playing at, rescuing you as if you're some damsel in distress?"

"I'm really not interested in discussing this, Sandys." Gaunt reached for the door.

"If he so much as looks at me funny, I'm breaking his face. I don't care how good-looking he is."

"You can't hurt him," said Gaunt, his voice suddenly raw.

Sandys stared at him for a moment, then laughed. "That's the most human I've ever seen you look, Gaunt. And I've seen you in all sorts of compromising positions."

"Say you won't hurt him."

"Good gracious, fine, I won't touch him."

Gaunt coughed and nodded, trying not to notice how curiously Sandys was watching him.

"He can take care of himself, you know," said Sandys. He pointed at his mangled face. "He's not exactly a hapless victim."

"I know," said Gaunt.

"Oh, Gaunt," said Sandys softly. "You'll have your shot at him next year, won't you? With Maitland gone."

"I don't want anything like this with Ellwood."

"You're wasting your time, you know," said Sandys, sidling closer. He put a hand on Gaunt's hip.

"You can't want—"

"I'm game if you are," said Sandys.

"You look like rotten fruit."

"Don't look at me, then," said Sandys, turning Gaunt roughly around. His mouth moved to Gaunt's ear as his hands fumbled with his belt. "You know, you'll regret being such a coward when you're married."

"I'm not *marrying*."

Sandys laughed and pushed himself closer. Gaunt braced himself against the wall.

"We're all getting married, Gaunt. To nice women."

"Stop talking."

.   .   .

"I've realised," said Sandys, as they dressed, twenty minutes later. "You're thinking ahead. That's why you won't kiss me, or tell Ellwood you're in love with him."

"I'm not in love with him."

"You're anticipating what they'll say about you, when you're forty and still a bachelor. 'Oh, Gaunt was utterly decent at school. None of that naughty schoolboy amorousness. No, Gaunt's an upstanding fellow.' That's what you're thinking, isn't it?"

Gaunt fixed his tie.

"I'm not thinking at all," he said, more honestly than he had intended.

———

Tuesday 13th April, 1915
Somewhere in France

Dear Gaunt,

It is most peculiar how grief affects you differently each time. My infant sister died when I was seven, and I remember every moment leading up to the funeral with a clarity that throws the rest of my childhood into darkness. Since hearing about Stephen, however, I am aware of time only as a blur of images. In billets, I saw a worm in the earth, an innocent thing in a flower bed, and I was struck suddenly with a blinding vision of Stephen, whose face I knew so well—and the worms don't distinguish—you and I know that. We have seen how they make feasts of Germans, French and English alike. What does it matter, now, that he had memorised half of *Paradise Lost*?

I was waiting for a letter from him. I've looked at the date of his death, and written to his commanding officer and servant, and I can't make sense of it, because he must have had time to write to me. He was such a reliable correspondent. Every time the post comes I break out in hot sweat, certain that his last words are coming to me, like the closing of a chapter. His life can't simply have stopped—surely it must have <u>ended</u>. Tell me this makes sense to you, Gaunt. You are <u>the only one who knew</u> what he meant to me.

You're a fool and a coward, yet I envy you. You were right to leave Ellwood alone. I have lost more than I can say, and what remains of me is not worth much. Stephen and I had a few happy weeks before we were expelled, but nothing could be worth what I now feel.

Sandys

OCTOBER 1913—Lower Sixth

"What the hell do you think you're doing, Sandys?" hissed Gaunt. It was the middle of the night, and Sandys had roughly prodded him awake. "Have you taken leave of your senses?"

"I had to talk to you," said Sandys, climbing onto Gaunt's bed.

"Are you mad? Get out! What if someone comes in?"

"They won't," said Sandys. "Shut up a minute, I'm trying to think."

It was the first year Gaunt had a room to himself, and he couldn't shake the feeling that there were twelve other boys in the room with him, waiting and listening. He sat up against the wall, as far away from Sandys as he could manage.

"If you've come here to—"

"I haven't," said Sandys. "That's what I'm here to talk to you about. Caruthers." He smiled dreamily. "Stephen."

"What *about* Caruthers?"

"I told him," said Sandys.

Gaunt froze. "Told him *what*, exactly?"

Sandys must have caught sight of his expression, because he laughed. "Not about that, idiot. About—well, about how I felt. With regards to him."

Gaunt stared at him. "You . . . you talked to Caruthers about your *feelings*?"

"Don't look so appalled," said Sandys.

"You're mad. Why on earth would you do such a thing?"

"I'm glad I did it," said Sandys. "Gaunt. He *feels the same way.*"

Although Gaunt was paranoid about making noise and drawing the attention of some patrolling teacher, he got out of bed. He had to put more space between himself and Sandys.

"He feels the same way," he repeated.

"Yes," said Sandys, laying his head down on Gaunt's pillow.

"Get off my bed," said Gaunt.

Sandys sat up, frowning. "You understand, of course," he said, "that this means you and I can't carry on—"

"Christ, Sandys, I couldn't care less if we see each other again. Get off my bed."

Sandys stood. He was broad and stocky, even in his childish pyjamas. Gaunt had never seen him naked, although he had seen every inch of his body.

"You should talk to Ellwood," said Sandys.

"You're mad. You're absolutely insane. I cannot believe you are saying any of this aloud," said Gaunt.

"We haven't got much time," said Sandys, and Gaunt didn't know if he meant that he would have to sneak out again in a minute, or if he meant it in a wider sense. That there wasn't much time before Oxford and Cambridge, before marriage and respectability and the putting aside of boyish, immature desires.

"Sandys," said Gaunt, and his voice sounded much less firm than he would have liked. "You can't *talk* like this."

"I can, with you," said Sandys. "And you can, with me."

Gaunt shook his head. "It's one thing to—to do what we do—to pass the time," he said.

"You behave as if you have so much time to spend," said Sandys, "but you haven't. You're squandering your years as if they're limitless—"

"It's the middle of the night; get out of my room," said Gaunt.

"Stephen loves me," said Sandys. Gaunt slammed his fist into his desk, and Sandys yelped.

"What the *hell* are you talking about," said Gaunt, "Stephen *loves* you, what absolute rot . . . !"

"Keep your voice down," said Sandys. "And stop punching things, for God's sake. Hasn't it ever occurred to you that Ellwood might love you back?"

Gaunt shoved at Sandys, but Sandys had clearly been expecting something of the sort, and braced himself. When Gaunt went to hit him, Sandys blocked him.

"Calm down," said Sandys.

"You don't know what you're talking about," said Gaunt.

"What's the worst that could happen, really, if you told him?"

It was as if Sandys was some visitation from another planet.

"What's the *worst that could happen*?" repeated Gaunt in disbelief. "I could be expelled. I could be sentenced to hard labour in a prison camp, and bring shame down on my family and everyone associated with me. I could be *hanged*."

"They don't hang people for that any more," said Sandys. "And none of those are the reason you won't tell him. You won't tell him because you're frightened of what he'll say."

"There's nothing to tell, Sandys."

They looked at each other for a moment, and Gaunt was struck by a strange desire to kiss Sandys on the mouth, just to see what it would be like. He clenched his fists at his side and stayed where he was.

"All right," said Sandys. He looked around at Gaunt's spartan dormitory, as if he were bidding it goodbye. "I just wanted to tell you. About Stephen."

"Well, now you've told me."

"Yes." Sandys continued to hover by the door. "I like you, Gaunt."

"Don't be revolting."

Sandys laughed and slipped out the door. Gaunt was left alone in his dormitory, Sandys' words echoing in his head. *You're squandering your years as if they're limitless.*

———

Friday 16th April, 1915
Somewhere in Belgium

Dear Sandys,

I don't make friends easily. I should say I have only three: Gideon Devi, who I knew in childhood. Ellwood. You.

Whenever I'm out of the line, I check *The Times* for your name and for Gideon's. I began this letter planning to tell you I could not imagine your grief; but that isn't true. I do imagine it, over and over. If you were killed, I doubt I should receive a telegram—our friendship has always been too tenuous for others to be aware of it. Still, in my imagination, I receive a telegram. I see your name and think, There goes the man I might have spoken to, had I only been able to open my mouth.

You say that what is left of you is not worth much. I can only respond by assuring you it is worth a great deal—to me.

Your friend,
Gaunt

———

His letter was returned to him a few days later, "RECIPIENT DECEASED" stamped across the front.

"Bad news?" asked Hayes.

Gaunt showed him the envelope.

"I'm sorry," said Hayes.

Gaunt tried to shrug, but his shoulders moved rather more jerkily than he had anticipated.

"Πάσιν ημίν κατθανείν οφείλεται," he said.

"Passing *what*?"

Gaunt shook his head.

"Sorry. Euripides. I forgot you hadn't read him."

" 'Death is owed to all of us,' " translated Maitland, from his corner of the dugout. "Who was it, Gaunt? Anyone I know?"

"Sandys."

Maitland paused, thinking. Gaunt could see him remembering the scandal.

"Awfully strong, wasn't he?" asked Maitland, finally.

It was a kindness.

Gaunt nodded. "Very," he said.

"That's bad luck, Henry. I'm sorry," said Hayes.

What a waste Sandys' last days had been, thought Gaunt. Pathetically attempting to overcome a grief that would never have time to heal.

"Anyone got a cigarette?" he asked.

Maitland gave him one. Later, Gaunt burnt the letter.

———

A German attack was coming, and Maitland was in a foul mood. Every spare moment was spent preparing for battle. It was to be Gaunt's first. Maitland had fought at Ypres the year before, and he became tense and irritable. He sent Hayes out to inspect the men's feet.

"No one is getting out of this because of fucking trench foot," he told Hayes.

"There's a few as have got it bad, John."

"Let them lurch at the Germans on their fucking stumps. I don't give a damn. You just tell them no man in this company is leaving before Friday afternoon."

Hayes and Gaunt exchanged a look, and Hayes nodded.

"Yes, sir," he said, and left.

"Ho! He didn't like *that*," said Huxton, the fourth officer in their company. "Still, good to teach him some manners, Maitland. I've always thought there's something insolent about that chap."

There was nothing remotely insolent about Hayes, thought Gaunt, other than the ambition he showed in being an officer when he wasn't a gentleman.

Maitland didn't even look at Huxton.

"Half our grenades are faulty. Report to Headquarters and enquire when we'll be receiving a fresh supply."

"I say," protested Huxton, "can't you send a corporal? It's jolly far."

"I gave you an order, and I expect for it to be obeyed," said Maitland.

"Send Kane, there's a good man," said Huxton.

"Get out!" said Maitland.

There was no arguing with him. Huxton left. Gaunt put on his greatcoat.

"Where d'you think you're going?" asked Maitland.

"Kohn said the men were feeling dispirited over by Regent Street. Thought I'd check they haven't let their trench get too straggly."

"Sit down."

Gaunt sank onto an ammunition case.

"What's the matter?"

"This!" said Maitland, waving what was unmistakably Ellwood's last letter to him—the one where he had said he was in love with Lantham.

"You had no right to read that," said Gaunt.

"I had *every* right," said Maitland. He was pale and thin-lipped with anger. "I'm your *captain.* I can censor your letters any time I like."

Gaunt kept his face a mask as he ran through all the things he had written to Sandys.

"Have you found enough to court-martial me, then?" he asked, lightly.

"You have no idea how careless you've been. Stop rapping your knuckles like that; you can't hit me."

Gaunt clasped his hands and put them in his lap.

"You're a hypocrite, Maitland."

"Shut up. I'm not reporting you. I'm trying to *help.* Can't you see that if you let Sidney write this sort of letter, you'll get him imprisoned?"

"Ellwood does as he likes. He always has."

Maitland slammed his hand down on the table.

"For *God's sake,* Henry! This isn't school. People won't turn a blind eye because Sidney's on the bloody First XI. Do you remember Caruthers?"

Gaunt gave a bitter laugh. "A little. Got mixed up with Sandys a few years back, didn't he?"

"Yes. He was killed in Artois a month ago. Walked straight into enemy fire. Do you know why?"

"No," said Gaunt, through clenched teeth.

"Archie Pritchard told me. See, Caruthers had written some rather compromising letters, and one was picked up by a superior officer. The day that Caruthers went over the top with such gallant bravery, he knew he was about to be summoned to Headquarters. Court-martial and disgrace, or a Military Cross for his grieving family. Not much of a choice."

Gaunt thought of Sandys, desperately trying to discover what had happened to the final letter he was so sure Caruthers had written. He was suddenly glad that Sandys was dead, so that he would never know.

Then, as always when Gaunt remembered Sandys, he turned his mind away.

"Ellwood's charmed," he said.

"He's an idiot," said Maitland. "You *must* make him see reason. I don't care how you do it."

"You don't seem overly concerned with *my* indiscretions."

"Yours?" asked Maitland. "I didn't read your letters. Only his to you."
He frowned. "I remember what he's like."

"I'm sure you do," said Gaunt.

Maitland went to the stairs. "Make him see. You may be killed in the
action we've got coming, and there's no one else he'll listen to."

"Rousing stuff," said Gaunt. He caught sight of Maitland's expression. "I . . . John. Of course, you're right. Thank you."

Maitland nodded. "We've got to look out for each other," he said.

We, thought Gaunt, *who's _we_?*

———

Tuesday 20th April, 1915
Somewhere in Belgium

Ellwood,

    I must insist that you don't write to me any more, unless you
can do so appropriately.

Gaunt

———

Ellwood didn't answer. Gaunt had known he wouldn't. If Gaunt was
killed, it would be the last letter Ellwood had from him. He tried not to
think about that; tried to think only of ammunition supplies and wire
reinforcements and the coming attack.

"I'm afraid I shall be a coward," he confessed to Hayes, late at night.

"You won't be," said Hayes. But Gaunt was still afraid.

FOUR

Tuesday 20th April, 1915
Somewhere in Belgium

Ellwood,
   I must insist that you don't write to me any more, unless you
can do so appropriately.

Gaunt

Ellwood turned the letter over, but there was nothing else.
"Anything interesting?" asked Pritchard.
"How many Boches has he killed?" asked West.
"Eighty," said Ellwood, "all with his bare hands."
He folded the letter away, conscious that his feelings were written
plainly on his face. Inappropriately, perhaps. He wished he were like
Gaunt, but he couldn't keep his character quiet, like a secret. He had
always skirted near the edges of Gaunt's tolerance, he knew that. He
had thought it would be easier not to antagonise Gaunt when he was
far away, and Ellwood didn't have to remind himself daily not to touch
him, never to touch him.
   "Is he all right?" asked Pritchard, in an undertone. He was often
careful around Ellwood when Gaunt came up. It was a painful sort of
thoughtfulness.

"He's fine," said Ellwood. "He's Gaunt; he's always fine." He grinned, knowing Pritchard would see how false it was. "I say, I want some sport. Shall we burn Burgoyne's French prep? He's been slaving away at it."

West brightened.

"Splendid idea! We haven't ragged on him in days!"

So they broke into Burgoyne's study. They burnt his French prep and smashed up his furniture. Ellwood was the fiercest of them all.

On the 30th April, there was a scrum at the door of Fletcher Hall.

"What's going on?" Ellwood asked Pritchard.

"Apparently there's been another battle at Ypres. Everyone's trying to get hold of *The Preshutian* to see the casualty lists."

"But that's in Belgium," said Ellwood.

THE PRESHUTIAN

VOL. L.—No. 749. APRIL 30TH, 1915. Price 6d.

⁓ROLL OF HONOUR ⁓

KILLED IN ACTION.

Bernard, Lieut. E., King's Own Scottish Borderers. Killed in action near Ypres on April 22nd, aged 25.

Blakeney, Capt. A. G., The Princess of Wales' Own (Yorkshire Regiment). Killed in action near Ypres on April 22nd, aged 23.

Finch, Lieut. L. D., The Suffolk Regt. Killed in action near Ypres on April 27th, aged 20.

Giffard, Lieut. R.O.C., Duke of Cornwall's Light Infantry. Killed in action near Ypres on April 22nd, aged 19.

Maitland, Capt. J. A., Royal Kennet Fusiliers. Killed in action near Ypres on April 22nd, aged 20.

Morris, Sec.-Lieut. R. K., Duke of Cornwall's Light Infantry. Killed in action near Ypres on April 23rd, aged 28.

Newton, Lieut. E. W., Royal Anglesey Royal Engineers. Killed in action near Ypres on April 26th, aged 19.

Straker, Capt. W. H., Ludhiana Sikhs. Killed in action near Ypres on April 22nd, aged 21.

Vaughan, Capt. F. P., Canadian Engineers. Killed in action near Ypres on April 25th, aged 23.

Ward, Sec.-Lieut. S. A., Duke of Cornwall's Light Infantry. Killed in action near Ypres on April 23rd, aged 17.

Wells, Sec.-Lieut. F. S., Bhopal Infantry. Killed in action near Ypres on April 22nd, aged 19.

Woodruffe, Sec.-Lieut. K.H.C., The Suffolk Regt. Killed in action near Ypres on April 23rd, aged 22.

WOUNDED.

Anderson, Sec.-Lieut. G. H., Durham Light Infantry.

Bowen, Capt. H. S., Royal West Kent Regt.

Brodie, Capt. J.G.R., Monmouthshire Regt.

Clayton, Sec.-Lieut. F. J., Royal Engineers.

Collins, Sec.-Lieut. E. R., Duke of Cornwall's Light Infantry.

Evans, Capt. J. T., London Regt.

Field, Sec.-Lieut. H. F., Middlesex Regt.

Forristal, Lieut. F. A., London Regt.

Gaunt, Sec.-Lieut. H. W., Royal Kennet Fusiliers.

Grimsey, Capt. L. M., Gordon Highlanders.

Lambert, Sec.-Lieut. S., Durham Light Infantry.

Mamet, Lieut. C. M., Queen's Westminster Rifles.

Miller, Lieut. D. T., Cheshire Regt.

Nott, Lieut.-Col. J.R.W., Welsh Regt.

Phillips, Sec.-Lieut. N. A., Liverpool Regt.

Pritchard, Lieut.-Col. A. M., East Yorkshire Regt.

Pritchard, Capt. C. S., East Yorkshire Regt.

Stein, Sec.-Lieut. A. N., Nofolk Regt.

Toles, Sec.-Lieut. T.Z.S., Durham Light Infantry.

Turner, Sec.-Lieut. C. P. J., Royal West Kent Regt.

Turner, Sec.-Lieut. M. P., Royal West Kent Regt.

Wall, Capt. I., Royal Fusiliers.

Wathen, Major H. A., Black Watch.

Wheatley, Lieut. A. D., West Riding Regt.

Wright, Capt. F., Seaforth Highlanders.

Young, Lieut.-Col., B.C.M., Liverpool Regt.

There were pages and pages more. After the long list of the wounded came those who'd died of wounds, those who had been killed accidentally, and those missing, believed killed. Ellwood handed the paper numbly to West.

"Your brother's all right," he told him.

Pritchard was frowning so hard his eyes were watering. Both his brothers were wounded, no way of knowing how badly. On the next table, Finch had his head in his arms, suddenly an only child. Grimsey was patting him on the back, but Grimsey's brother too was wounded, and all around the hall, boys stared unseeingly at the lists of the dead.

Ellwood's eyes had gone straight to "G." The brief moment of relief when he had not seen Gaunt's name had been immediately followed by something black and empty when his eyes fell on Maitland's.

"Come on," said Roseveare. Ellwood rose obediently and followed him to the graveyard. It was a bright blue day. The green leaves curled playfully into the sky, and daffodils burst out like exclamation marks among the tombstones. Ellwood stared at the one nearest him: "George Fuller (1663–1735)."

It felt like a boast. George Fuller had lived seventy-two years. He had probably grown fat and tired, splurging with time, outliving his eyesight and vitality. While Maitland—

Ellwood turned his back on the tombstone, and wondered just how wounded Gaunt was. It seemed almost worse to know so little than to know nothing.

"I remember that letter Maitland wrote you," said Roseveare.

Ellwood could not answer. He did not know why Roseveare had taken him outside, what he was trying to say.

"The one Burgoyne read. You know which I mean?"

Ellwood nodded, sharply.

"It was a good letter," said Roseveare. "I remember we were all spellbound. I had heard that Maitland treated you well, but I had never really believed it. That's not often how it goes, you know."

"I thought you were listening to find out if I was a despicable Oscar Wilde type."

Roseveare laughed. "No, I don't think any of us had any real doubts about that, Sidney."

Ellwood smiled at him weakly. "Is your brother Martin all right?" he asked.

"Yes. But I was friends with Harry Straker. I used to stay at his house and play cricket with his brothers. He had three." Roseveare paused for a moment, as if remembering long summer afternoons on an emerald lawn with young men who hadn't known how little time they had left. "Of course, he died in August. Battle of Mons, same as my brother Clarence. Now his brother Will, killed at Ypres. It's just a shame, that's all."

Roseveare had never mentioned his dead brother before. He did not look now as if he wanted to talk more about him.

"Simeon Ward was my age," said Ellwood.

"The Field House boys will be devastated. He was their only good bowler."

Boys had started trickling back to House through the graveyard. They walked sombrely, talking in hushed voices. Ellwood caught snippets of their conversations.

"Newton was on the hockey team, remember. . . ." "Giffard, you know, the one who always won the essay prizes . . ." "Poor old Ward . . . Still, he'll have been chuffed to have seen some action. . . ."

"I can't stay here," said Ellwood.

"Let's go kick a ball around," said Roseveare.

"No," said Ellwood. "You don't understand. I can't stay *here*, like a good schoolboy, while all my friends are killed."

Roseveare eyed him steadily.

"I suppose the fact you're only seventeen doesn't enter into your plans?"

"Ward was seventeen!"

"Yes, and he's dead."

Ellwood threw up his arms. "I *know that*!"

"Think about it for a day or two. The War will still be there on Monday." Roseveare peeled off and joined West, who had his arm around Pritchard.

———

On Monday, a letter from Gaunt arrived.

Thursday 29th April, 1915,
Somewhere in France

Dear Ellwood,

I suppose by now you've heard the news about Maitland. Incidentally, Sandys was also killed the other day, I haven't found out how yet. I hope it was in a decent show.

I only got a flesh wound in my thigh, which is a holiday compared to everyone else. I wish it had been a little more serious; then I might have been sent home for a spell. They're keeping me in France so that they can send me straight back once I'm healed.

It was Thursday evening, a week ago. We had just rotated back into the trenches—they give us a few days in the village every week or so, to let us shave and polish our buttons and catch up on sleep and sanity.

I was checking the sandbags. Half of them are rotting, which makes them liable to collapse suddenly, leaving anyone standing behind them totally exposed to snipers. There had not been any orders for that evening, other than the usual patrols and wire reinforcements, but of course, in the trenches, there is always the potential for horror. And horror came.

It appeared first in the form of a French Algerian soldier. He came racing through the trench and ran straight into me. My heart sank at the thought of having to shoot him as a deserter. I haven't had to do it, but Maitland ~~tells~~ told me how distressing he found it.

"What's the matter with you, you coward?" I asked him sternly, because my men were watching. And then the man pulled away from me, and I saw his eyes. They were bulging hideously out of his head, and he was taking great, gasping breaths.

"Gas," muttered someone.

"Don't be ridiculous. It was outlawed at the Hague Convention," I said.

I actually said that. I actually believed that the principles of our civilisation, our civilisation that has developed further than any other in the history of the world, giving us telephones and trains and <u>flying,</u> for God's sake, we can <u>fly,</u> I thought, surely such a civilisation, that prides itself on conquering the beast in man and seeks only to bend towards beauty and prosperity, surely, surely, surely, it would not shatter in such a vile and disgusting way.

The Hague Convention sought to make war more humane. We had reached a point in history where we believed it was possible to make war humane.

And then more Algerians came flooding by. Some were only choking, but others were coughing up scrambled bits of lung, their lungs were melting inside them and drowning them. They scrabbled at their throats—I have tried to keep things from you, Elly, you are so fresh and clean, and I did not want to be the one to open your eyes, but I must write, I must describe, I must tell you about the man I saw trying to claw open his own windpipe without seeming to realise that he was missing a hand and was only succeeding in smearing the blood and tendons of his blasted arm all over his blackening face—I stood as he pressed by, and I thought, Why are you at Ypres? Why are you not sitting in a courtyard in Algiers, eating a ripe orange? We have conquered the world with promises that could not be kept. We told those Algerians that their civilisation was no good, that they must have ours instead, we carried our white man's burden dutifully, enlightening Indians—Indians! They who built the Taj Mahal! And Egyptians! For we knew better than their pyramids! We swarmed through Africa and America because we were better than they, of course we were, we were <u>making war humane,</u> and now it has broken down and they are dragged into hell with us. We have doomed the world with our advancements, with our democracy that is so much better than whatever they've thought of, with our technology that will so improve their lives, and now Algerian men must choke to death on their own melted insides in wet Belgian trenches and I—

How I should like to be in England now. It must be spring. It will be brisk in the mornings, and the sky will be blue, with birdsong bursting out of the green, green trees, and women laughing in country lanes. I could read *A Midsummer Night's Dream* in the graveyard and think, England is magic. Surely everyone wants it. Surely they will be grateful for the gifts we bestow upon them, and will not mind the bitter price we demand in return.

The telephone rang in the dugout. I heard Maitland answer it, and in a few moments he emerged.

"There's a hole in the line four miles wide. We've been ordered to plug it."

Our eyes and throats were already beginning to prickle from the gas that was slowly spreading our way. David and I arranged for every man to have a wet flannel tied over his face. Maitland gave us our orders. Over the top, on his word. We split up with our men, and I waited for the signal. The gas smell grew stronger. It was like bleach. The men shifted on their feet, their eyes wild, as the poisoned Algerians continued to flee the thing I was asking them to go towards.

And then Maitland blew his whistle. I heard his men go over the top, and the answering barrage of machine-gun fire, ratatat-tat, like maniacal laughter.

"Over the top!" I cried, and began to climb up, but no one followed. "Over the top, I said!"

The men stayed still, paralysed by terror like nothing I'd ever seen. These were men who daily went on patrols right up to the enemy lines, but that smell was not something they could fight. It was like a phantom, it was like the spirit of God, come to kill every firstborn to show his anger.

"Over the top, you cowardly bastards!" I cried, my voice breaking, because I did not want to do it, I didn't, Elly, I <u>knew</u> those men, but what other choice had I? They were stupid with fear, and only more fear would move them. I shot my pistol into the trench, aiming for the sandbags. My hand was trembling. I missed and shot Harkins in the head. He'd signed up in 1914 and never been injured. No one would play him at cards, because he always won.

He fell to the ground. His blood and brains splattered onto his friends. Still they did not move.

"I will shoot you all!" I screamed, brandishing my pistol. Then, mercifully, they began to stir, and we climbed over the top. I was crying as I ran into the machine-gun fire—I could not see David on my left nor Maitland on my right. All No Man's Land was beginning to yellow with gas. I plunged forward and suddenly realised I was alone. All my men, every last one, had been hit.

I stood on the most God-forsaken patch of earth I hope ever exists and I thought: I wonder how Elly is.

Then something knocked painlessly into my leg, and I saw that I had caught a bullet. I couldn't feel it, but I knew I would soon, and the gas was coming. I picked up my nearest injured man and dragged him to the trench before my leg gave way.

Maitland was killed, and David was shot in the shoulder, but he'll be all right. I've been made captain. Seems a well-tailored uniform and the right accent make me a better candidate than Hayes, despite his years of experience.

My leg is healing nicely. Soon I will have to go back. I am terrified. I wish to God I could see you again before I die.

Yours,
Gaunt

———

Ellwood folded up the letter and put it into his pocket, glancing around at his bedroom. It was the nicest he'd had at Preshute, and he would miss it. Gaunt always said he'd lived a charmed life. It was true that Ellwood found most things easy: people liked him, he was good at sports, good at lessons. He had never been seriously teased nor bullied, despite the obvious reasons he might have been. Gaunt, meanwhile, had struggled along until he got so tall and strong and impenetrable that no one could hurt him. Gaunt, in fact, represented the only real trial Ellwood had ever gone through. Unrequited love was a difficult thing to live with, but Ellwood managed because Gaunt needed him.

He had never really known how much. This letter was not the way he would have chosen to discover the depths to which he was embedded in Gaunt's soul.

Roseveare had told him to wait a few days. The days had passed, and

Ellwood knew what to do. There was a part of him that felt as if it had always been inevitable that he would be forced to wander the Continent, homelessly drifting, like his ancestors through the desert. It was inevitable, because of how badly he longed to be rooted to England. Because of how happy he was at Preshute, the world unfurling, magical and beckoning, before him. Of course he could not have it.

"Oh, God! I'm so sorry!"

It was Pritchard. He tried to close the door and sneak away.

"It's all right, Pritchard, you can come in."

Pritchard sat awkwardly down on the bed next to Ellwood and patted him on the back. West would have made a joke, would have mocked Ellwood. But Pritchard was steadily kind, although he pretended not to be. His bland, forgettable face concealed a sensitive determination to be loveable, to make life easier for other people.

"There, there," he said.

Ellwood snorted.

"It's what girls say when someone is crying," said Pritchard, defensively.

Ellwood blew his nose and wiped his tears.

"I had a letter from Gaunt."

"Oh." Pritchard paused, perhaps thinking of his two brothers, one of whom had died on Sunday: Charlie. Ellwood suspected that Pritchard was secretly relieved it was Charlie who had been killed, and not his eldest brother, Archie, with whom he was much closer.

"Is Gaunt all right?" asked Pritchard, finally.

"No. I mean, yes. But really, no, he's not all right at all. And you know him, he's hardly forthcoming. If he's writing me a letter like this . . ."

"How much has he changed?"

"Yes."

The silence between them grew.

"I'm signing up," said Pritchard. Ellwood nodded.

"Me, too."

"Our mothers won't be pleased."

Ellwood was an only child, and Pritchard's mother had already lost a son. But Ellwood could not stand to read another letter like that, sitting helplessly in his cosy bedroom. If something dreadful was being done to Gaunt, he wanted it done to him as well.

FIVE

LLWOOD'S MOTHER WEPT inconsolably into the sofa cushions. Ellwood knelt by her, making soft, soothing sounds.

"How *could* you," cried his mother. "You *promised* . . . !"

"I'll be back in no time," said Ellwood, "and think how proud of me you'll be!"

". . . only seventeen . . ."

"I'm twenty-five in my head. Please don't cry, Mother, can't you see that I had to? I should have been too ashamed, finishing *lessons* while Gaunt and Pritchard and West were off fighting for king and country."

Mrs. Ellwood's shoulders heaved with sobs.

"I will *never* forgive your uncle," she said, "encouraging you to enlist . . . !"

"He *didn't*," said Ellwood. "He only helped with my commission. I thought you'd be proud."

Mrs. Ellwood sat up. She was still in her thirties. She was pretty and dark and slight; she could have married anyone after his father died, but she hadn't. *"Why should I, when I have you?"* she had told Ellwood when he was twelve, flattering and frightening him at once.

"You're not a soldier, Sidney," she said. "You're different from those boys."

"I'm not," said Ellwood, frowning.

"You're . . . sensitive," she said.

Ellwood knew exactly what it was that she wasn't saying. He bent his head to rest on her knee.

"That . . . may be," he said, suddenly tongue-tied by his desperate love for her, "but that doesn't make me a coward."

"It's not cowardly to finish school!"

"It's done, Mother." He sat next to her and took her into his arms. "I shall have a photograph taken of me in my uniform, and you can put it on the chimneypiece," he said. "And I'll write you such good letters; see if I don't."

"King and country don't *need* you. I do," said his mother.

Ellwood couldn't think how to answer her, so he merely kissed the top of her head.

————

Friday 7th May, 1915
Randall's Farm,
Leatherhead

Dear Henry,

When we next meet, I shall be a second lieutenant in the Royal Kennet Fusiliers, Third Battalion. I'm glad I was able to pick my regiment! (It's all about who you know.) You sit tight in France, I'm coming for you. We'll go to the front together and it will be like the cadets again.

Training is just as you said, hard work but rather peaceful. I've made friends with one of the horses, and I go riding in the afternoons. You weren't joking about the men being short, and their teeth give me nightmares. I'm sure they're the worst thing I'll see in the War. Ha ha.

Pritchard has joined up, too. He wanted to be in the same regt. as his brother Archie, but Archie was taken prisoner last week. I think Pritchard's relieved he's out of it, frankly—Charlie Pritchard died of wounds after Ypres, I don't know if you heard. Actually there was a bit of a rush on the Recruitment Office after we saw the casualty lists. Out of all of us, only Roseveare is staying behind.

"The War will still be there when I'm nineteen," he said. I

don't know where he gets that idea. Anyone with half a brain can see it isn't sustainable. The chaps here keep talking about the Big Push in autumn that will end the War by Christmas. I just hope it doesn't happen before I get there! I'd feel a chump, training away only to arrive in France for the peace celebrations.

I saw that Sandys had been killed. Pritchard heard through his brother Archie, before he was captured. Apparently Sandys was shot through the mouth. His captain said he was awfully brave about it, although it took him two days to die. I never did understand your friendship with him, but I hope you are all right.

I was very sad to hear about Maitland.

That gas attack sounded frightful and I wish I could have been there with you. I will be, next time. I promise.

Your (appropriate) friend,
Sidney

———

Tuesday 18th May, 1915
France

Ellwood,

Don't be an idiot. You are not old enough to enlist. Go back to school.

Gaunt

———

Monday 31st May, 1915
Randall's Farm,
Leatherhead

Dear Gaunt,

You sound just like my mother. She's simply furious with me. But I'm not a child, Gaunt, and it's patronising to treat me like one.

There are quite a few Old Preshutians here, including Arthur Loring. Do you remember him? Blond hair, firm features, makes the girls in town stare and stare. He and I have become chums through talking about Maitland. They were friends, back at school. I was telling one of the other officers about Maitland, about how he would describe a novel by only mentioning irrelevant details ("*Count of Monte Cristo,* jolly good tome about a girl running away with her piano mistress!"), and suddenly I realised they would never meet him. He was so charming, and they'll never know.

> When can their glory fade?
> O the wild charge they made!
> All the world wondered.
> Honour the charge they made!
> Honour the Light Brigade,
> Noble six hundred!

Did you hear that Rupert Brooke died? Infected mosquito bite on his way to Gallipoli.

Ellwood

———

Monday 14th June, 1915
Randall's Farm,
Leatherhead

Dear Gaunt,
Loring left for the front today. I shall miss him awfully. Maitland's mother wrote to me and asked if she could see his old letters to me. I told her I'd lost them. I'm itching to get to Flanders, I hate all this waiting about.
I wish you would write back.

Ellwood

———

Wednesday 23rd June, 1915
Randall's Farm,
Leatherhead

Dear Maud,

I hope you won't mind my writing to you. I haven't heard from Henry in a few weeks and was wondering if you'd had any news?

I'm in training in Surrey, heading to Flanders soon. I hope this letter finds you well. Do send my love to your mother.

Yours,
Sidney Ellwood

————

Friday 25th June, 1915
London

Dearest Sidney,

It is always a delight to hear from you. When will you be coming to stay with us again? Perhaps you could visit when you are on leave.

I have been training in secret with the VADs in a London hospital. I've told Mother I'm taking extra Greek lessons. Greek makes her think of Henry, and then she becomes quiet and guilt-ridden and asks no further questions. Do you think me cruel to lie to her? Only I can't stay in school, preparing for a way of life that vanishes more completely with each new battle. It drives me mad with helplessness to read the casualty lists, when all I am doing is Latin conjugations. Do you remember my friend Winifred Kempton? Her fiancé got a piece of shrapnel in the skull at Ypres. He's recovering in a hospital in Camberwell, but he was blind for two weeks. He kept trying to break off the engagement to save her marrying an invalid, which was well meant, but upset Winifred very much.

As to Henry, his leg is all healed and he is back in Flanders.

There hasn't been any fighting there for about a month, so Mother and I are very relieved. But I am surprised he didn't tell you himself! You two have always been so close.

I do hope you'll write to me, once you are at the front. Henry sends the most wooden little letters, and my imagination fills in the horror.

I shall worry about you.

Yours,
Maud Gaunt

———

Friday 2nd July, 1915
Randall's Farm,
Leatherhead

Gaunt,

You're punishing me for joining up. Well, it's not going to change a thing. I'm not bowing to your whim like some cowed scullery maid who's had her ears boxed.

Ellwood

SIX

THE SMELL WAS OVERWHELMING, but worse than that were the bits of corpses sticking out of the walls. The men had evidently tried to bury them, but in the rain the earth did not hold together. Feet and hands and faces poked at him as he walked by.

"*Bones galore, you've never seen anything like it,*" he had written in his letter to Gaunt, describing the Hermit Cave.

"*You're mistaken,*" Gaunt had answered.

"This is your dugout, sir," said the private. He had obviously dyed his white hair black so that he could enlist. "You'll be with Captain Gaunt. He's hard as nails."

"We were at school together," said Ellwood.

"So you'll know already, then, sir."

"Yes," said Ellwood. He hesitated.

"I'd best be off, sir," said the private. Ellwood smiled at him and went down the stairs.

The dugout was small and dank. It was lit by a few candles in bottles and smelt strongly of whisky. A man was at the rickety wooden table, censoring letters. From the look of his badly cut uniform, Ellwood suspected that it was David Hayes. He had a neat moustache and deep creases in his forehead—Ellwood thought he was probably in his late thirties. He looked up when Ellwood entered.

"Hullo. You must be the new second lieutenant," he said.

"Yes," said Ellwood, feeling quite shy. The guns were muffled down here, so that they sounded only like distant and continual thunder. "Ellwood."

"Lieutenant David Hayes."

Ellwood smiled.

"I know all about you, of course. My friend, Gaunt—" He stopped, painfully aware that Gaunt hadn't written to him in months.

"Yes, he'll be here in a minute."

Ellwood nodded vaguely and looked around.

"Which one's mine?" he asked, gesturing at the wire benches that served as beds. Hayes pointed at the bunk that seemed least stable. Ellwood put his pack down and it sagged almost to the floor.

"You'll want to watch out for the rats. They're friendly."

"Right."

"Known Gaunt a long time, have you?"

"Years. He's my closest friend. At least—" Ellwood broke off, confused. Silence fell.

"You mustn't expect him to be just the same, you know. We're all of us tired and . . . well, tired."

"I know."

Hayes looked disbelieving.

"Gaunt's always fine," said Ellwood.

Hayes seemed as if he wanted to say something more, but he closed his mouth and began cleaning his rifle with an old cloth.

Then Gaunt came down the stairs.

He could not stand upright because he was too tall. His eyes were bloodshot and bagged with deep, purpling shadows. He barely glanced at Ellwood before sitting at the table.

"Hullo, Ellwood," he said, and poured himself a mug of whisky. He sounded gravelly and hoarse.

"It's good to see you," said Ellwood quietly.

"Is it?" asked Gaunt, as if Ellwood had remarked that it was raining outside. "Have you found your bunk? Good. You can go on duty with Hayes in a moment. He'll show you what to do."

"Righto," said Ellwood. He hovered uncertainly near the table. Gaunt pulled out some paper and began a letter. "Er . . . how have you been?"

"Busy."

"It's very . . . muddy out here."

"Must I listen to your profound assessment of the War now, or might I get back to these letters?"

"Yes . . . sorry," murmured Ellwood, and Hayes stood.

"Come on then, let's show you around."

The first body Ellwood saw in its entirety was a Frenchman. He had mostly decomposed, and his long white bones gleamed in the afternoon light. Ellwood paused to look at him.

"Every company leaves him for the next," said Hayes. "Henry's been meaning for us to bury him for a while, but the ground is full up."

" 'He hath awaken'd from the dream of life,' " said Ellwood, in awe. Hayes cast him an amused look.

"Henry said you'd do that," he said.

A shell came yowling from the sky. Ellwood threw himself to the duckboards, which were springy with corpses.

Hayes chuckled as he pulled him up. The mud that now covered Ellwood was like nothing he'd ever seen before; a thick paste that smelt of blood and something vaguely chemical.

"Poor sod," said Hayes, taking a stick and scraping away the worst of it. "No changing clothes for six days, you know."

"Sorry," muttered Ellwood, ashamed of himself. His jaw was so tightly clenched that he had to touch it to release the muscles. "Thought it would land nearby."

"Crumps are easy enough. You'll learn to tell where they'll hit," said Hayes. "It's the whizzbangs you've got to worry about. Silent, and then . . ."

He made a soft sound with his mouth, spreading his hands to mimic an explosion.

"Is this a hot bit of the line?" asked Ellwood.

Gaunt poked his head out of the dugout.

"What's Fritz playing at, shelling us in the middle of the bloody afternoon?" he asked Hayes. "Go tell the machine gunners to give them hell." He retreated down the steps, mumbling something about *peace and fucking quiet*.

"Come on, then," said Hayes. Ellwood followed him down the trench, stumbling over the sprawled legs of the sleeping men. None of them had stirred at the sound of the falling shell. They were soaking wet, all of them. Ellwood watched as a haggard man huddled on the fire step peeled up the collar of his uniform to show his friend where the skin had been rubbed to bleeding by his rifle.

". . . it don't heal in the damp . . ." he said. The wound was dirty, infected.

"There's a general understanding that we won't use artillery on each other if we don't have to," said Hayes. "Hi, Kane, anyone hit by that latest?"

A scrawny-looking private stopped in his tracks. Something was splattered across his face. Ellwood stared at it, trying to figure out what it was.

"Three, sir," he said. "Flegg and Rawlins, and Molony caught fire."

It was brains, Ellwood realised. Greyish scraps of brain and blood, clinging to Kane's hair and eyelashes, dribbling down his chin.

Hayes whistled. "Direct hit?" he asked.

"Aye, sir."

"Molony get out all right?"

"Seemed pretty bad, sir."

"Never mind," said Hayes. "We'll get Fritz back."

Kane nodded. "Yes, sir."

"Clean yourself up, you look like a butcher's shop," said Hayes, and carried on towards the machine gunner's nest. "You've got to feel for Fritz, really," he said to Ellwood, over his shoulder. "He's not got half the artillery we have, and he knows, now, that he's in for a rough half-hour while we retaliate."

"Do you suppose an attack is coming?" asked Ellwood, who could not help but feel a throb of excitement at the notion that he was so near death, that he had really and truly come to a war. All his boyhood had been spent playing soldiers, and now he had *seen* it, *seen* splattered brains on a man's face, brighter and clearer than all the literature he had ever read.

"Doubt it," said Hayes. "Probably some ass of a colonel showing off for his superior, safe and sound behind the German lines."

In the machine gunner's nest, Hayes gave several short commands, and then motioned for Ellwood to cover his ears. The machine guns were so loud that Ellwood didn't really hear them so much as he *felt* them, vibrating thrillingly through his bones. The explosions tingled in his pelvis, filling him with so much exhilaration it was almost like arousal.

He went to sleep late that night, with the boarding-school feeling that he had been there a million years, and home was only a strange and self-indulgent dream.

Ellwood led his first patrol on his second night. He took six men over the top to the barbed wire, which had been shot to pieces in places. They worked as quickly as they could, reinforcing the picket irons with fresh wire.

There was only seventy yards between them and the German trenches. It was strange, thinking that the blasted, empty landscape concealed thousands and thousands of men. It reminded Ellwood incongruously of a grand game of Sardines they had once played at Cemetery House. Ellwood had been one of the last to find the other boys. He had looked all over, and found only ransacked rooms. But finally he opened the door into an empty room and was struck by a furtive silence, a silence that burst at the seams. He spotted a pair of shoes sticking out of the curtains, and then it was as if his eyes acclimatised and he could see boys hiding everywhere. There were three flattened under the mattress, and another two tangled up in the bed-covers. There was a boy behind the cheval glass, and another kneeling behind the fire screen. The whole room heaved with silent life, and Ellwood had hastily joined Gaunt beneath the eaves of a folding table. They had stared at each other in giggling silence when Bertie Pritchard came in, said "Not in here!" and left.

He remembered how Gaunt had leant his forehead into his under the desk. When Pritchard came in, Gaunt covered Ellwood's mouth with his hand. His eyes had been wide with stifled laughter.

As they unwound the coiled wire, one of Ellwood's men sneezed.

The men around him instantly edged away. When he sneezed again, he was shot in the leg by a German sniper, and began to groan.

"For pity's sake, you'll give us all away," said Ellwood.

"I've been hit," said the man. Ellwood's teeth were chattering so hard it was difficult to speak.

"Hayward, is it?" said Ellwood. "Now, listen. You've only nicked your leg, so be a man and keep quiet."

"There's a lot of blood, sir," said another man. Ellwood thought his name was Roberts. Ellwood crawled over to where Hayward lay moaning in the mud. The blood came out of his leg in crimson spurts. Ellwood pressed his hand over the wound, but it was useless. Within seconds, Hayward had bled to death.

Ellwood removed his hands from Hayward's bloodied leg. His men watched him. He was conscious that they were all much older than he was, and that he was new.

"Take him back, Roberts," he commanded. To his endless relief, his voice was steady. "We'll lie low for a quarter of an hour and then get back to work on the wiring."

Roberts dragged Hayward's body back to the trench by the arms, and Ellwood let himself breathe.

" 'Forward, the Light Brigade!' " said Gaunt, when Ellwood reported back. "Well, they'd better bury him, although I don't know where."

"He only sneezed," said Ellwood, who felt that there was something unsportsmanlike about shooting a man for sneezing.

"You ought to write his condolence tonight. Hayward? He had a wife."

"What . . . what do I say?"

Gaunt met his eyes with a dead look.

"That he died a gallant soldier's death for king and country."

Ellwood broke away first.

"Gaunt . . ."

"You'll be on duty from four to stand-to. Write that letter, then go to bed."

"He only sneezed," said Ellwood again. Gaunt wouldn't look at him. He drained his mug of whisky and went to see about the rations delivery.

Friday 6th August,
Somewhere in Belgium

Dear Mrs Hayward,

   On behalf of the Officers and men in my company I wish to offer you my deepest condolences for the death of your husband, Private William Hayward. He was shot while reinforcing our defences and died instantly & painlessly. I can only assure you that his loss will be felt by all, for he was a gallant gentleman and a brave soldier. Although his death is a tragedy, I hope you will find some comfort in knowing that he died protecting his country.

Yours sincerely,
Sidney Ellwood, Sec.-Lieut.

Ellwood soon learnt that it was not violence but sheer *ugliness* that made life in the trenches so unbearable. His boots were quickly soaked through, and Huxton, a slight, gloomy officer who shared their dugout, advised him not to remove them.

"It won't do any good, and it's hell putting them back on."

The flies plagued them, feasting on the dead and then coming to sit amicably on the men's rations. They got stuck in the jam, which was always plum and apple. Ellwood had never liked plum jam, but before two days had passed, he felt quite certain that if he ever saw a plum in the flesh he would be sick. As to apples, the sour, fly-covered substance that they ate with bread at five each evening had as little relation to *them* as the "meat cutlets" had to meat. Their servant, Daniels, tried to make the best of it, and occasionally would be inspired to try something a little more ambitious than yellow soup and bread.

"There'll be cake for dessert," he said. Huxton, Hayes, Gaunt and Ellwood sat around the dugout table.

"What sort of cake?" asked Huxton, suspiciously.

"Plum and apple," said Daniels. There was a groan from everyone except for Gaunt, who was silent. He had scarcely spoken to Ellwood since his first day. Whenever Ellwood asked him a question, he answered in monosyllables before ordering Ellwood away on some unpleasant duty. He treated Huxton as if he were senile, and Daniels was quite terrified of him. He was only patient with Hayes.

"Tell me it's not just bread and jam, Daniels," said Huxton.

"It's a cake," said Daniels stoutly.

"Sugar? Eggs? Flour?"

"We-ell, not that sort of cake, sir."

"What other sort of cake is there?" asked Huxton.

"I've baked some bread with sugar and jam."

"I knew it," sighed Huxton. "It's bread and jam. When I get home, I shall shoot bread and jam, for crimes against humanity."

"Shall I bring it out, sir?"

"Fetch more whisky," said Gaunt.

"Yes, sir." Daniels scurried away.

The discomforts were worse for the men, who had nowhere dry to sit or sleep unless a patch of damp fire step became free. The combination of blistering long marches in and out of the line with ankle-deep trench water led to putrid foot wounds. Their nails splintered to the quick when they attempted to clean their jammed rifles with their fingers—they weren't permitted to use gauze, as the officers were, because it was believed to deteriorate the weaponry over time. Amid this proliferation of small injuries was filth: the sandbags, for instance. When Gaunt wrote that they were rotting, Ellwood had not understood—how could sand rot? But the bags weren't filled with sand any more. They were a sickening mixture of sand and gut-smeared earth. They reeked of decomposing flesh, and sometimes would burst open, showering passers-by with gore and maggots. The rough hessian cloth of the empty sandbag was then used by the men for everything, from wrapping up cheese to bandaging cuts.

There were special trenches dug for the latrines. A long wooden beam was balanced across them, which sometimes broke, plunging the men into the pit of filth below. Mostly they did their business in German helmets, which were bowl-shaped, and then tossed the contents over the edge of the trench at night. It was too risky to attempt in the day, when a hand stuck out for even a moment was likely to get shot off. The constant indignities clotted the mind.

· · ·

It was dusk, on a Friday. The battered skeletons of trees tapered against the fresh starlight in No Man's Land. The sky offered curious glimpses of beauty, from time to time. The men wrote about it in their letters, describing sunsets in painstaking detail to their families, as if there was nothing to see at the front but crimson clouds and dusted rays of golden light.

Ellwood was overseeing a munitions delivery when one of the privates approached him. Ellwood knew who he was. His name was Isaac Kohn, and he was one of the only Jewish men in their company. Ellwood had noticed him immediately.

"Good Sabbath," said Kohn, quietly, hesitantly. There was no one else around.

Ellwood had somehow known this would happen.

"My mother's family converted before Benjamin Disraeli's," he said coldly, turning away to look for the quartermaster. Out of the corner of his eye, he could see Kohn's tentative smile flicker and disappear. He was much older than Ellwood, probably in his early forties. Most of the men were older than the officers.

"Meant no offence, sir."

Ellwood forced himself to stay cool.

"None taken, of course. Easy mistake to make. Now, stop dawdling and fetch that case of grenades."

Kohn bowed his head and obeyed. Ellwood patted his hair to check it was still under control. It was.

Between dinner and tea, they had about three hours in which to sleep and write letters. Gaunt never seemed to sleep. Sometimes Ellwood would return to the dugout to find him lying on his wire bench, candlelight glinting in his bloodshot eyes.

On their fifth day in the trenches, Daniels cleared away dinner and offered everyone a cup of tea.

"Bring out the whisky," said Gaunt, as he did at every meal. Daniels twisted his hands.

"There's only one more bottle, sir."

"What's happened to them all? Have you been at them?"

"No, sir! There were seven, and six have been drunk, sir."

"By whom?" demanded Gaunt.

"Well, sir, there was the one you had on our first day, and two the day Lieutenant Ellwood arrived—"

"All right, all right, no need to enumerate them like crimes. Fetch the last one, and we'll have rum tomorrow."

"Yes, sir." Daniels hurried away.

Hayes was watching Gaunt with concern. "You ought to get some sleep," he said.

"Can't," said Gaunt.

"You might lie down and rest your eyes," said Hayes. Gaunt smiled at him, and Ellwood's heart twisted with jealousy.

"Always looking out for my health, David."

"Well, I'm wired," said Huxton, comfortably. He pulled a pack of playing cards out of his rucksack. "What do you say to a game of cards, Gaunt?"

Gaunt stared at the cards as if he had seen a ghost, and then, to Ellwood's abject horror, he burst into tears. The three men watched him in utter silence as Gaunt howled, an insane, animal sound, his eyes wide open as the tears streamed out of them.

"*I missed and shot Harkins in the head,*" he had written in his letter to Ellwood. "*He'd signed up in 1914 and never been injured. No one would play him at cards, because he always won.*"

"Henry—" said Ellwood, reaching out a hand to touch Gaunt's shoulder. But Gaunt stood up with sudden violence and turned to him, his face full of unbridled fury.

"Don't 'Henry' me, Ellwood! I'm your captain, for God's sake!"

"I'm—I'm awfully sorry, Gaunt—"

"Get out! Go inspect the rifles!"

"But, Gaunt—"

"*Get out!*"

Ellwood fled up the stairs. A rotting hand had popped out of the trench wall that morning, and Ellwood watched as a private stopped and shook it.

"Good afternoon," said the man in an exaggerated posh accent. He didn't seem to know anyone was watching him. "Very fine weather we've been having!"

SEVEN

H E HAD ALREADY INSPECTED the rifles that morning, so the men were puzzled to see him again. Fortunately, Ellwood was used to having authority. It didn't bother him that most of his men were ten times more experienced than he was: he spoke confidently, as if addressing his House in a common room meeting.

"Now look here," he said. "Other companies might make do with grimy weaponry, but I want the Boches blinded by our gunmetal, understand? Lonsdale, wipe that grin off your face and get polishing."

"Yes, sir."

Ellwood had gone to the trouble of learning all the names of the men in his platoon in the first day or two. They knew *his* name, after all.

It was soothing, to command. By the time he returned to the dugout, he felt more steady.

"Hullo," said Hayes, from his perch on an ammunition case. He was alone.

"Hullo." Ellwood took off his greatcoat and hung it on a rusty nail in the wall. "Where's Gaunt?"

"With the gunners. D'you want a cup of tea?"

"Will it taste of disinfectant?"

"'Fraid so."

"Well, I'd better have it, all the same."

Hayes stood.

"Hayes?"

"Yes?"

"Have you seen him cry like that before?"

Hayes shifted on his feet.

"I—I don't like to say."

"Christ."

"He'll be all right," said Hayes. "He just needs a rest, that's all. He's tired. We're all tired."

Tired. A new word ought to be invented, if this was tired.

The next day, they gathered all the men and trooped back through the labyrinthine trenches leading to the village. It was five miles, and the men carried packs that seemed twice their size. The thin ones stuffed socks under their straps to reduce blisters. The officers had batmen to handle their luggage for them, of course. But the men were cheery as they withdrew from the reserve line, joking about what they would do to the Kaiser's daughter if they ever caught her.

As they got further away from the front, the trenches grew shallower, until they could see the plains of sinking mud in which the occasional hand or foot stuck out.

"See that fellow over there?" said Huxton, pointing at a few pale fingers in the sludge. "I saw it happen. He got thrown out of the trench by a shell, and no one was able to pull him out. The mud sucked him down like a cold drink on a hot day."

Ellwood did not answer, but turned his eyes away. He had a wincing memory of his answer to Gaunt's letter about the mud: *"It's funny thinking of you going to the front and complaining about mud, of all things."*

Gaunt marched ahead of him, rolling his shoulders back from time to time. He still hadn't said a word to Ellwood beyond giving him orders to pack up.

They passed the men who were to replace them. They looked clean and well rested, and some of them had faces shining with an excitement Ellwood recognised. They had not been to the front yet.

"How is it up there?" asked an eager young officer.

"Hell," answered Huxton, cheerfully.

"How topping!" said the officer.

· · ·

There was a holiday feeling when they got to the village. The men slung off their packs and raced for the brewery, where makeshift baths were set up. The officers were billeted in a small two-bedroom farmhouse.

"Share with me, Huxton," said Hayes.

Gaunt looked stricken. "We always room together."

"Yes, and you natter away in your sleep all night. I want a proper rest."

Gaunt seemed to bite back a retort. He pushed past Ellwood and went upstairs. Ellwood wondered what Hayes meant—Gaunt had not been known to sleep-talk in school.

The room was plain and whitewashed, with two cots, one on each wall. It seemed like the height of luxury to Ellwood.

It was bliss to bathe. Daniels collected their uniforms to be laundered and gave them clean clothes to wear, and after he had dressed, Ellwood felt like a human again. The men were giddy with relief at having survived, however briefly, and played a game of football in the falling light. For dinner, they had roast chicken. It was the best meal Ellwood had ever tasted.

When it was time for bed, Gaunt went slowly up the stairs, as if he were going to be executed. Ellwood followed and closed the bedroom door behind them.

"Well," said Gaunt. He looked dreadful.

"We don't have to talk, Gaunto," said Ellwood, softly. Gaunt smiled. Something in Ellwood seemed to break.

"Thanks," said Gaunt. They got into their separate beds, and Gaunt blew out the candle.

"Come on, you cowardly bastards, over the top!"

Ellwood was torn from the deepest sleep. He sat up, instantly alert. Gaunt was writhing about in his bed.

"I'll shoot you all! Over the top!"

Ellwood rushed over and shook him. "Gaunt! Gaunt, wake up!"

"I'll do it, I'll shoot you, I will—" Gaunt opened his eyes. He did not seem to recognise Ellwood, but he stopped shouting.

"It was just a dream," said Ellwood. Gaunt blinked and sat up, panting. "It was just a bad dream."

"Elly?"

"Yes, it's me."

Gaunt sagged into him.

"You're going to squash me, you big lump. Here, budge over."

Gaunt made space, and they both lay under the covers, facing each other.

"It was just a dream," said Ellwood again. Gaunt shook his head.

"No," he said. "I keep telling myself that, but it's all so *terribly* real."

"I know. I keep thinking of things I said in my letters—"

Gaunt laughed. "They were sweet." He sighed. He was growing saner and more awake. "I liked thinking of you at Preshute, reciting Tennyson."

"Before I spoiled it all by enlisting."

Gaunt reached out and stroked Ellwood's eyebrow with a trembling thumb. Ellwood kept very still, and let out a jagged breath when he stopped.

"I'm going to die out there," said Gaunt. "I thought . . . I thought it would be nice if you remembered me the way I was."

"You mustn't talk like that. Anyway, I like you the way you are."

Gaunt smiled bitterly. "Oh, yes? Sodden with drink and on the verge of tears?"

"You're not drunk now."

Gaunt was staring at him with an intensity Ellwood had feared he was no longer capable of. Gaunt's eyes were blank, in the trenches.

"No. I'm glad I'm not drunk," said Gaunt.

"I thought you hated me," said Ellwood.

Gaunt pulled him close and kissed him hard on the forehead. His every muscle was taut and shaking. "Idiot," he said.

Ellwood's heart was beating so fast he was sure that Gaunt could feel it.

"When I got here, and you couldn't even look at me—"

"I'm a mess, Elly. I'm so frightened all the time I can't think straight. I feel as if my skin's been burnt away, and I'm just a ragged skeleton walking—nerves without skin—" He frowned and edged away. "Sorry. I don't mean to go on."

"I don't mind one bit."

"Can't even *sleep* without embarrassing myself."

Ellwood brushed a floppy strand of hair out of Gaunt's eyes.

"You haven't embarrassed yourself," he said.

"Ha," said Gaunt. It came out uneven. Ellwood stroked his hair, his temple, so softly that he barely skimmed the surface. Gaunt let out a shaky sigh.

"You're just tired, that's all," said Ellwood, trying to convince himself. "You need to sleep; then you'll be right as rain."

Gaunt moved his face against Ellwood's hand.

"You make it sound so simple," he said.

"Just . . . lie still," said Ellwood. "You're trembling." And to show him what he meant, Ellwood swung his leg over Gaunt's, flattening Gaunt onto his back, draping himself over him. He had meant to still the quivering of Gaunt's muscles with his weight. He hadn't thought it out, hadn't considered what his leg would press up against. He froze when he felt the hard length of Gaunt along his thigh.

Instantly, Ellwood was more aroused than he had ever been in his life. He waited for Gaunt to say something. It was impossible that Gaunt could not feel him hardening against his leg.

Gaunt was silent, except for his laboured breath. Ellwood moved slightly, until they were almost rubbing against each other, so slowly that it might have seemed like an accident. He waited for Gaunt to move, or to push him off. Gaunt did neither.

Ellwood placed one hand on Gaunt's chest. It was much bulkier than his own; it felt as if it would take Ellwood's entire weight if he pressed on it. They weren't looking at each other, and Gaunt was still shivering, in abrupt, irregular vibrations. Ellwood slid his hand down lower, to Gaunt's waist. Gaunt's breath caught, and his hips moved slightly, almost imperceptibly, against Ellwood's. Ellwood breathed out in a surprised huff of air.

Then Gaunt pushed Ellwood off him.

"Get back to bed," he said. "You'll wish you had slept, tomorrow."

Ellwood lay completely still, flat on his back and breathing too hard. He could hear Gaunt next to him, could feel the hot length of his muscled body all along him. He waited for Gaunt to change his mind, to grab him and pull him close.

He didn't.

"Righto," said Ellwood, and sat up. "'Night then, Gaunt."

He was back in his own bed when Gaunt answered, his voice quiet.

"'Night."

Ellwood tried in vain to catch Gaunt's eye as they drilled the men that morning. Gaunt hadn't spoken to him all day.

"Game of football this afternoon, chaps?" asked Huxton, at lunch.

Gaunt glanced out of the window.

"Think I might take a walk."

"Mind if I come?" asked Ellwood, quickly; too quickly.

"Suit yourself," said Gaunt.

They walked in silence, although they could always hear the gunfire. If it hadn't been for that, they might have been back at Preshute, roaming the Wiltshire plains.

"What are you thinking of?" asked Gaunt.

"Guess."

"Poetry?"

"Always."

"Which?"

Ellwood hesitated before quoting. It seemed too revealing; as if he might as well shout *"I love you, I'm waiting for you!"*

But finally, he spoke.

> "*She is coming, my dove, my dear;*
> *She is coming, my life, my fate;*
> *The red rose cries, 'She is near, she is near;'*
> *And the white rose weeps, 'She is late;'*
> *The larkspur listens, 'I hear, I hear;'*
> *And the lily whispers, 'I wait.'*"

Gaunt plucked irritably at a poplar leaf as he passed under it.

"That's from Tennyson's *Maud*, isn't it?"

"Yes," said Ellwood.

"My sister is named after that poem."

"I know."

Gaunt grunted and lapsed into silence.

They talked idly of the War then, of the men, of the shells. Gaunt whipped at the hedges with a damp stick, as if he were beating back the enemy.

"Tireless droves of victims . . . clockwork corpses . . ." he muttered.

" 'Be still, sad heart! and cease repining,' " said Ellwood.

"Tennyson?"

"Longfellow."

"Do you always have a poem for everything?"

"Of course."

Gaunt put his arm around Ellwood and kissed the top of his head. So swiftly was it done that Ellwood hadn't time to capture the feeling before it was over. He stopped in his tracks, but Gaunt strode on as if nothing had happened.

They had reached a clearing when it began to rain. Gaunt sheltered under a palatial oak, but Ellwood turned his face to the heavens and laughed. The fat drops of water drenched him, and he stuck out his tongue to drink. It was sweeter because of the distant guns.

Gaunt watched him. Gaunt was always watching him, as if Ellwood was something important he wanted to remember, but this was different. He leant against the trunk of the oak tree, his teeth clenched, frowning. He seemed in pain.

Ellwood dipped under the shelter of the thick branches.

"Scared of a bit of rain, Gaunto?"

"Terrified," said Gaunt, in a low voice.

Ellwood came closer, closer, closer. He leant his forearm against the trunk by Gaunt's head.

"I used to think you weren't frightened of anything," he said.

"Shows what you know."

Gaunt's head was pressed against the bark. His eyes were fixed on Ellwood's.

"What are *you* thinking of?" asked Ellwood.

Gaunt's gaze dropped to Ellwood's mouth, then up again.

"I can't tell you," he said.

"Show me, then."

Gaunt hesitated, then tugged Ellwood's hips close by the loops of his belt. Ellwood came forward with a gasp, his face pressing into Gaunt's neck. Gaunt's fingers slipped to the front of Ellwood's trousers, fumbled with the buttons. Ellwood didn't dare move, terrified that any moment Gaunt would come to himself and stop.

Gaunt's hot hand was on him, had pulled him out of his clothes. Ellwood could not prevent the shocked sound that escaped him. Gaunt turned his head sharply and bit at Ellwood's neck, then twisted him round, propping Ellwood up against the bark.

Gaunt sank to his knees.

"Ahh," said Ellwood, "you don't have to—"

But Gaunt ignored him. It was surreal. Ellwood couldn't believe it was really happening, Gaunt's mouth so hot and busy around him—so un-Gaunt-like.

"Henry," said Ellwood, but Gaunt didn't look up, continued tending to him with disturbing proficiency, as if he were performing a duty for someone he didn't respect. It felt painfully good, but Ellwood stopped him. Put his hand on Gaunt's head and pushed him gently away.

"Just . . . try to relax," he said.

Gaunt looked up, his face taking on the cold, scornful look that Ellwood knew meant he was embarrassed.

"I've always been told I was rather good at that," he said.

"You've done this before?"

Gaunt laughed joylessly.

"Once or twice."

Ellwood knew that Gaunt had sometimes been siphoned off by the older boys, but he had never really let himself think about it. His own experience had been so different. Ellwood *had* wondered about Sandys, had never understood how Gaunt had befriended someone who forced him to—

Unless, of course, Gaunt had wanted . . . ?

"Have you ever—with anyone you liked?" asked Ellwood.

"*Liked?*" Gaunt looked incredulous.

"Someone you didn't *dislike*, at least," said Ellwood. "Someone you weren't angry with."

Gaunt's jaw tightened. His silence was answer enough.

"Perhaps, after *Lantham,* your standards are simply too high," he said, after a pause.

"Shut up about Lantham. I'm not saying you're no good." (He was *terrifyingly* good.) "You just don't seem to be enjoying yourself."

Gaunt frowned.

"Here, let me show you," said Ellwood. He sank down along the tree bark, sitting on the damp grass, then tugged Gaunt so that he was sitting beside him and unbuttoned his trousers. Gaunt's prick was a little smaller than his. Ellwood had noticed that a long time ago, at school, had found it ruinously attractive.

"On *me*?" said Gaunt. "But you can't want—"

He fell silent when Ellwood took him in his mouth. Eventually, he put a hand softly on Ellwood's head, breathing in faint, delicate tremors. He did not seem to mind about the wax in Ellwood's hair, and Ellwood was consumed by fierce affection. It was intoxicating, to know that his mouth could render Gaunt—Gaunt! with his austere, impenetrable stoicism!—so fragile.

"Elly—I'm going to—"

Ellwood held out an enthusiastic thumbs up.

"Well?" asked Ellwood, once he'd swallowed.

Gaunt drew him close.

"Marvellous," he said. He looked at Ellwood as if he had never seen anything like him before. "But you know you're marvellous at that, I assume."

Ellwood tilted his head down, intensely aware that they had not yet kissed, but Gaunt tipped up his chin with one finger. His pupils were wide and black. He kept his eyes open and leant forward a half-inch, then stopped.

Ellwood let his head drop towards him. They paused, a hair's breadth between their lips. It was strange how this seemed the point of no return, after what Ellwood had just done. For a moment, Ellwood was certain Gaunt would pull back, pretend none of it had happened.

Then Gaunt closed his eyes and touched his lips to Ellwood's.

It was tentative, curious. Ellwood matched it, terrified of scaring him, suspecting that Gaunt would be squeamish about kissing him when Ellwood hadn't had so much as a sip of water since finishing him off. But Gaunt's hand rose to Ellwood's jaw, held it delicately, and deepened the kiss.

"I didn't know . . . I didn't think you were that sort," said Ellwood, when they broke apart.

Gaunt's eyes flickered, hunted.

"Let me try again," he said.

"With pleasure," said Ellwood, biting back questions. Why did Gaunt want this? How long had he wanted it? Had he simply been driven mad by the War?

Gaunt returned to his task with a marked increase in passion.

I wish we had more time, thought Ellwood, before he stopped being able to think at all.

There were no prolonged kisses to nurse *Ellwood* back to earth. When he was done, Gaunt stood and walked away. Ellwood felt himself redden as he buttoned his trousers and caught up with him. The rain had stopped, and they were going back the way they had come.

You hate me, thought Ellwood, observing Gaunt's sharp, crooked profile, like a handsome face in a funhouse mirror. *You hate what you just did.*

"What poem fits us now, Ellwood?" asked Gaunt, in his trench voice, the same one he used when he ordered Ellwood to inspect the men's feet, in the line. It wasn't a voice Ellwood was used to. Gaunt had always been bitter, and occasionally cruel, but he did not use to forget that Ellwood was his friend. *That* had been a fact to carry them through, before.

In any case, the poem that ran through his mind was, once again, one that would betray him: Thomas Wyatt, bemoaning the loss of Anne Boleyn.

> *They flee from me that sometime did me seek*
> *With naked foot, stalking in my chamber.*
> *I have seen them gentle, tame, and meek,*
> *That now are wild and do not remember. . . .*

" 'The Charge of the Light Brigade,' " he lied.

"Recite it."

"Don't be an idiot, Gaunt, you hate that poem."

"Anything's better than this damned silence."

"We could *talk,* then."

"Just recite the blasted poem, Ellwood, since it's always on the tip of your fucking tongue!"

Ellwood clenched his jaw. Gaunt frowned and pushed his hands deeper into his pockets.

"I'm sorry," he said.

> "*Half a league, half a league,*
> *Half a league onward,*
> *All in the valley of Death*
> *Rode the six hundred.*"

"Elly."

"What, Gaunt? I'm doing what you asked. I always bloody do what you ask."

"Is that why we just . . . ? Because you think it's what *I* want?"

Ellwood tried to laugh. "No. You haven't a clue what you want. You're all scrambled up."

Gaunt sighed. "That's true enough." He sounded like himself again.

"Look. A magpie," said Ellwood, because it was all pointless.

"One for sorrow."

"Perhaps we'll see another before we get back."

"It'll be a good sky tonight," said Gaunt, craning his neck. "I think the sky is one of the few redeeming features of the War. I would pay a shilling to watch it, and yet it's free."

Ellwood wanted to punch him. He wanted to make him bleed, and then tend to the wounds.

"Yes," he said. "It's a good sky. I should like to fly up into it."

"Gideon Devi was in the RFC, before he was captured."

Ellwood tried to keep his expression from souring.

"Have you had any letters from him?"

"None. I'm not sure they're letting him send any."

"Beastly Huns."

Gaunt shook his head. "Yes, we're beastly, all right."

"You're not a Hun, Gaunt."

"Perhaps I'm not anything. I'm a ghost already. Wouldn't you look funny, strolling through Belgium, talking to yourself?"

"I wish you wouldn't joke like that."

Gaunt laughed softly, and it wasn't mired in anger the way Ellwood expected it to be.

"I'm sorry, Elly, I am. I'm being awfully unpleasant."

Ellwood let his shoulder knock into Gaunt's.

"I suppose I shouldn't be surprised that you're just as glum at the front as you were at the best balls of the London season."

"I think I'd rather be in a trench than at your cousin Ethel's birthday dinner."

"Ethel is a fine girl."

"Undoubtedly."

"You could do worse than Cousin Ethel."

"Trying to marry me off?"

He had closed again. They were talking too much, that was the problem.

"Oh, do as you like, Gaunt."

They did not speak any more. They went their separate ways when they got back to their billet.

EIGHT

GAUNT AND HAYES sat on a bench in the garden, talking in low voices. Ellwood went to bed early so that he wouldn't have to look at them, but he was still awake when Gaunt finally came upstairs.

He turned to face the wall.

"I know you're awake," said Gaunt, sitting on the edge of Ellwood's bed. "We ought to talk."

Ellwood rolled over to look at him. He remembered telling Macready that.

"All right."

"Our friendship means a great deal to me," said Gaunt, as if he were reciting something.

Ellwood sat up. "Me too, Henry."

"I don't want to risk it, not for anything."

"I was still friends with Maitland, after."

"And Macready? How did your friendship with *him* fare?"

Ellwood waved this away. "Oh, Macready brought that on himself. He took everything so seriously."

Gaunt chuckled softly. "But I won't?"

Ellwood frowned. "*Would* you?"

"No," said Gaunt, sharply. Ellwood put his cheek against Gaunt's shoulder. Gaunt let him.

"Lantham," said Gaunt.

"What about him?" asked Ellwood, surprised.

"You told me you were in love with him. In your letter."

"I'm not in love with Lantham," said Ellwood, quick as Peter denying Christ. "Not in the slightest."

This answer seemed to make Gaunt more uneasy than ever. He turned his face away, so that Ellwood could only see the edge of his strong jaw.

"Yes, but perhaps Lantham is in love with *you*," said Gaunt, and Ellwood could hear the frustration in his voice, although he didn't understand it.

"I doubt it. Anyway, that was at school. It's irrelevant."

Gaunt closed his eyes.

"Why is it irrelevant, please?"

"Because." Ellwood was bewildered by this line of questioning. Surely Gaunt didn't think that *Lantham* was a good reason for them to stop touching each other, not when Gaunt had suddenly developed a mysterious and hitherto non-existent sexual interest in men. "We were just . . . playing. You know how it is."

Gaunt swallowed. " 'Playing,' Ellwood?"

"Yes," said Ellwood. "Not real. Just . . . passing the time."

"Yes," said Gaunt. "I understand." He sounded dreadfully tired.

"Henry. How did it feel, in the woods today?"

Gaunt was breathing rather heavily, but he made no reply.

"Did it help you forget about the War?" pressed Ellwood.

Gaunt nodded once, jerkily.

"Well, then."

"And after the War?" asked Gaunt.

"It'll be as if it never happened. I promise."

"You promise, do you?"

"Yes. It doesn't mean anything, Henry. Only that we want to forget things, once in a while."

Gaunt suddenly gripped him around the waist, stamping kisses onto his eyes, his ears, his hairline.

"It won't change a thing," murmured Ellwood, terrified he would stop. "It doesn't mean a thing."

"Fine, *fine*," said Gaunt, pulling Ellwood onto his lap. "To hell with it. Forget it all."

"It doesn't mean anything," Ellwood reminded himself.

"Stop . . . stop talking," said Gaunt, kissing the spot where Ellwood's jaw met his ear.

I love you, I love you, I love you, Ellwood mouthed into Gaunt's hair.

"Have you ever slept with a man?" he asked aloud.

"Yes," said Gaunt.

Who? *Who?* Sandys? Gideon Devi? When? Why? Had he wanted to? Why hadn't he wanted Ellwood? Why did he want Ellwood now?

But these weren't questions Gaunt owed him answers to.

"So you know how it goes," he said.

"Yes," said Gaunt.

And indeed, Gaunt did know, although sex as he knew it could not have been more different from sex as Ellwood had been taught it by Maitland.

"Slowly," Maitland used to say. *"Or I'll hurt you."*

Gaunt didn't seem worried about pain. He hurried Ellwood through steps that he would gladly have lingered on.

They had barely discussed how they would do it. Ellwood knew what the assumptions were—Gaunt so huge and hulking, Ellwood lithe and delicate—but Gaunt's ideas of sex seemed to match up exactly with Ellwood's fantasies. He had always wanted to *take* Gaunt, to *own* him, had always been jealous and possessive. Gaunt, meanwhile, fell automatically into a rather submissive role, as if he thought Ellwood was so experienced that there was no other way it could go.

"I don't want to hurt you," said Ellwood.

"That's just *part* of it," said Gaunt, impatiently.

"Not if you do it right!"

Gaunt seemed to give up at that, as if he had been chastised. Ellwood didn't bother reassuring him. Cowed Gaunt was easier to manage, anyway. He became shy and skittish.

"I thought you'd done this before," said Ellwood, when Gaunt had jerked away from him twice.

"I have."

"We don't have to go on."

"I just haven't done it . . . like this. Facing someone."

"Would you prefer . . ."

"Would *you*?"

"No!"

Gaunt shut his eyes. He was sweating as if he was in the boxing ring. Ellwood resisted the temptation to lick him.

"Perhaps you're not ready," said Ellwood, preparing to climb off him. Gaunt grabbed him by the arms.

"No—Elly. I . . ." His eyes were all black with their pupils. "I want you to. Please."

Gaunt couldn't look at him the next day. It was as if he had gorged himself on the sight of Ellwood, when his pupils had swallowed up his eyes and he had begged for more. Ellwood tried not to think about it. *"I have seen them gentle, tame, and meek, / That now are wild and do not remember. . . ."*

The lines circled around his head. Gaunt barked orders at the men and terrorised Daniels, just as if nothing had changed.

Perhaps nothing had. But that night, they had sex again. It was better—slower, less furious—and Gaunt did not shrink away from his kisses as often, although he turned his head away from Ellwood's mouth at least half the time. Ellwood could not help but feel this was a baffling display of prudishness, given the circumstances. But Gaunt's behaviour as a whole was so mystifying and erratic that there was no explaining it. Ellwood wondered if he was taking advantage of the fact that Gaunt had clearly gone mad, if he should apologise and climb into the other bed and wait for Gaunt to come to his senses.

Instead, he planted kisses along Gaunt's collarbone and watched him shiver. Two could play at madness.

Gaunt kept starting at imaginary sounds.

"No one's going to come in," said Ellwood.

"You don't know that."

"Stop worrying so much."

"It's difficult when—ohh . . ."

· · ·

But on their last night, Gaunt could not sit still. He paced around their bedroom, chain-smoking.

"It won't be like this," he said.

"I know." Did Gaunt really think Ellwood was so depraved that he couldn't control himself in *a dugout on the front line*? What did he imagine—that Ellwood would dive at his groin between shell explosions?

"And you can't call me Henry."

"You and Hayes call each other by your first names."

"That's different."

"Why?"

"It just is." He flicked his cigarette onto the growing pile of stubs in the ashtray.

"Fine," said Ellwood. He did not want to return to the trenches either, but he didn't see any point in wasting their last night like this. "Gaunt it is. But you can't ignore me all the time."

"I'll damn well ignore you if I please!"

Ellwood flopped back in exasperation. "Will you come to bed?"

Gaunt shook his head and lit another cigarette.

"If nothing else, you need to sleep," said Ellwood.

"Can't sleep."

"You haven't tried!"

"Don't need to. I know."

When Ellwood finally coaxed him to bed, Gaunt kept him up all night. He would fall asleep for a few minutes and then sit bolt upright, his eyes glassy and wide. After a while, Ellwood went to his own bed. Twice, Gaunt woke up screaming.

Breakfast was a subdued affair.

"Impossible to get any sleep in this house with all that racket, Gaunt," said Huxton.

"As always, Huxton, you are the true victim of the War," said Gaunt. He drained his whisky. "Right. No point putting it off."

· · ·

It was worse returning to the trenches than it had been arriving for the first time. All novelty had worn off, and only the grim reality remained.

Gaunt spent most of his time with the men. He went on prolonged and dangerous patrols, and drank most of his meals. When he spoke, it was only to give orders. One afternoon, he stood quite suddenly, went to the wooden beam, and knocked his head into it, hard. It was as if his skull were an egg he wanted to crack. Then, without a word, he returned to the table to censor letters. Ellwood and Hayes looked at each other uncomfortably.

"Anything—anything the matter, Henry?" asked Hayes.

"Just a headache," said Gaunt.

But occasionally, his eyes met Ellwood's, and something in his face softened. It was reassuring to know that there was some connection still between the two Gaunts. Ellwood worried that if it were ever severed, Gaunt would remain the harsh, blank-eyed man he was in the trenches, long after the War had ended.

Monday 16th August, 1915
Ypres, Flanders

Dear Mrs Kohn,

It is with great sadness that I write to inform you of the death of your husband, Private Isaac Kohn. Everyone who knew him liked him very much, and he was awfully brave. He was hit by a shell that fell on his dugout, killing him and six others. I am told he was laughing when the shell landed, and that he felt no pain. We were very sad to lose such a gallant gentleman. I hope it consoles you to know that your husband laid down his life for his country, and made us all very proud.

Yours sincerely,
Sidney Ellwood, Sec.-Lieut.

Ellwood wondered whether there was some kind of Jewish phrase of comfort he ought to add to Kohn's letter. If there was, he had never learnt it. He could think only of Psalms. He had some dim recollection that Jews and Christians shared the Old Testament.

"P.S.," he added. "Yea, though I walk through the valley of the shadow of death, I will fear no evil: for thou art with me."

Writing Kohn's letter left Ellwood with a sense of rootlessness. How did Jews bury their people? Kohn would have known. Strange, drifting memories came back to him: a dark house, mirrors cloaked in black mourning cloth, ripped sleeves. A funeral he had attended as a small child. The images were so eerie that he wondered if he had made them up.

It didn't matter, in any case. Kohn had been blown apart by the shell that hit his dugout, and there hadn't been enough of him to fill a sandbag.

After six harrowing days, they were back in the village. They washed. The lice were laundered out of their clothes, although they could not shake them out of their hair.

Ellwood sat on his bed reading Tennyson's *In Memoriam A.H.H.* and waiting for Gaunt to come upstairs. He wasn't sure he would before supper, but his patience was rewarded when finally Gaunt came and sat next to him, leaving a careful distance between their thighs.

"It's only mutton for dinner," said Gaunt.

"Better than bully beef."

"Yes."

Ellwood closed his book and set it on the floor.

"Haven't you had the poetry scoured out of you yet?" asked Gaunt.

Ellwood frowned. "I need it now more than ever.

> *"Behold, we know not anything;*
> *I can but trust that good shall fall*
> *At last—far off—at last, to all,*
> *And every winter change to spring."*

Gaunt had closed his eyes. His face lost its hardened-captain look. He was only eighteen again.

He'd always liked it when Ellwood recited poetry. Ellwood wasn't sure why. All through Lower Sixth he had recited sonnets at Gaunt; it was probably the only thing that had stopped him from going completely mad and confessing wild, undying love for him, which he knew would have made Gaunt extremely uncomfortable. Anyway, Gaunt already knew that Ellwood loved him. Because of the sonnets.

Gaunt leant against the wall, and Ellwood went on.

> *"So runs my dream: but what am I?*
> *An infant crying in the night:*
> *An infant crying for the light:*
> *And with no language but a cry."*

He stopped. Gaunt opened his eyes.

"What sort of cry, do you think?" he asked.

He was so unendurably handsome.

"Touch me and find out," said Ellwood, boldly.

Gaunt grinned. "I doubt that's what Tennyson had in mind."

"Oh, I don't know. Didn't Sandys use to say Tennyson was a homosexual?"

He knew at once that he had made a mistake, although he wasn't sure which word had damned him: "Sandys" or "homosexual." Gaunt pushed away from the wall, resting his elbows on his knees and his head in his hands.

"Henry . . ."

"Don't."

Ellwood physically pulled back. It was true, he realised, what he had said in the woods: he always did as Gaunt told him. Ever since he was thirteen, when Gaunt found him crying under a desk and said *"Don't let them see you."* When Gaunt told him to be quiet, he was. When he told him to leave him alone, he did. The only time he hadn't was when he enlisted, despite Gaunt's furious letter telling him not to.

Except that had been a form of obedience, too, thought Ellwood—to a pre-existing command. He had been obeying the unwritten instructions in Gaunt's terrible letter after the Second Battle of Ypres: *"I wish to God I could see you again before I die."*

Come here, that letter had said. *I need you.* And Ellwood, obedient as ever, had enlisted instantly.

He wondered if Gaunt knew that he would do anything for him.

"My dust would hear her and beat, / Had I lain for a century dead," provided Tennyson, helpfully.

Gaunt stood and went to the door, but he paused before opening it.

"You hated Sandys," he said.

"Of course I did. He hit you."

"Everyone hits me. *You* hit me."

Ellwood stared at him.

In Shell and Remove, Gaunt and Ellwood had ragged on each other, bloodying noses and blackening eyes.

But he knew that wasn't what Gaunt meant.

MAY 1914—Lower Sixth

It was spring of Lower Sixth, and Ellwood was so in love with Gaunt that his thoughts ran wild with anger. Gaunt was woven into everything he read, saw, wrote, did, dreamt. Every poem had been written about him, every song composed for him, and Ellwood could not scrape his mind clean of him no matter how he tried.

He thought perhaps all the pain would sour the love, but instead it drew him further in, as if he were Marc Antony, falling on his own sword. And it was a magical thing, to love someone so much; it was a feeling so strange and slippery, like a sheath of fabric cut from the sky.

Sometimes, he imagined what Gaunt would look like when he was old, and knew with dizzying certainty that he would love him even when Gaunt was balding and wizened and spent.

He took up with Macready to distract himself, but it only made things worse, like one ironed sleeve of a wrinkled shirt. Macready's inadequacies made Ellwood's teeth ache. Macready wasn't clever like Gaunt. He smiled too easily. His laughter did not feel like a victory. After a few weeks, Ellwood forgot about him.

"You need to speak to him," said Gaunt. They had figured out how to crawl through the crumbling latticework of the Old Priory to get inside, and were smoking cigarettes on the altar.

"I've spoken to him plenty."

Gaunt tossed a balled-up sheet of paper into the air for Ellwood to catch. It was another of Macready's God-awful poems.

"I don't know why he keeps giving these to *you*," said Ellwood. "Oh, it's worse than ever: 'I'm sad and filled with strife, / I do detest my life'—have you noticed he always rhymes 'strife' with 'life'?"

"He gives them to me because *you* are avoiding him."

Ellwood sighed. "Why can't he just leave me be?"

"Because he's in love with you!" cried Gaunt, stepping away from the altar to face Ellwood.

"Of course he's not," said Ellwood, unnerved by this sudden display of emotion.

"You're blind," said Gaunt, staring at him. "He loves you desperately."

Ellwood stared back, wrong-footed.

"Just look at the poems," said Gaunt, breaking eye contact and gesturing loosely at the crumpled piece of paper in his hand.

"He's making himself ridiculous by drawing attention to himself like this," said Ellwood. "He's not playing the game."

"You're unfeeling, Ellwood."

Ellwood had to laugh at the irony of *Gaunt* telling *him* he didn't feel enough.

"Unfeeling? I'm not the one who can't talk to his own sister!"

Gaunt's eyes darkened, and Ellwood knew he had just burnt one of the fragile bridges of trust between them. Gaunt had told him that in confidence, as they walked drunkenly home from a Christmas ball in Mayfair. "*The words get trapped at my mouth,*" he had slurred. "*I can never say what I mean. . . .*"

"You're a cad," said Gaunt.

"Why are you getting so wound up about Macready? He doesn't *matter*."

"Perhaps *you* matter to *him*!"

It was too much. Gaunt shouting romantic advice at him in an abandoned medieval priory was simply *too much*.

"What happened that day with Sandys, last year?"

He wasn't sure why he had asked. The words had tumbled out of him; he hadn't even been conscious that it was a question he wanted answered.

Gaunt blinked, retreating into himself. (Ellwood could tell. He could always tell.)

"Nothing," he said, but he had not asked *which* day, which meant of course it had been something, and Ellwood needed to know, because there was some important truth about Gaunt hidden in his friendship with Sandys, a kernel of Gaunt's personality that Ellwood sensed might make a world of difference if only he could discover it. . . .

"Nothing?" asked Ellwood. Gaunt's face was expressionless.

"We ought to go back to House."

"He shut the blinds. You came out with a black eye."

"It was nothing."

And suddenly, Ellwood believed him. He was hot with anger.

"Of course it was nothing. There's never anything the matter with you. You're utterly indestructible." He knocked Gaunt in the shoulder, right where he knew Gaunt had a bad bruise from his latest fight. It was rather too hard for playfulness, but still Gaunt might have responded by knocking Ellwood mockingly back.

Instead, Gaunt stood still. He had been battered about in the ring the day before, so his face was littered with bruises and cuts. Ellwood wanted to hit each one of them in turn, in case one proved to be the weak spot that would crack Gaunt open. Ellwood smiled, as if he were joshing, and aimed a punch at the bruise on Gaunt's jaw.

"How about now?" he asked. "Still unbreakable?"

"I'm fine."

"You're always fine," said Ellwood, and he was so furiously hot, there was a fire at every pore; he couldn't even think beyond his fists as he hit Gaunt again and again, asking *"How are you?"* after each blow.

"I'm fine," repeated Gaunt, his voice cool and steady. He didn't even flinch. He was made of steel, and there was no getting inside the fortress. Gaunt wouldn't even block him; he was only a wall for Ellwood to throw himself against, and Ellwood was flying apart, breaking himself in the offensive.

"I don't want to fight you, Elly!" said Gaunt.

"Why not?" Ellwood punctuated his words with his fists.

And then, something shifted.

"Because!" shouted Gaunt. His voice cracked. He lashed out with the back of his hand, and it was nothing like how he fought in the ring, neatly and efficiently. It was wild, and Ellwood felt his nose break messily across the middle, blood rushing down his face. Tears sprang to his eyes, but he blinked them away. His heart soared.

There was a chink in the armour. There was something inside the fortress.

They stared at each other, panting, bleeding.

"I'll talk to Macready," said Ellwood.

Gaunt laughed, and helped Ellwood climb out of the priory window.

They never spoke of it again, but whenever Ellwood touched the flat spot Gaunt had punched into his nose, he remembered: there was something inside the fortress.

AUGUST 1915, FLANDERS

"That was different. Sandys persecuted you; I was just angry."

Gaunt leant his head against the door lintel.

"He didn't persecute me," he said, quietly.

"I'm sorry," said Ellwood. "I shouldn't have brought him up, it was thoughtless of me. I know how mixed up I feel when someone mentions Maitland."

"It wasn't like you and Maitland!"

"I know, I didn't mean—"

"It doesn't matter, he's *dead,* gallantly killed at the front, oh God—"

Gaunt turned his face to the door. Ellwood walked tentatively to his side, but didn't dare touch him.

"I'm sorry," he said again.

Ellwood hesitantly let his forehead drop between Gaunt's shoulder blades as they heaved.

When Gaunt stopped shuddering, he turned around. There was no trace of emotion left on his face. He had wiped it all away.

"Sorry about that," said Gaunt. "I'm getting morose in my old age."

"You're eighteen."

"Am I? I feel about eighty. We'd better get to dinner, or Huxton will have gobbled it all up."

"I'm sorry for hitting you, Henry."

"And I'm sorry about your nose. It's a shame, you used to be quite handsome."

"That still counts as a compliment. I'm writing it down."

"Peacock."

. . .

That night, Gaunt screamed in his sleep, but Ellwood lay in bed with him, and told him that it was all right, it was just a dream. The next day, Gaunt went to his knees for him in a field.

They did not talk much. If they were silent, Ellwood could pretend Gaunt loved him, and Gaunt could pretend . . . Ellwood wasn't sure what Gaunt was pretending. In any case, silence served them well.

As their four days drew to a close, Gaunt's eyes became vacant again.

"Can't you try to enjoy yourself? It's silly to lose two nights out of every four," said Ellwood, when they went to bed on the last night.

"Enjoy myself?" repeated Gaunt.

"Distract yourself, then," said Ellwood. "That's why I'm here, isn't it? To distract you?"

"You're here to be machine-gun fodder," said Gaunt.

It was cold, thought Ellwood. He hadn't noticed it before, but now he was shivering.

"I wish you wouldn't talk like that," he said.

"Oh, go to sleep."

So Ellwood did, and Gaunt stayed up, pacing back and forth, smoking.

He wasn't at breakfast.

"Did Henry sleep all right?" asked Hayes. "I didn't hear him last night."

"I don't believe he went to bed at all," said Ellwood.

Gaunt appeared in the doorway. "There's been a change of plan. We're being sent to France. There's going to be a Big Push."

"Goodie. Home in time for Christmas, eh, boys?" said Huxton, tucking into his bacon.

"Where to, Gaunt?"

"Some place called Loos."

NINE

THEY BOARDED a train to France. The men muttered super-
stitiously about the offensive.

"... battalion signaller over on Piccadilly said we're in the
first wave, for sure."

"Who, Ted? Ted said that?"

"Said it's a stone ginger."

"... Translate," said Gaunt to Hayes, as they climbed into the train
carriage. Hayes understood Cockney and trench slang far better than
the public school officers did.

"'A certainty,'" said Hayes. "Bastard signallers. Can't they keep their
mouths shut?" His eyes darted to Gaunt. "Have *you* heard anything?"

"No."

The train was crowded, although they had their own compartment,
shared with the officers of A and C Companies.

Ellwood's head drooped onto Gaunt's shoulder. Gaunt stiffened,
but when he looked around the carriage, he saw that the other officers were all in physical contact with one another. Huxton had his
feet in Hayes' lap. Hayes rested his head against the arm of an officer
from C Company. Men sprawled all over each other. In the hyper-
masculine atmosphere of war, they were not overly concerned with
manliness.

Gaunt let his head tilt so that it touched Ellwood's on his shoulder. Ellwood fell asleep, and Gaunt pretended to do the same, but he couldn't think beyond the parts of them that were touching.

If Ellwood were a girl, he might have held his hand, kissed his temple. He might have bought a ring and tied their lives together.

But Ellwood was Ellwood, and Gaunt had to be satisfied with the weight of his head on his shoulder. Loos hung over them, a word he felt sure would someday have black meaning, but now was only a whisper of dread in his stomach.

They detrained in France several hours later, and marched six miles to a nearby village. It was much larger than the one near Ypres, and the men yelled with delight when they saw the army brothel. There had been much grumbling about the lack of variety of women in Ypres.

The officers made their way to the abandoned château that served as Headquarters. A harassed orderly led Gaunt and Ellwood to a sumptuous bedroom with a large four-poster bed and set out Ellwood's fleabag on the parquet.

"That won't be necessary," said Gaunt. "I don't mind sharing."

"Very good, sir," said the orderly, and retired.

Gaunt rubbed the heavily embroidered bed hangings between his fingers, avoiding Ellwood's gaze.

"How's this for an army barrack?" he asked.

"Splendid," said Ellwood, coming to join him. Their shoulders touched.

"We shall feel like kings in here."

"Edward II and Piers Gaveston," said Ellwood. The comparison made Gaunt itchy. They had both met violent, untimely ends.

"I'd better report to the colonel," said Gaunt.

"I shall take off all my clothes and writhe around on the bed," announced Ellwood.

"Don't you dare."

Ellwood grinned. "Not until you get back, then."

Gaunt chucked him under the chin and went to find the colonel.

When he returned an hour later, Ellwood was curled up on the window seat, using his copy of *In Memoriam A.H.H.* as a surface on which to write a letter. He looked even more like a painting than usual. He radiated peace and prosperity. He was 1912; a world where savagery had been purged from the human spirit, for ever and ever. Gaunt paused at the door to study him.

"Hallo, ghost," said Ellwood, glancing up. "You haunting me?"

"Sorry, I didn't mean to startle you."

"Is the War over or something? You're positively glowing."

Gaunt sat next to him on the window seat. "We're to stay here on Divisional Rest for three weeks," he said.

"Three weeks!"

"Yes."

Ellwood's smile was slow and dawning.

"Three weeks in a four-poster bed with you," he said.

"If you're lucky. I could still make you sleep in your fleabag."

"Not if you want to touch me," said Ellwood, and something in Gaunt's chest turned with a clunk.

"I do," he said hoarsely.

Ellwood smiled, lowering his long, dark eyelashes.

"Do you," he said, in a voice so silky it made Gaunt want to crawl out of his skin. Ellwood leant forward a fraction. Their lips met, and things became simple.

"I can't understand a word he's saying," said Gaunt, as the old man finished his long and huffing monologue.

"Pouvez-vous répéter, monsieur?" asked Ellwood.

Gaunt rolled his eyes. "Repeating himself won't help," he said.

Ellwood waved a hand to quiet him.

They had set up in a cherry orchard in the château grounds. Ellwood had taken some shabby chintz chairs out of what must once have been a nursery, and Gaunt had begged a table from the servants' quarters. The cherries were mostly gone, but a few late-blooming trees still dripped with fruit. Every few hours, Ellwood abandoned Gaunt to his paperwork and filled his hat with cherries.

"Mais ce n'est pas possible, Capitaine, comment sommes-nous censés vivre normalement quand on pêche à la dynamite dans notre rivière—" said the furious old Frenchman.

"Ah," said Ellwood, and he laughed. "I begin to understand."

"Stop laughing," said Gaunt. "You're making him worse. He looks as if he'll pull out a guillotine in a minute."

"Sorry," said Ellwood. "*Monsieur—les hommes utilisent des explosifs pour pêcher dans la rivière?*"

"*Mais c'est ce que je viens de dire!*"

"Right," said Ellwood.

"I ought to have listened in Mamzelle Pardieu's lessons," said Gaunt.

"No one listened to her, the old hag," said Ellwood. "I should never have learnt French if Mother hadn't been friends with Alain-Fournier. Did you ever read *Le Grand Meaulnes*?"

"Not the time, Elly," said Gaunt.

"Well, he's dead now, in any case. Killed about a month into the War. He was *quite* handsome."

"Elly."

"*Les hommes seront punis, monsieur. Ne vous inquiétez pas,*" said Ellwood.

The old Frenchman let out a long breath, shouted a bit more, then touched his hat and disappeared.

"Are you going to explain?" Gaunt asked Ellwood.

"I thought you were good at languages," said Ellwood.

"Only dead ones," said Gaunt. "Pass the cherries. And stop looking so smug."

"That's just my face," said Ellwood, putting a handful of cherries onto Gaunt's supply form.

"Well, I hate it," said Gaunt.

Ellwood glanced quickly around. There was no one near, only a platoon from A Company practicing with bayonets in the field beyond the trees.

"Really?" he asked quietly, and put his index finger between his teeth, sucking cherry juice from the tip.

Gaunt tried to stop himself from smiling, although he knew it was a lost cause.

"Don't distract me," he said. "The Frenchman, what did he say?"

Ellwood grinned and leant back in his armchair. "Oh, all right. Seems the men have been *fishing with bombs.*"

Gaunt almost choked on a cherry stone.

"*Have* they?" he finally managed to say.

"Apparently," said Ellwood. "I wonder if it works?"

"It's not, technically speaking, what the munitions are for," said Gaunt.

"What, fishing? No, I suppose not. They ought to be used on the Germans, really."

"If we're going to be pedantic about it," said Gaunt.

They looked at each other and laughed. Then, without another word, Gaunt tidied the papers, and Ellwood collected the cherries into his handkerchief.

"Seems a shame to punish them, though," said Gaunt, as they walked towards the barracks.

"Only we can't have them blowing up half of France to catch some carp," said Ellwood reasonably. "Quite apart from anything else, it's inefficient."

"I'd give a lot of France for some carp, just now," said Gaunt. "At least a third."

"I wouldn't start with that," said Ellwood. "It may confuse the message."

Gaunt knocked his shoulder into Ellwood's, and Ellwood knocked him back. They told the men to use their rifles to shoot the fish, if they must, and pointed out that if the French didn't *hear* the explosions, there would be no complaints.

Two days later, Lonsdale approached them with a sheepish smile and a fresh carp.

"With the compliments of the men," he said.

"And that," said Ellwood that night, as they lay in bed, full of fish, "is why some things oughtn't be punished."

Gaunt turned over to face Ellwood and caught his eye. Ellwood smiled, and a sudden, dry bleakness spread over Gaunt's heart as he thought of Hercules, and Hector, and all the heroes in myth who found happiness briefly, only for it not to be the end of the story.

———

Apart from drilling in the mornings, and stand-to at six, they were free to do as they pleased. They played elaborate games of Prisoner's Base with the men and swam in the river. Ellwood went on long gallops across the countryside.

"I wonder what would be different if we had a leader as good as Pericles," said Gaunt, one night. They lay in bed, languorous and sated. Ellwood closed his eyes with a smile.

"You're tired," he said. "You talk about Thucydides when you're a certain kind of tired."

"A certain kind?"

"Mhm," said Ellwood. "Tired, not weary. Or ... when you can't think what to say."

There was a long pause in which Gaunt tilted his head to lean against Ellwood's on the pillow.

"You know me so well," he said. He was clearly trying to sound wry, but he had misjudged, and only sounded earnest.

"No," said Ellwood. "Barely."

"Better than anyone else," said Gaunt.

Ellwood doubted this. He remembered Gaunt pouring himself into his letters to Gideon Devi, who had known Gaunt since he was nine.

Ellwood propped himself onto his elbow to look at Gaunt. Gaunt opened one wary eye.

"What?" asked Gaunt.

"Tell me something," said Ellwood. "Something no one else knows."

"Oh, go to sleep, Elly."

Ellwood lay back down, feeling foolish. He forgot sometimes that Gaunt wasn't in love. That this was a convenient addition to their friendship, not a transformation.

"I used to pretend I was Perseus when I was a child," said Gaunt suddenly. Ellwood stared up at the canopy. He knew if he said anything, Gaunt would stop.

"Perseus' father was Zeus," said Gaunt. "But Zeus wasn't particularly interested in Perseus, at first. Perseus spent his childhood impoverished, in a fishing village."

"Ah," said Ellwood.

"What do you mean, 'Ah'?"

"Nothing. Go on," said Ellwood.

"That's all. I used to pretend I was Perseus. That's something no one else knows."

Ellwood opened and closed his mouth a few times, trying to think what to say.

"Your father must be awfully proud you've made captain," he said, finally.

"Yes, awfully," said Gaunt, in a strained voice.

"Do you suppose," said Ellwood, "that Perseus ever forgave Zeus? For not caring about him when it mattered?"

There was a long silence. Then Gaunt spoke.

"No," he said.

———

The only thing that prevented Divisional Rest with Ellwood from being the happiest time in Gaunt's life was the certainty that it would end, and the knowledge that what would follow would shatter him. Even if they should both, by some miracle, survive the War unharmed, Gaunt didn't know how he would stand by Ellwood's side at the altar and watch him marry Maud after these hazy, sunny weeks of kisses and poetry and sex.

———

Friday 20th August, 1915
London

Dear Henry,

Excuse my handwriting, I've blistered my fingers cleaning bedpans at the hospital. I'm so tired I can barely read, and only just found time for Russell's "The Ethics of War," which was brilliant, of course. Although I don't know if I agree with him entirely—I don't know <u>how</u> I feel about this war. It seems short-sighted to call it a war of prestige, as if Prussian militarism might have harmlessly spent itself on nothing. . . . Perhaps it would have. I don't know, I don't know. I've sent the essay to you, anyway. Even though you never read anything I send you.

Have you come across the Royal Welch Fusiliers at all in the line? I ask because that is the regiment of Winifred's fiancé, Charles. He's back at the front after his head injury (thank you for writing to her in May, that was kind of you). Will you let me know how he seems, if you see him? Winifred says his letters are all wrong. He gets too tired to write much, and can't understand her replies; says she uses too many words. I wish I could help her, she's so distraught on the days when she hears from him, because she says it's not like hearing from <u>him</u> at all. If you have any news of him, I know she would be grateful.

You asked after Mother and Father. Father works too hard and Mother complains about the servants: in short, they are unchanged. When you write to them, would you please ask them to let me stay in the nursing dormitories? I have to wake up so early to get across town, and it's just silly to act as if there will be some great attack upon my purity if I'm living in Brixton with eighteen girls and a matron. They'll listen to you. I can't tell you how much they talk about you. Father tells the story of your leg injury so vividly you'd think he was there when it happened.

Sidney wrote me a long poem about a horse. If I were to paint a picture of the War from his letters, I would assume it was made up entirely of clouds and fields and ruddy-cheeked French farm girls. Very pastoral, but I wonder: does he think I don't <u>know</u> about the brutality? He can be so Victorian. Anyway, send him my love, and stay safe.

Love,
Maud

"The Ethics of War" wasn't long—she only sent Gaunt short essays, because she thought he found them boring. He was somehow quite unable to tell her how much he valued her taste, the way she opened doors in his head. They had been close as children, but when he went to Grinstead and began to see her only at the holidays, something had snapped between them, like the breaking of a wishbone. Then had come Ellwood, inevitably enchanted by Maud's independence, her cleverness, her good looks, and any remaining chance there was of regaining that childhood friendship had been lost. Gaunt wanted to talk to her, knew she was worthy of his confidence, and yet was completely incapable of saying what he meant. Her letters built a tongue-tied loneliness in him. He kept them all.

Monday 23rd August, 1915
Somewhere in France

Dear Maud,
   I don't think it would go well if the men caught sight of me reading a conchie like Bertrand Russell. Hard to sympathise with conscientious objectors when you're eating meat from a tin the second year running. The other day I heard a man say he'd like to garrote Mr Bertrand-bloody-Russell with a Union Flag. . . .
   All well today. Ellwood too. Nothing to report. Have written to Father with regards to the dormitory, he's behaving absurdly.
   Poor old Winifred. Am sure Charles will buck up once he's had a bit of rest. Will let you know if I come across the Royal Welch; haven't yet.
   Good luck with the bedpans—keep at it.

Love,
Henry

———

"You've been quiet this afternoon," said Gaunt. They were lying by a riverbank, letting the sun dry them after their swim.
   Ellwood made a noncommittal noise in the back of his throat.
   Gaunt nudged him.
   Ellwood covered his eyes with his forearm. "I had a letter from Roseveare. Here, you read it." He stretched out a hand to fumble in the heap of clothes at his head, and withdrew a crumpled letter. Gaunt sat up to read. Ellwood rested his head on Gaunt's shoulder, his curls untamed by wax after their swim.

Tuesday 31st August, 1915
Kingswood Court, Surrey

Dear Sidney,

Hope you're well. It's jolly nice to get your letters. Glad you and Gaunt are having a bit of a rest.

We had some bad news this week. My brother Martin was killed at Gallipoli. Apparently his death was instantaneous and he did not feel any pain, which is some comfort. We got the telegram the same day as the letter from Preshute telling me I'm Head Boy. Mother is perfectly wild, she wants me to refuse, says it's cursed. Well, you can see her point. First Clarence, then Martin, both Head Boys, both dead. We went to town to see about the memorial service and some girls gave me a white feather. Mother nearly scratched their eyes out. I do wish school would start. It's simply awful at home, what with Mother—well.

You asked for news about the others. Pritchard's at Gallipoli, he says the Australians are frightfully brave. West, Finch and Aldworth are all in France, waiting around for something to happen. Grimsey was injured at Gallipoli. He's in a bad way, to tell you the truth; I visited him in hospital in London. Bit of shrapnel right to the groin, so it's no kids for him, no anything really, and it's not like there's any honour in a wound like that. He'd be furious if he knew I'd told you. They're sending him back to the front once he's healed. I think he's rather hoping he'll be killed.

I'm sorry to write you such a gloomy letter. School starts soon, and then I'm sure I'll cheer up.

Your friend,
Cyril Roseveare

Gaunt folded up the letter and slipped it back into Ellwood's jacket pocket.

"That's rotten luck about Roseveare's brother," he said. He had never liked Cyril Roseveare—had always thought him lofty. When Ellwood was fiercest and cruellest, Roseveare never tried to stop him. He smiled indulgently and went along with things, no matter how unjust. Boys thought him brave because he never complained, but Gaunt didn't call that bravery. Bravery was not so unquestioning.

He couldn't understand why Roseveare hadn't enlisted. It went against everything Gaunt knew of him.

" 'All in the valley of Death / Rode the six hundred,' " said Ellwood. Gaunt tried not to grimace.

"Do you think his death really was instantaneous and painless?" asked Ellwood.

Gaunt gave him a long, cool look.

"Well, no need for Cyril to know that, I suppose," said Ellwood to his knees.

"He'll find out for himself when he enlists. Why hasn't he?"

"He's very close with his mother," said Ellwood, frowning. "Very. He told me once when he was drunk with the Ardents. Said he had dreams about all three of them dying, and her not being a mother any more."

Ellwood put his head in his arms. He was close with his mother, too. Gaunt nudged his nose gently against Ellwood's bare shoulder and Ellwood gave a small laugh.

"Pritchard's letters have been more cheerful than usual," he said. "He's always so *jolly* when things go wrong."

"It sounds as if the fighting's pretty hot at Gallipoli," said Gaunt.

"I can't bear to think of anything happening to him," said Ellwood.

"He'll be all right," said Gaunt. "He's not the sort to die tragically young. Too prosaic."

Ellwood's shoulders shook with soft laughter.

"You're right," he said. "He's got to live. He's destined to have six boring children and a boring job."

"Exactly," said Gaunt.

Ellwood tilted his head up, resting his chin on his arms.

"I used to wish I had brothers," he said.

"Me, too," said Gaunt.

TEN

THEY WERE DRILLING the men when Gaunt saw him. Burgoyne. He was standing with the colonel, taking notes on a pad of paper.

Ellwood found him when they were done. "Did you see him? Did you see Burgoyne?"

"Yes," said Gaunt.

"Repulsive little coward. He's going to spend the rest of his life claiming to have been at the front, when he's done nothing more than swan around a château, eating lamb shanks."

"Perhaps he didn't qualify for armed service. His eyesight isn't good, after all."

"You've gone soft in the head if you think he hasn't squirmed his way out of it, just as he used to squirm out of swimming in the winter."

"*I* didn't want to swim in the winter. That pool was damnably cold. Don't you remember how pneumonia used to fly around in the Lent term?"

"Oh, well, take his side, then. He burnt my poems."

They had both been growing argumentative and belligerent. The bombardment of the German defences had begun, so there was no forgetting that the assault was imminent. The hammering of the coffin makers unnerved the men, who alternated between spreading rumours that they would soon all be sent to a cushy spot in Palestine, drinking too much, and writing evasive letters to their families.

Gaunt wasn't sleeping well any more, and he knew Ellwood wasn't either, although Ellwood never said anything. Each night, Gaunt dreamt of a cloud of unbreathable air sinking over the world. The savage stumps of trees spread away from him in the empty, wasted landscape. Somehow, he knew that a hundred years had passed, and that it was all happening again.

The sex became feverish, panicked, frequent, as if they were trying to stock up memories. Gaunt was sore, and didn't say anything about it, but Ellwood noticed all the same.

"That's not the only kind of sex I enjoy," he said.

"I never said it was."

"Would you stop *suffering* all the time? I don't *want* to hurt you."

"You talk too much," said Gaunt, turning his face to one side. "Just do it, it's fine."

Ellwood worked his way down Gaunt's chest, kissing each rib.

"Hold still," he said, and Gaunt tried to focus, to appreciate, to remember. But as always, the minute Ellwood's mouth touched him, he lost himself.

It had been such a marvellous few weeks, but now Gaunt had a morbid feeling that he had not noticed its passing, that he had been too childishly involved in enjoying it. He felt that if he could only capture one blessed moment with Ellwood—the way his mouth tasted, perhaps, or the look on his face when Gaunt did something that pleased him in bed—then he might hold on to it in the trenches and feel that some part of him had survived.

On the last day before the assault, they ran into Burgoyne on the stairs.

"Hullo, Burgoyne," said Gaunt, wearily. Ellwood's lovely face was cold and haughty.

"Hello, Gaunt, Ellwood. Looking forward to the show tomorrow?"

Gaunt was struck with sudden pity for the gangly boy standing a step or two above him. Burgoyne had never stood a chance, really. He was clever enough to know he didn't fit in, but not clever enough to know how to change.

"I can't say I am, no," he said.

"We've got a jolly good plan. We'll show the Boches what's what!"

"*We*, is it, Georgie Porgie?" said Ellwood, venomously. "Will *you* be going over the top?"

"A little less cheek from you, Ellwood. Remember, I am your superior."

"He doesn't mean anything by it, Burgoyne. But it's hell out there, you know."

"He *doesn't* know," said Ellwood. "I'll bet he hasn't even been to the trenches. Too scared he'll get his ugly teeth knocked out."

"Shut up, Ellwood," said Gaunt. "Burgoyne, I'm sorry, we're awfully distracted just now. I hope you're well."

He took Ellwood physically by the elbow and dragged him up the stairs before Burgoyne could answer.

"You disgusting little suck-up!" said Ellwood when they got to their bedroom. Gaunt lit a cigarette. "He *burnt my poems*!"

"Blast your poems! He has the power of life or death over us, Ellwood, in case you've forgotten!"

"He called me a Jew."

"You *are* Jewish."

"Don't do that."

"Look, he's ghastly, all right? Doesn't mean we have to be ghastly back."

"Gaunt, the son of God, always turning the other cheek."

"That's nonsense and you know it."

"He's a revolting little snake. He's probably never *seen* a dead body."

An agonising laugh broke out of Gaunt. "Oh, God, Elly, is that how we judge men now?"

Ellwood didn't answer.

That night, Gaunt sat in the window seat and smoked. He thought Ellwood was asleep until his voice pierced the dark.

"Behold me, for I cannot sleep,
And like a guilty thing I creep
At earliest morning to the door."

"Tennyson?" asked Gaunt, although he knew the answer.

"Yes. *In Memoriam A.H.H.*"

"Poem written upon the death of a friend," said Gaunt.

The whites of Ellwood's eyes glittered like glass in the candlelight.

"Will you write about me when I die, Elly?"

"Yes," said Ellwood. His voice was thick with sudden and inexplicable anger.

"What will you call it? *In Memoriam H.W.G.*?"

"Maybe. I haven't decided yet."

Gaunt made a sound that was somewhere between laughter and choking.

"Come to bed," said Ellwood.

"Pray tell, O illustrious poet, how will you versify fucking me?"

"Maybe I'll just change your name to Maud and be done with it."

Gaunt shook with laughter, the kind of laughter that prickled at the eyes and balled up in the throat. Ellwood did not come to him, and Gaunt didn't know how to ask him to.

"Go to sleep, Elly," he said, when he had control of his voice.

"Henry . . ."

Their eyes caught each other. Gaunt's heart beat savagely in his ears.

"Never mind," finished Ellwood. "Good night."

All their anger had been spent. Gaunt nodded.

"Good night, Elly."

So Ellwood lay in bed, pretending to sleep, and Gaunt began to drink.

At 6:30 a.m. on September 25th, they assembled the men and waited. The battle had begun. They stood-to for hours before they were finally given their marching orders. The men were restless with anticipation. Even the most fearful among them felt a desire to finally *see* No Man's Land, to walk through it in daylight.

When they arrived at the trenches, everything was in chaos. The

British were using gas for the first time, but the wind had blown it back over No Man's Land, towards their own troops. It was impossible to move without stepping on the wounded, who groaned pitifully for water. A young man with the yellowing complexion of the nearly dead turned his head away from them with a resentful look, as if he did not want to be watched. Another man asked every passing soldier to describe his wound to him—"Please, I don't want to look at it!" The truth was that his entire body was stuck with metal splinters, too many to count, like a pincushion. Next to Gaunt, Ellwood twitched. He had not yet built up that remorseless indifference to pain that was a prerequisite to survival at the front.

Gaunt ignored the groaning wounded and divided the men into their platoons. Everywhere was the peppery-sweet smell of gas.

"Ellwood," he said, before they split up. Ellwood glanced at him. His shoulders were so narrow and boyish, even in his well-cut uniform. "Good luck."

Ellwood nodded, unsmiling.

"You, too."

Gaunt wished the War had been what Ellwood wanted it to be. He wished they could have ridden across a battlefield on horseback, brandishing a sword alongside their gallant king.

He put on his gas mask. His men followed. They looked like strange, monstrous insects.

"Over the top," he said. He had practiced saying it out loud, so that his voice wouldn't quaver, so that he wouldn't remember Ypres, but the shells were so loud no one could hear him. Blood pounded in his head, keeping pace with the explosions of the artillery. He brandished his pistol and stepped onto the fire step.

His men followed.

They climbed out of the trench and past their wire into the thick green gas. All around them, other platoons were forming themselves into blocks, like on a parade ground. They marched forward in columns.

The machine guns mowed them down.

"Get down!" cried Gaunt. "Open covering fire!"

They all fell into the mud and shot wildly into the impenetrable gas. There was no way of knowing whether they were shooting at Germans, or at the troops they were supposed to be relieving. It was almost impossible to see through the clouded panes of glass, and even harder to breathe. All his exposed skin was beginning to sting.

The platoon next to them fell down and began firing.

"They're covering us! Advance!"

They got clumsily to their feet and ran forward, but a shell erupted near Gaunt and he flew through the air, landing heavily on old corpses. Their distended stomachs burst open on impact. His gas mask had been blown off. His first shocked breath filled his lungs with fire, and he looked wildly about for the mask. A bullet came whistling past his ear, and he threw himself into a nearby shell hole, holding his breath.

A young private turned his gas-masked head weakly towards him. His intestines glistened where they had spilled against the bloodied rags of his uniform.

Gaunt's eyes burnt. The gas was worse here, for it had settled. He had a little water in his pack, and he fumbled for it, pouring it on his sleeve and taking an agonising breath through the cloth.

The man pulled at his gas mask.

"Here," he said. "Take mine."

"I couldn't," said Gaunt, coughing.

"I . . . insist," said the man, taking off the mask and holding it feebly towards Gaunt. He looked about twenty. Gaunt shook his head.

"You keep it," he said.

"Please," choked the man, holding the mask out.

Gaunt took it and put it on. Clean, breathable air rushed into his lungs. He guessed that he had taken only one full breath of the gas, and it had been diluted in No Man's Land. He was still coughing and gasping, and his eyes were streaming with tears, but he would not face the same fate as the Algerian soldiers at Ypres.

The man was beginning to choke. Gaunt soaked some linen from his field kit in water and strapped it over his face.

"What's your name?" he asked.

"Billy Selton," coughed the man.

"I'll write to your mother, Billy."

The man nodded loosely.

"Morphia?" he asked. Gaunt shook his head, but found his hip flask. He helped Billy lift the makeshift mask so that he could drink.

"Can you breathe?" he asked, when the linen mask was back in place.

"Just about," said Billy. His eyes were screwed up, poisoned tears oozing out of them like pus. "It hurts."

"I'm going to tell your mother how brave you are."

"It hurts," said Billy again. Gaunt took his hands and squeezed them. Billy began to cry, quietly, like a child ashamed of himself.

"I'll tell your mother," said Gaunt. "She'll be awfully proud of you, Billy."

"Will I . . . live?" asked Billy.

"Of course you will, old boy," said Gaunt.

Billy whimpered. When he died he shook his head gently from side to side, as if he were trying to say no.

Gaunt climbed out of the hole. He deduced which way the Allied trenches lay by the sheer quantity of bodies in that direction. It was only about twenty feet, but it felt like an unimaginable distance. It seemed that he had always been scraping along on his belly through mud and gore, as if there had never been anything else.

He came to a corpse that looked so much like Ellwood that he actually stopped to check, despite the constant bullets that flew past him. It wasn't Ellwood, however. It was some other handsome eighteen-year-old. The back of his head had been blown off. Gaunt was violently glad this boy was dead, because it seemed he must have died *instead* of Ellwood. He kept pulling himself forward, and then he had reached his own trench, and he fell over the side, onto a man who lay moaning on the ground.

"Ohh!" cried the man when Gaunt landed. He wasn't wearing a gas mask. None of the men were. Gaunt tore his off.

"Royal Kennet Fusiliers, Third Battalion, B Company," he said.

"That way," said one of the injured men on the floor. Gaunt raced in the direction he had pointed. He had to get to his dugout. He had to find Ellwood.

ELEVEN

S OON HE STARTED recognising the wounded.

"You're alive!" said a private named Ramsay, as he passed.

"We both are," said Gaunt. "Seen Lieutenant Ellwood anywhere?"

Ramsay shook his head. "Haven't seen any of the officers. They got it pretty bad, sir."

Gaunt stormed towards the officers' dugout. He practically fell down the steps.

"Ellwood?" he called.

"Is that you, Gaunt?"

Ellwood was at the dugout table. He was alive. He was alive.

In a matter of seconds, Gaunt was kissing every inch of him he could reach, which was made more difficult by the fact that Ellwood was doing the same to him.

"You're alive," said Ellwood, "Henry, oh God—"

"I passed a body that looked like you—"

"I saw a shell hit you; are you wounded?"

"It blew me into a tricky spot but I got out all right—"

"Huxton stepped on a mine, I got a bit of him on my sleeve, look—"

"How's David?"

"I don't know, I didn't see— Henry, I thought you had been killed—"

Ellwood started to cry. "I want to go home. . . . We're not nineteen yet, we could still go home. . . ."

"We can't, Elly. We've got to stick it out."

"They're going to send us back out there tomorrow. . . . I don't care about me, Henry, but all that time I thought—I thought you were dead—"

Gaunt kissed him. His stinging eyes were still leaking tears; they mingled with Ellwood's.

"Don't think about it, Elly. You'll go mad if you think about it."

"I want to go home," sobbed Ellwood.

"Well, this *is* a surprise," said a voice. Gaunt sprang away from Ellwood, terror lancing through him, stark and bright, like facing open fire.

Burgoyne was on the stairs.

"What are you doing here?" asked Ellwood savagely. His tear-streaked face held all the bitter helplessness of an angry child.

"You said I had never been to the trenches, so I thought I'd visit. I must say, I didn't expect to find you snivelling for your mummy, Ellwood."

"*Snivelling*—why, you cowardly little worm, you'd claw your own eyes out if you'd seen the things I've seen—"

"Ellwood, go find out about Hayes. Burgoyne . . ." Gaunt held out a trembling, pleading hand. "It was a pretty bad show out there."

But Ellwood did not leave.

"A 'bad show'?" His hands were balled into fists. Gaunt tried to position himself in between him and Burgoyne. "It was *carnage*. It was criminal. You and everyone who planned it ought to be shot."

"You don't understand the first thing about military strategy, Ellwood," said Burgoyne, in a high voice.

"Maybe I don't, but you lot don't seem to understand how machine guns work, when men come marching at them in lines of ten. We wear cloth fucking hats, Burgoyne!"

"Ellwood—" warned Gaunt.

"Steel helmets have been issued in limited numbers—"

"How do you justify yourself? What pathetic excuse have you used to save your worthless little life?"

"My eyesight—"

"Your eyesight! Ask Gaunt about his headaches!"

"Enough!" shouted Burgoyne. "I am your *superior,* Ellwood!"

Ellwood pushed past Gaunt and struck Burgoyne, hard, across the face.

"You're a shameful coward."

Burgoyne was pale, except for his cheek, which was scarlet. His nostrils flared.

"Striking a superior is punishable by death," he said.

"Burgoyne," said Gaunt, his voice cracking. Burgoyne turned to look at him with the sudden sharpness of a snake about to strike.

"I knew *he* was a pervert, Gaunt, but I didn't think *you* were."

Gaunt hung his head.

"Burgoyne . . ." he said again, without much conviction. But Burgoyne had climbed the steps and left.

Gaunt sank onto an ammunition case. Ellwood laughed, bright-eyed.

"Someone had to tell him, Gaunt."

"In this war he's a *god,* Ellwood." He put his face into his hands. "You've brought the anger of the gods upon us."

Twenty minutes later, Hayes stumbled into the dugout. Gaunt and Ellwood wordlessly put their arms around him. Their three heads touched and they stood that way for a moment before Hayes spoke.

"Huxton—"

"Dead."

"Daniels, too."

Gaunt peeled away and poured out three whiskies.

"I've assigned Ramsay to be our servant for now," said Hayes.

"Can he cook?" asked Ellwood.

"Could Daniels?"

Hayes went out and took roll call. He returned, grim-faced.

"How many?" asked Gaunt.

"A hundred and four casualties," said Hayes.

"There'll be a counter-attack tomorrow," said Gaunt.

"I've got Lonsdale attending to the rations," said Hayes. "There'll be more to go round, at least."

"That'll cheer up the men," said Gaunt. "They deserve it."

They drank their whiskies in silence and began writing letters. Gaunt grew increasingly aware that the right side of his body had been ripped up by shrapnel. Now that the shock of battle had worn away, the pain was building. He determined to write to Billy Selton's mother before going to the dressing station.

He spent a long time on the letter, but he omitted that Billy's last words had been "It hurts."

The telephone rang.

Gaunt went to it slowly. He listened to the orders and asked a few questions. Ellwood and Hayes were looking at him when he hung up. He took out his cigarette case, but his fingers were trembling too much to open it. Hayes stood, opened the case easily, and put a cigarette in his mouth. Once he had lit it, he handed it to Gaunt.

"Thanks." Gaunt took a drag and spluttered as the smoke hit his gassed lungs. When he had caught his breath, he looked at Ellwood. "They want more information on the German troops. You and I are to take three men and capture a German prisoner."

There was an awful pause.

"When?" asked Hayes.

"Tonight."

"But that's impossible!"

"Ellwood and I have enemies in high places," said Gaunt, with a small laugh.

"But it's useless, anyway," said Hayes. Ellwood stared unseeingly at his bunk. "We already know who the enemy troops are. Bavarians. The subaltern here before us said one of them spoke English, and they would chatter away across the trenches, talking about Munich."

"Oh," said Gaunt weakly. "So it was Bavarians we were shooting at all day? Poor fellows. It's Oktoberfest now, in Munich." He held up his mug of whisky unhappily and sang under his breath:

"*Ein Prosit, ein Prosit*
Der Gemütlichkeit
Ein Prosit, ein Prosit
Der Gemütlichkeit!
Oans, zwoa, drei, gsuffa!"

He drained his mug.

Hayes stared at him as if he had gone completely mad.

"You speak *German*?"

Ellwood laughed.

"Heinrich Wilhelm Gaunt? His mother knows the Kaiser."

"Go find some volunteers for tonight, won't you, Ellwood?" said Gaunt. "They'll have double rations of rum for a month."

Ellwood nodded. Once he was gone, Gaunt turned to Hayes.

"Don't tell him."

"Tell him what?"

"That it's murder."

TWELVE

Y ou might make it out all right," said Hayes. Gaunt looked at him. "Well. You might!"

"I rather think the point is that we won't." He smiled tightly. "Still, at least you'll be captain."

"Don't say that."

Gaunt shrugged and pressed his hand to the shredded mess of mud, cloth and skin on his ribs.

"Is that your blood, or someone else's?" asked Hayes.

"Mine, I think," said Gaunt. "Caught a bit of shrapnel in the side."

"You ought to go and get it dressed. I'll do the mission for you."

"I'm fine."

"Don't be a hero. You're injured."

"I'm not letting Elly go out there without me."

Hayes considered him. "You won't budge, will you?"

Gaunt laughed. "No."

"I like you, you know that?" said Hayes. "You're all right."

"I like you too, David."

"I suppose you wouldn't have looked twice at me, if it weren't for the War."

"Probably not," said Gaunt. "My loss."

Hayes lifted his drink.

"To unlikely friends."

They clinked mugs.

"If he lives and I don't . . ." said Gaunt.

"Drink," said Hayes, rough-voiced.

By nightfall it was raining heavily, which Gaunt told the men would make it harder for the gunners to spot them. In reality, it would scarcely make a difference, except that it would be miserable to die in the cold, wet mud. He handed out the rum, and went back to the dugout to wait a quarter of an hour for the spirits to soak in. Ellwood sat alone, his face white but determined.

"Here, let's look at the map," said Gaunt. "When I say the word, you'll go right here, and throw your bombs at the wire. Then, when it's clear, I'll dart in with the men, nab the nearest Fritz, and pass him up to you."

"How long will it take?"

"With any luck, no more than ten minutes, start to finish."

"That's good."

"Yes."

"Henry?"

Gaunt looked up.

"Would you have kissed me, if it hadn't been for the War?"

Gaunt let his eyes trace the curve of Ellwood's jaw. The stark, messy blackness of his eyebrows, each hair growing like a miracle out of his smooth, olive skin. The dreadful, seductive arch of his lips. Would Gaunt have kissed him, if it hadn't been for the War? Of course not—he would never have dared. He had been a coward, perhaps, or perhaps he had simply valued his heart intact. It was only because he knew he would die that he could be so reckless with it.

"No, I wouldn't have," said Gaunt.

Ellwood fiddled with the frayed edge of the map.

"How vain am I! / How should he love a thing so low?" he said.

Gaunt had a headache. His head was filling up with salty water, that was why.

"Tennyson," he said.

"In Memoriam."

"We ought to look at the map again," said Gaunt, because it was ridiculous, incongruous, for Ellwood to be bandying about words like "love" when they were preparing to venture out into No Man's Land—

"I sometime hold my tongue, / Because I would not dull you with my song," said Ellwood. "Shakespeare."

It wasn't the time for Shakespeare. How painfully typical of Ellwood not to know that.

"There's a hole in the wire already from the artillery, so your bombs will just be clearing out debris," said Gaunt.

"'My spirit loved and loves him yet, / Like some poor girl whose heart is set / On one whose rank exceeds her own.' That's Tennyson again."

"Ideally we'd capture a lieutenant, but I doubt we'll have time to be choosy," said Gaunt, without any idea of what he was saying. Ellwood was standing, and Gaunt found that he was standing too, that they had stepped away from the old ammunition boxes that served as a table and stools. Ellwood ran his hand through his hair, loosening the curls so that they stuck out at odd angles. He looked as if he hadn't yet made up his mind as to whether he wanted to kiss Gaunt, or to punch him.

"Elly," said Gaunt. "Elly, we have to focus. We—look at where we *are*."

But Ellwood only had eyes for him.

"I wish I could tell you in my own words," he said. "But I can't. And you don't want me to. 'Love is my sin, and thy dear virtue hate, / Hate of my sin, grounded on sinful loving—'"

"I don't hate you, don't be absurd," said Gaunt, although he *did* hate Ellwood a little, just then, hated him for his useless, incomprehensible eloquence, which did not belong at Loos, which reminded Gaunt of Preshute and England and things he did not want to think of until he could be sure he would have them again.

"That was Shakespeare. But sometimes Keats is best!" said Ellwood, his voice swelling with unshed tears. He seized Gaunt's waist (Gaunt bit his tongue as Ellwood's hands split his wounds), he tugged him close, and even though Hayes was due to return at any moment, Gaunt didn't care; he would die, he knew he would, and Ellwood was looking at him as if he was the world.

> *"O! Let me have thee whole,—all—all—be mine!*
> *Yourself—your soul—in pity give me all,*
> *Withhold no atom's atom or I die!"*

He looked insane. Feverish. The kiss he pressed against Gaunt's lips was violent in its desperation.

"Elly—" said Gaunt, breaking away.

"Do you understand?"

"I—"

"Do you understand?"

"But—what about Maud?"

"Maud?" cried Ellwood. "What do you *mean,* Maud? How *can* I make myself clearer, Henry?"

"Well, maybe if you used your own words for once, instead of speaking in cryptic fucking quotations—"

"Cryptic? How thick are you?"

"It's time," said Hayes softly from the entrance.

"Thank you," said Gaunt.

He put on his pack. Ellwood did the same, neither of them looking at the other.

"Henry," said Ellwood, as they approached the stairs. "Promise me you'll talk about it when we get back."

Gaunt couldn't look at him. If he looked at Ellwood now he would lose his head completely; he would refuse to fight, become a conscientious objector on the spot, shoot himself and Ellwood through the feet. Anything to keep them both alive.

"When we get back," he repeated.

"Promise me."

Gaunt thought of the letter he had tried to write that evening. He had given up after four words. The sheet of paper that might have told Ellwood how he felt was still attached to his stationery set. It had been hopeless to love Ellwood because Ellwood did not love him back, and now it was hopeless even though he did.

"Yes," said Gaunt. "I promise."

· · ·

Outside, Cooper, Allen and Kane were putting on their sodden packs.

"All right, men," said Gaunt. "It's possible that what our prisoner tells the colonel might save the lives of hundreds of thousands of British soldiers. It may mean the difference between winning or losing the War. So we won't give up until we've got him, no matter what they throw at us, understand? Let's put on a good show!"

The men nodded. Gaunt wondered whether they knew that it was all irrelevant nonsense, that they were being sacrificed because of a schoolboy quarrel that had festered and blossomed into evil.

The rain came down in ropes. They climbed quietly out of the trenches and crawled through the poisonous, corpse-studded No Man's Land. It was usually silent, but tonight, the thousands of wounded groaned like a ship in a storm.

"Now," said Gaunt, and Ellwood threw his bombs at the barbed wire. Instantly the Germans began shooting at them. Cooper was killed in the first few seconds, shot through the eye. Gaunt did not wait for the rubble to clear away, but rolled through the still-burning wire. He could hear Ellwood, Kane and Allen following him, as well as a German officer shouting orders at his men in a painfully familiar accent. He jumped into the trench and grabbed the nearest German by the waist, flinging him up to Ellwood. A dozen men blinked at him, including—

"Ernst? Sind Sie das?"

Something shattered into his chest. He looked down and saw with strange, coolheaded curiosity that blood was blooming across his front.

"Henry!" cried Ellwood.

Poor Elly, he thought, as he fell. It's so much harder to be left behind.

II

THIRTEEN

H E'S DEAD, SIR," said Kane, urgently. It did not seem to
Ellwood that he was speaking English. A bullet came flying
past him and the world clicked back into focus. The German
boy was trying desperately to escape—the German he had gained in
exchange for Gaunt's life. Ellwood gripped the boy's legs so hard that
he yelped in pain. Allen and Kane were dashing through the barbed
wire, and Ellwood followed. The guns roared. Kane was blown apart
by a grenade. Ellwood did not even pause at the sight, although he had
joked with Kane the day before, flicked his forehead and called him a
miserable bastard.

Allen was hit as he ran. He tumbled into a shell hole, and Ellwood
and his captive dropped in after him. The boy shouted in German, so
Ellwood punched him, and he stopped.

Allen was only hit in the arm. He held his hand over the wound,
trying to stem the blood.

"What now, sir?" he asked.

"Christ," said Ellwood, meaning to swear—but somehow it came out
as prayer; agonised, pleading. "Look," he said, brandishing his rifle at
the German. "*Sprichst du Englisch?*"

"A . . . a little! Very bad!"

"Well, I don't want to die, do you?"

The boy looked at him, wide-eyed. Ellwood ripped through his
memories, trying to remember the phrases he had used that summer

in Munich, but it was simply unbearable, because Gaunt was in every gleaming recollection—

"*Ich möchte leben,*" he said, hastily pairing words together. "I want to live."

"*Ich auch,*" said the boy earnestly. *Me, too.*

"*Ja,*" said Ellwood. "So just shut up, won't you?" He put his finger to his lips. "Here, Allen, keep your rifle on him while I tie him up."

It was quick work. The German boy had become extraordinarily cooperative now that they had established a mutual desire to survive. The guns were dying down. Ellwood took off his hat and stuck it out of the shell hole. It was immediately shot out of his hand.

"Have you any grenades left, Allen?"

"Two, sir."

"On my word, throw them at the Boches, and we'll run like blazes."

Allen nodded at him, his eyes round with fear. Ellwood picked the boy up and settled him over his shoulder.

"*Spinnst du? Sie werden uns töten!*"

"Well, what other choice have we? Now, Allen!"

Allen lobbed the grenades with his good arm, and they scrambled out of the hole and ran. The ground was slick in the rain, and twice Ellwood almost fell. Bullets whizzed around him, but Ellwood paid them no mind. He only ran.

And then they were at the gap in their barbed wire. They tore through it and leapt into their own trench.

Ellwood dropped the German boy on the duckboards.

"Are you all right?"

"*Ja,*" answered the boy, shakily. "You—will—hurt—me—now?"

"*Nein.*" Allen was throwing up. Hayes came hurrying down the trench.

"You made it!"

"Two of us."

Hayes' eyes skipped from Ellwood to Allen. He set his teeth.

"How?"

"Shot in the chest." A sound came out of him like laughter, except that it tilted unpredictably. "Honour the charge they made! / Honour the Light Brigade, / Noble six hundred!"

Hayes looked at him in consternation.

"You'd better go lie down."

"No. Gaunt—Gaunt said we had to bring the prisoner straight to Headquarters."

"I'll take him."

"Gaunt *said*," repeated Ellwood.

Hayes looked as if he wanted to argue, but only nodded.

It was nearly eleven by the time Ellwood and the German boy arrived at the château. Ellwood had walked in a state of total blankness, unaware of anything but the slight pinching of his boots.

An orderly led them to an elegant sitting room, where the colonel sat with half a dozen men, smoking cigars and drinking port. Burgoyne put his glass down when he saw Ellwood.

"Ah! Our German prisoner! Well done, Lieutenant," said the colonel. "Bring him here."

Ellwood prodded the boy forward. The colonel spoke to him in halting German for a few minutes, then beamed around the room.

"Yes, just as we thought, a Bavarian regiment. Well, it's good to confirm our information. Thank you, Burgoyne, for suggesting it. You've got a real sense of strategy." He cast his eye over Ellwood. "I will overlook your dishevelled appearance this once, Lieutenant, but I will not be so lenient if I see you again with unpolished buttons. You may go."

"I apologise for the buttons, sir," said Ellwood, every word sharp and precise. "You see, I had expected Captain Gaunt to deliver the prisoner to you."

The colonel looked at him coldly.

"But he was killed, I suppose?"

Burgoyne made a strange noise. Ellwood ignored him.

"Yes, sir. Along with two other men. But I am glad you were able to confirm your information."

"Careful, Lieutenant. You're coming rather close to insolence."

Ellwood shut his mouth tightly and waited.

"That's all. You may go."

"Thank you, sir." Ellwood turned and left the room.

He was halfway down the corridor when he heard Burgoyne.

"Ellwood! Wait!"

He did not stop walking. He couldn't. He was so tired he thought he might collapse if he stopped.

Burgoyne caught up to him at the stairs.

"Is Gaunt really dead?"

"Yes."

"You aren't . . . you aren't playing a prank?"

Ellwood leant heavily against the bannister, numb with hopelessness.

"A prank, Burgoyne?"

"Yes. To give me a scare."

Ellwood was hit by a dizzying wave of nostalgia for Preshute. For ripping up studies and playing cricket and lounging in beech trees, eating scrumped apples.

"No, it's not a prank, Burgoyne."

Burgoyne looked utterly astonished.

"What did you expect?" asked Ellwood, gently, curiously. He was too weary to hate Burgoyne, just then. Hate would come later. It would make him strong and brittle and warped, a brave and furious soldier— but it had not come yet.

"I thought you'd get a bit of a fright and . . . and see that you couldn't treat me that way," said Burgoyne.

"A bit of a fright," said Ellwood blankly.

Burgoyne nodded. He looked eerily green and corpselike in the dim hall lighting.

Ellwood started to descend the stairs. His heart was heavy with something he couldn't understand because it was too huge and too futile. His mind was repulsed by this grief that felt like infinity: impossible.

"Ellwood," said Burgoyne. Ellwood did not stop. He did not care what Burgoyne had to say: it could not matter. Nothing could. It was all so blindingly meaningless. His buttons weren't polished. The regiment they would slaughter tomorrow came from Munich, where the girls wore dirndls and they ate white sausage for breakfast.

"Ellwood, wait—*how*?"

Ellwood trod heavily down the stairs, so tired.

"He was shot in the chest," he said, without looking around. "We had to—we had to leave him behind."

He had almost reached the door when Burgoyne spoke again.

"Ellwood—I—what can I do?"

Ellwood stopped and faced him, then.

"Nothing."

This time, Burgoyne did not follow when he walked away.

West was in the dugout when he returned. His ears were comically, boyishly large, Ellwood had forgotten how much they stuck out, and his greatcoat was askew.

"Ellwood!" he exclaimed joyfully. Ellwood practically fell into his arms. West hugged him, although he seemed taken aback.

"Hullo," said Ellwood, pressing his face into the fabric of West's coat. His voice sounded thick and strangely childish. He swallowed before speaking again. "What are you doing here?"

West thumped him a few times on the shoulder, and Ellwood forced himself to move away.

"We've been sent as reinforcements for morning," said West.

He looked just as he always did. There was something comforting about how unchangeably, cheerily *normal* he was.

"Seen any action yet?" asked Ellwood.

"No. I'm raring to go. Only they kept us fifty miles behind the front and made us march here in two days, so we're simply exhausted."

"Did you meet Hayes?"

"Yes. Somebody ought to tell him his tailor is deranged."

"You don't notice it so much after a while. Hayes is a good sort." Ellwood sank onto an empty ammunition case. "Fifty miles in two days? Your men will be dead on their feet."

"Yes, they're a bit dispirited." West cleared his throat. "Hayes told me about Gaunt."

Ellwood poured himself a whisky without answering. He wasn't in control of his voice.

"I was sorry to hear it," said West. "I always rather liked him, although he did break my collarbone."

"You were trying to steal his mattress while he slept!" said Ellwood, outrage pulling the words from him.

"I'm not saying I didn't deserve it!"

Hayes came trudging into the dugout.

"Half of your men are underage, and they've had about eight weeks' training between them," he said to West.

"Yes, but they're frightfully keen."

Ellwood pushed the heels of his hands into his eyes. "Frightfully keen!" he said. "Yes, I'm sure they are."

"You ought to get some sleep," said Hayes.

"Does anyone ever tell *you* to get some sleep?" retorted Ellwood.

"I'm twenty-seven years old. I can put myself to bed."

He looked so much older. Ellwood shook his head. "I've got to write Gaunt's parents a letter."

"I'll write it," said Hayes.

"It's my fault he's dead, it's the least I can do."

"What a horrid thing to say!" said West. "I'm sure that's not true."

Ellwood did not answer.

"Ellwood," said West. Ellwood looked up. West's face shone with earnest concern. "It's bad enough without you thinking that, you know."

Ellwood considered throwing himself into West's arms again.

"Have your men synchronised their watches?" he asked, instead.

"Oh—yes. Of course I'll check them again before we go over the top," said West, and then continued to chatter in the background like the ghost of a Preshute common room as Ellwood pulled out a sheet of paper and began to write. It was like all the other letters: patriotic and dishonest.

At 5:30 a.m. the telephone rang. Hayes answered it and wrote down the orders of attack.

"Well, Captain Ellwood, you'd better come here so I can brief you," he said after he'd hung up.

"You're joking."

"I'm not."

"I say, Sidney, congratulations!" said West. "Won't the boys at school be sick!"

"Burgoyne," said Ellwood, realisation dawning. "Burgoyne's arranged it. To atone." He felt queasy. He hadn't eaten anything since breakfast the day before.

"Really?" said West. "What for? That's awfully decent of him. Captain Ellwood. It *does* sound fine!"

"I'm sorry, Hayes. It ought to have been you."

"Don't talk rubbish," said Hayes, stiffly. "You're the obvious choice. *My* school didn't train me to rule an empire."

"I think what we're doing now is losing an empire."

"What rot!" said West. "Losing the empire—look at how the Gurkhas fight! They love England just as much as we do, anyone can see that."

Ellwood went to look at the map.

"We press forward at nine," said Hayes. "We'll be providing covering fire for the troops to the right of us."

Mercifully the gas had been dissolved by the rain, so they did not wear their gas masks. West's men all looked about fifteen, and Ellwood caught one of them trying to load a cartridge into his gun the wrong way round. It did not inspire confidence.

At nine, they went over the top. West's head was shot off before they had gone two feet. Ellwood paused to look at his brains. Pritchard had always said he didn't have any, but there they were, grey and throbbing and clotted with blood.

When they were twenty feet into No Man's Land, they lay down and opened fire. The noise was deafening, deadening. A platoon from another regiment came marching past them. Ellwood saw, as in a mechanical nightmare, that they were led by his friend from the Ardents, Finch. A moment later, Finch was smashed up by a shell.

"Keep firing," Ellwood told his men. He crawled to where Finch had fallen. Finch opened his eyes weakly. His left hip had been ripped away, and half his rib cage torn off.

"Hallo, Ellwood," he said.

"All right, Finchy?"

With a strange lurch of intimacy, Ellwood realised he could see Finch's exposed lung.

"Don't cry, Sidney, old friend," said Finch. His voice was breathy. It sounded as if it hurt to speak.

"Do you think you could move a bit?" asked Ellwood. "It's not so far."

Finch tried to sit up, and gave a low groan of pain.

"No, I don't think so."

"I could drag you."

"All right."

Ellwood took him under the arms and tugged.

"It's no use, Sidney," gasped Finch. The blood gushed out of his chest, arterial-bright against his khaki uniform.

"It's a Blighty one all right. You'll be going home after this," said Ellwood, taking Finch's hand and squeezing it.

Finch smiled, but he could not seem to squeeze back.

"I should like that."

"I have to go back to my men," said Ellwood, bending his head.

"That's all right, Sidney. I'll see you back at the Hermit Cave."

"At midnight."

Finch started to laugh but it turned into a little cry of pain. Ellwood kissed him on the forehead and crawled back to his men, leaving Finch to die alone.

THE PRESHUTIAN

VOL. L.—No. 753.　　　　OCTOBER 14TH, 1915.　　　　Price 9d.

⁓ROLL OF HONOUR ⁓

KILLED IN ACTION.

Adams, Sec.-Lieut. H. R., The Norfolk Regt. Killed in action
near Loos on September 26th, aged 21.

Bates, Lieut. O.H.L., The Royal Warwickshire Regt. Killed in action
near Loos on September 28th, aged 25.

Blackett, Sec.-Lieut. D. A., The South Wales Borderers. Killed in action in
Gallipoli on August 13th, aged 19.

Burkill, Capt. A. H., Cheshire Regt. Killed in action in Gallipoli on
August 10th, aged 25.

Feetham, Sec.-Lieut. B. E., The Seaforth Highlanders. Killed in action
near Loos on September 26th, aged 22.

Finch, Lieut. J. P., The Worcestershire Regt. Killed in action
near Loos on September 26th, aged 19.

Gaunt, Capt. H. W., The Royal Kennet Fusiliers. Killed in action
near Loos on September 25th, aged 18.

Harbord, Capt. J. W., The Black Watch (Royal Highlanders). Killed in action
near Loos on September 28th, aged 21.

Lecke, Lieut. C. B., Public Schools Battalion. Killed in action in Gallipoli on
September 5th, aged 30.

Lyde, Sec.-Lieut. G. G., The Duke of Edinburgh's (Wiltshire Regt.). Killed in
action in Gallipoli on August 10th, aged 21.

Nepean, Lieut. C. G., The Gloucestershire Regt. Killed in action in Gallipoli
on August 8th, aged 25.

Prickett, Sec.-Lieut. R. E., The Seaforth Highlanders. Killed in action
near Loos on September 26th, aged 20.

Rotherham, Capt. H. G., The York and Lancaster Regt. Killed in action near Loos on September 26th, aged 19.

Spooner, Lieut. R. P., The Bedfordshire Regt. Killed in action near Loos on September 26th, aged 24.

Wells, Lieut. W. W., The London Regt. Killed in action near Loos on September 28th, aged 22.

West, Sec.-Lieut. E. W., The Royal Warwickshire Regt. Killed in action near Loos on September 26th, aged 18.

Whitling, Sec.-Lieut. C. M., The Rifle Brigade. Killed in action near Loos on September 26th, aged 20.

———

WOUNDED.

Aldworth, Lieut. E. H., Yorkshire Light Infantry.

Aubrey, Capt. F. C., Royal Fusiliers.

Bird, Sec.-Lieut. T. L., King's Royal Rifle Corps.

Carr, Lieut. E. C., Royal Irish Regt.

Cowley, Capt. A., Bedfordshire Regt.

Charlton, Sec.-Lieut. P. A., York and Lancaster Regt.

De Sausmarez, Capt. J. M., Royal Scots.

Henderson, Sec.-Lieut. N. C., Royal Highlanders.

Loftus, Capt. R. P., The Worcestershire Regt.

Loring, Lieut. A. O., Royal West Surrey Regt.

Mastroianni, Lieut. A. M., Bedfordshire Regt.

Nozieres, Sec.-Lieut. C., Norfold Regt.

Sheppard, Major C.R.B., Sussex Regt.

Sorley, Lieut. H.H.G., The Suffolk Regt.

Stansfeld, Lieut. K. L., The Seaforth Highlanders.

Symonds, Lieut. M. H., York and Lancaster Regt.

Taylor, Lieut. D. R., Dorsetshire Regt.

I

Half a league, half a league,
Half a league onward,
All in the valley of Death
Rode the six hundred.
"Forward, the Light Brigade!
Charge for the guns!" he said.
Into the valley of Death
Rode the six hundred.

II

"Forward, the Light Brigade!"
Was there a man dismayed?
Not though the soldier knew
Someone had blundered.
Theirs not to make reply,
Theirs not to reason why,
Theirs but to do and die.
Into the valley of Death
Rode the six hundred.

III

Cannon to right of them,
Cannon to left of them,
Cannon in front of them
Volleyed and thundered;
Stormed at with shot and shell,
Boldly they rode and well,
Into the jaws of Death,
Into the mouth of hell
Rode the six hundred.

IV

Flashed all their sabres bare,
Flashed as they turned in air
Sabring the gunners there,
Charging an army, while
All the world wondered.
Plunged in the battery-smoke
Right through the line they broke;
Cossack and Russian
Reeled from the sabre stroke
Shattered and sundered.
Then they rode back, but not
Not the six hundred.

V

Cannon to right of them,
Cannon to left of them,
Cannon behind them
Volleyed and thundered;
Stormed at with shot and shell,
While horse and hero fell.
They that had fought so well
Came through the jaws of Death,
Back from the mouth of hell,
All that was left of them,
Left of six hundred.

VI

When can their glory fade?
O the wild charge they made!
All the world wondered.
Honour the charge they made!
Honour the Light Brigade
Noble six hundred!

Tuesday 5th October, 1915
London

Dear Sidney,

Thank you for your letter. I cannot tell you how much I
appreciate your candour. One hears so often of men killed
quickly and painlessly, but it is all too clear from my work
at the hospital that most men die slowly and in agony. Your
description, while difficult to read, was . . . I suppose I cannot
say reassuring. But I have an active mind, and you gave it
something to grasp. I am grateful.

A letter from him arrived yesterday. It had been delayed,
I suppose. It included our code for a coming attack: "μᾶλλον
γὰρ πεφόβημαι τὰς οἰκείας ἡμῶν ἁμαρτίας ἢ τὰς τῶν ἐναντίων
διανοίας." Do you recognise it? It's Thucydides, of course.
"I am more afraid of our own mistakes than of the enemy's
plans."

It was strange, receiving a letter of premonition about something that had already come to pass. And from a ghost, no
less.

Mother hasn't stopped crying since she got the telegram.
Father appears to be pretending nothing has happened. Both of
them want me to leave my job at the hospital, but I can't stand
the thought of giving up my small contribution to the War. Now
that the thing has begun, what other choice have we but to try
to end it?

I feel rather blank and angry. Sympathy of any kind
makes me want to respond with cruelty. I believe you would
understand—it was you who truly knew him. We were linked,
the three of us, from the moment he met you. At least, I always
felt that way. I don't know that Henry did. I don't know that
Henry ever thought of me, once he went to school. Henry was
good at leaving things behind.

I'm sorry. I am angry, as I said. I work twelve-hour days in a
hospital full of men in varying states of rot and decay, and the
War does not end, yet I don't know how it can possibly go on.
I am so frightened you will die, or be blinded or maimed or

disfigured. My fear for you is like a weight that must be carried even in my sleep. Please write back.

Yours,
Maud

———

Thursday 14th October, 1915
Cemetery House
Preshute College

Dear Sidney,

I just saw the casualty list in *The Preshutian*. I'm terribly sorry about Gaunt. (And Finch, and West, and every other poor fellow we knew by name and face and now will never see again.) How are you holding up?

The school is so strange after *The Preshutian* comes out. No one knows how long to wait before behaving normally again. For the younger boys, the period of dignified quiet seems to grow shorter and shorter. For the upper school, it stretches longer each issue. We know more of the dead, I suppose, and look round at each other wondering which of us will join their ranks in the coming year.

I liked Gaunt. I know it's not the first word most people associate with him, but he was kind. Gloomy, too strong for his own good, bafflingly interested in Thucydides, but kind. It seems strange that someone so strong could have been killed by a little piece of lead, doesn't it? I remember thinking that about my brother Clarence.

I hope you are managing.

Your friend,
Cyril Roseveare

———

Friday 22nd October, 1915
Somewhere in Belgium

Dear Cyril,

Thanks awfully for writing.

We fought at Loos for six days, until the regiment was so depleted that they had to pull us back. I can't give you numbers, of course. Now we're back in Flanders, which seems relaxing in comparison. I've become something of an expert at detecting where a shell is going to land just by the way it hisses. The men have taken to calling me "Lucky Sid." I think a year ago I would have thought that impertinent, but now I rather like it.

I avoid thinking about Gaunt. I'm trying to pretend he never existed. He's making it jolly difficult, though. Keeps popping up in the most unexpected places. When I go on patrol, there's always some corpse who morphs into him and opens his eyes at me. Disconcerting. Then he comes into the dugout and hovers by the stairs, watching me. I wish I knew what he wanted.

Well, I know what he wanted. Same as all of us. Punting and lectures and drinks at the pub. 1912, forever.

Hope the Ardents are burning strong. Did you hear that Aldworth is all right? It was only a flesh wound. Of course, what you really want is a nice broken arm. That's a proper holiday. Still, there's always next time. They're saying there's going to be another Big Push in summer.

I live in a constant state of anxiety about Pritchard. He writes me the cheeriest letters, but his regiment is in a tight spot. Each letter I receive only proves he was alive a week ago, and I go mad imagining what may have happened in the interim. His mother has promised to telegraph if he is killed or wounded. I am inexpressibly grateful that you are in England.

Your friend,
Sidney Ellwood

Tuesday 16th November, 1915
The Dardanelles

Dear Sidney,

I just heard about poor old Gaunt. You must be a wreck. I know I am, about West. Thank you for telling me how it happened, I'm glad it was quick.

I am absolutely determined not to feel sorry for myself. It's lucky we're so busy over here. The fighting's a bit hot, so I get plenty of action. Whenever I see something ghastly I think: What ho! I am becoming a man! Just as Kipling promised I would, in *The Jungle Book,* if I was brave enough. Did you hear that his son was killed at Loos? It sounded like a pretty bad show.

I keep starting to write West letters in my mind. But, then, poor sod was practically illiterate, wasn't he? He probably never read my damned letters in the first place. I shouldn't have thrown so many things at his head. Oh, I don't like to think of his head any more.

Aren't I boring? Are you boring, about Gaunt? I'll bet you are.

Beastly Turkish snipers are shooting away at us. Guns rumbling like a purring cat. Comforting! Tell you what, war isn't as colourful as in the illustrations in *Our Island Story.* Where are the banners? I want BANNERS, dash it all!

The poor old rats get sick from eating the dead. The bodies rot quicker out here, see. I'd feel for the squeaky buggers if they'd stop snacking on my rations, after they've snacked on my friends.

I may not see you again; things over my end are rather bloody. I'll make an appointment with you by the pearly gates, how's that? Am I stable? West kept me from capsizing. Christ, the guns don't stop. The Turks are tireless; you've got to admire them.

I know you're keeping safe, you lucky devil. Chin up! The only thing to do in times like these is be a man!

Yours with love,
Bertie Pritchard

———

Wednesday 29th December, 1915
Hampshire

Dear Ellwood,

Please don't rip up this letter when you see who it's from. You have every right to, but please don't.

I've re-enlisted as a private and am in training as I write this. I'll be going to the front in a few months. I know that nothing I say or do can make up for what happened, but I am trying.

I keep remembering the way you looked when you said there was nothing I could do, the night Gaunt was killed. I don't think I'll ever forget that, as long as I live. Fact is, I liked Gaunt. At least, I always felt he had more sympathy for me than the other boys did, even if he did break my nose in Hundreds. He didn't even want to fight in the War in the first place. I will always regret his death, and the part I played in it.

I don't expect, or even ask, you to forgive me. But I thought it might bring you satisfaction to know that your words had effected a change in me.

Your humble servant,
George Burgoyne

FOURTEEN

Ellwood and Hayes soon came to the quiet, unspoken understanding that their company was cursed. Officer after officer came through to replace Gaunt and Huxton. None lasted longer than a month.

Keary was shot in the windpipe while on patrol. Fanshawe was blown up by a trench mortar; his head came rolling back, and the men watched in silence as it rocked appallingly on the duckboards. Wilding was captured in a raid. Langhorne and D'Olier were killed together, when D'Olier lit a cigarette while they stood at watch on the fire step. Langhorne's last words were, "Put out that damned cigare—"

Yatman was luckiest. He only lost an arm.

"You owe me a shilling," said Hayes, as the stretchers took him away.

"It doesn't count if they survive," said Ellwood.

For Ellwood, the officer who represented his worst fears was a young man named Crawley. He was a delicate boy of nineteen, quite handsome, and he had read Ellwood's latest antiwar poem, which had been published in *The New Statesman*.

"You're very good," said Crawley. "I write a bit myself."

He showed Ellwood. They were pretty little poems:

> *Green sunlight slanting through the winds of spring,*
> *A dream in which my heart takes flight, grows wings!*

It was his first time in the trenches. Within three weeks, his eyes were dull, and he spoke no more of England. Ellwood returned to the dugout one morning and found that he had put a shotgun in his mouth. They recorded that he had been killed while on patrol, and Ellwood wrote Crawley's mother a letter telling her how gallant his death had been.

Crawley was replaced by Lansing, one of those rare men at the front who loved killing. He carried grenades in his pocket at all times, even in billets, and crowed when the bombs fell on the German line.

"God! Wouldn't you pay to hear them shriek? *Kamerad! Kamerad!*"

Hayes and Ellwood looked at each other in disgust. Neither answered. This did not discourage Lansing in the least. He seemed, in fact, to take their frequent and prolonged silences as admiration. He strutted in and out of the dugout like a puffed-up cockerel, always poking Ellwood, ribbing him.

"Need some help with loading your rifle, Captain? You're about as good with a gun as you are with the girls," he said, one afternoon. Ellwood, who had been rubbing at the gunmetal with an old rag, lifted the barrel ever so slightly, training it at Lansing's chest.

"Your mother's never had any complaints," he said. Lansing roared with laughter.

"He doesn't rag on you," said Ellwood, later, when they had sent Lansing out on a particularly foolhardy scouting mission.

Hayes scoffed. "Doesn't think I'm worthy. You don't rag on plebs."

"I'm sure that's not it," said Ellwood. Hayes twisted his mouth and didn't reply. Ellwood had the uneasy feeling he had misspoken, that it was like all the times in Shell when boys had called him miserly and Gaunt had told him it wasn't because he was Jewish. It occurred to him now that Gaunt had meant to reassure him. It had only ever made Ellwood feel alone.

Their first night in billets, Lansing got drunk and boastful. He leant across the little farm table, addressing Ellwood. He never spoke to Hayes if he could help it.

"You ever killed a German?" he asked, his breath thick with whisky.

"I imagine so," said Ellwood.

"In cold blood. With your bayonet."

"No," said Ellwood. Lansing sighed and slouched in his chair.

"There's nothing like it. Nothing. You've been hunting?"

"Yes," said Ellwood. Hayes' eyes glittered dangerously, watching, waiting for Ellwood to align himself more closely with Lansing. Ellwood sometimes wondered how Gaunt and Maitland had managed to bridge the class divide, to make Hayes trust them, when he appeared to see *Ellwood* as the physical embodiment of oppression. He wondered if it was his mother's blood that made him so untrustworthy. It was what he always wondered when people didn't like him.

"The feeling of hot gore on your skin," said Lansing, gazing somewhere past Ellwood's left ear. "Holding someone's life in your hands . . . !"

"What battle?" asked Hayes, briskly puncturing Lansing's daydream.

"Wasn't a battle," said Lansing. He did not look at Hayes. "It was prisoners."

"You killed *prisoners*?" asked Hayes.

"Three fewer Boches," said Lansing, with a shrug.

"Go on," said Ellwood, making his voice smooth and inviting. "Tell us. Were they big?"

Hayes curled his lip. Ellwood ignored him.

"One of them was," said Lansing. "Have you got a cigarette? Thanks."

"One of them was big, you were saying," said Ellwood, flipping his cigarette case open and shut. The shadows were long across the floor. Distantly, he could hear the men singing. "He must have been hard to kill."

"Not for me," said Lansing, grinning. "And he squealed like a little girl when I slit his throat."

"With your bayonet?" asked Ellwood.

"No, with his own trench knife." Lansing pulled a knife out of his pack. It was six inches long, and glinted dully in the flickering light.

"My goodness," said Ellwood. "The irony. That must have pleased you. Did you pity him?"

"Pity him? He was *German*," said Lansing.

Ellwood nodded. "No, of course. Truly, your bravery is to be commended."

Lansing seemed finally to hear the ice in Ellwood's voice.

"Got something to say?" he asked, his voice lowering.

Ellwood took out a cigarette and lit it, leisurely slow, at the candle.

"No," he said, when he had let out a curl of smoke. "Not at all. I'm impressed by your talent for murder. I wonder, can you fight?"

Lansing lunged across the table at him, still brandishing the knife. Ellwood did not move.

"Assaulting a superior officer now, are we?" he asked, taking another drag of his cigarette. Lansing froze, then sank back into his chair.

"You bloody well know I can fight."

"Well. We'll see," said Ellwood.

It wasn't fighting that killed Lansing, in the end. He was fumbling in his pocket for a box of matches, and his fingers caught on the ring of a grenade, blowing himself up, along with two others.

His replacement, Carrington, came to them already half mad. Ellwood had played him at cricket, for he had been on the Wellington First XI. Carrington had been eighteen when the War broke out and enlisted immediately. Now the grinning batsman of two years ago was almost unrecognisable. His hair had receded halfway up his scalp, and every thirty-five seconds he spasmed violently. He also had the disquieting habit of looking Ellwood in the face and screaming in terror.

"Will you stop that!" shouted Ellwood impatiently, the third time it happened. "You are an officer in the British Army!"

Carrington closed his mouth sharply and put his hand to his chest.

"I'm awfully sorry," he whispered. "I thought you were someone else."

When he did it to Hayes, Hayes screamed back. At first, Ellwood thought he was trying to wind Carrington up, but he soon realised that Hayes was quite as terrified of Carrington as Carrington was of whatever memories changed their faces in the candlelight.

"Hayes! Pull yourself together!"

"Oh God," said Hayes, white and glistening with sweat. "He's mad. He's utterly mad."

"I'm terribly sorry," said Carrington. "I thought . . . I thought you were someone else."

"The men will think our dugout's haunted if you carry on like this," said Ellwood. He did not mention that the dugout *was* haunted. When he tried to sleep, Gaunt sat by his bunk, watching. Sometimes he wore his uniform, his chest caved in and cracked with dried blood. More often, however, he was in his Preshute tailcoat, unspeakably wistful.

"Carrington's just trying to get sent home," said Ellwood, while Carrington was on patrol.

Hayes lit a cigarette with trembling hands. "That's what's waiting for all of us, if we survive," he said. "Madness."

Hayes refused to be alone with Carrington. He walked up and down the trenches while Ellwood was on duty, and only slept when Carrington was out.

"Nonsense," said Ellwood.

"You're passing your prime, Ellwood. After six months, your nerves start to go. You'll see."

Ellwood drummed his fingers on the table. "Is that what you fear most? Shell shock?"

It was a common conversation. In 1913, you might ask a new acquaintance where he had gone to school, or what he did for a living. In 1916, it was this: what part of yourself did you most fear losing?

Hayes gave a small shrug. "If you get your legs blown off, you're still *you*."

Ellwood passed a hand over his forehead. Crawley's shattered face came to him often in dreams; the fragments of grisly bone, the jellied eyes, the complete end to all that Crawley had been.

"What about you?" asked Hayes. "What keeps you up at night?"

Ellwood forced himself to smile. "Ramsay's cooking. I say, Hayes, why are you smoking those nasty army cigarettes?" The Belgian girls in the village sold Woodbines. The army ones tasted like tar.

"They've raised the prices in the village," said Hayes.

Ellwood looked away. He didn't like to discuss the prices of things.

"Only by a few francs," he said.

Hayes glared at him.

"Golly, I'll give you the money if you need, Hayes. Lord knows I smoke enough of yours."

"I don't need you to buy me cigarettes," said Hayes, with an angry jerk of his head.

"Don't be silly, Hayes," said Ellwood. "I buy things for my friends all the time. Anyway, it's depressing to see an officer smoking that junk. I would have thought your pay would be enough for a few measly packets of cigarettes."

"I send my pay home to my wife's family," said Hayes, sourly.

"You have a wife?"

"*Had* a wife."

"Oh."

Hayes tapped his cigarette into the old bully-beef tin they used as an ashtray.

"Pneumonia."

"I'm sorry."

Hayes didn't respond.

"I . . ." began Ellwood, uncertainly. "I don't know much about money, really."

Hayes gave a mean laugh. "I find that hard to believe," he said.

Ellwood was stung. He took to buying extra packs of Woodbines and leaving them on the table, but Hayes never smoked them.

In April, Ellwood went home on leave. He had tea with Maud in London without a chaperone.

"Are you sure it's all right?" he asked, several times. He felt an awful cad, risking her reputation.

"Things are different from how they were," said Maud. She was at once less and more beautiful than she had been: she was worn and tired, but Ellwood could make out Gaunt in the curve of her eyebrows.

"I can see that," said Ellwood. "Can you imagine what your mother would have said if we had gone out alone together in 1913?"

"I should have been banished to Australia, like the fallen women in Dickens," said Maud, with a smile.

Ellwood's china cup was so delicate. He felt too strong and clumsy to drink out of it, as if he were a wild beast being trained for the circus.

It was easier to talk to Maud than he had anticipated because of her work in the hospital. She had no ideals about the War, and did not remark on his dour ill humour when the scones came and there was no clotted cream, only an anaemic sliver of butter. The food shortages were not so noticeable at the front. The best was reserved for the soldiers.

"You don't answer my letters," she said, when they had finished eating. He had the impression that she had been thinking how to mention it all afternoon, without coming up with any more tactful way than the simple, wounding truth.

"I'm rather busy," he said, trying not to sound as ferocious as he felt.

"Henry wrote every day," she said.

Ellwood looked up, surprised. He hadn't known. It was astonishing to learn new things about Gaunt, like discovering a long-lost Shakespeare poem. Maud, however, was not looking at him. Her gaze was fixed on her hands, clasped around her teacup.

"He didn't write to *me* that often," said Ellwood.

"Are you much busier than he was?" asked Maud.

"There's nothing to write about, in any case," said Ellwood.

"I think of things to tell you," said Maud. "Or do my letters bore you?"

"No," said Ellwood. "I scarcely notice them."

Maud's teacup clattered on its saucer as she clenched her hand.

"Maud—"

She met his eyes. She was so fierce that her features seemed to broaden. It was like seeing Gaunt through a fog. Ellwood shrank back in his chair.

"Please forgive me," he said. "That was inexcusably rude. I only meant that I find it difficult to remember England exists at all, when I'm . . ."

He trailed off.

"I'm sorry," she said. Her eyes filled with tears. She tried to brush them away without Ellwood noticing. "I know. I know how dire it is, out there. I haven't any right to ask things of you. I'm the reason Henry signed up, anyway."

Ellwood reached across the table and drew her hand away from her face.

"He was always going to enlist," he said. "He would have joined the moment I did."

Maud tipped her eyes up to the ceiling.

"He was always so jealous of your company," she said. "I used to wonder if he hated me."

Gaunt would have hated the idea of Maud and Ellwood having tea together. Ellwood felt suddenly that he was the worst sort of traitor, sitting with Gaunt's pretty sister, eating scones and enjoying himself, as if his heart wasn't buried with Gaunt's in the crowded French earth. He caught the waitress' eye and motioned for the bill.

"Of course he didn't," he said breezily. "Don't be silly."

Maud frowned. "Are you going?"

"What? Oh, yes. I've got to buy a compass from the Army and Navy Stores."

"I'll come with you," said Maud. "I arranged to have the afternoon off."

The waitress brought the bill. Ellwood paid, not looking at Maud.

"It'll be boring," he said, once the waitress had left.

"Sidney."

Ellwood stood.

"Oh, come along, if you like," he said.

Maud stayed seated.

"You aren't the only one who has suffered," she said.

"I know," said Ellwood. "You're right. I'm sorry. The fact is . . ." He took a deep breath. "The fact is, Henry *was* jealous. He never liked the idea of our being friends."

"Why ever not?" asked Maud, desperately. "Surely you can see how different our friendship is from yours with him?"

"Of course," said Ellwood. He didn't know how to explain himself. "Of course it is. Don't listen to me, Maud, I'm . . ."

Maud's hand was on his arm.

"Sidney," she said, softly.

"I'm just a selfish . . ."

"It's all right," she said.

He blinked and blinked until the tears stopped coming. Everyone in the tea shop was looking at him. ". . . making a damned fool of myself . . ." he muttered.

Maud guided him gently out of the tea shop. She talked about the hospital as they walked to the Army and Navy Stores. She complained about the Victorian regulations imposed on the VADs, intended to preserve their moral purity. Ellwood let her sensible voice wash over him. Occasionally he stole a glance at her. Her long, straight nose; her thick, fair hair. She had a rather masculine jaw.

". . . and nurses are obliged to resign if they marry," she was saying.

"Do you want to get married?" he asked.

Maud raised her eyebrows. "Are you asking?"

Ellwood was taken by surprise. "Do you want me to?" he asked.

She stared straight ahead as they wove through the crowded street.

"The headmistress gave a speech at my school before I left. She said, 'Only one out of ten of you girls can ever hope to marry. This is not a guess of mine. It is a statistical fact.'" Maud glanced at him. "One in *ten*."

Ellwood didn't want to marry, but he didn't want anything much, so what did it matter?

"Well, you've got me," he said.

Maud grimaced. "Be serious. Anyway, you may not—" She stopped herself. The word "survive" hung heavily between them.

"No," said Ellwood, bleakly. "I may not."

There was a pause as they crossed the street.

"I didn't mean to say that," said Maud.

"I'll marry you now, if you like," said Ellwood, reckless and miserable. "We can go to Gretna Green."

Maud looked just as unhappy as he felt.

"Oh?" she said. "Because we're so in love?"

"We get on. Lots of married people aren't in love," said Ellwood, not sure why he was arguing. He had decided at fifteen to marry Maud because she was clever, and a nice sort of girl, and it would mean Gaunt would be there every Christmas for the rest of his life. It was only occurring to him now how stupid a plan it had been.

"I want to be a politician," said Maud. "You don't want a politician for a wife."

Ellwood laughed. "You can't even vote."

Maud did not answer. They had arrived at the Army and Navy Stores. Ellwood bought a compass, and they parted ways as if they hadn't talked about anything meaningful at all.

Had she changed, he wondered? Had the War distorted her, too?

If it had, it hadn't stopped with Maud. As he walked to the train station, the women he passed were strange and unrecognisable. The poor ones were better dressed, and the rich ones walked alone through the streets, even young girls. London seemed to belong to them. They wore black: Maud had mentioned this, that black had become stylish. It was short-sighted to buy colourful clothes when the bereavements came so quickly.

One of these confident women approached him as he took the train back to East Sussex. He was dressed in a light wool suit, as his housekeeper had said his uniform would need to be thoroughly laundered to remove all the lice.

"For Sir Chickenheart," said the woman, holding out a white feather. "Who dodges trenches so gallantly!"

Ellwood actually snarled at her, like a dog. She started back, dropping the feather at his feet. He spent the rest of the train ride glowering at the other passengers. He knew he might have explained that he was on leave, but he didn't feel he should have to. It seemed as if it should be obvious from his face where he had been.

He had learnt his lesson, however. From then on he only left the house dressed in his uniform. Girls smiled at him. He could not smile back. He wondered what would happen to a country full of spinsters. It was unimaginable.

He went to Preshute to visit Roseveare. The boys swarmed around him.

"*Captain* Ellwood!" they said. Mr. Hammick insisted on making a speech at dinner about what a credit Ellwood was to Cemetery House.

Roseveare, however, did not remark on Ellwood's smart uniform. He looked thinner than before, and the emblazoned Head Boy tie seemed to weigh heavily around his neck.

They escaped the Cemetery boys and went deep into the graveyard. It was heart-wrenching to be there without Gaunt. He knew Roseveare was grief-stricken too, although they didn't talk about it. But Roseveare now wore three signet rings—his own, and those of both his brothers. They were stacked unevenly on a cluttered little finger, as if he was keeping them safe for when Martin and Clarence came home.

"Did you hear about Burgoyne?" asked Roseveare.

"That he enlisted as a private?"

"That he was killed."

"Oh," said Ellwood.

Roseveare looked pensive.

"All this has taught me the limits of my hatred," he said. "I always thought I loathed Burgoyne, but apparently not enough to be glad he's dead."

"How did he die?"

"Oh, painlessly killed in gallant action, said the 'In Memoriam.' But Grimsey was there. Apparently he fell into a flooded shell hole and was drowned."

Ellwood was surprised to find that he was not glad either, although his hatred grew and grew. But he could not hate soldiers. He longed to destroy, to hurt, to kill, but he wasn't sure whom. Possibly the civilians on the train, who had looked so shocked when he snarled.

"When will you be eighteen?" he asked Roseveare.

"Next month."

The age of recruitment had been lowered to eighteen, and conscription had begun in March. Ellwood touched the mossy top of a headstone.

"Do you think you'll be killed?" he asked.

Roseveare's face darkened.

"I don't know why I said that," said Ellwood. "I—"

Roseveare shook his head. "Doesn't bear thinking about."

"I can't seem to hold my thoughts together," said Ellwood.

Roseveare didn't look at him for several seconds, and Ellwood remembered that drunken night, not so long ago, when Roseveare had told him about his recurring dream.

"It's just a telegram," he had said. "It's only my mother opening a telegram, and there are two others on the table. I wake up from the horror of it. Just a telegram."

"You weren't close with Finch, as I was," said Roseveare.

Guilt curled up in Ellwood's chest. He had almost forgotten about Finch. It was strange to think that at one point, he would have cared deeply about his death. It hadn't occurred to him that this was yet another grief Roseveare carried, along with the loss of both his brothers. Ellwood had always been selfish. He was sure Gaunt would have remembered.

"I'm sorry," said Ellwood.

"Don't be," said Roseveare. "I only meant . . . I don't think about whether I'll be killed. I think about whether *you* will be. And Grimsey, and Aldworth."

"One develops a list of names," said Ellwood.

Roseveare gave a quiet laugh. "Yes. And my list is rather depleted. You have a duty to me to survive, Sidney."

Ellwood peeled moss off the grave. He couldn't look at Roseveare. It was bad enough feeling certain he would die, without being told of the misery it would cause his friends.

"I'll be all right," he said. "I'm charmed, remember?"

Roseveare did not reply.

"I'll be nineteen in July," said Ellwood, after a moment. "Older than Gaunt ever was. All my life I've been younger than him. Isn't it funny?"

Privately, he did not believe he would reach his nineteenth birthday. Everyone knew the summer offensive would begin sometime in June.

"Do you still see his ghost?" asked Roseveare.

Ellwood sat down behind the headstone and ran his fingers through the blades of grass. He did not see colours the way he used to. He knew that the grass must be a vibrant, aching green, but it did not seem so to him. More vivid were his memories of Gaunt's strangely feminine hands, which Ellwood had always thought better suited to piano playing than to boxing. It was as if Ellwood hovered in some unreal place where the living faded and the dead took form, and all the world was vague.

"I shouldn't have told you that," he said. "It makes it sound as if I'm going mad."

"I don't think you're going mad," said Roseveare.

"I wish I might have buried him, that's all. Here. He should have liked that."

The birds chattered merrily on the wet brown branches. Daffodils sunned out among the headstones. How alive it all seemed, and how gracious—to die in an era when your death bought you a brief moment at the centre of something. To be important, rather than one of millions.

·   ·   ·

"You've hardly told me what it's like," said Ellwood's mother, that evening. She sprawled on a Napoleon III chaise longue, darning a sock to send to the front. She had joined the war effort with more enthusiasm than effectiveness: she was so proud of the knobbly wool muffler she had knit, for instance, that Ellwood hadn't told her she'd made it too wide. Regulations decreed that the men couldn't cover their ears, no matter how bitter the cold.

"What would you like to hear?" he asked, staring unseeingly at his book of Thomas Hardy poems.

His mother sat up slightly. "I don't know, darling. You know you can always speak to me. We're friends, aren't we?"

"Yes," said Ellwood, because that was simpler than explaining to her that there was no vibrancy to a friendship not threatened by violence.

"Is it . . ." She nibbled her bottom lip. She was no good with words. Ellwood had always found it endearing, but now it made him furious. "Is it . . . *very* dreadful in France?"

"I was mostly in Belgium."

She flushed scarlet.

"Yes, of course—I know that," she said, stumbling over herself, red-faced and miserable. She didn't know what to say, how to look at him, and Ellwood was too numb with anger to care. A strange impulse to hurt her surged through him. He put down his book.

"It isn't very agreeable to see your friends die, no," he said.

His mother's eyes filled with tears, and the anger vanished. He just wanted to be left alone.

"But it's jolly most of the time," he added. "Just like school. Don't cry."

"I wish—I don't suppose you could find a way to—your uncle could arrange to have you sent somewhere safer," she said. "Won't you consider . . ."

He thought, strangely, of Hayes. The idea of pulling strings to escape the front became disgusting in a new and unexpected way.

"I'm quite safe," he said, knowing he couldn't explain. "It's not as if I'm in the RFC. I'm in the reserve line, mostly."

She gave a small sigh, as if she had expected this answer.

"The reserve line," she said. "That's good. You know I . . . I was terribly sorry to hear about Henry. I liked him very much."

"Oh," said Ellwood. "Yes. That was a shame. Couldn't be helped. What's for dinner?"

His mother brightened. "I'm having some lovely friends over; they ought to cheer you up. Do you remember Lady Emma?"

Ellwood nodded, picking up his Thomas Hardy once more.

"Oh!" cried his mother. She held her hand out to him. She had pricked her index finger, and a fat, globulous drop of blood sat on the tip. "I'm quite certain the last maid stole my thimble, and here's what comes of it," she said, laughing.

Ellwood's stomach lurched. His vision blackened at the edges, and he felt suddenly, breathlessly faint.

"Sidney? Are you all right?" asked his mother.

"I," said Ellwood, then collapsed backwards in his chair, light-headed darkness seeping across his eyes.

"It's very unusual for him to be so squeamish," Ellwood's mother explained to her friends at dinner.

"It must have been quite the pinprick to intimidate a soldier." Lady Emma laughed.

Ellwood did not say anything. He could not explain why that drop of blood on his mother's finger had so appalled him, when he had seen West's brain pulse with his last heartbeats and felt nothing but dispassionate curiosity.

Before many days had passed, he longed to return to the front. With the exception of Roseveare, no one seemed to know what to say to him. His mother looked at him too much, as if she were trying to fix him in her memory. Her friends watched him expectantly over the cheese course, as if they thought at any moment that he would burst forth with a thrilling tale of heroism and chivalry.

"My Peter was killed at Loos," said the farmer when he brought the milk. "Were you at Loos?"

Ellwood was forced to admit he had been.

"What was it like?"

He did not know how to answer. *It was the Hell you'd feared in child-*

hood, come to devour the children. It was treading over the corpses of your friends so that you might be killed yourself. It was the congealed evil of a century.

So he had simply stared at the farmer, speechless, until his mother took his arm and led him away, as if he was a drunken old fool.

"He's very tired," she'd apologised to the farmer. Yes. He was very tired.

FIFTEEN

IT TOOK HIM A LONG TIME to realise he was dreaming. He was boxing, or trying to box, but he was so breathless that every movement was a punch to the chest. His opponent—Sandys?—was ruthlessly quick. He landed blow after blow, each one boiling sharp, twisting into Gaunt's lungs like a white-hot drill. The pain was so acute—Gaunt couldn't breathe—he gulped for air, but there was never enough.

"Stop," he tried to tell Sandys, but no sound came out, and he knew then that he was dreaming. The pain continued. He was conscious of a terrible wetness on his chest.

"Breathe," said a man, and Gaunt tried, but he couldn't, he was suffocating.

Then strong hands were pushing his body, propping him onto his side, and he sucked in a panicky lungful of air.

"Don't be frightened," said the man soothingly.

Gaunt opened his eyes. Another breath, and another. His terror became less animal.

"They're going to move you," said the man, and Gaunt realised he had spoken in German.

Wait, Gaunt tried to say. Wait, I don't understand. But as he opened his mouth, the pain wrung through him with fresh, burning throbs, and the sound he made was one he recognised. He had walked past men making sounds like that, and ignored them.

"Don't be frightened," said the man again. "You're going to live."

SIXTEEN

Ellwood returned to the front brimming with a sort of hard, wretched joy. England was filthy with ignorance, and the trenches were clean by comparison.

Gosset was in his dugout.

"Hallo, Ellwood! Oh—ought I call you Captain now?"

Hayes threw Ellwood a disgusted look.

"What are you doing here?" asked Ellwood. "How can you possibly have convinced anyone you were eighteen?"

Gosset grinned widely. "Well, I'm almost fifteen, you know! And the man at the Recruitment Office got so tired of turning me away, and Mummy got so tired of catching me, that finally my uncle wrote a note saying I really *was* eighteen. He came to the Recruitment Office himself! Wasn't he a brick?"

Behind Gosset, Hayes held up a finger. *One week.* Ellwood gave a tiny shake of his head. Hayes shrugged.

"I say, is that whisky? Can I have some? It's jolly damp in here, isn't it? I met the other fellow, Carrington, already. He's a bit mad, isn't he?"

"Screamed his bloody head off when Gosset came in," said Hayes.

"He does that," said Ellwood. "Where is he now, Hayes?"

"On patrol. I hate to send him, he's a total fucking liability."

Gosset giggled when Hayes swore. Ellwood ignored him.

"Did you send him with Lonsdale?"

"Yes. Only it riles the men up to have to play nanny to public school boys in No Man's Land when they get only a fraction of their pay."

"Well, *I* don't know what to do about it," said Ellwood.

"It's all frightfully interesting," said Gosset, apparently unperturbed by Carrington's insanity. "Hayes has explained everything to me already, Ellwood, about rifle inspections and the morning hate and wire reinforcements. He couldn't believe I'm a duke!"

"I told you at school, Gosset. You mustn't go around telling everyone that. It rubs people the wrong way."

Gosset slouched happily down in his chair.

"Oh, well, you're probably right. Only I *am* a duke, you know."

"Can I have a word?" said Hayes.

"Gosset, go stand outside."

"Goodie! I've been longing to look around!"

"Don't touch anything!" shouted Ellwood after him.

"Well, what are we to do?" said Hayes, when he was gone.

"If his guardian signed off on it, I don't think there's anything we *can* do."

"He's a *child*."

"Yes, I can see that, Hayes."

Hayes leant his elbows on the table. "He followed me to the latrines, you know."

"He'll settle down. We'll just have to keep him alive for . . . for a few years. . . ."

The hopelessness of the task stretched between them.

"Maybe one of us should shoot him in the arm," said Hayes.

"I'm not getting court-martialled over Gosset."

"He'll be dead within a week," said Hayes, glumly.

"No. Listen. He'll go on patrol with me tonight—"

"With you? Are you trying to get him killed?"

Ellwood was drawn up short. "What do you mean?"

Hayes straightened up. "You've got a death wish."

"No, I haven't," said Ellwood.

"No? Then why do you insist on lobbing grenades at Fritz whenever you go on patrol, even if you're only fixing up the wire?"

"Because I want to kill—" He stopped. That was it. There wasn't an intended victim, just an act.

"Six months, Ellwood. That's when the nerves start to fray."

"Your nerves seem fine," said Ellwood testily.

Hayes laughed. "Do they!"

"Well, you take Gosset, then."

Hayes sighed. "He won't be pleased. He hero-worships you. I can't think why."

"I'm sure you'll set him straight on that account."

Hayes flicked ash at him on his way up to collect Gosset.

Their last day in the front line, Carrington returned from his patrol looking paler than usual.

"My legs feel rather queer," he said, and collapsed. When Ellwood checked him for wounds (Hayes refused to touch him), he seemed entirely unharmed.

"What's happened to him, Ellwood?" asked Gosset eagerly.

"Go check the sandbags over by Regent Street," said Ellwood. He and Hayes were constantly banishing Gosset from the dugout. It put Gosset at risk, but they couldn't stand to look at him.

Ellwood asked Lonsdale about the patrol. (He was uncomfortably aware that he liked Lonsdale too much. It was difficult to strike the right balance with the men—if you did not know them and care for them, you could not lead them, but if you loved them, their constant deaths were devastating.)

"It was quite ordinary, sir," said Lonsdale. "We fixed the wire up and came straight back."

"Lieutenant Carrington says he can't move his legs."

"Can't he?" Lonsdale looked puzzled. "Nothing happened to them."

"Did anything strange occur?"

"Well—an enormous rat was rummaging around the bodies, and at one point he propped up a dead Frenchman. It did look rather as if the Frenchman was sitting up all by himself. We all chuckled a bit, but Lieutenant Carrington went white as the Cliffs of Dover."

Trying not to think about how much he should like to see the Cliffs of Dover, Ellwood returned to the dugout. Hayes was hovering outside.

"He's mad," he said.

"He's malingering," said Ellwood grimly. "There's nothing wrong with his legs."

But no matter how much Ellwood shouted at Carrington, no matter how many times he called him a shameful coward who would rather let his men die for him than get up and walk, Carrington would not move from his bunk.

"I know," he whispered. "I know I'm a coward. But I can't move my legs, Ellwood, I just *can't*."

Ellwood threatened to shoot him if he didn't get up. Carrington tried and collapsed again. Ellwood trained his pistol at his head.

"You'd better do it," said Carrington. "I'm a dreadful coward. I know I am."

Hayes came in at this point and wrested the pistol from Ellwood.

"He fought at Mons and Artois, Ellwood, he's hardly a shirker!"

"There's nothing the matter with his legs, he just wants to go home!"

"I do," said Carrington, miserably. "I do want to go home. I know that's shameful."

"He's mad, that's what he is," said Hayes, and he insisted, finally, that they call the stretcher-bearers. Carrington was taken away, whispering "I'm a dreadful coward!" in between spasms.

Hayes sat at the table, censoring letters, and Ellwood lay on his bunk. Gosset was on patrol, under Lonsdale's watchful eye.

Gaunt leant against the wooden beam, dressed in his Preshute tailcoat.

Ellwood closed his eyes, itchy with rage. After a few minutes, he couldn't stand it. He sat up and glared at Gaunt, who only continued to watch him steadily, as if waiting for him to speak.

"Did you know that Gaunt and I were fucking?" said Ellwood. Each word seemed to burn his mouth. Gaunt turned away and was gone.

Hayes glanced at the stairs, then put down his pen.

"Don't talk about him like that," he said.

"Spoiling your happy memories of him, am I? It's true. We fucked in billets—" continued Ellwood, sick with anger, but Hayes interrupted him.

"Shut up. I don't want to hear."

Ellwood tilted his head back to look at the ceiling.

"What did you expect, Ellwood? Did you want me to have you court-martialled?"

"No," said Ellwood, quietly.

"Well?"

"Oh, forget I said anything."

Hayes raised his eyebrows.

"What?" asked Ellwood belligerently.

"It was just a rather extraordinary outburst."

Ellwood got up and poured himself a glass of whisky. It was no use trying to sleep.

"Do you know that everyone I've ever told has been kind about it? Gaunt used to say I was charmed."

"I imagine you're usually less crass than you were just now."

"Why don't you like me, Hayes? Everybody likes me."

"Go to bed, Ellwood."

"'Ellwood.' How come you never call me by my first name? You called Gaunt and Maitland by theirs."

Hayes looked surprised. "Henry read me that bit in your letter—where you said it was *untoward*. 'Like a child or an American,' I think you said."

"I don't remember. I was probably trying to be witty."

"Were you? I don't think you would have liked me calling you Sidney when we first met."

"It's intimate." Ellwood rubbed his nose. "Gaunt never called me that. I don't think he felt close enough to me. Anyhow, I shouldn't mind it, if you did."

They looked at each other for a moment.

"I'd better go inspect the rifles," said Hayes.

Although Gosset was only a second lieutenant, Hayes and Ellwood automatically let him have his own room in the officers' farmhouse, rather than condemn each other to share with him. Ellwood went upstairs immediately after dinner. He sat on the bed Gaunt had slept in and tried to write.

He had not been trying very long when Hayes knocked.

"Do you have a minute?"

Ellwood nodded, and Hayes sat on the bed, leaving six careful inches between them. Ellwood felt like telling him *I wouldn't sleep with you if you asked,* although that wasn't true. Ellwood would have done anything to blot out his thoughts.

"I found something of Henry's that I think you should see," said Hayes.

Ellwood's hand shook slightly as he took the stationery pad that Hayes held out to him. He lifted the cover and looked at the first sheet of paper, instantly recognising Gaunt's neat blue handwriting:

My dearest, darling Sidney,

There was nothing else. Only dead white paper, blank and meaningless. A comma, followed by nothing. Death summed up by grammar.

"Where's the rest of it?" said Ellwood, his voice rising unpredictably.

"That's all," said Hayes. "I didn't think to give it to you, until you said that he'd never called you that."

"But where's the rest of the letter?" howled Ellwood, brandishing the empty page as he stumbled to the window. "Where's *the rest of it*?"

"He must not have finished it, Ellwood," said Hayes.

Ellwood mouthed the words. *"My,"* just the word *"my"* would have been enough to live on, if Gaunt had ever called him that to his face.

"He never called me Sidney. Not once, in five years." He looked up at Hayes. "What does it mean?"

"I don't know," said Hayes. He sat stiff and upright on the bed.

"Why didn't he finish it?"

"I don't know," said Hayes.

"He knew he was going to die."

"He thought you both would."

"But he never called me Sidney."

He never called him any of it. *My, dearest, darling. Sidney.* Ellwood leant back against the window, his throat stretching long as he looked up.

"If Gaunt had been a girl, I should have married him in an instant," he said.

The silence stretched, awkward and painful. He had misjudged, he had finally misjudged, and Hayes would report him now. Ellwood couldn't bring himself to care.

"*Gauntette*," said Hayes.

Ellwood was taken aback by how hard he laughed. He wasn't sure why it was so funny, but it felt marvellous to laugh without bitterness or horror.

When he opened his eyes, Hayes was watching him.

"Henry used to read parts of your letters out loud," said Hayes. "He thought they were charming even when they were heartless."

The laughter seemed to have loosened something in Ellwood's head. His brief joy was transfigured into the horror of discovering something new about Gaunt, and knowing there was a limit to how many more discoveries could be made. Perhaps this was his last one.

Ellwood turned to the window so that Hayes couldn't see his face. The tears fell easily. There were so many of them, they kept falling, and Ellwood could not stop them, no matter how much he blinked and breathed.

"Ellwood," said Hayes.

"I'm all right," said Ellwood. His voice was normal, unquavering. "I'm fine."

"Good," said Hayes, sounding relieved. He did not know that it was the first thing homesick little boys in their dormitories learnt at boarding school: how to cry in silence.

On their third day in the farmhouse, Carrington's replacement arrived. His name was Watts. He was twenty-three and shy and exceedingly *pretty*.

Ellwood lounged against the door frame to the small room Watts would be sharing with Gosset while in billets.

"Where are you from?" he asked. "Cigarette?"

"Oh! Thanks," said Watts, taking one. He had curly blond hair. "I'm from just outside Buxton."

"Beautiful," said Ellwood, looking at his soft, languid blue eyes.

Watts smiled and dropped his gaze.

"It is. I mean. Thanks," he said. He had a thick Derbyshire accent. Ellwood found it desperately new and different.

"Well, I'll leave you to rest," he said. "Let me know if Gosset drives you mad; I'm sure I could persuade Hayes to swap with you."

"Oh, I'll manage," said Watts. "I mean—not that there is anything to manage! I'll be fine wherever, Captain."

"You may call me Ellwood."

Watts looked up. His lashes were very pale.

"Ellwood," he said.

Ellwood held his gaze for a few seconds too long, then rapped on the door frame.

"See you at dinner, Watts. You'll want to get a bath while you can. I suggest you take a dip in the river."

"The river! Yes, I will. Thank you, Captain. I mean, Ellwood. Thank you."

Hayes lay outside on the grass. Ellwood went to lie beside him.

"Two weeks," said Hayes.

"Don't," said Ellwood.

Their colonel began to insist on scouting missions, peculiarly miserable tests of mental endurance in which men went out into No Man's Land alone at night, crawling on their stomachs until they reached the German wire. The idea was to listen for how many soldiers were in the German trench, and how much work they were doing, in order to gauge the likelihood of an impending attack.

It was always shattering to go into No Man's Land, but to go alone was so isolating that the scouts tended to develop neurasthenia within weeks.

Watts volunteered as a scout. He did well for a while, but it told on him. He shivered for hours after each mission. It tore up Ellwood's heart.

After one particularly tense scouting mission, Watts came back and threw up outside the dugout. Ellwood helped him down the stairs and handed him a tin cup of water.

"Thanks," said Watts.

"I'll go for you tomorrow," said Ellwood. Watts put his tin cup on the table with a slow, cautious movement to hide how his hand trembled.

"No, no," he said. "I can do it, Captain. I mean, Ellwood. I can, I'm not trying to get out of it, honest, I'm not."

Ellwood took his hand and pressed it. Watts stared at where their skin touched, then at Ellwood.

"I know you're not," said Ellwood.

Watts licked his lips.

"Watts," said Hayes, from the entrance to the dugout. His voice was hard. "The munitions delivery has just come through; will you go and check they've sent enough rifle grenades?"

"He's been scouting all night," said Ellwood. Watts removed his hand from his and stood.

"That's all right, I can do it," he said.

Hayes watched him go with an unfriendly expression. Once he was out of earshot, Hayes turned to Ellwood.

"Don't even *think* about it," he said.

Ellwood took out his writing paper and his fountain pen from his pack.

"Think about *what*, Hayes?"

"You know perfectly well what. Don't touch that boy."

"He's older than I am," said Ellwood.

Hayes put both his hands on the rickety table and leant forward.

"*Ellwood.* I know you find it difficult to think of anyone but yourself, but please try to remember that unlike you, Watts didn't go to Eton."

"Preshute. And I don't see what that has to do with anything," said Ellwood.

"No, you wouldn't, would you," said Hayes.

Ellwood rested his elbows on the table.

"Go on, Hayes. Let's hear what you think of me, shall we? What is it that troubles you, exactly? I have one or two guesses, but I'd simply *hate* to assume."

Hayes' eyes gleamed, but he spoke as if Ellwood hadn't said anything.

"Do you know what would happen if someone caught you and him? They'd say he'd assaulted you. That it was all his fault. He'd be court-martialled and shot so fast for daring to besmirch his precious public school captain—"

Ellwood stared at Hayes. It hadn't occurred to him, any of it.

"I wouldn't let them think that," he said.

Hayes laughed. "Really, Ellwood? Given the choice between hard labour and a brilliant career? You'd stand up for him? Grow up."

Ellwood tried to hold his gaze, but couldn't. Hayes was too scathing, too right. Ellwood looked at his writing paper.

"The fatigue party will be getting in any minute now," he said quietly. "I'd like there to be hot tea ready for them when they arrive. Go see about it, please." He didn't look up.

Hayes laughed unpleasantly. "As you command, sir," he said, and left.

Ellwood barely glanced at Watts, after that. Watts was clearly confused by the sudden lack of attention, but he said nothing about it. In fact, he stopped saying much at all. He developed a stutter and stank of whisky. It was a blessing when he caught a venereal disease from a French prostitute and was sent to a hospital in Amiens.

"Thank God," said Hayes. "He set me on edge."

"Me, too," said Ellwood darkly, and Hayes, to Ellwood's very great surprise, laughed.

"Yes, I could see that," he said.

That evening, Ellwood volunteered to go scouting. He didn't mind it as much as the others did. It gave him a curious sense of elation to go out into No Man's Land alone.

He reached the German trenches without incident, and lay in the mud for half an hour, listening to them cough and stamp their feet and mutter. When he felt he had enough information to satisfy his superiors, Ellwood began to crawl back.

It was then that he realised his compass was broken, the new compass he had bought with Maud. The arrow swivelled wildly whenever he managed to get a look at it by the light of the soaring star shells.

Horror spread through him in juddering waves. It was every scout's blackest nightmare: he was lost. If he tried to make his way back to the British line, there was every chance he might accidentally crawl right into the German wire. He could not see any of the landmarks he used to locate himself on patrols: the young German soldier with the shot-up jaw who had been slowly decaying near their line; the three rotting horses; the battered old brick wall that might once have been someone's garden shed. He did not dare lift up his head when the star shells illuminated the sky, but it was impossible to see in the dark.

His panic grew as the night drew on. If he did not get back before dawn, he would be stranded until night fell again, for it was death to move a muscle in No Man's Land in daylight. Each breath he took smelt sickly sweetly of corpses.

His jaw began to ache. He held his teeth so tightly together to stop them chattering that he worried he would break them. He crawled forty yards towards what he hoped was the English wire, and found only more crump holes, more dead. It appeared he had managed to trace a parallel line alongside the trenches.

A dirty sunrise leached across the sky. He was totally exposed, and he still had no idea in which direction his trench was. He lifted his head, and instantly bullets hailed down on him, splattering muddy water into his eyes. He sprang to his feet and ran about three steps before one hit him and he threw himself headfirst behind a small pile of dead Canadians. The bullets caught on the bodies with the hard sound of someone slapping a wet plank.

Had they been British bullets, or German ones? He did not know. He could not risk moving to study his wound. It hurt too much to be serious, he hoped. His tongue was thick and dry in his mouth.

When the morning hate began, and both trenches shot at each other with rifles, he pressed himself closer to the corpses. There must have been a dozen of them. He wondered whether they had been friends.

The day passed in agony. Whenever he moved an inch, he was shot at, although fortunately it seemed that the snipers could not see him clearly for the bodies. The sun burnt a headache into his temples. He fell asleep once or twice, only to wake up with a jolt and, a second later, machine-gun fire.

The Canadians smelt in the heat. He studied their uniforms, thought about how far they were from home. His hip no longer hurt where the bullet had touched him. He didn't know what that meant. Pain was an unpredictable marker of damage.

If he could not find his way back to the trenches that night, what would become of him? Would Hayes come to look for him? It was a pointless risk, when it was so unlikely that anyone stranded in No Man's Land for twenty-four hours would still be alive when found.

The sky grew cool. Down the line, there came the distant sound of shells. But where he lay, it was quiet.

SEVENTEEN

ELLWOOD WAITED until it had been dark for an hour before he moved. He drank from his water bottle. It heightened his hunger. Then he examined the wound on his hip. To his dizzying relief, it was only a graze, nothing a tetanus shot and some clean gauze wouldn't fix.

He took a deep breath, and stood. When the next star shell went off, he did not fall to the ground: he turned his head and methodically searched the landscape.

And then he saw it. The old brick wall. It was in exactly the opposite direction from where he had thought it would be.

He dropped to the mud just in time. Rifles fired at him from both directions.

He crawled forward, faint with hunger, desperate with fear and determination. It took him an hour to go twenty feet. He felt like an animal, like prey.

Finally, finally, he reached the brick wall. He was, if anything, in more danger now than he had been before: the British would certainly shoot him as he approached the wire.

He glanced at his watch. The wiring parties would be out in fifteen minutes. He waited.

Lonsdale led the first wiring party. Ellwood recognised his voice and crept slowly forward to the three dead horses.

"Lonsdale," he hissed.

The wiring party stopped moving, each man going still at the horror of an unfamiliar sound in No Man's Land.

"Lonsdale," said Ellwood again.

"Who goes there?" whispered Lonsdale.

"Captain Ellwood. Come get me, I can't come closer by myself or the sentries will shoot."

"Captain . . . !" said Lonsdale. He made his way over to Ellwood on his stomach. "We thought you were a goner, sir!"

"So did I," said Ellwood, and followed him back to the wire. The men smiled at him, a few of them touching his arms to show their relief. "Keep at it," said Ellwood, then he slipped through the gap in the wire, back to the safety of his own trench.

Hayes stood with the sentries.

"Ellwood?"

Ellwood swayed on his feet.

"Hallo Hayes. Did I miss much?"

Hayes took a step forward, staring at Ellwood as if he were a ghost.

"You're alive," he said.

"Seems that way," said Ellwood.

Hayes just looked at him.

"I'd better get to the dressing station," said Ellwood. "I can feel the tetanus warming up nicely in my hip."

"You're wounded?"

"Hardly," said Ellwood, showing him the graze.

"That's not so bad," said Hayes.

"I know," said Ellwood. "No chance of impressing the girls with it."

Hayes laughed, bright and sudden. He took one more decisive step forward and slapped Ellwood on the back.

"I'm glad you made it," he said.

Gosset kept hugging him.

"Oh I *am* glad," he said. "Was it very exciting? Did you kill anyone? I wonder if you'll get a medal. Wouldn't that be grand?"

"They don't give out medals for getting lost in No Man's Land, Gosset," said Ellwood, disentangling himself from his embrace. Hayes laughed quietly from his bunk.

"I could talk to my uncle's friend about you. He's a general. General Haig, have you heard of him?"

Hayes laughed harder.

"Yes, in fact I have," said Ellwood. "Please *don't* mention me to him. My God."

"Oh, all right. He's very important, you know. Did you hear that Hayes was temporary captain while you were dead? He was awfully good."

"Shut up, Gosset," said Hayes, not laughing any more.

"*Temporary* captain?" asked Ellwood.

"They were going to send someone else in to take over next week," said Hayes.

"That's . . ." Ellwood glanced at Gosset. "Gosset. Have you checked the sandbags recently?"

"This afternoon."

"Go do it again."

Gosset sighed.

"We must have the neatest trench in Belgium," he said, but he did as he was told. Ellwood turned to Hayes.

"*Temporary* captain? What utter nonsense!"

Hayes sat up in his bunk. "I sent men out to look for you," he said.

Ellwood blinked. "Did you? That was rather irresponsible."

"Well, I was scared out of my mind at the prospect of having only Gosset for company."

Ellwood laughed and took another bite of his meat cutlet.

"He *has* lasted longer than expected," he said.

"He'll make it out all right," said Hayes. "His uncle is friends with General Haig, don't you know."

Watts' replacement was named Thorburn, and he never so much as blinked when shells went off near him.

"He'll last, that one," said Hayes. "Nerves of steel."

Perhaps it was in contrast to Thorburn that Ellwood first noticed how bad Hayes' nerves had got. Ellwood knocked a mug off the table, and it landed with a dull thud on the packed earth floor. Hayes threw himself to the ground and covered his neck with his hands.

"Just a mug, Hayes," said Ellwood, staring at him.

Hayes sat up slowly. There was white all around his irises.

"Sorry," he said. His voice was raspy.

"Are you feeling all right?"

"Yes," said Hayes. "What time is it? I'd better get going. See if Ramsay will bring me a cup of tea, would you?"

"Hayes. Sit down. You're not on duty for another ten minutes," said Ellwood.

Thorburn came into the dugout.

"Bloody Boches have attached a bell on a string to our wire and keep ringing it," he said. "It's driving the sentries perfectly mad."

"Mad!" cried Hayes.

"It's almost dark," said Ellwood. "I'll go out in half an hour and cut the string."

"I should think they'll shoot you for it," said Thorburn, sounding uninterested. Ellwood sighed and went to go look at the bell, leaving Hayes pale and sickly in the dugout.

In billets, Hayes and Ellwood continued to share a room. Hayes slept on the floor. The bed gave him dreams about drowning in mud.

Ellwood woke up one night to the sound of Hayes repeatedly calling his name, so quietly that Ellwood would never have heard it before the War: he had been a deep sleeper. He opened his eyes, confused, and found Hayes kneeling by his bed, head in hands.

"Ellwood . . . Ellwood . . . Ellwood . . ."

"Hayes? What's going on?"

Hayes looked up with wild eyes. "I'm going mad," he said.

Ellwood sat up and swung his legs off the bed. He was so tired. It was only in billets that he could count on more than two hours of sleep at a time.

"What are you talking about?" he asked. "What time is it?"

Hayes buried his face in Ellwood's mattress.

"Hayes," said Ellwood. Hayes muttered something, but Ellwood could not make it out. "What was that?"

Hayes sat back up and looked at Ellwood, although, eerily, it did not seem as if he could *see* him.

"I'm glad Henry died," he said. "I'd rather have him dead than lose his mind."

Ellwood was speechless. He wasn't fully awake yet, and he couldn't think of a thing to say.

Hayes lunged suddenly forward and clutched at Ellwood's knees.

"You'll kill me, if I go mad," he said. "I saw. With Carrington. You'll shoot me."

"Don't be stupid," said Ellwood.

"I'm losing it," said Hayes, looking beseechingly up at him. "I'm going to bottle it, I know I am. I'll lead the men out somewhere and lose my nerve and get everyone killed. I can't afford to go mad, Ellwood, I've got people depending on me, I can't—"

Ellwood stood and backed away. "Get a grip."

"You don't know what it was like, with John and Henry. They showed up bright and young and hopeful—"

"Gaunt was never hopeful," said Ellwood, despite himself.

"Unravelling . . . seeing someone's mind spool out of them . . ."

Ellwood had admired Gaunt for his impenetrability, but he had also wondered what it was *for.* What use was there in being so guarded that no one could get in, and nothing could get out? Watching Hayes convulsing against the bed, he understood, as he never had before, why a man might need to forcefully hold himself together.

"We know how long it takes to recover from a broken arm," Hayes was saying. "We know how long it takes to die of a stomach wound. But how long will Carrington—how long will I—"

"You're fine, Hayes. David. You're fine."

"I'm not, I'm not, I'm not," said Hayes.

Ellwood dropped to his knees beside him and put one hesitant hand on Hayes' back. Hayes put his head on the bed and panted.

"David."

Hayes looked up.

"You're not mad," said Ellwood. "Don't you think I'd tell you, if you were?"

Hayes closed his eyes, breathing deeply.

"You didn't believe Carrington was mad," he said. "You thought he was a coward."

"Well, you're certainly not that," said Ellwood.

"Every sound I hear scrapes down my spine."

"I think you're so frightened of losing your mind that you're driving yourself insane," said Ellwood.

"All my dreams are about motor accidents. I don't know why. Getting knocked over by a hansom cab. Or train crashes."

"You can't go mad. You bet me three shillings that you would last out the War."

Hayes laughed a little, a choking sound, and Ellwood pulled his hand away. He had spent so much time trying to knock through Gaunt's defences. He didn't know how to build the walls back up.

"If I write to the colonel, we could get you sent to an officer-training course for a few weeks. You could have a bit of a rest."

"The men don't get *a bit of a rest* when they go mad. We just leave them in the line until they're killed," said Hayes.

"Well—that's different," said Ellwood.

"Is it!"

"They're less likely to be killed than we are, for one thing."

"God, you're a comfort," said Hayes.

"Let me write to the colonel," said Ellwood. "You'll feel much better if you—"

"*No.*"

A silence passed.

"Did you ever want to go to war, as a boy?" asked Hayes.

Ellwood smiled. "All the time. I used to steal saucepans from the kitchens for helmets."

Hayes nodded. He seemed calmer now. He got up and sat on the bed. Ellwood sat next to him.

"I thought I would be brave," said Hayes.

"You are. You have been."

They looked at each other. Ellwood spoke slowly, deliberately. "You're fine. You're all right," he said.

Hayes shut his eyes and gave a shuddery sigh. "Sorry," he said.

"You're fine."

"Yes. I know. I am," said Hayes. He opened his eyes and smiled weakly. "Thank you."

"Don't mention it," said Ellwood.

The men grew uncommonly fond of Gosset. They called him "the Little Duke." However irritating Ellwood found him, it was worth it to watch Hayes seethe when Ramsay gave him his bowl of yellow soup with a deferential "Your Grace."

It could not last, of course. Gosset was killed by a shell that tore through the trench while he was on sentry duty.

"Some lucky fellow just inherited a dukedom," said Hayes, when they went to look at what was left of the body.

In June 1916, they received orders that they would be leaving Ypres. There was to be another Big Push. They packed their things, and marched towards the Somme.

EIGHTEEN

B Y THE TIME HE WAS LUCID, Gaunt was in a makeshift German hospital in a bombed-out village behind enemy lines. He lay on his right side, a thick pad of browned gauze covering the hole in his chest, and every breath he took was both excruciating and ineffectual.

"I can't breathe," he said to a passing nurse. She looked at him, uncomprehending, and he realised he had spoken in English. "I can't breathe," he tried again, this time in German.

She was at his side in an instant, calling for the doctor. They stabbed into his lung to let out the extra air and he screamed in choking agony.

"Get him some morphine," said the doctor.

"We're running low—"

"He needs it."

The nurse administered the morphine, pushing Gaunt's hair out of his eyes. He gulped for air, panting and straining against the pain, which seemed to block out everything but terror.

Then the morphine dropped like a curtain between him and his chest.

Time passed. He lay in a daze, letting German wash over him. If his mother had had her way, he would have grown up in Munich. These would be his men dying around him. He would have been shooting at Ellwood—he wouldn't have known Ellwood.

"Hallo," said a young officer, coming to sit beside him. Gaunt blinked at him. It was the man he had seen in the trench, the man who had told him not to be frightened, but Gaunt could see now that he had been mistaken in thinking it was his cousin Ernst.

"Hullo," said Gaunt. "You rescued me."

"So I did," said the officer. "Who is Ernst? You speak good German."

"My cousin. Ernst Grisar."

The officer beamed. "I know Otto Grisar!"

"Yes, they're brothers."

"I'm Lukas Hohenheimer."

They shook hands.

"Thanks awfully for getting me out," said Gaunt. "I thought I'd had it."

"How could I leave you, when you looked me in the eye like that?"

"Most men wouldn't have bothered."

"It didn't hurt that you had a Munich accent."

Gaunt smiled. "Always knew that would come in handy one day."

"That man you captured in the trench raid," said Hohenheimer. "Will he be all right?"

Gaunt started. A stab of pain burst through the morphine.

"They got away?"

"Two of them did," said Hohenheimer.

"Which two?"

"How should I know?"

Gaunt covered his eyes with his arm.

"A friend?" asked Hohenheimer.

"Yes."

"I'm sorry."

"He's charmed," said Gaunt forcefully. "He's fine, I'm sure of it. And don't worry about your man. He'll be safer in one of our prisoner-of-war camps than you are at the front."

Hohenheimer came to visit each afternoon during his four-day break from the trenches. He gave the staff cigarettes and called Gaunt "Heinrich Grisar." The result was that Gaunt was treated as well as any German, and they did not move him to the prisoner-of-war tent.

No one knew what to make of him. He spoke German with a Bavarian accent and answered to "Heinrich." Had it not been for his khaki uniform, no one should have known he was the enemy.

The Battle of Loos raged on, supplying the hospital with a constant flow of badly wounded men. The day after Hohenheimer returned to the front, the bed next to Gaunt was filled by a young second lieutenant named Alex Pfahler. His side had been ripped up by a trench mortar, so he lay on his left flank in a morphine stupor. He and Gaunt stared at each other for hours on end, blinking messages. They hardly spoke the first week, except to explain a new code. It was an intimacy born of pain.

"If I close my eyes for five seconds, I am thinking of a hot bath," said Pfahler. Gaunt blinked once for yes.

"If I wink my right eye, it means the man they've brought in will die within the hour," said Gaunt.

"Don't make me laugh," grimaced Pfahler. "It hurts to laugh."

I miss Munich, Pfahler blinked, fifteen times a day.

I hope Ellwood is alive, Gaunt blinked back.

"Some friendship you had," said Pfahler, after a few hours of silence had gone by.

"You've no idea."

Six days later, Hohenheimer returned to tell him that the man they had killed near their trench was not an officer, but a private.

"Your friend must have got away."

Gaunt closed his eyes, guilt tingeing his relief. That meant that either Kane or Allen was dead, and he had liked them both.

"I've got to get back," he said.

"Don't even say things like that. Do you want to get me court-martialled? What do you think will happen to me if you run away from here?"

"I'm English. I can't stay."

"You're German, too. Wait out the rest of the War in a camp."

Gaunt turned his head into his pillow.

"The rest of the War . . . ! That might be years!"

"It can't be," said Hohenheimer. "We can't go on like this."

Gaunt didn't answer. He was beginning to think the War would continue until No Man's Land enveloped the world, and the last two men alive shot at each other from their ditches in the mud. Had Edward III known, when he declared war on France in the fourteenth century, that it would last 116 years?

"The nurse says you've been having nightmares," said Hohenheimer, casually.

Gaunt's heart warped with shame. He knew he kept everyone in the ward from sleeping. At night he sprang upright, shouting at the dead. The sudden movement would rip at his chest wound, so that he would follow his harrowed yelling with howls of pain. It was the only time the men in the ward heard him speak English: *"Over the top, you cowardly bastards! I'll shoot you all!"*

"I'm sorry," he said.

"I suppose there's not much you can do about it."

"I try to stay awake."

"Not a very good long-term solution."

"No." Gaunt sighed. "The nightmares aren't so bad when I'm at the front."

"Brilliant. We'll just send you right back to the Tommies so you can shoot at us in peace."

"I wish you would."

He asked every new patient how the battle was going. It was inconclusive, they said, and bloody. Hayes and Ellwood were constantly on his mind. Sandys had once told him that the average British officer lasted only three months before he was killed or wounded.

By the time the Battle of Loos was over on the 8th October, Germany had won, although the men in Gaunt's ward were too weary to rejoice at the victory.

Pfahler and Gaunt had both had their morphine reduced as the hospital bulged with patients. They talked to distract themselves from the pain.

"What's it like, over there?" asked Pfahler.

"Hell," said Gaunt. Then he reflected. "Better food."

"Is it true your officers get meat three times a day?"

Gaunt thought of the "meat cutlets" he had hated in the trenches. German food shortages meant a great deal of black rye bread and potatoes.

"Yes," he said. "It's true."

Pfahler sighed enviously. "I keep thinking of a meal I had in 1912, at a small country inn near Augsburg. It was simple, yet excellent. I dream about it, but always I wake up when I pick up my fork."

" 'For he on honey-dew hath fed, / And drunk the milk of Paradise,'" quoted Gaunt, in English.

Pfahler wrinkled his nose. "It's unsettling when you do that."

"Do what?"

"Become English all of a sudden."

"I *am* English."

Pfahler rolled his eyes. He was deeply patriotic, and seemed to think Gaunt's insistence on his nationality amounted to little more than a passing phase.

"Tell me, Kapitän Grisar-Gaunt—"

"It's just Gaunt."

"Who do *you* think will win this great war?"

"I hope we will."

"And by 'we,' you mean . . ."

"The British, of course. The Allies."

"Impossible. They cannot win."

"I don't see *British* field hospitals reusing their gauze," said Gaunt, putting his hand to the ugly brown dressing on his chest.

"It's been disinfected!"

"It doesn't *look* right."

"But, you see, this is why you will lose. The English, they are too sympathetic, too casual. And Germany has the finest army in all human history."

"I won't deny that."

"So?"

"I suppose I simply don't *want* you to win."

Pfahler brought his finger playfully to the corner of his smile.

"Ah, but you *should* want us to. Everyone should. Under a German Empire, there would be centuries of prosperity. We would teach the world to succeed."

"How very high-minded. I'm sure we'd all be grateful for such instruction."

"There's always an empire, Kapitän. Why not a German one? With our art, our medicine, our philosophers? We have a great deal to offer."

"I think we're all so busy *offering* that we forget how much we *take*."

Pfahler tried to shrug, and winced. "I doubt the barbarians minded the Romans, once they had their roads and baths."

"On the contrary," said Gaunt. "I think they minded extremely."

"Oh, it's no use talking to you. You don't understand history."

Gaunt shut his eyes. Morphine made the vast sweep of history more logical to him than the chaotic present, which had not yet shaped itself into meaning. In his mind, he saw empires rise and fall like the swelling and abating of the tide, perpetual, each society blindly throwing its tragedies and flaws onto foreign shores. It seemed inevitable, and yet, from the perspective of the sanded beaches, devastatingly corrosive.

Pfahler died a week later, blinking at Gaunt: *I miss Munich. I miss Munich.*

Hohenheimer was away when the Oberst came to inspect the hospital. Gaunt's lung had improved to the point where he could lie on his back, a particularly welcome development given the bedsores that now peppered the right side of his body. He lay with his eyes closed, trying to strike a balance between thinking, which was unpleasant, and sleeping, which was blood-curdling.

"What's that Tommy doing in here? Why isn't he in with the other prisoners of war?" came a booming voice.

"Lieutenant Hohenheimer brought him in, sir," said a nurse. "He's German."

"Then why is he wearing khaki?" The voice was louder now; the Oberst had come to look at him. "Hello Tommy," he said in faltering English. "What's wrong with you?"

"Shot in the lung, sir," said Gaunt in German.

"Ho! Little traitor wanted to fight for the wrong side, did he? You're as German as I am."

"No, sir," said Gaunt, opening his eyes. "I'm English."

The Oberst was comically similar to the colonel of the Royal Kennet Fusiliers. Commanding officers, it seemed, were universal characters.

"You should be dead." He looked at the doctor. "We don't make a habit of rescuing Tommies with fatal lung wounds, do we, Doctor?"

"The Hague Convention provides clear guidelines as to the treatment of prisoners—" said the doctor.

"Oh, the Hague Convention! No one abides by that any more, do they? There's a train going to an Offizierslager. Put him on it."

"He's not well enough to travel, sir," said the doctor.

The Oberst's whole face went red. "Put him on that train. *Now.*"

So it was that Gaunt ended up on the floor of a railway carriage filled with downcast British officers, on his way to a prisoner-of-war camp in Germany.

NINETEEN

G AUNT'S FELLOW PRISONERS carried him gently to his
dormitory and deposited him on a bed that reminded him so
much of his one at Preshute that his morphine-limber mind
continually tricked him into thinking he was indeed at school again.

"Elly?" he asked, each time someone entered, before remembering
that Ellwood was at the front, and that he was in a prison camp.

"'Fraid not, old friend," said Nicholson, the second time this happened. He distantly knew Nicholson, who had been at Sherborne in
the year above. Most of the two hundred British officers in the camp
had gone to the same twenty-odd boarding schools. The four hundred
remaining prisoners were French or Russian.

"Henry?" said someone, after a few hours. "Henry Gaunt?"

Gaunt tried to sit up, but could not. "Yes?"

A handsome young Indian man knelt by his bed.

"*Gideon?*" said Gaunt.

"It *is* you! Henry!" Gideon Devi draped himself over Gaunt's body.
"My God, am I glad to see you!"

Gaunt cringed in pain.

"Oh, I say, I'm not hurting you, am I?" asked Devi.

"Just a bit sore in the lung. How did you get in here?"

"Some clever Hun shot down my plane."

"Sounds awfully glamorous."

"This doesn't look too good, Henry, are you all right?" asked Devi, pulling aside Gaunt's shirt to look at his wound.

"I'm fine."

Devi threw him an exasperated look, and Gaunt grinned.

"It hurts like blazes," he said.

"Better." Devi had always rather forcefully *made* Gaunt talk, whereas Ellwood would only ask delicate, knocking questions, and retreat the moment Gaunt glowered. "I heard there was some injured giant in here shouting every time someone came in, so I had to investigate. I'm in this dorm, you know."

"It'll be like Grinstead House all over again."

Devi smirked. "More than you know. It's astonishing how well an English boarding school prepares one for prison. There's a fellow in here who says he wishes his parents had sent him here instead of Preshute. Calls Preshute a 'House of Tortures.'"

"I can't tell you how glad I am to see you," said Gaunt. "I've been going mad inside my head."

Devi climbed onto the bed, facing him.

"How's your friend Ellwood?"

To his humiliation, Gaunt began to cry. Devi looked tactfully away, handing him a handkerchief.

"I don't know," said Gaunt, when he had regained control of his voice. "He's still at the front. I haven't had a letter from him."

"We're not allowed to send or receive mail," said Devi.

"But the Hague Convention—"

Devi laughed. "Yes, Henry? The Hague Convention? Go on."

"No. I see your point."

A spindly man in glasses came bursting in, covered in dirt.

"Hi, Devi, it's your turn downstairs. Hallo, you've woken the giant."

"This is Henry Gaunt. We were friends at Grinstead."

"Small world. I'm Oliver MacCorkindale. Nice to meet you, Gaunt. Planning on staying here long?"

"I've got to get back to the front," said Gaunt. He looked at Devi. "Elly's wild when he's unhappy. He'll get himself killed just for the fun of it."

Devi and MacCorkindale exchanged looks.

"Well, he's not much use now," said MacCorkindale.

Gaunt stared, confused. Were they talking about Ellwood?

"No, but he's strong as an ox when he's healthy. And he speaks German," said Devi.

"Does he, now? That's very interesting."

"What are you two on about?" asked Gaunt. Devi took back his handkerchief from Gaunt's hand and jumped off the bed.

"Nothing yet, Henry. You just heal up. Hi, MacCorkindale, why don't you keep him company for a bit? You two are both Greek fiends, you'll have plenty to talk about."

He swept out of the room.

"Where is he going?" asked Gaunt.

MacCorkindale gave a noncommittal shrug. "You like Classics, do you?" he asked, settling himself down on the floor by Gaunt's bed and taking off his glasses to clean them.

"Rather."

"We aren't allowed paper—a week of solitary confinement if you're found with so much as a scrap. I'll tell you what, I never expected reciting the *Iliad* would bring me so much popularity."

"No books?"

"The Red Cross sends some from time to time, but somehow it's always George Eliot's *Adam Bede*. Every chap in here must have read *Adam Bede* a dozen times. It's not half bad, but one tires of love triangles."

"What does everyone *do* all day?"

"We've invented a rather boisterous chair-leaping game that we play in the dining hall. And of course, everyone tries to get free."

"Has anyone ever escaped?"

"From here?" MacCorkindale smiled broadly. "Not yet."

TWENTY

*O*VER THE TOP, *you cowardly bastards! I'll shoot you all!"*

"Henry!" Someone was shaking him.

"Elly?" His eyes focused. Of the eleven men in his dormitory, half of them were glaring at him from their beds.

"No, it's me. Gideon."

Gaunt managed, with great difficulty, to sit up. "I'm awfully sorry, did I wake everyone?"

"That doesn't matter," said Devi. The man in the bed next to Gaunt's huffed.

Gaunt put his hands to his heart, which was beating as fast as it had at Ypres.

"Help me get to the corridor, Devi. I'll sleep there."

"Don't be absurd! You're wounded!"

Gaunt started to hoist himself.

"Steady on!" said Devi.

"It'll just keep happening. No one will get any sleep as long as I'm around. Don't make me beg."

Devi made an exasperated face, then half-carried Gaunt out of the dorm. He dragged Gaunt's mattress and thin coverlet to the freezing corridor.

Gaunt lay down and faced the wall.

"Henry."

Gaunt didn't answer.

"Henry, it's nothing to be ashamed of."

Eventually, Devi left. Gaunt reflected that Ellwood would have waited at his side all night, waiting for him to talk. But the gentle parts of Ellwood were more patient than Devi, just as Ellwood's savage streak was crueller and more violent. Devi was honour and charm down to the bone. Ellwood was fierce contradictions.

The next morning, Gaunt discovered his nightmares had earned him the enmity of a bitter young man named Windeler. He deliberately stepped on Gaunt's stomach as he went downstairs for roll call. Gaunt gasped in pain.

"Sorry, old boy," said Windeler. "Don't start screaming like a little girl again."

Gaunt said nothing. Ellwood had always been quick to think of clever retorts, but Gaunt found refuge in silence—silence, and his fists. It had been years since anyone had insulted him without him thumping them. But he was barely able to stand, let alone challenge Windeler to a duel.

Then there was the fact that he privately agreed with Windeler's disdain. His powerlessness over the nightmares terrified him almost as much as the nightmares themselves.

Devi helped him back into the dorm after morning roll call.

"That Windeler chap didn't seem too keen on me," said Gaunt.

"Oh, Windeler's all right," said Devi. Gaunt had forgotten Devi's propensity to like everyone. As a defence mechanism, it was startlingly effective. At Grinstead, Devi smiled at his bullies and laughed at their unkind jokes, until they started to feel that *he* was really the audience they sought, and bullied someone else for his amusement.

Gaunt had been dreadfully bullied at Grinstead. He had arrived, eight years old, still clutching his Steiff teddy bear. A well-meaning matron had sealed his fate when she loudly proclaimed that he looked just like Little Lord Fauntleroy. There was almost nothing little boys in 1904 despised more than Little Lord Fauntleroy, that paragon of feminized masculinity, with his long blond ringlets and sickening habit of calling his mother "Dearest." Gaunt had been instantly reviled. The precious teddy bear was shoved down a toilet, and Gaunt locked in all manner of cupboards and boxes, where he remained for hours before being found by Devi. The masters would consequently beat him for missing lessons, for of course he could not reveal why he had not been in Arithmetic. He wasn't a *sneak*.

Yet despite all the heartbroken nights he spent sobbing quietly into his pillow, he had loved Grinstead. In London, he had taken sedate walks around Hyde Park with Maud and his governess. At Grinstead, he and Devi climbed high into the treetops, scaling beeches and oaks and even, one heady afternoon, managing to scrape their way up the long, branchless sides of a Wellingtonia. The boys were cruel to him in unpredictable spurts, but often quite happy to have him join in their elaborate fort-building games. At night, they stayed up talking until the matron would pounce on a scapegoat, drag him out by the ear, and beat him with a shoe.

It was marvellous fun.

And then, of course, there was Devi, with whom he rolled about in the vast fields, practicing violence—for even Devi, with his shieldlike good temper, could see that the safest trait to develop at Grinstead was strength. They spent long Saturday afternoons trying to knock each other out. By the time Gaunt was eleven, the boys in his year no longer frightened him. In fact, nothing visibly frightened him. He had begun to acquire that ineffable coat of studied ease that was slowly painted over all the boarding-school boys between the ages of eight and eighteen.

When he arrived at Preshute, still pretty in that saccharine, Lord Fauntleroy way, he was introduced to a whole new world of dominance and power. Lonely without Devi (Gaunt's father had gone to Preshute, and had refused point-blank to send Gaunt to Eton with his friend), Gaunt had endured the sexual equivalents of being locked in cupboards and missing lessons. But just as tree climbing with Devi had tipped the scales at Grinstead, Ellwood had shone so brightly into his life at Preshute that the shadows had been burnt away. Ellwood, like Devi, swam into a feeding frenzy of power and cruelty, and emerged unscathed. Gaunt was convinced that the thirteen-year-old Ellwood had targeted Maitland as a likely protector, and burrowed under his wing with Machiavellian savoir-faire. Devi, too, had always managed to spin his liabilities into assets. The Grinstead boys never stopped calling him "Maharaja," but Devi skilfully convinced them it was an affectionate and even reverent pet name, rather than an insult. Gaunt found both Ellwood and Devi fascinating, although he knew he would never learn to weaponise charm as they did.

But Gaunt's tactic—hitting people until they grudgingly respected him—was not useful now. He could only hope that Windeler would torment him in ways he was immune to. Because of boxing, he was quite used to taking punches. But his nightmares were soft and painful, and he did not like to think how vulnerable he was to attacks in that direction.

MacCorkindale was keeping him company the day Gaunt first encountered a guard. The guard was about seventeen, and his head was too big for his painfully thin body. He might have been good-looking if he hadn't been so malnourished.

"Captain Gaunt?"

"Yes?"

"You were not at roll call," he said, in heavily accented English. MacCorkindale leant his elbows on the bed next to him and glared at the poor guard.

"Of course he wasn't. One of *your* lot only went and shot him in the bloody lung, didn't they?"

The guard clearly did not understand the meaning of MacCorkindale's speech, but there was no mistaking the intent.

"You must come to roll call," he said roughly. "Or there will be punishments."

"I'm sorry," said Gaunt, in German. "I'm injured, you see. It's quite tricky for me to get out of bed."

"You speak German!"

"My mother is Bavarian."

The guard was transformed. He beamed. "Bavaria! Such beautiful country."

"Yes. What's your name?"

"Oberjäger Christian Lüneburg."

"I'm sorry that we must meet in these circumstances, Oberjäger Lüneburg."

"I will come to you for roll call until you are better."

"That's very kind of you."

Lüneburg glanced at MacCorkindale.

"What is that?" he said in English, pointing with his chin at an empty peach tin in which MacCorkindale had been mixing together lard and beeswax with the handle of his razor.

"A paste, for Gaunt's bedsores," said MacCorkindale. Gaunt translated, and Lüneburg's face softened.

"You are in pain?" he asked Gaunt. "I can send for the doctor."

"He's coming this afternoon. I'm well cared for. Thank you."

Lüneburg smiled and left.

"Golly. You *can* speak German," said MacCorkindale.

"Have you really made me a paste for my bedsores?"

MacCorkindale laughed.

"No. Thought awfully fast, though, didn't I?"

"What is it for, then?"

"You just heal that chest of yours, Gaunt. Then we'll talk."

It was several months before Gaunt was able to make his way downstairs for roll call without help. In that time, he was able to get a pretty firm understanding of how the camp worked. He soon found that MacCorkindale had accurately summarised it. The men spent their time galloping around the dining hall, antagonising the guards, reading and rereading *Adam Bede,* and, most notably, plotting elaborate escapes.

Fishwick was growing out his hair in long blond ringlets. He and a Frenchman who spoke fluent German were planning on pretending to be an amorous Saxon couple. The idea was that Fishwick would appear so desperately in love with his companion that the guards would be too delicate to question them.

Woodbridge was making himself a pair of ice skates so that he could cross the moat when it next froze. The moat was the great disadvantage of the Fürstenberg prison camp, which Gaunt soon deduced was the last stop for the most inveterate escapers, men who had already broken out of three or more camps. Still, the prisoners were not discouraged. In the time it took for Gaunt to recover, three officers had been shot trying to swim across it, including one artistic fellow who had painted his face to look like a lily pad and swum on his back, making it nearly to the other side before he was caught. None of the officers were fatally wounded. They were simply put on the waiting list for solitary confinement, although they were usually transferred to another prison before they could serve their time. This was typical: solitary confinement was the most frequently awarded punishment, and as such was vastly oversubscribed. It was, in fact, not solitary at all, and the men in the dank cells passed their time in much the same way as the men who roamed free—rereading *Adam Bede*. (At one point, a shipment of books from the Red Cross arrived, and the men fell upon it in frenzied excitement when they saw that it contained a different George Eliot novel: *Felix Holt*. They were devastated to discover that there had been a clerical error. The two dozen books were, in fact, copies of *Adam Bede* with *Felix Holt* covers.)

Every escape attempt made by an Englishman had to be approved by the senior British officer, a Kiplingesque Victorian named Evans, who coordinated escapes to ensure that one attempt did not endanger another.

Gaunt had expected there to be more animosity between the British, the French, and the Russians, but there was none. The British were the most active escapers, but the French and Russians were always keen to help. The French were uniformly good at swiping things. The Russians were dour and hungry but generous with their home-brewed alcohol. Soldiers from all three countries were united in their total disregard for German authority.

As the nights grew longer, the prisoners' lamp-oil allotment did not increase, so that they had only enough to keep the lights on until nine o'clock.

"I feel as if I'm in bloody first year again," said Devi.

"It's not to be borne," said MacCorkindale. "There's plenty of oil in the lamps lighting the corridors. Let's take some from there."

So they did, siphoning oil away each night, until the Kommandant discovered them and posted men to guard the lamps.

"We'll just have to be clever about it, that's all," said MacCorkindale, who developed a simple and routine procedure to steal the oil from under their noses. The hapless guards were spread too thin as it was, so there was never more than one to a corridor. First, Devi would linger suspiciously near a lamp at the far end of the corridor. The guard would stride towards him, leaving the lamp at the other end of the corridor completely open to be emptied by MacCorkindale. Surprised by the sudden darkness, the guard would turn sharply around, seeking a perpetrator, in which time Devi would rob the second lamp of its oil. The guard would then be left in total blackness.

Gaunt still spent every night in the corridor, shivering through the sleepless dark. Devi and MacCorkindale would help him back to his bed in the morning, although usually not before Windeler had kicked him in the ribs. Gaunt didn't mind that so much. What he hated was when Windeler mocked him in a high voice—*"Oh, gosh, I'm frightfully frightened of going over the top, I wish my mummy were here to give me a kiss before I went. . . ."*

He only said it when no one else was around. They both knew perfectly well on whose side the other officers would be. Gaunt said nothing.

Lüneburg came to check him in at 9:00 a.m. and 6:00 p.m. When no one else was there, he leant against Gaunt's bed and struck up a conversation.

"You look awfully hungry," said Gaunt.

Lüneburg bit his lip. "It's a strange thing, Kapitän, when the prisoners are better fed than the guards."

"Come by at lunchtime tomorrow. I've not much appetite at the moment, I'd be glad to share."

Lüneburg looked cautious. "I cannot give you anything in exchange," he said.

"I know."

Lüneburg scratched behind his ear in a sweet, embarrassed gesture. "When I first saw you, I thought you looked kind," he said.

MacCorkindale was disgusted to discover that Gaunt was sharing his meals with a guard.

"You're a British officer. It's your job to make his life miserable."

"His life is plenty miserable without my help."

"He's our *captor*."

"I'm not suggesting otherwise. But it's ungentlemanly to taunt starving boys." He had made his way to the mess hall that day, and been appalled to see officers ostentatiously throwing their German rations into the bin in favour of the far superior Red Cross supplies that only prisoners received. The guards had followed the wasted food with their sunken eyes, powerless and hungry.

"It was *ungentlemanly* of them to use gas at Ypres and to invade Belgium."

"Lüneburg didn't invade Belgium."

"I swear, if you had been in Germany when the War broke out, you would have enlisted on their side."

"Lay off, MacCorkindale. I fought in the damned war, didn't I?"

It wasn't until March that he was able to walk with any degree of confidence. In April, the doctor pronounced him officially healed.

"So you're good as new?" asked Devi at lunch.

"Not fit for combat, apparently. As if that matters. They'll send me to the front all right, if I get back to England."

"How are you in enclosed spaces?" asked Devi.

"Snug. Why?"

"Well, you want to get out of here, don't you?"

"Rather."

"Come with me."

Gaunt hadn't eaten his German rations. He wrapped them in a napkin and slipped them to Lüneburg on his way out. Lüneburg's eager face lit up with excitement. It reminded Gaunt of the glowing fervour that possessed Ellwood when he spoke of Tennyson.

Devi led him into the orderlies' basement. It was empty, except for some old stuffed mattress covers under the stairs.

"Obviously, you must swear to secrecy, etc., etc.," said Devi.

"I swear it."

Devi flicked a splinter of wood on the wall, and a tiny door popped open in the wooden panelling.

"Come on," whispered Devi. Gaunt ducked through, and Devi closed the door behind them.

They were in a brick crawl space in the foundations of the building. MacCorkindale was in his shirtsleeves, sweating like a coal miner as he operated a rudimentary set of bellows made out of an old leather jacket. The air from the jacket came out of one sleeve, through a series of cut tin cans, and into a small hole in the brick wall.

"You're *tunnelling* your way out?"

Devi and MacCorkindale nodded enthusiastically.

"Pretty good, eh?" said Devi. "Did you guess?"

"But . . . the moat!"

"We're aiming to go deep enough beneath it that it will hold."

"It's bloody slow going," put in MacCorkindale.

"But what will we do when we get out? They'll set the dogs on us."

Devi grinned at MacCorkindale.

"What did I tell you, Mac? I knew he'd be game."

"You'll help us?" asked MacCorkindale.

"Of course I'll help you," said Gaunt. "I've got to get back to the front."

"That's the rope," said Devi. He went to the hole and tugged on a long, thin cord. Eventually, a shallow enamel dish filled with earth emerged. There was a sound like rats in the walls, and a few minutes later Nicholson came wriggling out of the hole, feetfirst and covered in dirt. He immediately sat and put his head in between his knees.

"How's the air?" asked MacCorkindale.

"Can't be good," said Nicholson. "I've got a splitting headache."

"Well, Gaunt, do you want to have a go?" asked Devi. Nicholson looked up curiously.

"Hallo, it's the wounded giant! Are you one of us?"

"I'd like to be."

"It's a bit tight," said Devi. "You worm your way along about twenty-five yards. We've got spoons and cups to dig with. Try to keep your mouth closed, you'll last longer."

"I say, it's rotten to send him straight in, isn't it, Devi?" asked MacCorkindale.

"Oh, Gaunt's always fine," said Devi.

"Yes," said Gaunt, slowly. "I can do it."

Nicholson looked uncertain. "I shouldn't like to go down there with half a lung."

"I'll be all right," said Gaunt. He lay on his back with his head in the hole.

"Tuck your arms in," said Devi. "You won't be able to move them much once you're inside."

Gaunt put his hands to his chest. Nicholson handed him the empty enamel basin with the rope attached, and Gaunt edged into the tunnel on his back.

The air was thick and humid. He felt an instinctive, clutching panic. It was not like being locked into a cupboard, for the ground pressed narrowly in on him like a coffin. Broken bed slats were shoved haphazardly every few feet as supports, which only served to highlight the amateur nature of the whole enterprise.

"It won't . . . it won't collapse on me, will it, Gideon?" he asked, when he could no longer see the dim light from the crawl space.

"If it does, tug on the rope like anything, and we'll pull your feet out," said Devi.

"Maybe you ought to come back," said MacCorkindale. "Start with the bellows."

"I'm fine," said Gaunt, and he inched down the tunnel.

"I know you're fine," said Ellwood, smoke drifting out of his exquisite mouth as they stood on Fox's Bridge. "But are you all right?"

The thought of Ellwood spurred him to work faster. Soon he was so deep in the belly of the earth that the air was rank. His lungs felt as if they were tearing each time he tried to breathe.

Conditions improved as he reached the end of the tunnel, for the long tin-can tube stopped there, and quick gulps of breathable air puffed out of it. He felt around in the darkness for the digging tools. His hand fell on an old tin mug. He took it and delved into the earth. The angle of his arms was extremely awkward. To fill the mug took him almost ten minutes. He emptied it into the enamel basin and began again.

Maitland was buried like this, he thought. Maitland once roved the Wiltshire downs, feeling the rain on his face and the air in his lungs, but now he lay still in an unending bed of earth. The sun would never find him again. Maitland, who had loved Ellwood so much, and yet still been kind to Gaunt. Gaunt realised he didn't even know what Maitland had wanted to do after the War. Perhaps Maitland hadn't known.

"Are you still awfully close with Ellwood?" Maitland had asked him, their first night away from the trenches.

"I am."

Maitland dipped the tip of his finger into the candle wax and rolled it into a ball. "I care about Sidney very much," he said.

"I know you were particular friends, in school."

Maitland smiled. "Yes. I never superseded you in his affections, though."

"Ellwood absolutely worshipped you," said Gaunt. "He was devastated when you left."

"Oh, Ellwood likes playing at emotions," said Maitland, watching him intently. "It distracts him from the real thing."

Gaunt hadn't asked what Maitland meant by "the real thing." He had thought he knew: had thought it meant Maud.

He hacked at the damp earth, each blow punishing his lungs. *Fool. Blind, wasteful, cowardly fool; all those sonnets in Lower Sixth . . . ! All those months you might have had!*

Finally the enamel dish was filled with earth. Gaunt tugged on the rope and it was pulled down the length of his body. He followed after it. He had no idea how long he had been underground, but his head felt as if it were being squeezed by a tight iron circlet. The tunnel seemed to get smaller as he shimmied back, and he was keenly aware that some part of it might collapse and prevent him from escaping at the last moment. The air got worse and worse, and he began to gasp for breath. *I'm going to die here,* he thought, and all his muscles cramped at once; they were filled with an insane itching to stretch that was so powerful he tried forcefully to straighten his arms. It was impossible. There was only space for him to keep his elbows tucked in at his sides.

"Oh God!" he cried aloud.

"Don't panic," said a voice from the end of the tunnel.

"I can't breathe, I can't move!"

"Just stay calm," said the voice.

"I can't breathe!"

"Pull yourself together!" It was Devi.

In the dark, Gaunt nodded. He was an officer in the British Army. He had to keep his head.

He resumed his slow, inching pace down the tunnel. The air improved. Light pierced the black. Then someone grabbed hold of his ankles and pulled.

He was out.

"Oh, God," he said.

"Put your head between your knees," said Nicholson.

Gaunt did so, taking great, shuddery gulps of breath.

"Henry, you ox, look how quickly you dug! It takes me an hour and a half to fill the dish," said Devi.

"Oh, God," said Gaunt again. Devi put his arm around him.

"You all right, old thing?"

The question steadied him.

"I—yes. I'm fine." He lifted his head. MacCorkindale, Nicholson and Devi were looking at him admiringly. "It's . . . a bit of a tight fit, that's all."

"It's always worst when you're almost free," said Nicholson.

"How long was I in there?" It had felt like a week.

"Forty-five minutes." Devi squeezed him. "You're like a mole, Henry. We'll be out of here in half an hour, now that you're digging."

The tiny wooden door popped open, and Archie Pritchard entered. He was the older brother of Ellwood's friend Bertie Pritchard, and had been in Cemetery House, two years above them. Charlie Pritchard had been a bully, and Bertie Pritchard (to Gaunt's mind, although Ellwood had disagreed) was an idiot, but Archie had been a scholarship boy. He was placid and quiet, inconspicuously popular—quite a feat, considering his red hair and freckles.

"Hallo, Gaunt, is that you?"

"Pritchard Major!"

They hugged each other like old friends, although they had scarcely known each other at school. But there was something of Preshute about him, and the sight of him was as comforting to Gaunt as his own mother might have been.

"I say, have you had any news of my brother?" asked Pritchard.

"He was all right in September, but I've been rather out of the loop since then."

Pritchard fluffed his hair distractedly. "Ever since we lost Charlie at Ypres, I've been like a clucking mother hen about Bertie. He's such a dimwit, you know. Probably hasn't figured out which way round a rifle goes yet."

"Buck up," said Gaunt. "He'll manage."

Pritchard smiled. "With any luck, I'll be back at the front to look after him soon. How did you find the hole?"

"Oh, marvellously, you know, *holey.*"

"He had a bit of a panic on his way out," said MacCorkindale. "I *told* you we should have started him on the bellows, Devi."

"Nonsense," said Devi. "You underestimated him. Henry is the strongest man I know." He hooked his arm around Gaunt's neck and kissed the side of his head. "Indestructible Henry Gaunt. Now, who'll take the bellows while I go in?"

"I'll show you how they work, Gaunt," said MacCorkindale, as Devi wriggled effortlessly into the tunnel, like a fish in water. Nicholson filled an old mattress cover with the earth Gaunt had dug up.

"We're going to need to steal some more covers soon," he said.

Pritchard and MacCorkindale groaned.

"The guards kick up such a fuss when things go missing," said Pritchard.

"Well, where do *you* suggest we hide another fifteen cubic yards of earth?"

"Cubic yards? Don't make me laugh. If that tunnel were a yard wide, I should spend my afternoons in there, picnicking," said Pritchard.

"Oi!" shouted Devi from inside the tunnel. "Stop mucking about and get me some air in here!"

MacCorkindale showed Gaunt how the bellows worked. It transpired that the strange beeswax-and-lard paste MacCorkindale had mixed had been to line the seams of the leather jacket so that it was airtight. It was a remarkable feat of engineering, although within a few minutes of pumping, Gaunt was completely winded, and his lungs ached as though he had run a mile.

"You look a bit peaky, Gaunt," said MacCorkindale.

"I'm all right," said Gaunt, although grainy darkness encroached on his vision.

"Oh, don't be such a martyr. Go have a lie-down."

Gaunt left gratefully, and lay on the grass outside the barracks for a few hours, drinking the sky.

He remembered Master Larchmont teaching them about the Battle of Poitiers. He had described it in fascinating, painstaking detail, and left off just when it seemed as if the Black Prince was in desperate trouble.

"But sir! Did the Black Prince live?" asked West. Master Larchmont widened his eyes.

"They're all *dead*, West. It was *hundreds of years ago*."

Against the vast spread of history, Gaunt's fears dwindled into insignificance.

The next day, in the tunnel, the walls seemed to close in on Gaunt. He thought he smelt sweet, cloying gas, that strange pineappley scent, and he could not get out quickly enough; the faster he tried to move, the more wholly stuck he became, until he kicked too violently and clumps of earth rained down. He would be buried alive. He remembered stories of corpses discovered with broken, bent-back nails, long claw marks streaking the insides of their coffins. He tried, illogically, to sit up—but he wasn't thinking any more, he was drowning; he was merely a pair of lungs, yearning for air.

"Henry!" Devi cried from the mouth of the tunnel. "Stop panicking!"

But Gaunt could not. He thrashed around in chaos until Devi crawled in after him, and dragged him out by the ankles.

Pritchard had been on the bellows. When Gaunt would not stop gasping, he slapped him. The shock calmed Gaunt, and he breathed again.

Devi was looking at him as if he had never really seen him before.

"I say, Henry, you look rotten," he said.

"I'm fine," said Gaunt, although this was undermined by the fact that he had started to cry.

He heard the door open and shut. He didn't have to look to know that Devi and Pritchard had left. He was grateful for their tactfulness.

· · ·

That night, Pritchard came to sit on his mattress in the corridor.

"I've lost it," said Gaunt, surprising himself with his candour. But Pritchard had been at Ypres. He understood.

"You'll be fine," he said.

"I'm no use to anyone. Screamed like a bloody girl because I thought I smelt gas."

"Ah, I wondered if that was it. You were at Ypres too, weren't you?"

Gaunt nodded.

"That was a pretty bad show," said Pritchard.

"I got out of it all right." Gaunt sighed. "Gideon keeps looking at me as if I've gone mad."

"He's a fossil. You know how trench time works. Six months is a generation. Anyone who fought in 1914 has no clue what it's like out there now."

"If I could just sleep—"

Pritchard laughed.

"That would be something, wouldn't it?"

The dormitory door opened and Devi came out. Gaunt felt himself grow still with shame.

"Look, Henry . . ." began Devi.

"You don't want me to help with the tunnel any more."

Devi looked relieved. "I knew you'd understand."

Gaunt glanced at Pritchard, who sighed.

"Your lungs are too bad, anyway," he said. "Even if you were . . . more rested."

Gaunt knew that if he spoke, his voice would betray him. He nodded and lay back on the mattress.

"How are you, Henry?" asked Devi, tentatively.

Gaunt could only swallow.

"He's fine," said Pritchard. "Let's go back to bed."

Gaunt had marched into gunfire, but he was too much of a coward to keep his head in a tunnel. The thought occurred, flickering and insubstantial, that he might have preferred being killed at Ypres to discovering such a weakness in himself.

TWENTY-ONE

R IGHT, GAUNT, you'll have to play Hector," said MacCorkindale.
"You said *I* could play Hector," complained Nicholson.
"That was before I found out Gaunt was a Classicist. Hector
has the most lines, after Achilles."

"Can I play Achilles?"

MacCorkindale cast Nicholson a withering look. "*I'm* Achilles."

"I don't really want to play Hector," said Gaunt. "I don't know the
Iliad nearly as well as you think I do, MacCorkindale."

"We can do the Peloponnesian War another time, Gaunt. For the
moment, by popular demand, it's the *Iliad*. And you have to play
Hector—you speak Greek better than the others."

Nicholson groaned.

"Ohhh, we're not doing it in *Greek,* are we?"

"Problem, Nicholson?" asked MacCorkindale icily.

"No, no. Carry on."

Gaunt reluctantly recited what he could remember of the *Iliad* to
the other actors, teaching them their lines orally. It passed the time. So
did the performances, which were well attended. Gaunt had thought
MacCorkindale mad to insist on performing in Greek, but he soon saw
his logic. The French and the Russians had studied ancient Greek more
than English, and were able to enjoy the *Iliad* better in the original. The
performances provided an opportunity for the whole camp to gather
together in the dining hall, which facilitated escape plotting. While

some people did indeed watch Gaunt and MacCorkindale as they re-enacted the final fight between Hector and Achilles ("No need to actually punch me," complained MacCorkindale), mostly they exchanged information, homemade compasses, hand-drawn maps, and food supplies. Even the men who intended to spend the War in safety were more than happy to help others escape.

Every few days, a new plan was foiled. Lovell sneaked through the sewers and got his head stuck in a pipe. Campbell stole lumber from a visiting carpenter and built a bridge over the moat. It collapsed the moment he stepped on it. Robinson and Harley drugged two guards with a sleeping draught they had bought from the Russians. Dressed in the guards' uniforms, they got past the moat, but were caught in the nearby village when the baker engaged them in a conversation and recognised their strong English accents. The camp was very bitter about this—it was always a joyful thing when prisoners successfully crossed the moat.

"Just wait out the War," Pritchard told Gaunt. "If you were home, they'd probably lock you up for neurasthenia, anyway. Gideon says you still scream bloody murder every night."

"Charming, loyal friend, that Gideon. How's the tunnel going?"

"Swimmingly."

Gaunt raised his eyebrows.

"Ah, poor choice of words. No water, as yet, thank God. We're plugging away."

Gaunt tried to relax. Devi and Pritchard were right. He would be too much of a liability in any escape attempt. He slipped away into shivering, shuddering panic too easily. When Windeler whispered "Who's Ellwood? Your girlfriend?" one morning, after Gaunt had spent another night embroiled in tense, sweat-filled nightmares, he found quite suddenly that he couldn't breathe. Archie Pritchard was at his side in a moment, rubbing his back and muttering to him.

"Steady on, old boy, you're all right," he said, until the hazy blackness had drained away from Gaunt's vision, and his heart had stopped pounding.

"What if it's another Hundred Years' War?" he asked, when he could speak.

"Nothing we can do about it if it is," said Pritchard with a shrug, although Gaunt could tell the thought perturbed him. "Are you always this much fun?"

Gaunt laughed. "Yes."

"Look, this'll cheer you up—a box from the Red Cross arrived this morning."

"I've already read *Adam Bede*."

"You should give it another go. I've read it twice this month and like it more each time. But regardless, I've heard there were newspapers in this box."

Gaunt sat up. *Newspapers!* Newspapers had lists of the dead. Fear stole over him as he imagined (as he so often did) seeing Ellwood's name on the Honour Roll. *Ellwood, Sec.-Lieut. S. L., Royal Kennet Fusiliers. Killed in action, aged 18 . . .*

He followed Pritchard blindly to the dining hall, which was more than usually chaotic. Evans, the senior British officer, was slowly and methodically reading out the list of the dead from an issue of *The Times*. As more and more men trickled in who had missed the beginning of the list, cries of "What about Ainsworth? Captain J. Ainsworth?" or "I say, have we already had the 'G's? Did anyone hear about a Goodwin? Second lieutenant?" rippled through the room.

"Hush," chided the others.

"Prentis, H. W., Lieutenant," read Evans. Pritchard gripped Gaunt's arm so tightly it hurt. "Quaid, C. K., Private."

Pritchard released Gaunt. He was pale, his forehead sweaty. It was strange to think of *Bertie Pritchard* mattering so much to someone.

"It only means he didn't die in the last week or so, of course," said Pritchard.

"That's not nothing," said Gaunt, who knew he wouldn't rest until he had searched the paper himself for Ellwood's name.

"Hi, no one's reading this one," said Pritchard, picking a magazine off the floor. He looked disappointed when he saw the cover. "*The New Statesman*. Bunch of conchies."

"Might tell us something, though," said Gaunt, who was an enthusiastic reader of *The New Statesman*. It had been against the War from the beginning. He felt a grudging, confused admiration for conscientious objectors, who he suspected were braver than he was, yet whom he could not help but resent. They, at least, would survive the War.

He and Pritchard retreated to the edge of the room and pored over the pages, gorging themselves on information. It was only as they looked through it that Gaunt realised how isolated they really were, how bleary the outside world had become.

And then he saw something that made his heart jolt.

"Stop—"

Pritchard had been about to turn the page, saying, "It's only poetry."

It *was* only poetry. A long poem, lyrical and neat. Quatrains.

"What will you call it? In Memoriam H.W.G.?"

"Maybe. I haven't decided yet."

Gaunt knew Ellwood's poetry. He had read all of it, at Preshute; knew the dreamy, delicate way Ellwood spun nature into words. He had watched as it changed when the War broke out, puffing up with heroism and the promise of soldier glory.

It had changed again now. There was no more Pre-Raphaelite loveliness, nor any boyish optimism. Ellwood wrote colloquially, with occasional, startling bursts of reluctant beauty. Despite the poem's having Gaunt's initials, there was almost no reference to him at all—that Gaunt could make out, at any rate. Two stanzas were given over to a description of a colonel chiding the poet for his unpolished buttons, three to the scrambled body of a butchered duke, one to a wistful suicide. The poem as a whole seemed to pace back and forth with restless, bristling rage. Gaunt recognised that anger. It was what had driven Ellwood to gather half a dozen friends and beat Sandys to a pulp. It was the same fury with which Ellwood had hit Gaunt in the Old Priory. Reckless, scorching hatred ran through every word of *In Memoriam H.W.G.*, but only in one stanza could Gaunt discern any real reference to himself:

> *I hear the breaking bodies scream.*
> *Thankful I have hit my mark,*
> *I slither through the trenching dark.*
> *You bleed to death in all my dreams.*

"He thinks I'm dead," said Gaunt.

"It does seem that way," said Pritchard. " 'S. E.' That's Ellwood, isn't it?"

The poem was structurally Tennyson, down to the last iamb. But the words—the anger—it could only be Ellwood.

"Let me help with the bellows," said Gaunt.

"What?"

"I know I can't dig. Let me help with the bellows, I'll pump like anything, and then we'll get out faster."

"Henry, old boy, I'm not sure—"

"He thinks I'm dead! I can't hang about waiting for peace to break out, if it ever does, while he . . ."

Pritchard looked at him with understanding.

"All right. I'll talk to Gideon, if you're sure you can manage."

"I can," said Gaunt. "I can."

And he could. His chest ached for hours after he pumped the bellows: a gritty, dangerous pain that felt like something going wrong. He didn't care. He was stronger than the others, and when he was on the bellows the air quality in the tunnel was better. They could work for longer, make more progress. The tunnel grew in length, although Mac-Corkindale complained that the earth was suspiciously damp.

"We ought to dig deeper. We don't want the moat to flood in."

"That could add months!" said Gaunt.

"Faster than starting a whole new tunnel when this one caves," said MacCorkindale. So they delved deeper, where the air was worse, and Gaunt pumped harder than ever.

They began assembling materials for their escape. The guards frequently conducted room searches, but the prisoners had discovered a thousand ways to hide contraband. Everything that ought to have been solid was hollow and concealed some forbidden item. A Frenchman made them tiny compasses, and MacCorkindale copied maps in the crawl space in the attic. The attic crawl space was a camp secret—some months ago, an industrious young Russian had smuggled in photograph developer and constructed a camera out of an old shoebox. The French provided a diversion while he sneaked into the Kommandant's office and photographed all of the maps. (The French were always happy to provide diversions. This particular one took the form of five histrionic Frenchmen angrily accusing the Kommandant of insulting them by allowing French orderlies to work on a Catholic holiday that Gaunt later discovered they had invented. As the Kommandant defended himself, more and more incensed Frenchmen arrived, and the crowd grew increasingly volatile, until the bloodthirsty cries of "Liberté! Egalité! Fraternité!" and threats of camp-wide revolution could be heard even in the tunnelling basement.)

The map photographs were left for reference in the attic crawl space, and it was part of every escape to procure paper and spend hours tracing in the dark. The Germans were baffled by the sheer quantity of accurate, hand-drawn maps in circulation throughout the prison.

As it was spring, the guards had relaxed some of their more Draconian measures. The moat had thawed, which meant they no longer had to patrol it all night to catch the droves of men who attempted to skate over it. The ban on paroles was lifted, so Gaunt, Pritchard and Devi took long walks every afternoon, scouting their escape route. Before each excursion, they were required to sign a card promising not to escape. No one ever broke his word. To do so would have earned the disdain of their fellow prisoners, for what sort of officer gave his word of honour only to break it?

When prisoners were caught, they were always taken to the Kommandant's office, where their supplies were stripped and locked in a large metal chest. Devi concocted a plan to retrieve these stolen treasures, enlisting the help of the French and the Russians. When Hammond and Awdry were caught (they had hidden in the laundry barrels, but Awdry had packed so many cans of tinned food that the wicker bottom of the basket broke under his weight), they were brought to the Kommandant's office, and Devi set his plan into motion.

It began, of course, with a French diversion.

TWENTY-TWO

*S*ALE *TYPE! C'est indigne! C'est insupportable!"*

Devi and Gaunt waited in a dark spot in the corridor left by a lamp whose oil had been siphoned off in the usual way. They watched as the Kommandant warily emerged to find a Frenchman slapping a guard in the face with his glove.

"Was nun?" asked the Kommandant, who looked as if he hadn't slept in days.

"Ce barbare m'insulte, monsieur," said the Frenchman, haughtily.

"C'est vrai!" cried his friend.

"Jamais de la vie je n'ai subi un tel outrage!"

Evans, the senior British officer, came forward.

"Calm yourselves. What seems to be the problem?"

"I said nothing!" protested the unfortunate German guard, at which all three Frenchmen babbled over each other in outrage.

"Menteur!"

"Et dire que vous vous prétendez civilisé!"

"Ah, c'est raté, ça!"

"Evidently you have done *something* to distress these gentlemen," said Evans. "The Hague Convention and the laws of human decency both suggest that we be treated with respect, sir, although we *are* your prisoners."

"I said nothing! They are so easily offended!" cried the guard.

All three Frenchmen puffed up, exclaiming that they had never heard anything so unfair, that they simply hoped for a little common decency, but what could you expect from a country full of barbarian Visigoths—

"*Ruhe!*" said the Kommandant. "I am tired of your complaining. Take them to the cells."

"I refuse to go to the cells with this pig," said one of the Frenchmen, in sniffy English. "You may accompany us yourself, Kommandant, or face a revolution!"

The Kommandant tugged on his whiskers. The threats of revolution always unsettled him, because the fact was that although any prisoners revolting would eventually be court-martialled and shot, there were certainly enough desperate men at Fürstenberg to murder the Kommandant and all his guards first.

"Very well," he said. He and his guard took the Frenchmen by the arms and marched them down the corridor.

"I think you've got a clean shot, boys," said Evans. Gaunt and Devi darted into the Kommandant's empty office. Hammond and Awdry grinned when they saw what they were doing. The metal chest was open, having just been filled with Awdry's numberless cans of tinned meat. Gaunt and Devi picked it up with difficulty and brought it to the nearest Russian barrack, where a young officer from Moscow waited with a few rudimentary tools. As he dismantled the metal chest, men entered in groups of two or three, took what they needed from the treasure trove, and disappeared.

By the time the Kommandant realised what had happened, not a scrap of the chest or the supplies remained. The camp was searched from top to bottom, but nothing was found, save for a few decoy supplies the men hid in obvious places: under the mattresses or in the toilet cisterns.

The tunnellers acquired all the materials they needed to escape—all, except for German identification papers.

"Tricky," said MacCorkindale. "I thought there'd be something we could use in there."

"How have other people procured them?" asked Pritchard.

"They haven't, mostly," said MacCorkindale. "And consequently, they've been caught."

"The Kommandant's secretary would be our best bet," said Gaunt.

"I've tried her." Devi sighed. "She's an ice queen."

"Is she?" Gaunt had never thought so. Whenever he walked by Elisabeth, the Kommandant's pretty young secretary, she always had a smile for him.

"Famously frigid," said Nicholson. "We'll have to think of something else."

They carried on plotting, but Gaunt's mind wandered. Elisabeth was slender and dark-haired. She was friends with Lüneburg. Gaunt resolved to ask him about her.

"What do you want to know?" asked Lüneburg.

"Anything." He paused. "Has she a sweetheart?"

Lüneburg shot him a knowing look. "No."

"Hmm," said Gaunt.

"She's a good girl," said Lüneburg.

"I'm sure."

"I've talked to her about you before. She thinks you're kind."

"That explains the smiles," said Gaunt.

"Maybe partly."

When Gaunt next walked past Elisabeth, he stopped and talked to her for a few minutes in German before sneaking her an apple and a bar of chocolate. The interaction was enough to confirm his suspicion: Elisabeth was sweet on him.

He watched her small white teeth nibble on the chocolate, and thought of Ellwood.

"Would you like to go for a walk with me tomorrow?" he asked her. She blushed furiously red.

"Yes—all right," she said, falsely casual.

Gaunt let his eyes soften towards her. It felt strange, how easy, how permissible it was. He had to be so careful when he looked at Ellwood.

The next day, they walked arm in arm and he asked her questions about her family. She seemed delighted to answer, and leant heavily against him.

"Look," she said. "Isn't this a pretty view?"

She had quick, brown eyes. She was soft where Ellwood was hard, but she was as delicate as he was. Her long, dark hair hung around her shoulders in limp curls. Her lips were rather shapeless. He wondered, scientifically, what it would be like to kiss them.

Easy, he thought.

"You are a very kind man," said Elisabeth. Her words came out in little clouds, for it was cold.

"I don't know if that's true," said Gaunt.

"I don't feel—that you would be unkind to me," she said.

He tilted her jaw up. It was so small, like a cat's. It fit incorrectly in his hand, and he felt nothing.

"May I kiss you?" he asked. She nodded breathlessly.

He had kissed girls before. The summer of 1914 had been a whirl of balls and parties. Ellwood frequently disappeared with some society beauty or another, only to re-emerge half an hour later, lips stained red and eyes bright. Gaunt had not wanted to be left behind.

But he had never kissed a girl like this: sober, in a forest. It felt real. It was deadening. His skin was asleep; no matter how she touched it, it would not react.

"You are so handsome, Heinrich," she whispered.

"Call me Henry."

"Henry."

It was worse. Her accent—the pitch of her voice—it was just worse. He put his mouth on hers again and wondered how kissing could feel so different, kiss to kiss, when it was such a simple action.

The pain in his lungs was indistinguishable from anguish as Elisabeth wrapped her arms around him.

"Henry," she said. "What's wrong?"

"I'm fine."

She crowded her face into his. Strangely, he did not mind.

"You can tell me."

"I'm fine."

"Women are good for listening, Henry."

"Don't—don't call me that."

She looked surprised, but continued to place kisses where she could reach him. It was so *easy*. Was this how it was, for other men? Did they allow themselves gentleness, when women offered it so graciously?

"This horrible war," she said, her voice rich with concern. "I am so sorry."

She wiped away his tears with her fingers.

"I'm in love—" he said. He ought to have been embarrassed at the way his voice cracked, but he couldn't be, not while she kept her face so close to his that they could not look at each other.

"That's wonderful, Heinrich. She's a lucky girl."

"Oh, God."

"I don't mind," she said. "I don't mind."

"I'm sorry."

"It's all right, shh, just kiss me. I'm here."

Was Ellwood alive? He had been when that poem was published in *The New Statesman*. But Gaunt had seen what happened to poetic young men in the trenches. It was more than bodies that were blown apart by the shells. Perhaps he wasn't even Ellwood any more, but some hollowed-out version of himself, angry and ugly. Perhaps he was dead. It was likely, in fact. He was dead, or maimed, or in pain, or—

"Shhh," said Elisabeth. She was crying now, and Gaunt held her close, burying his face into her hair to comfort her.

"I'm sorry, I didn't mean to upset you," he said.

"My brother is at the front," she said. He pressed her tighter. "The girl you love, is she safe?"

"No," said Gaunt.

"At the front?"

"Yes."

"A nurse?"

"I don't want to talk about it."

Elisabeth nodded into his chest. He wondered if he could marry her. She would lean her dark head against his shoulder when she was tired. He would hold her hand in restaurants. It would be romantic when they touched each other. People would admire their affection.

When he and Ellwood were gentle with one another, there was a sense of awe to it. Their tenderness was hesitant and temporary, like a butterfly pausing on a child's hand.

"I'm afraid I haven't shown you a very good time," he said.

Elisabeth shook her head and smiled.

"Tomorrow," she said. "It will be better, now that we understand each other."

She did understand him, a little. They walked back to the camp and she let him kiss her in the corridor outside her office.

It was nice enough, thought Gaunt.

Between Elisabeth, pumping the bellows, performing in various Greek plays and rereading *Adam Bede,* time passed quickly.

He did not tell anyone that he was seeing Elisabeth. He met her every few days in a quiet spot. They did not talk much, after that first day. Gaunt undressed her with a dispassionate calm that she seemed to take as a sign of good breeding.

"I don't want to have a baby," she said, when they came close to having sex.

"We don't have to do anything," he told her, masking his relief.

Sometimes she asked about Ellwood.

"Are you engaged?"

Gaunt laughed. "No. It's not like that."

"But surely you want to get married?"

"It has never crossed my mind."

"But she must—"

"I don't want to talk about it."

One time, he accidentally called her Elly.

She froze. "That is what my mother calls me," she said. "Say it again, please."

"I ought to go. It'll be dinner soon."

"Is that her name?"

"I don't want to talk about it."

"I'm good at listening, Heinrich."

He was better at kissing her now, because he liked her.

"You're very good, Elisabeth. But I—I just *can't.*"

"You don't trust me."

"I don't trust anyone."

"That's terrible!"

"Is it?"

"Yes," said Elisabeth. "You'll fill up your head with sorrow if you don't let it out."

"Little poetess. I'll be all right."

He told himself that he was seducing her to procure identification papers, but when he lay awake at night, avoiding his dreams, he knew that was only an excuse. He was kissing her because of what Ellwood had told him in the dugout, through Keats and Shakespeare and Tennyson. He felt as if there was a decision to be made, and he needed to accrue information before making it.

Unfortunately, the more time he spent with Elisabeth, the more apparent it became how fruitless it was to try to want her. He could appreciate her beauty in an artistic sense, as if she were a sculpture in a museum, but it was a flat, textureless sort of admiration. If love was stepping off a cliff in the hope of flying, there was a wall at the precipice that had never been there with Sandys, or Ellwood, or even Devi, whom Gaunt had hopelessly adored at thirteen. He felt no fear around Elisabeth, because there was no chance of falling. He was fond of her, but he would never say to her, " 'Withhold no atom's atom or I die!' "

It was full spring, and snippets of information about the War trickled through the camp. News of Verdun made the French edgy and hostile. The gas attacks near Loos in late April intensified Gaunt's dreams. He often woke up gasping, Devi's hand on his shoulder to remind him where he was.

Shortly after Lord Kitchener's death at sea in June 1916, the tunnel was completed. Devi, Pritchard, MacCorkindale, Nicholson, Gaunt and Evans met in the basement to plan.

"This is an ambitious affair," said Evans. "We will have to schedule it carefully."

"We can't wait too long," said MacCorkindale. "The tunnel might collapse at any moment."

Gaunt shifted uncomfortably. He had not been inside since the time he had lost his head and thought he smelt gas.

"Have you assembled your supplies?" asked Evans.

"Yes," said Nicholson. "All except for identity papers."

Evans sighed. "That's a shame. It would make everything a great deal easier."

Gaunt cleared his throat. "I believe I may be able to get them."

Everyone turned to look at him.

"I've . . ." He paused. ". . . befriended the Kommandant's secretary."

"Well, aren't you a sly dog!" said Nicholson. "Right, in that case, we've got everything we need, I should think."

Evans nodded. "Once you have the papers, I will schedule your escape at the nearest possible opportunity."

They discussed a few more technicalities, and Evans inspected the tunnel. Gaunt was distracted by the unreadable looks Devi threw at him.

Finally, the meeting was done. They exited the secret basement room at ten-minute intervals.

Pritchard and Devi were waiting for him in their dormitory. Pritchard lay on Gaunt's bed, and Devi leant laconically against the wall. He smiled when he saw Gaunt, but waited until Gaunt had closed the door to speak.

"So," he said, "you're sleeping with Elisabeth, are you? How do you manage it? Do it from behind and close your eyes?"

Gaunt crossed his arms. "She's quite good-looking."

"Oh, certainly," said Pritchard. "I wouldn't say no."

"But then," said Devi to Pritchard, "*you're* not a pansy."

Gaunt felt something like a lurch, as if he were being dragged backwards into a nightmare.

"No," said Pritchard, "I'm not. Still, Henry, it was good of you to grit your teeth and bear it, for the sake of king and country."

Gaunt didn't know what to do with his face, his hands, he had forgotten how to *breathe*. But even through his rising panic, he could see that neither Pritchard nor Devi looked disgusted. In fact, they both looked just as they always did: Devi, laughing and mischievous; Pritchard, placid and comforting.

"I don't know what you're talking about, but it isn't funny," said Gaunt.

Ellwood would have known what to say. Ellwood would have made just the right joke, and no one would ever have brought it up again. But Gaunt was clumsy and ineloquent and he did not know how to use words to chisel his way free of accusations.

"Oh, don't look so glum," said Pritchard. "You're not the only invert ever to have roamed the earth. I'm friends with Aldworth."

"Aldworth . . . !"

"Yes, did you ever go hunting with him, in Kent?" asked Pritchard. "He's an excellent shot."

"I . . . there isn't some secret *club*!" said Gaunt. Too late did he realise what he had admitted to.

Devi looked triumphant.

"I think the real question is, which of us do you fancy more?" he asked, gleefully. "Me, or Archie? Because I'm taller. I really think my height should be taken into consideration."

Gaunt yanked the door open and walked out, slamming it behind him. But he couldn't think. He was frozen. Eventually the door opened, and Pritchard poked his head out.

"Don't be a chump," he said, so Gaunt followed him back into the dormitory and sank onto the bed opposite his own.

Devi sat next to him, crowding close.

"I must say, that *you* should be the one to melt the ice queen is truly a killing irony," he said.

Gaunt jerked away. "Gideon. Fuck *off*."

Devi smiled even wider and turned to Pritchard.

"He doesn't swear often, but when he does, it's because he's *upset*."

"Hmm," said Pritchard, moving to sit on the other side of Gaunt. "Why are you upset, Gaunt? Didn't you like the pudding at dinner?"

"He's crossed in love," said Devi. "Hi, Gaunt, remember when you kissed me, at Grinstead?"

"I did not!"

"For the school play," said Devi. He leant forward so that he could grin at Pritchard across Gaunt's body. "He was the Juliet to my Romeo. He wore a wig with long ringlets. He was ever so pretty."

"As I recall, I insisted that we stage the kissing," said Gaunt. It was true. Gaunt had pretended to suffer through wearing a nice dress and a wig, but he knew he wouldn't be able to strike the appropriate balance of disgust if he had to kiss Devi. He refused point-blank. Eventually it was settled that Devi would take Gaunt's face in his hands, put his thumbs on Gaunt's lips, and kiss his own fingers. Gaunt agreed with very bad grace.

"You *were* a sour Juliet," said Devi. "Miss Fairfax despaired of you. Anyway, I had a pretty good idea of what was going on."

"Oh, you did, did you?" said Gaunt, faintly. He kept waiting for—he wasn't sure what for. Something awful.

"I've always known you were a bit funny," said Devi.

"How . . . are *you* . . . ?"

Devi looked horrified. "Oh, God, no! No. No! I'm not—no."

"Yes, all right, Gideon, no one here thinks you're deviant," said Gaunt testily.

"No, I don't mean . . . only, I'm Indian. I've got quite enough trouble to be getting along with."

"It isn't illegal to be Indian," said Gaunt, staring at his balled-up fists in his lap.

"Yes, yes, woe is you."

"It isn't illegal everywhere," put in Pritchard. "Aldworth plans to move to Brazil."

Gaunt thought of the darkling fields behind Cemetery House, the chalk horse carved into the hill, Ellwood in his billowing tailcoat saying, *"England is magic."*

"Or you could try hypnosis," said Devi.

Gaunt collapsed back on the bed and covered his face with both arms.

"I've heard that doesn't work," said Pritchard, just as if Gaunt hadn't moved.

"Of course it doesn't, if you don't *believe* it will," said Devi.

"I'll hit you," said Gaunt. "Both of you. I don't care."

"I suppose he might grow out of it," said Devi, ignoring him.

"I doubt it," said Pritchard. "What do you think, Henry? You strike me as incorrigible. You and Ellwood, you know."

Gaunt groaned.

"Henry, is this Ellwood fellow better-looking than I am?" asked Devi. Then, to Pritchard: "He can't be."

"Don't look at *me*," said Pritchard. "I'm no use in judging something like that."

"If a friend of mine is going to bugger men, I'd like him to have good taste," said Devi.

"I think that's reasonable," said Pritchard.

"Christ! Will you be quiet!" said Gaunt.

"We've upset him," said Devi.

"*You've* upset him," corrected Pritchard.

"I'm not upset!"

Devi lay down on the bed next to Gaunt. A moment later, Pritchard did the same. Both of them, pressed close beside him.

Gaunt swallowed, hard. He knew what it meant that they were touching him so readily.

"Do you really think you can get us those papers?" asked Pritchard.

"Of course he can," said Devi. "He's Henry Gaunt, Great Seducer of Men and Women the World Over. I say, Henry, don't you think it'd save time if you just slept with the Kommandant?"

"I'd rather get shot in the lung than discuss any of this ever again," said Gaunt.

"Oh, stop boasting about your battle wounds," said Devi. "Everyone thinks you're very brave, no need to lay it on so thick."

Pritchard didn't mention it again. Devi made jokes, but he was careful, Gaunt could see that—he was so careful in ensuring that his jokes would never be overheard, and to Gaunt's immense surprise, he found that he could tolerate them. That they even brought him relief. To have something that he had thought so grave be treated lightly and playfully—it was reassuring. He felt as if he had shed something, some weight he had not known he carried. His mood lifted. He would forget why, sometimes, and then remember: *I have no secrets from Archie and Gideon.*

It took Elisabeth a few days to find them identity papers, and in the interim she tried to convince Gaunt to stay. He was safe in the camp, she pointed out. He was touched that she cared, not about the risk she faced in smuggling him papers, but the one he faced in returning to the front.

"I'll miss you," he told her, truthfully.

He had begun to understand Ellwood's relationship with Maud better, through his own with Elisabeth. Friendliness that led nowhere. A knot of tangles in his heart was unsnarling, and things were much simpler than before.

If Ellwood were there, they would have been simpler still.

TWENTY-THREE

ONCE THEY HAD RECEIVED the papers, Evans told them they could escape the next evening. The moon was waxing, which would make them more difficult to spot as they emerged from the tunnel, and they would have the additional coverage of a field of barley that grew at the tunnel's exit.

The day before the escape reminded Gaunt very much of the day before the Battle of Loos. He had the same jittery feeling of anticipation, although it was a more pleasant experience, because he was more excited than nervous. It was strange to go through the motions of the day as if everything was normal. He promised Hinton to help him learn his Greek lines the next day. He shared his food with Lüneburg, he took Elisabeth to the woods and kissed her. He didn't dare say goodbye.

Whenever he caught the eye of one of his fellow escapers, he could not stop himself from grinning.

"It's a bit like a midnight feast, isn't it?" said Devi.

"Less wholesome by about half."

"Much naughtier."

"Rather less cake."

Devi laughed. He sounded slightly unhinged. "I am going to eat my *weight* in cake, Gaunto. Just you watch."

They went to bed at the usual time. Gaunt settled himself in the corridor, as always, and waited.

At a quarter to one, Evans shook him awake from delicious, dreamless sleep.

"It's time, my boy," said Evans.

Gaunt was the first to arrive in the basement. The others came in one at a time, loaded with supplies. They put on their dirty tunnel clothes, and wrapped their things in waterproof jackets tied with string.

"Gideon ought to go first," said Nicholson. "It was his idea."

Everyone nodded. This would give Devi the greatest chance of escaping.

"Are you sticking together, once you're out?" asked Evans.

"Not me," said Nicholson. "I'm trying the trains. *Eine Fahrkarte nach Münster, bitte!*"

"The rest of us are going on foot," said Devi. "If anyone talks to us, Gaunt will tell them that I'm a madman and they're escorting me to an asylum near Emsdetten. I'll just drool a bit; it should be all right."

"Everyone here will be rooting for you," said Evans. "I've organised for a few men to answer at your names in the morning *Appell*; that ought to give you a few hours."

They helped Devi tie his pack on. Gaunt gave him a tight smile.

"You'll be all right, Henry," said Devi. "You always are."

"Don't worry about me."

Devi got to his knees and climbed into the hole.

MacCorkindale estimated that it would take Devi about twenty minutes to get through the tunnel. They would wait fifteen before sending another person through, to avoid disturbing the tunnel's foundations.

Fifteen minutes passed without incident, and Nicholson was just tying his pack on when Pritchard spoke.

"Listen!"

There was a low rumbling sound coming from the hole.

Gaunt didn't hesitate. He got down on the floor, stuck his head in the tunnel, and shouted.

"Gideon!"

Distantly, Devi's voice answered.

"Help!"

"Gaunt, wait," said MacCorkindale. "If the tunnel's flooding—"

Gaunt slid into the tunnel on his stomach.

"I'm coming," he called.

"I'm stuck," Devi called back. "The water's rising!"

"Try to get free; I'm coming!"

The tunnel was formed in a sharp V. From the sounds of it, it had collapsed near the surface, and water was pouring in, pooling at the lowest point of the tunnel and rising from there. As Gaunt progressed downwards, it grew steeper and steeper.

"Henry . . . !"

Devi's voice was faint. His face burst into Gaunt's memory like a firework.

"Remember the grass forts we built at Grinstead, Gideon?" he asked desperately.

Devi didn't answer.

"Remember the feeding frenzy when there was toast as a treat at elevenses? Remember—remember the day we climbed the Wellingtonia?"

Silence. Gaunt pushed forward. It was hard to find enough breath in the tunnel to speak and move at once.

"Can you hear me?"

The earth was damp, and then it was wet. He had reached water, freezing, muddy water. It was pitch-black, and the air was almost unbreathable.

"Gideon!" cried Gaunt. There was no answer. He estimated the tunnel continued another twenty-five yards, all flooded. Devi was stuck somewhere, drowning in a hole too narrow to move his arms. Devi, who had taught him how to climb trees.

Gaunt took a deep breath—the foul air made his head spin—and edged forward into the submerged tunnel.

At Preshute, Gaunt could hold his breath for several minutes at a time, but since his injury, even going up stairs winded him. The air in the tunnel was so bad that the breath he had taken to prepare barely served him at all. Within seconds, his lungs were throbbing. He continued to half-swim, half-dig his way forward. Devi was in there somewhere, if he could just get to him.

He felt oddly clear-headed, despite the pain in his chest. It was much easier to be brave for your friends than for yourself.

The slow darkness of the water did not ease up. It was not the kind of black that eyes could adjust to. Gaunt pressed on. The water dug into his ears. He felt so calm. His body was neither cold nor hot. He moved forward steadily, like a soldier.

His hand felt something hard and rubbery. It was a boot. Gaunt's mind jolted, and he grasped around until his hands fell upon what he thought must be an ankle. The leg kicked slightly—Devi was alive.

Suddenly aware that he didn't have enough air to get them both out safely, Gaunt edged furiously back, tugging Devi's leg. After a brief tussle, Devi's body began to move.

There wasn't space in the tunnel for Gaunt to turn around. He was crawling backwards, uphill, dragging a body through water. It should have been impossible. Perhaps it would have been, if Gaunt had allowed himself to believe for a second that it was. But he simply pulled. The water made Devi's body almost weightless. It was all Gaunt could do not to open his mouth to draw breath. Desperation built in his chest. It was increasingly difficult to move his limbs, which buzzed with a helpless need for oxygen.

And then a hand grabbed his ankle and pulled.

Someone had come for him. He redoubled his grip on Devi, and the hand pulled him further, until suddenly his head breached the water, and he took a dizzying gulp of air.

"Keep going," he gasped.

"Righto," said Pritchard, and Gaunt heard him continue to crawl backwards. Gaunt pulled Devi painstakingly out of the water. He knew the instant Devi's head was free, because Devi spluttered and coughed like a gas victim.

"He's alive!" said Pritchard, behind him.

"Keep going," said Gaunt again.

Gaunt continued to drag Devi backwards, because it was evident that Devi wasn't yet capable of moving on his own. It was much more difficult with the full weight of gravity. But soon Devi spoke.

"I'm all right now," he said.

"We ought to get out sharpish," said Gaunt. "I don't fancy sticking around while the whole place collapses."

He felt Devi adjust himself, and then he was worming his way backwards, his feet kicking into Gaunt's face.

"How far, Archie?" asked Gaunt.

"I can see the light," said Pritchard.

"The water's rising," said Devi.

And then Gaunt could hear the others in the basement room, including—his heart quailed—the unmistakable sound of German.

TWENTY-FOUR

H ENRY," SAID DEVI URGENTLY. "Hide your compass in your mouth."

With great difficulty, Gaunt extracted his tiny homemade compass from his pocket. It was flat, and only a little bigger than a marble. He stuck it between his cheek and his teeth.

There was a loud yelp and a dragging sound. Pritchard had been pulled out of the tunnel by his ankles. Gaunt continued shuffling backwards, and then, for a second time, he felt someone grab him by the feet and pull.

He was out of the tunnel, blinking in the dim light of the secret basement. It was Lüneburg who had pulled him out, and he cast Gaunt a betrayed look before leaning back into the tunnel entrance to feel for Devi.

Lüneburg was not the only German in the basement.

"*Steh auf,*" barked the Kommandant. Gaunt got unsteadily to his feet. Nicholson and MacCorkindale were facing the wall with their hands on their heads. Evans, Gaunt was pleased to see, must have got away before they were caught. Pritchard gave him a quick grin.

"A sentry heard you shouting in the tunnel," he said.

"*Sei still!*" said the Kommandant, pointing a rifle at Pritchard, who held out his hands placatingly.

There was a scuffling sound, and Lüneburg reappeared, followed closely by Devi, who looked quite grey.

"*Er braucht einen Arzt*," said Gaunt, speaking carefully around the compass in his mouth. "He needs a doctor."

"Quiet!"

"Lüneburg," said Gaunt. "*Help him.*"

But Lüneburg only glared and dragged Devi to his feet.

The Kommandant kept his gun trained on them as he marched them up to his office. They lined up in front of his desk. Pritchard had his arm around Devi's waist to hold him up.

"I will not search you if you give me your word of honour to hand over all your supplies," said the Kommandant. They each in turn promised. Gaunt had no scruples about lying. The Kommandant was not behaving like a gentleman, keeping Devi from a doctor.

They took off their packs and turned out their pockets. Nicholson even took the coins out of his shoes. That was clever of him, thought Gaunt—they all knew that he kept the bulk of his money in paper form, taped to his back.

"Where did you get these?" asked the Kommandant in English, holding out their identification papers.

They were all silent.

"Where did you get these papers?" repeated the Kommandant, his voice rising.

"I procured them," said Gaunt.

"From whom?"

"I'm afraid I can't say. It's a point of honour."

The Kommandant looked as if he would like to hit Gaunt, but held back.

"Only a German could have given you these. Surely, Kapitän, you can see how this information is necessary for me."

"I can quite see that. I'm sorry I'm unable to help," said Gaunt sincerely. The Kommandant turned to Lüneburg.

"I have heard reports that Kapitän Gaunt gives you food."

"It wasn't Lüneburg," said Gaunt quickly. "That, I can assure you."

"I say," said MacCorkindale. "If you're done grilling us, might we get Gideon here to a doctor?"

"Be quiet!" said the Kommandant, waving his rifle at MacCorkindale.

"Now, look here—" said MacCorkindale.

"Shut up, Mac," said Gaunt. MacCorkindale fell silent.

"You will tell me who gave you these papers!" said the Kommandant.

"I will not," said Gaunt. "I'm truly sorry to disappoint you."

"You will have no Red Cross parcels! You will be put in solitary confinement!"

Gaunt tried not to smile. Both these threats were empty. One was automatically put in solitary for an escape attempt, after all, and Evans would arrange for Red Cross food to be smuggled to them, as he did for all British escapers.

"Oh, get on with it," said Nicholson. The Kommandant whacked him on the head with his rifle. Everyone started talking at once.

"I say!" cried MacCorkindale. "What a dirty, brutish thing to do!"

"German swine," said Pritchard, his cheeks flushing red under his freckles.

"That's a clear violation of the Hague Convention," said Gaunt.

"We won't forget this when the War is over," said Devi.

"*Seid still!*" said the Kommandant.

"Settle down, men," said Gaunt. "I think he's getting agitated."

They stopped talking. None of them wanted to get shot, although they knew the Kommandant wouldn't dare wound any of them fatally. It would likely get him sent to the front if he did.

"*Bleib wo du bist,*" said the Kommandant.

"German is such a charming language," said MacCorkindale.

"Stop antagonising him," said Gaunt.

The Kommandant cast MacCorkindale a poisonous look before pulling Lüneburg aside. They talked together in lowered voices for a few minutes. Gaunt tried to listen, but couldn't hear over Nicholson and MacCorkindale's mutinous mutterings.

Whatever they discussed, Lüneburg looked more furious than ever afterwards.

"You will go to solitary now," said the Kommandant.

"That's rather flattering," said Devi, as they were marched down the corridor. "We've been bumped to the top of the waiting list."

"I suppose the tunnel *was* impressive," said Pritchard.

"Might have been, if it hadn't caved," said Gaunt. "Are you all right, Gideon?"

"Fizzing. I like a good swim."

"I say, Gaunt, that guard is looking daggers at you. What *have* you done to him?" said Nicholson.

"Betrayed him, I suppose." He slowed down, so that he could speak to Lüneburg. "You're angry with me," he said in German.

"Be quiet."

"I'm awfully sorry if I've got you in trouble."

Lüneburg made a horrible sound that Gaunt supposed was meant to be laughter.

"Trouble? You've got me sent to the front."

"Oh," said Gaunt, guilt opening wide in his chest. Lüneburg ground his teeth and stared straight ahead. He looked at once much older than before, and much younger.

"It's not so bad," said Gaunt. He meant to reassure, but the look Lüneburg gave him was withering. "Yes, well, it's no picnic. But you'll manage. Everyone does."

"Oh, yes," said Lüneburg bitterly. "Everyone manages."

Gaunt couldn't think of anything to say. He felt rather as if he had shot Lüneburg, or punched him when he wasn't expecting it. He dropped his gaze to the ground.

Solitary confinement was, as always, rammed. It was a row of cells with no windows, each intended to house one prisoner, but instead filled with three. Everyone cheered as they came in.

"Foiled?" asked a large-nosed Scotsman. Gaunt vaguely remembered that he had been caught cutting holes in the walls of his dormitory in some convoluted escape plan that had involved, among other things, poisoned mushrooms and a great deal of lead piping.

"Tunnel collapsed," said MacCorkindale.

"Tunnelling? Did you forget about the moat?"

"Completely. Someone ought to have reminded us."

They had to let five men out to find room for them. To Gaunt's pleasure, he, Devi and Pritchard were put in a cell together. There wasn't any furniture, only a bucket and a blanket.

"I really am sorry, Lüneburg," said Gaunt, as Lüneburg locked them in. "I wish you luck. Perhaps we'll meet again, after the War."

Lüneburg swallowed. "I'll let Elisabeth know what happened," he said. "You won't see her again."

"Send her my love."

Gaunt watched Lüneburg leave.

"Don't worry about your German," said Devi. "He'll be fine."

"Will he," said Gaunt.

"He'll get more food at the front, anyway," said Pritchard. "He looks as if he could do with it."

Gaunt thought of Lüneburg's small, thin body being hit by a shell, and shuddered, and decided never to think of him again.

They extracted the compasses from their mouths and checked them against each other. They were both in functioning order.

"I say, that was some quick thinking," said Pritchard.

"I wish I'd thought to hide a map on me," said Devi. "I left it in my pack." He sighed and surveyed the cell. "Well, this is about as nice as first-year digs at Eton, really."

"Rather nicer than Preshute," said Pritchard. "No older boys who'll shove us into barrels and roll us down hills."

"Your brother Charlie shot at us with rifle blanks, you know," said Gaunt. A dreamy look crossed Pritchard's face.

"Yes," he said. "He was fierce, wasn't he?"

"I wish I weren't so *wet*," said Devi. "We'll have to huddle for warmth."

"I'm not touching either of you," said Pritchard. "I'm dry, in case you hadn't noticed."

"Come here, then, Henry," said Devi. Gaunt sat next to him, and Devi wrapped an arm around him. "You saved my life, you crazy bastard."

"Archie here saved us both."

"And none of us are getting out any time soon," said Pritchard gloomily.

Devi grinned. "Don't be so sure."

"What? Have you been digging holes in the cells in your spare time?"

"No," said Devi. He leant closer to Gaunt, so that their bodies warmed each other. Gaunt found it rather touching that Devi wasn't suspicious of physical contact with him. But then, if what Devi said was true, he had always known Gaunt was homosexual, and never treated him differently.

"You have that look on your face," said Pritchard. "That Sherlock Holmes, plot-hatching look."

"They're going to move us to a new camp," said Devi. "They always do. By train. Let's just say that I've thought a lot about trains, and the opportunities they offer."

"How many times *have* you tried to escape, Gideon?" asked Gaunt.

"This is my eighth attempt. Pathetic, isn't it?"

"Eighth? What were the other seven?"

Devi counted on his fingers.

"Seduced a nurse; jumped off a boat; threw sand in a guard's eyes and sneaked past him while he cried; slipped away during a riot; hid in a cart of manure—very unpleasant, can't recommend; scaled the walls . . . In the first camp I just walked out with so much confidence that no one stopped me. I was captured after six days, half starved, by some overzealous schoolchildren."

"Christ," said Gaunt. "You *are* keen to get back to the front."

Devi shrugged. "It's something to do."

Pritchard settled himself under the blanket.

"Right, I've come to some new conclusions about *Adam Bede*," he said. "Get comfortable, because I've got a lot to say."

TWENTY-FIVE

THEY WERE IN SOLITARY for two weeks. Within three days, they were thoroughly sick of each other. Pritchard complained of the bucket smell, and Gaunt explained in painstaking detail how the British Empire would self-destruct after the War, no matter who won.

"Wouldn't that be dreadful," said Devi, with a charming little smile. "Imagine, India ruled by Indians. The horror!"

He was always smiling. He drove them mad with his relentless good humour.

"Mind over matter," he said cheerfully, about eight times a day. Gaunt took to reciting Thucydides. Pritchard called him an insufferable swot. Gaunt told him his *Adam Bede* theories didn't hold water. Pritchard hit him, Gaunt hit him back, and Devi instigated an afternoon of silence.

Harry Windeler visited once a day and smuggled them food—Gaunt assumed Evans had intimidated him into obedience. Without his visits they would have starved, for the German rations were so measly that Gaunt didn't know how anyone could possibly live off them.

No matter how much they fought, Devi or Pritchard would shake him gently awake when he had a nightmare.

"Quiet down, old boy," Pritchard would say. "You're all right."

Pritchard had been in a different dormitory from Gaunt and Devi, so Gaunt hadn't known that Pritchard walked in his sleep. Almost every night, he rose from the ground and stood on an imaginary fire step, keeping watch for snipers.

"Mad, the pair of you," said Devi comfortably.

By the second week, they had moved past aggression into peaceful tranquillity. They played games, including Truth.

"Do you believe Bertie's alive?" Pritchard asked Gaunt.

"How should I know?" said Gaunt. "It's a percentage game, isn't it? Eighteen percent of officers are killed, last I read."

"Bertie's always the first to put himself in the line of fire, the idiot," said Pritchard. "I'll bet he's trying for a Victoria Cross. He's thick as two planks, you know."

"It's all those billiard balls West throws at him."

"Oh, stop glooming," said Devi. "My turn. Henry, come on, you were never in love with me?"

Gaunt sighed. "Gideon."

"Is it because I'm Indian?"

"I don't care that you're Indian."

"Am I not your type?"

Gaunt's poisonous expression appeared to give him away. Devi cackled.

"I knew it! I always thought that Ellwood chap sounded rather simi-lar to me."

"I think he was jealous of you, actually," said Gaunt.

Devi preened. "Well, of course he was. I came first."

"Let's not torture Henry unduly," said Pritchard.

"One for you, Gideon," said Gaunt. "Archie and I want to find Ell-wood and Bertie. Why do you want to get to the front so badly?"

"Have you ever been in a plane?" asked Devi.

"No," said Gaunt.

Devi's mouth stretched into a boyish smile. "It's the most wonderful freedom in the world. I long for it. Just think: we're the first people in history who can *fly*."

They exercised as much as they could, in preparation for their next escape. Devi explained the plan to them in the mornings, when the guards were more relaxed and less likely to overhear.

"Everyone focuses on getting out of prison, but the most dangerous part of any escape is the walk through Germany," said Devi. "That's when people starve, or are shot by farmers. We'll be at a particular disadvantage because we won't have many supplies. I've some meat lozenges sewn into my shoulder pads, but they won't last long."

"Has anyone any money? Perhaps Henry can buy us something to eat," suggested Pritchard.

"We'll be wearing prisoner uniforms," said Gaunt.

Devi shook his head.

"No. Evans has managed to convince the Kommandant that British officers have an 'at ease' uniform that's essentially mufti. They'll give us that to change into before we travel."

"Evans is a national treasure," said Gaunt.

"That he is."

It was just as Devi said. The day before they were to be transferred, a guard brought them a change of clothes that looked almost civilian.

"The tricky thing is that we haven't got the right hats," said Devi, as they dressed.

"Nothing to be done about it," said Pritchard.

"It means we'll have to travel by night. Never mind, I'm sure we'll manage. Henry, how's your lung? Jumping from a moving train's no joke."

"Oh, it's—"

"Fine," said Pritchard and Devi at once.

Gaunt laughed. "Ellwood used to say, 'I know you're fine, but are you all right?'"

Devi cocked his head. "He's got your number, then." He paused. "I'm glad."

The next day, they were bundled out of Fürstenberg by a pair of frazzled-looking guards. It was bizarre to cross the moat they had spent so long tunnelling under.

There were fourteen of them being transferred to another camp. Devi whispered to Nicholson as they were marched to the train station.

"*Seid still!*" yelped one of the guards.

Devi inclined his head submissively and was quiet, but Gaunt could see from the glint in Nicholson's eye that he had managed to explain the plan to him. Nicholson quickly passed it on to the other prisoners, until Gaunt was sure everyone knew.

The train was waiting for them at the station. They were divided into two groups of seven. Gaunt, Devi, Pritchard, MacCorkindale and Nicholson positioned themselves so that they were all sorted into the same train compartment, along with the large-nosed Scotsman (Liddell) and a furtive young Frenchman named Templon. Devi caught their eyes one at a time, and they both nodded minutely.

Gaunt, Devi and Pritchard took the seats nearest the window. The guard threatened them with his gun until they were all seated.

"This journey will be much nicer if you promise not to escape," said the guard. They were silent. The guard sighed. "If you give your word not to escape, I can put away my gun," he said.

"Ever read *Adam Bede*?" Pritchard asked the Frenchman. "Capital novel."

Liddell answered for him. "Poor buggers, they only had Flaubert."

Templon brightened. *"Vous parlez de Flaubert?"*

"Seid still!"

"I say," said MacCorkindale, reasonably. "It'll be a jolly boring train ride if we've got to be quiet all the time."

"What part of Germany are you from?" asked Gaunt.

"Dresden," said the guard suspiciously.

"Beautiful city," said Gaunt.

"Donc aucun d'entre vous n'a lu Flaubert?" asked Templon.

"I don't mean to be rude, but can't you speak any English?" asked Nicholson. Templon glared at him.

"Can't you speak any French?" he asked, icily.

"Henry can speak ancient Greek," said Devi.

"No, I can't. It's a dead language."

"Seid still!"

The train sped up. It was going south, taking them further and further away from neutral Holland.

Devi's head lolled onto Gaunt's shoulder and he pretended to sleep. Gaunt knew quite well that he was only pretending, because Devi chewed imaginary food when he was really sleeping; had done since he was a little boy. Gaunt stared out of the window and wondered what would happen if he broke his leg jumping out of it. His heart pounded so hard that he could feel it in his face.

The train came to a stop at a station. Still Devi pretended to sleep, but Gaunt could feel that his muscles were clenched.

When the train started moving again, he sat up from Gaunt, cricked his neck, and spoke to the compartment at large.

"Chilly, isn't it?"

It was the signal. At once, all seven of them stood and tried to get baggage down from the overhead compartment, loudly exclaiming in agreement—"Awfully cold!" "Damned freezing in this train!" "You'd never believe it was June!"

The guard shouted at them to sit, but he could scarcely be heard over the commotion. In all the chaos, no one noticed when Devi and Gaunt pushed down the window.

Devi caught Gaunt's eye and grinned.

TWENTY-SIX

THEY CLAMBERED OUT at the same time, dropping from the slow-moving train into the fields below. Pritchard followed almost immediately, curling into a ball as he fell, just as Devi had advised, and rolling to a stop. They stayed still until the train had passed, for they knew there was a guard with a rifle posted on the final carriage.

When the train had gone, they got to their feet, crossed the train tracks and started to run west. This was the moment they were most likely to be caught, Devi had warned. It all depended on how much time their fellow prisoners were able to buy them on the train. They sprinted. Freedom, exhilaration and fear lent them speed.

Finally, Devi gasped that they could slow down a little.

"We need to find somewhere to hide until nightfall," he said. They carried on running at a more measured pace, reassured that the train had not come back for them. After almost an hour of steady jogging, they reached a pine forest. Devi put his finger to his lips, and they found a secluded ditch far away from any paths.

They spoke only in whispers as they sank into the pine needles to rest. It was common knowledge that the Germans loved to go on country walks, particularly on Sundays, and many a British officer had been caught by a rambling family on an afternoon constitutional. They were thirsty, but it was too risky to look for a spring until nightfall. They lay in a heap and closed their eyes.

One of the concerns Gaunt faced was that his nightmares would give them away, but, to his surprise, they did not come when he slept in the forest. He suspected it was for the same reason that he slept better in the line than out of it: suspense prevented him from remembering.

They woke when the sun went down. It was summer, which was a mixed blessing: they would not suffer snow, but the nights were short. They would have to make good progress, and they did not have a map, only compasses. As soon as they found a place-name, they would be able to orient themselves, however. MacCorkindale had insisted that everyone memorise the names of all the villages and towns, for which they were now most grateful. They walked west through the pine forest, stopping when they found a stream. There, they filled their tobacco tins with water, for none of them had bottles.

They walked all night in silence, only stopping when the sun came up. Then they found a quiet place to shelter and fell asleep again.

When they awoke, they were ravenous. Pritchard had strapped several pounds of Red Cross chocolate to his stomach with his belt, and Gaunt had tucked a not inconsiderable number of Horlick's malted milk lozenges into his sleeves. Gaunt could have eaten the entire stock of food for breakfast, but they only had four lozenges each—two milk, two meat—and a quarter-pound of chocolate.

Then they waited out the long summer day. Seventeen hours of sunlight. Hot, impatient, and silent by necessity, they waited. They slept in shifts, but it was difficult, even when they threw their arms over their eyes, to block out the sun.

On the second night, they passed a signpost. Pritchard stood on Gaunt's shoulders and struck a match so that he could read it. They recognised the name. If their calculations were correct (which was by no means certain), they had over a hundred miles to walk.

By the second day, Devi's feet had started to bleed. He kept up with Gaunt and Pritchard throughout the night, but when the sun rose and they stopped in a field of tall grass, he took off his boots with a groan. His feet were covered in vicious blisters.

Pritchard and Gaunt exchanged looks. In the trenches, the difference between a dead man and a live one was often the condition of his feet.

"My socks are thicker," said Pritchard quietly. "They'll help."

So they swapped socks. It was a revolting process, and not one that would make a difference, but it cheered Devi, and that, Gaunt supposed, had been Pritchard's intention.

They developed several rules: they would not walk through a village before 11:00 p.m., they would avoid trains and cities unless they were on the verge of collapse, and they would always follow the counsel of whoever was most cautious at that point.

On the third day, they encountered their first German. They were walking down a country lane just after dusk, and a man passed them on a bicycle. He stopped when he saw Devi. They all three looked dirty and peculiar, clothed as they were in plain matching outfits, without hats. All of that might have been explained away quite easily, however, if Devi weren't Indian.

"Good evening," said Gaunt in German.

"Where are you from?" asked the man suspiciously.

"Munich, originally. I'm helping my cousin take this lunatic to the asylum in Emsdetten."

When Gaunt gestured at him, Devi groaned ferociously and gnashed his teeth. Pritchard held him tightly by the arm.

"Is he dangerous?" asked the man.

"Only when angry, or hungry, or tired. He is all three, at present."

"Well, good evening," said the man, jumping back on his bicycle and pedalling away as fast as he could.

"It's ironic," said Devi, once he had gone, "given that I'm quite the sanest out of the three of us."

There was almost nothing they dreaded more than dogs, especially after they were chased by a pack of them in a darkened village on their sixth night. They managed to get away by wading through a river, which made Devi's blisters rupture. He was now in so much pain that they had to slow their pace considerably. He never complained, and his temper never flagged, even though they had finished all the chocolate long ago, and were nearing the end of their supply of meat and milk lozenges. They ate berries when they found them, and on the fourth day Devi had produced some salted pork strips he had saved "as a surprise." All the same, hunger weighed heavily on them, making them faint and headachy and irritable.

"If I get any hungrier, I won't be human any more," said Pritchard. "We've got to send Henry into a village with some money."

"Too risky," said Devi. "He looks like a filthy convict."

"We're never going to get to Holland," said Gaunt. "We're going to expire by the roadside like the Little Match Girl."

"Oh, stop griping," said Devi. "All adventures have their discomforts."

"*Discomforts?*" repeated Pritchard in disbelief. "We can't keep going like this, Gideon!"

"Something'll turn up," said Devi. "It always does."

He was right. That night, they came across a potato field. It was too early for them to have formed, but the seed potatoes had not yet rotted. They filled up Pritchard's jacket with those and ate their first real meal in over a week. It was amazing how much it affected their outlook. Suddenly Holland seemed so close they could practically touch it.

"If we're caught, we'll have to dump the lot," warned Devi. "What with German food shortages, they're not likely to take well to potato thieves."

Devi's feet hurt him so badly that he had to hold on to Gaunt and Pritchard for support when he walked.

"But we aren't far now," he said, cheerfully. In any case, it added to the realism of their cover story.

They skirted dangerously near a farmhouse on their tenth night. It was a risk, but the alternative was to walk all the way around a hill, and Devi's feet had to be taken into consideration. They thought they had passed through to relative safety when a bullet came ricocheting into the trees near them.

"Halt!" cried a man. "Who goes there?"

"Run," said Pritchard.

They grabbed Devi by the waist and sprinted through the trees. The man set his dog on them, but it was dark, and Pritchard spotted a small wall for them to clamber over. Once they were over it, they carried on running, dragging Devi between them, until they were so exhausted they could not go on.

"That was close," said Pritchard.

"It was in the right direction, at least," said Devi, irrepressibly optimistic.

More than once, they were caught while they rested up in the day, but each time Gaunt talked them out of trouble.

They had passed Emsdetten by now, and were nearing the Dutch frontier. It was no easy matter to get over the border, and all three felt how bitter it would be to fail at this advanced stage. They were running low on food again.

"We'll have plenty to eat in the Netherlands," said Devi.

They did not dare speak much, since it would be disastrous for them to be overheard conversing in English. On busier roads, Gaunt monologued in German, pretending to chide Pritchard. This proved surprisingly effective at warding off questions from strangers.

Their good luck made them reckless.

They had been walking for two weeks, and hoped they would be able to cross the border that night. Impatient, they started earlier than was advisable. The sun had barely set when they got back on the road.

It was still light when they turned a corner and walked straight into a German soldier. He had just come out from a little wooden hut by the road. Gaunt could see other soldiers inside.

"Good evening," said Gaunt, suddenly aware that none of them had shaved or washed in weeks.

"Who are you? What are you doing here?"

"I am helping my cousin accompany this lunatic to an asylum near Overdinkel. Would you be so kind as to point the way to the Dutch border?"

"Do you have papers?"

"Of course," said Gaunt, his heart sinking. "Am I correct in thinking the border is just past those trees? Carting around a madman is hard work, I don't mind telling you."

The soldier took out his gun and aimed it at him.

"Papers."

Several more soldiers emerged from the hut, also armed.

"Ein Problem, Heinrich?" asked Pritchard quietly.

"Nein, nein," said Gaunt, patting down his pockets, trying to think.

He felt Devi squeeze his arm. He knew Devi was trying to communicate something, but he didn't know what.

Fortunately, it soon became apparent. Devi broke free from Gaunt and Pritchard with a whooping battle cry and launched himself at the German soldiers.

Gaunt and Pritchard did not hesitate. They bolted into the trees, leaving Devi behind.

TWENTY-SEVEN

JUNE 1916, THE SOMME

THEY COULD HEAR the artillery from the Somme while they were still on the train. The village where they disembarked swarmed with activity, and the roar of the guns provided a thunderous backdrop. Thorburn instantly disappeared into the officers' brothel. Hayes and Ellwood were making their way to their billets when Ellwood was swept off his feet by a gang of young men.

"Sidney!"

"Look at this, it's Ellwood!"

"How are you, old boy?"

Bertie Pritchard and Loring had him on their shoulders, and Roseveare, Grimsey and Aldworth clamoured around him.

"It's a regular Preshute reunion!"

"Have you had a rough time of it?"

"Roseveare already has about six French girls trailing after him, the cad—"

"How are your men? Do they fancy a game of football?"

"Apparently Lantham's around here somewhere—d'you remember Lantham?"

"Aren't the guns splendid? Enough to make you feel sorry for the poor old Huns!"

Ellwood looked from one friendly face to another and was filled with a riotous joy that was immediately overshadowed by despair. *They were all here.* All his friends, together in one place, as if attending some ghastly wedding. They leapt about him like puppy dogs, haloed in doom, and he knew each of them had realised the same thing.

Hayes stood slightly apart, looking almost comically uncomfortable next to all these immaculately dressed, crisply spoken, bounding public schoolboys.

"This is Hayes," said Ellwood, rather desperately, for Pritchard was arguing with Grimsey and had considerably loosened his hold on Ellwood's leg. Loring struggled to hoist him, and Ellwood rolled around on their exuberant shoulders like a sack of potatoes.

"Hallo, Hayes," said Roseveare, kindly. "I'm Roseveare. It's awful being the only one who doesn't know everybody, isn't it? Where were you at school?"

It was exactly the wrong thing to say. Hayes' arms crossed themselves even tighter.

"The local one in Lewisham."

Ellwood saw—and he knew that Hayes saw, too—Roseveare's surprised look, and then the quick flickering of his gaze as he took in Hayes' pitiful uniform, and realised.

"Oh. Right," he said. "I'm afraid I don't know it."

Ellwood struggled down from Loring and Pritchard.

"Hayes is terrific. I don't know what I should do without him as a friend."

Hayes flushed.

"You poor sod," said Roseveare. "Imagine having to put up with *Ellwood* as well as the trenches!"

"He's all right," said Hayes.

"You must tell me everything about how he is in the army. Does he cheat at cards? He's an untrustworthy fellow. You ought to watch out for yourself, Hayes."

Hayes gave a crooked smile.

"I don't know about cards, but he nearly punched my eyes out the other day because he lost an earwig race."

"You cheated!" cried Ellwood.

"Earwigs? Who said earwigs?" said Pritchard. "I have the prize earwig of my battalion. Ozymandias, King of Kings! Look upon him, ye mighty, and despair!" He took out a folded handkerchief and opened it reverently, but there was only a crusty smudge inside. "Oh, Grimsey! You must have squashed him when you bashed into me earlier! What a beastly thing to do."

"My orderly's a marvellous cook," said Loring. "Shall we all have dinner together?"

"What do you say, Hayes?" asked Ellwood. Hayes put his hands in his pockets.

"I'm not sure—"

"Do come," said Roseveare earnestly. "Any friend of Sidney's is a friend of ours."

"Well, all right, then," said Hayes, rather shyly.

Ellwood never laughed as much as he did that night. They were on top form, shouting over the droning cacophony of the artillery. Loring persuaded Aldworth to tell them how he had been injured at Loos; a meandering tale that culminated in Aldworth being accidentally stabbed with a bayonet by one of his own men as he tried to explain to them how to use it. Pritchard made them all cry with laughter describing Gallipoli, which in his stories sounded less like a battle and more like a hilarious romp through Turkey in the vein of Jerome K. Jerome's *Three Men in a Boat*. Even Grimsey smiled, although he had been there too, and come back changed. Ellwood told them how Hayes used to shout puns at the Germans.

"Was that *you*?" said Loring. "My word, Maitland worshipped you."

Hayes glowed with pleasure. When he left for a few minutes, the boys all leant in to ask Ellwood questions.

"I say, is it really true he was a factory worker before all this?"

"He's awfully sharp, isn't he?"

"Do you think he'd take offence if I recommended him a new tailor?"

"Yes," said Ellwood, flatly.

"Oh, all right," said Loring. "But he'll never make captain, looking like that."

"Well, he's the best officer in the company," said Ellwood.

Later in the evening, Lantham appeared. Ellwood had forgotten how good-looking he was.

"Hallo, Sidney," said Lantham softly. "I've just found out I'm to be your second lieutenant. Isn't that a bit of luck?"

"What are you doing here, Maurice?" said Ellwood. "You're only sixteen!"

"I'll be seventeen in August."

"But you didn't even like cadets. What are you playing at?"

Lantham lowered his long-lashed eyes.

"Some girls gave me a white feather in town. I felt so awful I went and signed up that afternoon."

"I'd like to drag those girls into the trenches by their hair," said Ellwood darkly.

"Oh, they're just doing their bit—we've all got to do our bit, you know, Ellwood. I think it's awfully hard on the girls. They're losing their brothers and fathers and sweethearts and there's so little they can do about it."

"Saint Maurice the compassionate," said Ellwood, ruffling Lantham's silky copper hair. Lantham blushed furiously.

As it turned out, Lantham was in their billet. Ellwood and Hayes automatically went to share one of the two bedrooms, leaving Lantham with Thorburn.

"Another one who hero-worships you?" asked Hayes, when they were alone. "What did you *do* at that school?"

Ellwood didn't answer. He was worried he had been rather cruel to Lantham. He had somehow never got round to answering his letters.

"You seemed to get along with Roseveare," he said.

"Mhm," said Hayes vaguely.

"Cyril's a gentleman," said Ellwood. "Through and through."

Hayes did not remark on this, which Ellwood found concerning. He had been sure that Hayes would have opinions on the use of the word "gentleman." But Hayes just sat on his bed, frowning as he pulled off his boots.

"Penny for them?" asked Ellwood.

"You told them we were friends."

"Oh," said Ellwood. His face felt hot. He sank down onto the bed opposite Hayes. "Sorry. Should I not have?"

Hayes folded his greatcoat over the back of a chair, put his pillow on the floor, and lay down. Ellwood blew out the candle.

"Henry asked me to look out for you," said Hayes.

Ellwood settled himself under his covers. He tried to imagine the conversation, but couldn't. Somehow, he could never imagine Gaunt talking about him. It had always felt as if Gaunt must forget about him when he wasn't there.

"That's why you sent men out looking for me when I got lost," he said.

"I would have sent them after anyone. But I was glad when you came back," said Hayes.

There was a long pause. The sound of the artillery swelled the silence. Ellwood wondered whether he would still be alive in twenty-four hours.

"There's going to be quite a bit of action when we get up there," he said.

"Yes, I think you're right."

"The colonel says the barbed wire will have been blown into dust, and the survivors will come out with their hands up when we attack."

Hayes breathed out a heavy sigh.

"They said that at Loos," he said.

"It seems unfair, doesn't it? Our parents got to live their whole lives without anything like this."

"Busily building up the world that led to this."

"I suppose they thought they had their own problems," said Ellwood.

"No one ever thinks their life is easy."

And then they were both quiet, as they tried not to think of what inconceivable horror waited for them, when the shelling stopped and the men were sent in.

TWENTY-EIGHT

THE NOISE as they approached the front was unfathomable, but the larks continued to soar overhead in the mournful sky, and scarlet poppies drooped over the edges of the communication trenches. As always, when his mind found nothing to latch on to, it clung to Tennyson.

> *My heart would hear her and beat,*
> *Were it earth in an earthy bed;*
> *My dust would hear her and beat,*
> *Had I lain for a century dead,*
> *Would start and tremble under her feet,*
> *And blossom in purple and red.*

With Gaunt dead, there was no one Ellwood spoke to about poetry. He kept the lines in his head. He supposed they had returned to him because of the funny way the ground moved with the force of the explosions. It was as if the dirt had a heartbeat, and it pounded to be saved, urgently alive. He wondered when Europe had last felt such destruction. *Waterloo*, he thought. The land had lain for a century dead, but now it had awoken, demanding blood.

The colonel spoke to the assembled battalions in the village before they left.

"You have your orders. Slow and steady, and don't stop until you reach Berlin!" He clopped back and forth on a glossy chestnut mare. It made Ellwood think of autumnal hunts in East Sussex, of sniffing the cold, damp air and knowing that there would be tea and crumpets by the fire in the evening. "I don't expect you will encounter much opposition. You can hear our shells, you know what fearful things they are doing to our German friends. Few Englishmen have had the opportunity to heap so much honour upon themselves at so low a cost. March with your heads held high into victory, for yourselves, for your king, and for the Empire!"

The men cheered lustily. Most of the battalions were made up of Kitchener's Army, eager young boys who had never seen battle.

But as they approached the front, even the most cheerful among them grew silent. Ellwood remembered what Gaunt had said, about gunfire: how it made you feel as if you were at the centre of the universe. It was more than that, at the Somme. It was like watching the universe split in half.

He had written a letter to his mother the night before.

Wednesday 28th June, 1916
Somewhere in France

Dear Mother,

There's going to be a terrific show tomorrow. I am quite certain I will be fine, but I wanted to send a quick word to tell you I love you. I'm only being superstitious, really. We've been bombarding poor Fritz relentlessly for almost a week now, and he's probably quite desperate to surrender.

Thanks awfully for the food package, the men particularly liked the tinned pineapple. I love you. I shall see you soon.

Your boy,
Sidney

He was sure the letter would bring her no comfort. He had become used to the idea that he would die. There wasn't anything else to think. He only wished he wouldn't have to see any more of his friends killed before it happened.

Lantham walked palely at his side. Ellwood remembered that Lantham had never even liked Bonfire Night because of the fireworks.

"Cheer up, chum," said Ellwood. "We're making history."

Lantham's neck muscles strained, like those of an animal trying to escape its rope.

They were held up at the support trench.

"It's been postponed," came a rumour from the firing line. "Postponed for forty-eight hours."

Ellwood's heart sank. His men had steeled themselves for battle, not the agony of anticipation.

Two of his men killed themselves in the night. Ellwood felt no sympathy for them. They were going to die anyway, and it struck him as selfish to contribute to the general feeling of despair that pervaded the trenches.

Roseveare came to visit them in their dugout. He was white and fluttery. It was his first battle. Ellwood couldn't decide if he wished that Bertie Pritchard had come as well, or that Roseveare hadn't come at all. It was hard to look at him and remember all the years they had spent together, not knowing what violence awaited them.

"I wish it would start," said Roseveare.

"Try not to think about it," said Hayes.

"Yes, that's a good idea," said Roseveare. He paced around the dugout. Thorburn was reading an old newspaper as if he hadn't a care in the world. Lantham sat huddled and empty-eyed on his bunk. Ellwood and Hayes censored the men's fatalistic letters home. It was dispiriting work, particularly when they had to scratch out with black pen all references to the men's blood-dimmed horror. Fear was not good for civilian morale. Ellwood wondered how the widows of Britain would interpret the great smudges of the censorship pens, whether they would imagine far worse things under the black ink than the muted versions of reality the men described.

"Do you play football?" Hayes asked Roseveare. Ellwood smiled at him. He knew Hayes didn't care, he only wanted to distract Roseveare, whose fingers jittered as he walked back and forth in the dugout.

"Yes," said Roseveare. "My brothers and I used to play at home. They're both dead now. Mons and Gallipoli. God, I wish it would start."

"I used to play with the boys in my street," said Hayes. "Did you ever see boys playing in the streets of London? We were practically feral, looking back on it."

"No. I grew up in Surrey. Although I feel as if I'm from Wiltshire, because of school. Do you think the wire's really been cut by the shells?"

"I'm sure it has," said Ellwood. "And I feel that way too. School was always more home to me than my mother was."

"If my mother had had money, you can be sure she'd not have spent it paying strangers to raise me," said Hayes.

"Oh, but it's not strangers!" said Roseveare, and his eyes focused. "It's your peers. Your friends. You can't imagine how much we loved it, even when it was awful."

Ellwood nodded. "I know it isn't fair to send some children to stately homes to be educated, when others get practically no school at all. But it's difficult to disapprove of a place that gave me so much joy."

Roseveare smiled dreamily. "I don't think I'll ever be so happy as I was galloping around Preshute with the Ardents."

"I hated it," said Lantham, unexpectedly.

Roseveare and Ellwood turned to look at him.

"I used to be woken up by the sound of the boys talking about me. I would lie perfectly still and listen as they said the most terrible things you could ever hear about yourself."

"Oh, we all had *that*," said Roseveare, dismissively.

"It was character-building," said Ellwood, who would never forget the things Burgoyne used to say about him at night, when he was thirteen.

"You beat me," said Lantham. He looked from Ellwood to Roseveare. "Both of you. You tied me to a chair and beat me all night."

Hayes swore under his breath, but Roseveare laughed fondly.

"I forgot about that. God, weren't we rotten! I'm awfully sorry, Lantham. I didn't know you'd take it so personally."

"We did it to everybody," said Ellwood. "And it was done to us. It was character-building."

Lantham shook his head. "It didn't build my character any more than *this* does. It tore me apart."

A particularly loud shell made the hanging ceiling light swing crazily on its wire.

"Christ," said Roseveare. "I wish it would begin."

. . .

The night of the 30th June, they got their orders. They would attack at seven-thirty the next morning.

Thorburn laughed when he heard. "Daylight," he said. "That'll be fun."

Ellwood spent all night at the wire, which he had noticed was too thick for them to march through. He knew what happened to troops who got bunched up in a daylight attack. In the dark of night, he took Hayes and some men to hack at the wire in their leather gloves, jumping into the trench whenever shells landed near them. The army wire cutters were blunt and badly made, and the men discouraged by the casualties they suffered as they worked. When dawn broke, Ellwood was dismayed to find that the wire still looked dreadfully thick.

"We've got to go in," said Hayes. "They can see us."

"Just another ten minutes," said Ellwood. But soon even he had to admit that the snipers were shooting at them with unsettling accuracy, and they returned to the dugout.

"Bavarians," Hayes said, tapping his fingers against the table. "I heard a battalion signaller say. That's who we're shelling. Wasn't Gaunt's mother from Munich?"

A bit of chalk fell into Ellwood's hair as the shells rumbled. He shook it out. It felt as if some other person had got drunk with Gaunt's cousins in 1913; some happier, luckier young man.

They stood-to at 5:30. The men were unspeakably drunk.

"Probably for the best," said Hayes. The guns were so loud that Ellwood sometimes almost forgot them. It was impossible to pick out any individual explosion. Lantham, who had been shivering for two days straight, looked distinctly unwell. His eyes were red and inflamed, and he had bitten his nails to the quick.

"I can't think," he said to Ellwood. "I can't think."

"That's all right, Maurice, old thing. No need to think just now."

At 6:45, the guns reached a fever pitch. Huge mines erupted, tossing all of No Man's Land up in shapes that Ellwood thought bizarrely similar to Easter eggs. A wave of detached good humour crashed over him—it was all so ridiculous. A minute later, it was gone, replaced with bleak resignation.

"Oh, Jesus!" cried Lantham. His eyes bulged out of his face obscenely, like those of a horse Ellwood had once watched die after badly missing a jump. He didn't seem to know what he was saying.

"It's all right, Maurice, it's all right," said Ellwood, emptily. Lantham tilted his head back at the sky, every muscle toiling to stay still.

Ellwood produced a football and showed it to his men.

"Now, we're to walk slowly forward. Whenever you spot the ball, kick it on. Whoever kicks it into the Boches wins. Got it?"

A few of them smiled weakly.

"What if they kick it into our trench?" asked Lonsdale.

"Then they've won the War, I'm afraid. I don't make the rules." Ellwood grinned. Pretending made him feel braver.

At 7:20, the guns stopped. The men were silent, except for a low, harsh, grating sound, which Ellwood soon realised came from Lantham. He was gnashing his teeth like a mad dog. Ellwood forced him to drink some whisky, which Lantham seemed quite unable to swallow.

At 7:25, they waited in the firing line. Roseveare had returned to his company. Ellwood had the most curious feeling of spinelessness, as if his whole body were filled with turbulent water. Hayes grabbed Ellwood and enveloped him in a tight hug. Ellwood hugged him back, just as hard. It made him feel, for a minute, as if he had bones.

At 7:29, he put his whistle in his mouth, his eyes fixed on his wristwatch. Lantham was groaning, but Ellwood could not help him now.

At 7:30, he blew the whistle, and climbed onto the fire step. The battle began.

TWENTY-NINE

GAUNT HEARD A GUNSHOT, and a terrible cry, but neither he nor Pritchard stopped. The soldiers were after them, shooting haphazardly in their direction, but Gaunt and Pritchard hadn't spent countless hours in No Man's Land for nothing. The trees provided them with cover, and they raced, neck and neck, away from the road.

Adrenaline spurred Gaunt on at first, but soon his starved body ached with weariness. Just when he thought he would have to stop and turn himself in, Pritchard touched his arm.

"They've given up," he panted. "Listen."

Gaunt stopped. The woods were silent.

"Is Gideon . . ."

"I don't know," said Pritchard.

They stared at each other.

"He wouldn't want us to go back," said Gaunt.

"No," agreed Pritchard.

Another long pause.

"There are an awful lot of places you can get shot without being killed," said Pritchard.

"Yes," said Gaunt.

"We ought to . . ."

"Yes."

They pressed on. It was dark now. After about an hour, they spotted the railroad track that they knew ran along the border. They skirted along it, hiding in the bushes. When they were quite sure no one was around, they crawled out of the undergrowth and crossed the tracks.

"The moon's rising," said Pritchard. If they didn't get across the border in the next hour, they would have to wait until the following evening, and they would almost certainly be caught in the interim. The soldiers would have pieced together who they were by now, and the honour they would gain from capturing three escaped British officers would be a powerful incentive to continue their search.

"We have to do it now, no matter what," said Gaunt. He was immensely grateful for how absorbing their task was. There was no space to think about Devi; about that scream.

Gaunt had studied this part of the map obsessively. He had dreamt about the little stream that marked the Dutch border. When he saw it, right where the map had said it would be, he was filled with a swelling gratitude for the nameless Russian officer who had stolen the maps and made copies all those months ago, not so that he could escape himself, but so that others might.

Of course, there was a sentry pacing the stream. He was alone, however. Gaunt and Pritchard ducked into a ditch and bent their heads together.

"He's got his rifle slung up on his back," said Gaunt. "It'll take him a minute to shoot at us."

"Are you sure this is the border?"

"Almost positive. Once we're past that stream behind him."

"We could crawl. Evade notice."

Gaunt shook his head. "No chance. It's a sprint, or nothing."

"All right. On three."

Gaunt counted to three, and they came barrelling out of the ditch.

"Halt!" cried the sentry, struggling to shoulder his rifle. Gaunt and Pritchard sped past him. Gaunt was sure he had never run so fast. He was approaching the finish line of a race that had begun nine months ago, at Loos. Ellwood was at the other end, and Gaunt would not stop until he reached him.

They scrambled down the bank as the sentry began to shoot at them. Clods of earth erupted in their faces. As always when under gunfire, Gaunt was oddly clear-headed. The gunshots sounded distant and muffled, because they were so near.

He waded through the stream, and clambered up the other side. Pritchard slithered forward on his belly, and Gaunt dropped to all fours. The sentry stood less than twenty feet away from them, and could see them easily in the moonlight.

But there were no more gunshots. When he was quite sure his ears weren't playing tricks on him, Gaunt turned to look at the sentry.

He had lowered his gun.

They were in the Netherlands.

THIRTY

A T 7:20 A.M. on the 1st July, the guns finally stopped. For the first time in a week, Ernst Grisar could hear his own breath. Deep in their chalk trenches, hungry and thirsty, the Germans had waited out the bombardment. They had suffered few casualties. The shrapnel shells blew harmlessly above their heads. Occasionally, parts of the trench wall were knocked down, burying soldiers in dirt. But they were soon dug out, more or less intact. Many of the shells, perhaps half of them, did not explode at all.

Now they had stopped. The attack was coming. Ernst and his machine-gun team crawled tentatively to their gun on the firing line. Ernst stuck a periscope over the top.

Nothing.

"Why don't they come?" asked Private Weigand. Ernst cast him an anxious look.

"I don't know. They can't get past the wire, anyway." The wire was entirely undamaged by the shelling. Ernst doubted whether even a rabbit could get through.

Weigand looked unconvinced.

"Depends on how many of them try it."

"We have the upper ground. Don't be so fainthearted."

In truth, Ernst felt rather weak himself. They were so very hungry. Even though they had been mostly sheltered from the shells, the noise of it had driven men mad. As to sleep, it had been quite impossible for days now. And now they had to face an attack whose scale was bound at least to match that of the heart-stopping artillery. For the third time since leaving his dugout, Ernst checked his ammunition. There, at least, they were well supplied.

For ten minutes, the landscape was quiet. Birds glided easily against the deep blue of the sky.

"Why don't they come?" asked Weigand again.

"Be quiet," said Ernst. "You'll get your chance to shoot at Tommies." Weigand shifted on his feet.

"It's this waiting. Feels like a trick."

It did. It was unnaturally calm. For a moment, Ernst entertained the idea of simply jumping into No Man's Land and throwing himself to the sky. It seemed as if the trenches opposite were empty. It was such an unappealing patch of land. Perhaps the Tommies didn't want it, after all. Ernst certainly didn't.

And then heads began to appear above the deep gash of the British trenches.

"Fire!" said Ernst, and the machine gun let out a sigh of bullets, knocking the heads back. But more heads appeared, and men climbed out of the trenches, only to get stuck in clumps at the small gaps in the British wire. Ernst didn't even have to aim. Every bullet hit flesh, because the field seethed with it. It was like shooting into a crowd. No—in a crowd, people would have scattered, but these men walked calmly forward, trudging over their fallen comrades before being struck down themselves. It was absurd.

"This can't be their plan," he said. Weigand couldn't hear him over the sound of the machine gun. Another wave of men had come out of the trench, and the guns cut them down like a scythe through grass. It was laughable. Ernst couldn't comprehend the scale of it. He was reminded of the way his mother would wipe her finger along the window mullions, clearing away the dirt with her index finger. *Sweep.* A hundred men hit. *Sweep.* A hundred men hit. They just kept coming. They had not advanced more than ten feet, and they were already wading through bodies.

This must be all of England, he thought. *The women will come next, and then the children, and we will kill every last one of them.* He thought of his cousin Heinrich, and his friend Ellwood who had come to visit him in Munich, not so long ago. A sparkling, mirthful boy, who had laughed in delight at the moving clock in the Marienplatz. They had gone for a walk in the mountains, and when they reached the peak, Ellwood had spread out his arms like wings.

"Land of Goethe, Schubert, Wagner, take me!"

"Ignore him," said Heinrich, indulgently. "He's just showing off."

Ellwood had dropped back into the grass, a blissful smile on his face.

"Aren't we the luckiest boys alive?"

Ernst forced the memory away. It wasn't boys marching at him, but soldiers, who would kill him the moment they broke through. Over and over he loaded the ammunition and cut down the advancing men who drove on, unwavering, relentless as the sea. They did not even run, but plodded to their deaths, like—

There was no comparison. No animal on earth would have suffered it. No creature would walk so knowingly, so hopelessly, into the jaws of death. Weigand's lips moved in prayer. Tears stained his face.

When will they stop? Surely some general even now was telephoning the front line, saying Call it off, it's a massacre, nothing will be gained, perhaps we can save a battalion or two?

He had no idea how long he had been at the gun, how many men he had killed. Soldiers had started to find the gaps in the German wire. The machine gunners picked them off leisurely at the bottlenecks. They fell on the bodies of those who had gone before, and the men behind them stepped on their corpses before being killed themselves. Ernst couldn't even think of them as human. Humans did not die like that, in droves. They began to seem like ants to him, and he was a child crushing them with his fingers. It was the only way he could continue to load the ammunition, now that he could see their glazed, terrified faces. A shell went off to his right, blowing up a wave of British soldiers who had nearly reached the German line. As the debris cleared, Ernst noted, with nightmarish calm, a pair of disembodied hands still clutching at the wire.

"Oberleutnant Grisar?" A private hovered behind him.

"Yes?"

"They've lost two officers over in A Company. I was sent to fetch you as a replacement."

Ernst followed the private back down the trenches to A Company, which had been thrown into chaos by a well-aimed grenade. He had the wounded removed, and the men returned to the fire step with their rifles, continuing their grim butchery. Here and there, the British trickled through holes in the wire, inexorably marching forward. They were killed, and more followed. There were so many of them. Soon it would be a question of hand-to-hand combat. Ernst had just checked that his bayonet was securely attached when a British officer dropped into the trench.

He was utterly wild, covered in blood, and seemed to have no fear. He aimed his bayonet first at one German and then another, as if they were all at his mercy. One of Ernst's men pulled back his own bayonet to kill—and suddenly Ernst recognised him.

"Halt!" he cried, and stepped forward. "Ellwood?"

Ellwood blinked as if he had seen a ghost. There was something diabolical about him, as if he were a body filled with fire, desperate to burn.

"I'm not surrendering, Ernst," he said, in a high voice. "You'll have to kill me."

THIRTY-ONE

A HALF-HOUR WALK brought them to a town.

"What if we're still in Germany?" asked Pritchard.

Despite what had happened with the sentry, Gaunt, too, had his misgivings.

"Do you think we ought to walk further on?" he asked Pritchard.

"I don't know that I can," admitted Pritchard. "I'm so hungry I might faint."

"Then let's knock and ask," said Gaunt. "We've had a good run, if they catch us."

He did not add, *"And then we'll find out about Gideon."* He knew they were both thinking it.

Pritchard nodded. They approached a small stone cottage with candles lit in the windows, and knocked.

A man in nightclothes opened the door. He eyed them with great suspicion. Given how wild Gaunt and Pritchard looked at this point, Gaunt could not blame him.

"Is this Overdinkel?" asked Gaunt in German.

"Jawohl."

"We are in the Netherlands?"

"Jawohl," repeated the man.

Gaunt could not stop the joy and relief from spilling out into laughter. Next to him, Pritchard made an uncharacteristic giggling sound. The Dutchman stared at them as if they were mad.

"We've escaped from Germany," said Gaunt. "We're British officers. Have you any food you could sell us?"

A woman appeared in the doorway.

"British?" she said.

"Yes," said Gaunt.

"Come in, come in!"

Gaunt and Pritchard followed her into the little cottage. A fire was dancing in the hearth. Pritchard couldn't seem to control his giggling.

"Have you any food?" asked Gaunt again, because he suddenly felt as if his insides were caving in. "We have money." Gaunt peeled up the sole of his boot to retrieve his small supply of coins.

The Dutchman waved it away.

"No, no," he said, in German, "you are our guests. Sit, sit!"

Gaunt held out the money insistently.

"Sit!" barked the Dutchman.

Gaunt and Pritchard obeyed him like schoolboys. They stared and laughed as the woman brought them beer, cold bacon, bread and three large eggs each. To Gaunt, it might have been manna from Heaven. He had thought he could eat three times as much, but once he had finished the eggs he felt rather sick, and had to stop. He had been eating with such focus that it was only when he lowered his fork that he registered that the woman had spoken to him.

"Would you be so kind as to repeat yourself?" he asked, as if the politeness of his words could counter the savagery with which he had devoured his eggs.

"You do not sound English," she said.

"Oh, I'm English, all right," said Gaunt.

"Ask if we can stay the night," said Pritchard.

Gaunt asked. The Dutchman shook his head.

"We must give you to the Frontier Guard."

Gaunt bristled. "And be held in some cell until the end of the War? Out of the question!"

"It cannot be helped."

Gaunt explained the situation to Pritchard, who shrugged.

"Don't fuss, Gaunto. We'll escape from any old Dutch holding centre. I want a *bath*."

"Fine." He turned to the Dutchman. "Very well. You may take us to the Frontier Guard."

They thanked the man and his wife for the food, and tried once more to pay. Neither of them would accept the money.

It was bright with moonlight, and Gaunt was still luxuriating in the unfamiliar feeling of fullness after so many weeks of privation. They crossed a cobbled courtyard and entered the police station. Gaunt and Pritchard spotted some mattresses on the floor and went to lie down without speaking to anyone. Let the Dutchman explain, thought Gaunt.

They fell asleep instantly.

The next morning, an affable Dutch guard brought them a bucket of warm water, a cake of soap and two razors. They washed up as best they could. When Pritchard undressed, Gaunt was alarmed to see how thin he was.

They felt better once they had shaved, but they still had only their torn and muddy clothes to wear. There was no chance they looked like anything but escaped prisoners.

"We will take the train to Hengelo now," said the guard.

"Ah," said Gaunt, apologetically. "We're going to Amsterdam, actually."

"I'm afraid that's not possible."

"We thought you might say that," said Gaunt, with utmost politeness. "Only we didn't escape from Germany to hang about in Hengelo. I'm sure you understand."

"My orders are to take you to a holding centre in Hengelo."

"I can quite see how difficult this must be for you. Unfortunately, we will be going to Amsterdam, with or without you."

The guard looked pained. He evidently did not have the authority to shoot at them, but his hand twitched for his rifle, all the same.

"Trouble, Henry?" asked Pritchard.

"Poor chap wants to take us to Hengelo."

Pritchard looked sympathetic. "I hate to disappoint him."

"Me, too. Shall we pretend to agree so that he'll take us to the train station?"

"Yes, that seems kindest. Poor fellow, he looks distraught."

Gaunt addressed the guard. "Very well—take us to Hengelo."

The guard looked enormously relieved. After a lovely (albeit half-eaten) breakfast, during which Pritchard surreptitiously stole a train timetable out of the guard's pocket and showed Gaunt that there was a train to Amsterdam leaving in under an hour, the guard led them back into the village square.

"Roseveare's father is a diplomat in Amsterdam," said Pritchard, when the guard was a few steps ahead of them. "He'll help us out."

The station was tiny, but it had a telephone. Gaunt politely but aggressively insisted on being allowed to make a call, although he had Pritchard talk to the embassy. Pritchard had been good friends with Martin Roseveare, who had been killed at Gallipoli. He quickly got through to the embassy and explained their situation.

"Hang up," said the guard. "Our train is here!"

"Oh, we're not getting on that," said Gaunt.

"What?" said the guard, ashen-faced.

"We'll be taking the nine-ten to Amsterdam. It's all been arranged." The guard glanced helplessly at his rifle.

"Now, don't be like that," said Gaunt. "I'm happy to call your superior and explain."

"But you must be taken to the holding centre in Hengelo," said the guard unhappily.

Pritchard hung up.

"I say, he does look miserable, Henry. What have you been saying to him?"

"It's not my fault he's so damned *dutiful*. Budge over, will you, I'm going to call this holding centre he keeps banging on about."

Once put through, Gaunt explained in clear, unwavering terms that he was sorry to inconvenience anyone, but that he and Pritchard would be meeting their friends at the British Embassy in Amsterdam that morning. He repeated this several times, as each guard he spoke to passed the call to his superior, until finally he was on the line with a major.

"Yes, yes, that's fine," said the major impatiently.

"Would you mind confirming that to our guard? He seems to be in the depths of despair at the prospect of disobeying orders."

The guard protested weakly.

"Here," said Gaunt, passing him the telephone, and then joined Pritchard on the station bench.

"All that time in the wild makes one appreciate things like furniture, doesn't it?" said Pritchard.

"Yes," said Gaunt. "Benches are marvellous inventions."

It was easy to be optimistic, now that they were safe and fed. Devi would have been in his element. It did not seem fair. At the thought of the word "fair," Gaunt gave an unhappy laugh. Pritchard glanced at him, seemed to understand exactly what he was thinking, and turned away.

The guard came to join them, looking prickly and resentful.

"I'm sorry to have tricked you like that," Gaunt told him. "But we'd only have caused more trouble if we'd escaped from Hengelo, you know."

The guard sighed but did not answer.

Once they were comfortably situated in a second-class carriage on the train, Pritchard announced that he was hungry again.

"Isn't he supposed to feed us?" he asked, gesturing at the guard.

"Well, he has," said Gaunt.

"I'm starving. Let's go to the dining car."

They got up and left without warning the guard, who stumbled after them, muttering insults. They ignored him, and used the money in Gaunt's boot to buy champagne and sandwiches. Gaunt offered the champagne to the guard, who just glared at him.

"More for us," said Pritchard. He had only eaten half his sandwich. Gaunt stared at it, knowing it would be thrown away, or scarfed down by some starving train-worker.

"I wish Gideon were here," he said.

Pritchard didn't look at him. He topped up their champagne, even though they didn't need it.

"He's a sturdy bastard," he said, after they had clinked glasses. "Fell out of a plane and landed on his feet, didn't he?"

"I don't think it was quite like that."

"Whatever it was, he survived. A bullet's a piece of cake, after that."

They could both hear the straining optimism in Pritchard's words. They did not mention Devi again. There wasn't any point.

. . .

Mr. Roseveare was waiting for them at the station.

"Good heavens!" he exclaimed, when he saw them. "You look on the verge of death! Well, come on, then. I've got a taxi waiting."

"I have orders—" interjected the guard.

Mr. Roseveare handed him a crisp bill. "Yes, thank you, I'll take it from here."

The guard stared at the money, perplexed.

"But—"

"Thanks awfully," said Gaunt. "Sorry for any trouble we've caused you."

And then Mr. Roseveare swept them into a taxi. He was immaculate, as were all the Roseveares. Gaunt felt clumsy and inadequate in comparison.

"You must be terribly hungry. You look like a pair of skeletons. You ought to stay here in comfort for a few weeks and let us fatten you up."

"We haven't had any news of the War," said Pritchard. "How's it going?"

Mr. Roseveare's face darkened.

"I wouldn't worry about that just yet," he said.

"Why? What's happened?"

"Only a bit of a skirmish at the Somme," said Mr. Roseveare. "Some rather heavy casualties on our side."

Gaunt felt his stomach drop. Next to him, Pritchard had gone very still.

"How heavy?"

Mr. Roseveare looked out of the cab window.

"Nearly sixty thousand British casualties on the first day alone."

"Sixty thousand?" repeated Gaunt in disbelief.

"They're calling it the biggest military disaster in British history," said Mr. Roseveare, lightly.

Pritchard, as always, was more sensitive than Gaunt.

"Was your son there, sir?"

"Yes." He paused. "I haven't heard from him yet." He smiled a peculiar, unpleasant smile.

Gaunt and Pritchard were silent for a moment.

"I'm so sorry about Martin and Clarence," said Pritchard. "Martin and I were close."

To Gaunt's shock, Mr. Roseveare's eyes filled with tears. Gaunt had seen soldiers cry, of course, when they were shell-shocked and broken and pushed beyond endurance. But to see an elegantly dressed diplomat in his fifties break—so quickly and easily—*that* was not an effect of the War that Gaunt had foreseen. He had not realised that the cracks would spread so far, nor so deeply.

He and Pritchard looked away as Mr. Roseveare wiped his tears.

"I'm very proud of them, of course," he said thickly. "Very proud. As the saying goes, *Dulce et decorum est pro patria mori.*"

Pritchard cast Gaunt a warning look, as if expecting Gaunt to start ranting about war aims and the betrayal of the generals and modern weaponry as a crime against humanity. But nothing could have been further from Gaunt's mind. As Mr. Roseveare put away his handkerchief, Gaunt thought only of how cruel it would be to disillusion him.

"I'm sure any one of us would be glad to die for England," he said.

"Yes, exactly," said Mr. Roseveare. "And Cyril will . . . I'm sure he . . . he'll pull through."

"Have . . . have you had any news of my brother? Bertie?" asked Pritchard.

Mr. Roseveare shook his head.

"No, I'm sorry. It'll be in the papers. Ah, we've arrived."

Mr. Roseveare set them up in a grand hotel in central Amsterdam and gave them tickets for a boat to England the following day.

"You'll both be up for Military Crosses, I should think."

"How topping," said Pritchard, exploring the bathroom. "Oh, I say, I call that a *bath*!"

"I'll meet you for dinner tonight at the restaurant. Order anything you please; the embassy will foot the bill."

"Thanks awfully," said Pritchard.

"Not at all. We old Preshute boys have got to help each other out, haven't we?"

Gaunt thought unwillingly of Hayes. Had Hayes escaped from a prisoner-of-war camp, he would have been sent to the holding centre in Hengelo, and no one would have done a thing about it.

He wondered if Hayes was still alive. There was only so much luck a junior officer could have.

Pritchard turned to Gaunt. "Let's not look at the papers today. I can't stand it. I want a bath, and a good meal. I couldn't bear to see him on the Honour Roll just now."

Gaunt nodded. "Yes. We'll look tomorrow, on the boat."

"Sixty thousand casualties," said Pritchard.

Gaunt forced down his fear. It was amazing, all the different textures fear could have. He thought he would prefer to face machine guns than look at the papers and find Ellwood's name there, permanent as a tombstone.

"You take the first bath," said Pritchard.

"Thanks."

"Do you think Gideon—"

"Tomorrow. On the boat. Let's not think about any of it until then."

"Yes," said Pritchard. "You're right."

THIRTY-TWO

Ellwood was burning. He would die with the fire in his bones, because when it went out, there would be nothing left. Everything was ash.

Distantly, he realised that Ernst was looking at him with a strange, drowning sorrow. Then something in his eyes shifted. He opened his mouth to speak—

The bottom half of his face was shot off. Roseveare stood above the trench. Ernst's eyes widened as he felt the empty space where his mouth used to be.

Roseveare held out a hand to Ellwood, who grabbed it and leapt away from the startled Germans. Roseveare pulled him away from the trench, through the wire, and into the relative safety of a mine crater. Ellwood landed on a headless torso, soggy with blood. Next to Roseveare, a charred body stirred feebly with pointless, painful life.

Roseveare and Ellwood stared at each other, speechless.

"They're all dead," said Roseveare, eventually.

"Yes."

"All my men."

"All mine, too."

"We've got to get back to the line," said Roseveare, glancing up.

"Our orders are to press onwards."

"Damn our orders, Ellwood! We can't press on, it's impossible! Everyone is dead!"

"*We're* not. Our orders are to press on."

"Ellwood—"

"'Don't stop until you reach Berlin,' the colonel said."

He stood and began to climb.

"If you're going, I'm going," said Roseveare, climbing, too.

Ellwood stopped. "Don't be stupid."

Roseveare tilted his chin up, stubborn and determined, and Ellwood realised for the first time what it meant to be one of those precious names on Roseveare's mental list.

"Stay here," said Ellwood.

Roseveare shook his head. "All for one and one for all," he said.

They clung to the wet earth, and then Ellwood nodded, and they climbed on. They crawled on their stomachs towards the German trenches, back through the same gap in the wire they had come through. A handful of British soldiers were engaged in hand-to-hand combat with Germans. The bullets flew past Ellwood, and somehow he knew they would not hit him—or perhaps it would not matter if they did. He stood, and a German boy ran at him. Ellwood stabbed at him with his bayonet. In bayonet practice, they attacked sandbags, but sandbags did not have ribs. His blade caught on the boy's bones. Ellwood had to tug it, like jiggling a key stuck in a lock. The boy watched him, dazed, his mouth opening and closing like that of a fish. Finally, Ellwood fired his rifle into the boy's stomach, and the force of the recoil ripped his bayonet out of his body. He fell to the ground, clutching his belly.

"*Mutter,*" he said.

But another German had taken his place. Ellwood cast off his pack so that he could move more easily and stuck the approaching soldier through the eye. His helmet fell off as he tumbled back, revealing a bald head, and Ellwood had a painful flash of a family silently passing around a telegram. He pushed it away. He was too hot. He tore off his new steel helmet and threw it on the ground with his pack. He dipped and parried; it was like drilling on the parade ground; it was killing as they had done at Agincourt, and it would wash him clean. *England is magic. Nothing is worth this.* His mind began to wander crazily through time, and he thought of King Arthur—bowels falling out of bodies—of the Hundred Years' War—his rifle was slippery with blood—

THIRTY-THREE

I T WAS THE MOST HEAVENLY BATH Gaunt had ever experienced. The hot water never ran out, so he ran it twice over, scrubbing himself raw. Mr. Roseveare had given them a clean set of uniforms to change into, and when he emerged from the bathroom, Gaunt felt like a man again.

"You took your time," said Pritchard.

"You're lucky I came out at all," said Gaunt. "I was halfway to buying the place and living there for all eternity."

Once Pritchard was clean and dressed (he still looked deathly thin, as did Gaunt—they both had to punch new holes into their belts to hold up their trousers), they went for a walk around the city. Mr. Roseveare had left them money at the front desk, and they stopped every hour to eat, because they were always hungry. The food shortages were extreme, and they often had to try several bakeries before finding one with bread.

"They've mixed the flour with sawdust," said Pritchard, looking sadly at the bread roll he had just bitten into.

"I don't even care," said Gaunt.

They cringed at the shell-like screech of the trams. They looked at tulips and Rembrandts and girls on bicycles, and did not speak much.

Dinner was in the hotel restaurant, and it was a splendid affair, compared with the sawdust bread. Here, too, food shortages could not be avoided, but the hotel was clearly well acquainted with the black market. There was steak—tough and stringy, but steak nonetheless—and potatoes in real butter.

"Enjoy those," said Mr. Roseveare. "Potatoes are gold, these days."

The flavours were almost too intense after their weeks of meat lozenges. Gaunt ate less than half his steak, despite how wonderful it was.

Mr. Roseveare wanted to hear about their escape in detail, and plied them with champagne to loosen their tongues.

"This Gideon Devi chap sounds as if he masterminded the whole thing," he said.

"He did, rather," said Pritchard.

"And then sacrificing himself so that you might stand a chance!" Mr. Roseveare's expression turned serious. "War brings out the best in men."

Gaunt bit back his response.

"It bonds them together," said Pritchard, diplomatically.

"Clarence's servant wrote to me, to tell me how Clarence was really killed," said Mr. Roseveare, swirling his wine. "None of that 'instantly and painlessly' claptrap to comfort the women. Said that Clarence had his hip and leg shot away in No Man's Land, but wouldn't scream for fear of drawing out stretcher-bearers to their deaths. Bit down on his arm so that he wouldn't. They found the teeth marks."

Gaunt's hands were shaking too badly to hold his champagne glass. He set it down and hid his hands in his lap. Pritchard, too, looked rather pale, his skin stark against his red hair.

"He was so brave," said Mr. Roseveare. "Only twenty-two. I was . . . so proud. . . . Excuse me." He dabbed at his eyes.

"Sometimes I think the War is harder on parents than on soldiers," said Pritchard. Gaunt could tell he was lying, but Gaunt would have lied too, if he had thought of it. Instead, all he could think of was No Man's Land at night, when the star shells lit it up, and it seemed to contain the world. The steak and champagne disgusted him. The fine china and silverware were sticky with something intangible, something fouler than the mud of the trenches. Next to him, Pritchard dropped his fork with a clatter. Gaunt still knew the names of all the men in his company. Where would they sleep tonight? How many were left alive?

"My wife thinks she can speak to them," said Mr. Roseveare, staring into the distance. "She's in England. She attends, you know, these *séances*. Perhaps she *can* speak to them, I don't know—" His voice broke, and he coughed. "I pray you never have to bury a son," he said. "Let alone two." He opened his mouth to go on, then closed it again.

Gaunt and Pritchard watched him powerlessly. He was evidently thinking of his third and final son, still not accounted for.

After a moment, he shook his head and smiled.

"But I want to hear more about your adventures. You mentioned a tunnel. Whatever happened to that?"

THIRTY-FOUR

R OSEVEARE FELL, grimacing and clutching his shoulder.
   "Ellwood. Help me," he said.
   Ellwood paused, but only for a moment. He threw down his rifle, swept Roseveare into his arms, and ran.

It was not so far, after all. No matter how immense No Man's Land was in terms of the lifetimes lost there, it remained a patch of land not much wider than a rugby pitch. He was conscious that very few bullets came their way: the Germans were avoiding killing men as they retreated. In minutes, Ellwood was back at their trench. Stretcher-bearers passed up and down the line, lugging men to the dressing station.

"Are you all right?" he asked Roseveare.

"Yes. I can walk from here."

Ellwood went to the fire step.

"Ellwood!"

"What?"

"You can't possibly go back out there. For God's sake, wait until dark!"

Ellwood didn't even try to understand him. He simply climbed back into No Man's Land and began searching for men who might survive. Those he found, he dragged back to the trenches. Half of them died on the way, but he couldn't stop. *Hayes' blood splattering into his eyes. Pritchard's body blown apart. My name is Ozymandias, King of Kings—*

Grimsey had propped himself up behind a small hill of bodies and torn-up earth. One of his arms was gone, and with the other, he was shooting his pistol, over and over, although it had long ago run out of bullets.

"Leave me alone," he said to Ellwood. "I want to die."

In the trench, Grimsey was immediately loaded onto a stretcher.

Gaunt leant forlornly against the trench wall, wearing his Preshute tailcoat. Ellwood could not look at him. He went back over the top.

He had lost track of how many trips he had made when he caught a bit of shrapnel to the face. It was like being hit in the head by a football. He stumbled and fell to the ground, dropping the injured man he had been carrying. Something covered his left eye; Ellwood couldn't see out of it. His hands were filthy, thick with dirt and gore. He had used them to staunch wounds, to poke intestines back into stomachs, to drag mangled men through the corpse-studded mud to the trenches. He used them now to touch his face.

It didn't feel like his face. It felt like hot butcher's meat.

The injured man he had been carrying groaned, and Ellwood remembered himself. He hoisted the man up and continued to drag him, disoriented by the loss of half his vision. He fell three times before he got back to the trench. The third time, he fell face-first into a body. He spat the dead man's blood out of his mouth and staggered on.

When he finally reached the clearing station, he was relieved of his charge. He made to leave.

"Where do you think you're going?" asked a frazzled doctor. Ellwood gestured vaguely towards the front line. The doctor took him by the arm and guided him to an empty patch of grass next to a man whose hands had been blown off.

"I'm all right," said Ellwood. "I don't feel a thing."

"You will," said the doctor. "Half your face is gone."

At least, that's what it sounded like he had said, but Ellwood was sure he had misheard. He was tired. He lay down on the grass and stared up at the deep blue sky, the larks circling overhead.

"*To faint in the light of the sun she loves, / To faint in his light, and to die,*" he thought. He felt no pain at all.

THIRTY-FIVE

"FOR THE LOVE OF GOD, HENRY!"

"I'm sorry," gasped Gaunt. "I'm sorry."

The sheets were wet with sweat. Pritchard lit two cigarettes, passing one to Gaunt.

"Thanks," said Gaunt. "I'm awfully sorry. I'll stay up for a bit so you can sleep."

"It's no use. I'm just keeping watch on the fucking fire step."

They smoked their cigarettes in silence.

"It'll be better when we're back at the front," said Gaunt, eventually.

"What will we do when the War ends? Never sleep again?"

Gaunt laughed. "As if the War will end!"

"Has anyone ever told you that your pessimism is a form of selfishness?"

Gaunt blinked. "No."

"Well, it is," said Pritchard. He was curled up at the end of the bed, his chin on his knees. In solitary confinement, Devi would have woken up. Devi would have said something inane, like "Cheer up, chums!" and Pritchard and Gaunt would have been united in temporarily loathing him.

You could be shot in the head and live. In the lung, in the stomach. Gaunt had seen men die from harmless-looking leg wounds, and seen them live through violent explosions. It was utterly useless to conjecture about Devi's fate, yet impossible not to.

"Let's take a walk," he said. "If I have to shoot Harkins in my dreams one more time, I don't know what I'll do."

"All right."

They dressed and drifted out into the silent streets of Amsterdam.

"What happened, with Harkins?" asked Pritchard. "I've pieced it together, but not entirely."

"They wouldn't go over the top. Gas."

"At Ypres."

"Yes. Funny thing: everyone was hit once we went over, so what difference does it make?"

"Shooting your own countrymen will always feel wrong, of course."

Gaunt laughed again.

"But I was *always* shooting my own countrymen."

"You mean Germans."

"Yes."

They watched the lamplight reflect on the quiet water of the canal.

"This is enough, just now," said Gaunt.

"Amsterdam, at night, with a friend," said Pritchard.

They did not speak again. The peaceful loveliness of the night absorbed them completely.

A grey dawn broke, and the noise of life began again. They did not return to the hotel—they had nothing they wished to bring with them. They wandered loosely to the train station and boarded the train to Hoek van Holland.

"Do you think we'll ever stop being hungry?" asked Pritchard.

They went to the dining car and bought mealy meat sandwiches.

"What sort of meat?" asked Gaunt.

"Meat," said the man selling the sandwiches, and would not elaborate.

In Hoek van Holland, they boarded the ferry that would take them to England, provided they did not encounter any German submarines.

There were not many people on the ferry. Travel across the Channel was dangerous. Gaunt and Pritchard went first to the canteen to buy more food, then to the empty central lounge. Looming large in the middle of the room was a low coffee table covered in newspapers, both Dutch and British.

Pritchard and Gaunt hovered nearby, watching the newspapers as if they might at any moment come to life and shoot at them.

"I don't want my mother to have to tell me," said Pritchard.

"Bertie might not even have been at the Somme. For all you know, he's sunbathing in Palestine," said Gaunt.

"Sixty thousand casualties," said Pritchard. "They must have sent a hell of a lot of troops to France for that."

"Why don't I look for Bertie, and you look for Ellwood?" suggested Gaunt.

Pritchard breathed a sigh of relief.

"Yes, good idea."

There were several copies of *The Times*. They sat down and looked at each other before reaching for them. Gaunt flipped to the Honour Roll. It went on for pages and pages. He found the names beginning with "P" and scanned for Pritchard. His eye fell continually on the names of boys he knew from Grinstead, from Preshute, from the balls he had attended the summer of 1914. Pritchard sat next to him, making small and distracting exclamatory sounds.

"Hugo Elliot! I went hunting with him, he had an awfully nice grey mare. . . . Percival Ellis—Gaunt, did you know him? He was in River House, your year, I think. Played the piano like an angel. I used to hear him in the practice rooms. He was frightfully modest."

Gaunt barely listened. He had already found the name he was looking for.

"Archie," he said hoarsely.

"Sorry," said Pritchard. "Sorry. It's just so many people I know." A pause. "Ellwood's not here."

The sunlight filtering through the dirty windows had a strange, unreal quality.

"Are you sure?" asked Gaunt.

"Positive. I'll look under 'Wounded.'"

It did not occur to Gaunt to rejoice. There were too many variables. Ellwood might have been killed in an earlier battle. He might be fatally wounded.

Meanwhile, he had to tell Pritchard. The name glared at him in small black print. It was only ink, and yet it was the cruellest thing Gaunt had ever seen.

"Archie," he said again, but Pritchard kept prattling, his voice rising excitably.

"Clement Edwards! He was at prep school with me. I wish they gave more information than just 'wounded.' I knew a fellow who slipped on the duckboards before a nasty show and broke his ankle. Listed as wounded just the same as my brother Charlie, with his fatal bullet to the stomach."

"Archie . . ."

"Ellwood, Capt., Royal Kennet Fusiliers."

"What?"

"He's wounded."

Gaunt couldn't breathe.

"Show me."

Pritchard handed him the paper, leaving his index finger on Ellwood's name. Gaunt mouthed the words. Ellwood, Capt., Royal Kennet Fusiliers. Wounded.

"Did you find Bertie?" asked Pritchard.

Gaunt met Pritchard's eyes and nodded.

"Is he . . . is he wounded?" asked Pritchard.

Gaunt shook his head.

Pritchard wordlessly held out his hand. Gaunt gave him the paper and pointed at where it said "Pritchard, Second Lieutenant Herbert Wollaston, Royal Scots Fusiliers, killed in action on July 1st, aged 18 years."

Pritchard put the newspaper down. The ship rocked them like a cradle.

"I'm sorry," said Gaunt.

Pritchard did not answer. He was still, so still that Gaunt thought he was holding his breath. Gaunt put a hand on his shoulder.

"My mother will be awfully—upset," said Pritchard.

"I'm sorry," said Gaunt again.

"That's—that's all right," said Pritchard, his voice light and breathless. "Oh, look, they have the Indian cricket scores. Can you read them, Henry, I'm—I can't see—"

He was blind with tears. In a low, steady voice, Gaunt read out the cricket scores.

THE PRESHUTIAN

| VOL. LI.—No. 763. | JULY 12TH, 1916. | Price 6d. |

⁓ROLL OF HONOUR ⁓

*WE ARE GLAD TO PUBLISH DETAILS SENT
BY PARENTS OR FRIENDS.*

KILLED IN ACTION.

Aldworth, Captain and Adjutant Edmund Hamo, Royal Irish Rifles,
killed in action on July 1st, aged 19 years.

Birley, Lieutenant George, Northumberland Fusiliers,
killed in action on July 1st, aged 23 years.

Blumenfeld, Second Lieutenant Leslie Frederick Chamberlain,
Lancashire Fusiliers, killed in action on July 1st, aged 20 years.

Cathcart, Second Lieutenant Lancelot Owen, East Lancashire Regiment,
killed in action on July 1st, aged 26 years.

Davidson, Lieutenant (Temporary Captain) James Ainslie,
London Regiment, killed in action on July 1st, aged 22 years.

Ellis, Second Lieutenant Percival, Somerset Light Infantry,
killed in action on July 1st, aged 18 years.

Elmhirst, Lieutenant Francis, Brigade Machine Gun Company,
killed in action on July 1st, aged 27 years.

Farlow, Lieutenant Ronald, R.F.C.,
killed in action on July 1st, aged 20 years.

Holmes, Second Lieutenant Guy Geoffrey, K.O.S.B.,
killed in action on July 1st, aged 21 years.

Lantham, Second Lieutenant Maurice Morton, Royal Kennet Fusiliers,
killed in action on July 2nd, aged 16 years.

Pritchard, Second Lieutenant Herbert Wollaston, Royal Scots Fusiliers,
killed in action on July 1st, aged 18 years.

Robinson, Captain Cecil Lionel Charles, York and Lancashire Regiment,
killed in action on July 1st, aged 26 years.

Spooner, Second Lieutenant I. Robert, R.F.A.,
killed in action on July 1st, aged 22 years.

Yule, Private Richard Alexander, Middlesex Regiment,
killed in action on July 1st, aged 19 years.

DIED OF WOUNDS.

Bell, Second Lieutenant William Percy, The Suffolk Regiment,
died of wounds on July 3rd, aged 18 years.

Davies, Captain Alistair Westcott, R.F.A.,
died of wounds on July 10th, aged 28 years.

Fairbanks, Captain Edward John, Leicester Regiment,
died of wounds on July 5th, aged 22 years.

Goode, Second Lieutenant Philip Francis Ewbank,
King's (Liverpool) Regiment, died of wounds on July 3rd, aged 20 years.

Gordon, Lieutenant Clifford Thomas, Middlesex Regiment,
died of wounds on July 8th, aged 23 years.

Hugo, Lieutenant Charles Woodhouse, Dorset Regiment,
died of wounds on July 9th, aged 22 years.

Long, Lieutenant Lawrence Archibald, Royal West Surrey Regiment,
died of wounds on July 2nd, aged 20 years.

Lovegrove, Captain Rollo Christie, York and Lancaster Regiment,
died of wounds on July 7th, aged 20 years.

Meyrick, Captain Edward Mann, R.E.,
died of wounds on July 10th, aged 28 years.

Pittar, Second Lieutenant Lawrence Dale Montagu, Royal Fusiliers,
died of wounds on July 2nd, aged 18 years.

Rosing, Captain James Devereux, Middlesex Regiment,
died of wounds on July 4th, aged 21 years.

Streatfeild, Lieutenant Cedric D'Aubigne, 5th Lancashire Fusiliers,
died of wounds on July 6th, aged 19 years.

DIED.

Cathcart, Lieutenant Roland Henry Richard, S. Lancashire Regiment, died July 10th of pneumonia following wounds received on July 1st, aged 22.

Iles, Corporal Gerald Vincent, Cambridgeshire Regiment, died of sickness on active service, June 30th, age 29.

Kinloch, Captain Errol Musgrave, R.A.M.C. and Essex Yeomanry, died in London after an operation on July 5th, aged 30.

———

WOUNDED.

Alington, Lieut.-Col. A. W., West Kent Regt.

Ashfield, Lieut. G. M., Royal West Kent Regt.

Barnes, Maj. H. N., Lancs Fusiliers.

Bartlett, Lieut. S. H., Northants Regt.

Belben, Capt. A. P., Border Regt.

Bellhouse, Lieut. H.U.S., Royal West Kent.

Brown, Sec.-Lieut. B. C., North Staffs Regt.

Buchanan, Capt. C., Guards.

Burt, Lieut. L., South Wales Borderers.

Butler, Brig.-Gen. W.B.R., C.M.G.

Cameron, Sec.-Lieut. G. M. Royal Sussex Regt.

Campion-Lock, Lieut. F. M., Royal Sussex.

Charlesworth, Sec.-Lieut. H. B., Queen's (Royal W. Surrey Regt.)

Coke, Sec.-Lieut. S. W., Loyal North Lancs.

Cornwall, Sec.-Lieut. M. T., Hampshire Regt.

Dent, Sec.-Lieut. L. T., Middlesex (attd. R.F.C.)

Dexter, Lieut.-Col. C. S., Indian Cavalry.

Donnison, Sec.-Lieut. C. H., R.F.A.

Ellwood, Capt. S. L., Royal Kennet Fusiliers.

Farrow, Capt. J., Norfolk Regt.

Formby, Lieut. A. F., R.F.A.

Fox, Capt. R. G., Cambs. Regt.

Gardiner-Lewis, Capt. J. V., R.G.A.

Geoghegan, Lieut.-Col. T.S.H., Lancs Fusiliers.

Godfrey, Capt. N.A.C., Argull and Sutherland Highlanders.

Gray, Lieut. R. J., R.F.A.

Grimsey, Sec.-Lieut. H., S. Lancs Regt.

Grosvenor, Sec.-Lieut. G. M., Royal Sussex Regt.

Hancock, Sec.-Lieut. J. W., R. Munster Fusiliers.

Harper-Paul, Capt. C. W., R.F.A.

Herbert, Sec.-Lieut. V. R., R.F.A.

Hilder, Sec.-Lieut. F., Rifle Brigade.

Holland, Capt. L. A., Kings Royal Rifle Corps.

Howell, Capt. W.E.M., Royal Berks Regt.

Leach, Lieut. T. C., K.R.R.C.

Letts, Lieut. T.E.T., King's Own Scottish Borderers.

Lowth, Sec.-Lieut. J. L., Oxford and Bucks Light Infantry.

Lushington, Capt. and Adjt. R. J., Loyal North Lancs.

Mallinson, Sec.-Lieut. D. M., R.G.A.

Mansell, Capt. J. B., "Queen's" attd. K.R.R.C.

Mansergh, Capt. and Adjt. G.C.R., South Staffs Regt.

Milford, Sec.-Lieut. G. T., Royal Warwick Regt.

O'Shea, Sec.-Lieut. S. E., R.F.C.

Parsons, Maj. N. A., R.F.A.

Pegler, Capt. E. M., Cheshire Regt.

Penlington, Sec.-Lieut. P. V., Indian Army, Reserve of Officers, attd. Cavalry.

Philpott, Lieut. D. G., Royal Berks Regt.

Pratt, Capt. T.G.C., London Regt.

Preston, Lieut. E., King's Own Scottish Borderers.

Rees, Lieut. L.T.N., R.G.A., attd. R.F.C.

Ridley, Capt. O. V., West Yorks Regt.

Rodman, Sec.-Lieut. G.A.N., London Regt.

Rose, Lieut. A.C.V., Oxford and Bucks Light Infantry.

Roseveare, Sec.-Lieut. C. M., E. Yorks Regt.

Schiele, Lieut.-Col. J. C., Royal Fusiliers, attd. West Yorks.

Shelmerdine-Jessop, Maj. W. H., R.G.A.

Sillem, Private C., R.A.M.C.

Simpson, Lieut.-Col. H. B., Manchester Regt.

Skene, Capt. R., Manchester Regt.

Smith, Lieut. C. F., Durham Light Infantry.
Spence, Lieut. R.G.W., Somerset Light Infantry.
Swayne, Maj. R. H., London Regt.
Tucker, Lieut. R. D., Trench Mortar Battalion.
Tuckerwell, Lieut. F.R.B., West Yorks Regt.
Waldergrave, Lieut. J. B., Rifle Brigade.
Wallis, Sec.-Lieut. E.G.C., Grenadier Guards.
Watson, Sec.-Lieut. L. B., Rifle Brigade.
Westmacott, Sec.-Lieut. G.A.N., London Regt.
Woollcombe, Lieut. G. M., Royal West Kent Regt.
Wordsworth-Block, Maj. W. H., R.G.A.
Wright, Lieut.-Col. A. W., West Kent Regt.

———

MISSING.

Campion, Sec.-Lieut. T. M., Somerset L.I.
Cooper, Sec.-Lieut. G. F., R.F.A.
Gunner-Pratten, Lieut. H. R., R.F.C.
Mallet, Sec.-Lieut. A. W., R.F.C.
Saville, Sec.-Lieut. L.A.N., King's (Liverpool).

———

WOUNDED & MISSING.

Harbinson, Sec.-Lieut. J.M.V., Machine Gun Corps.
North, Lieut. J. N., King's (Liverpool).
Shaw, Capt. P. B., R. Berkshire Regt.

———

PRISONERS OF WAR.

Bardsley, Maj. A. J., Indian Vol. Artillery.
Calver-Prescott, Sec.-Lieut. C. H., R.F.C.
Newington, Capt. G. C., R. Warwickshire Regt.
Spicer, Maj. F. L., Hampshire Regt.

In Memoriam.

SECOND LIEUTENANT HERBERT WOLLASTON PRITCHARD

Killed at the Somme on July 1st, aged 18.

It is difficult to believe that Bertie Pritchard can really be dead. He was quite the liveliest boy I ever knew. He was a true soldier at heart, on the battlefield or off it. His simplicity and cheerfulness, and above all his loyalty to his friends, ensure that he shall be missed by all who knew him. Although his letters continued to display his typical good humour until he was killed at the Somme, he was greatly affected by the deaths of first his brother Charlie Pritchard at Ypres, and then his friend Edgar West at Loos. "I keep thinking of tricks to play on West and then remembering," he told me once. Extract from his Sec.-Lieut.:—"Your son was hit by a shell almost the minute he went over the top. It was over in an instant." Bertie Pritchard was a true Englishman, and as such would have been proud to give his life for his country.

C. M. ROSEVEARE

SECOND LIEUTENANT PERCIVAL ELLIS

Killed at the Somme on July 1st, aged 18.

I think it is Percival's eyes that made him so magnetic. When anyone spoke, he would observe them intently, no matter how uninteresting their remark. Under his unwavering gaze, one felt on the verge of becoming extraordinary, and indeed he brought the best out of everyone. He was hero-worshipped by all who knew him, for he was the best of us— kind, uproariously funny, decent and brave. His modesty is particularly worth mentioning. In Lower Sixth, he was one of three chosen to perform at Blenheim Palace for the Duke of Marlborough (Percival was an excellent pianist). When asked when the performance would be, he not only gave incorrect dates, but also refused to tell anyone where they might procure tickets. Consequently, none of his friends were able to attend the concert.

"How did it go?" we asked upon his return. He made a small grimace.

"The others were good," he said.

Only later did we discover that the Duke of Marlborough was so impressed by his performance that he invited him to stay for Christmas. This is only one example of Percival's almost aggressive modesty. He seemed incapable of understanding the extent of his worth. I hoped adulthood would teach him how much we loved him.

He was shot in the head while gallantly leading his platoon in an attack, and lived only long enough to ask that others should be attended to before himself.

The War was abhorrent to him, and he agonised over questions of murder and fear. Ultimately, he fought because he loved peace. It is impossible for me to think of him at the front. The very sight of him in a khaki uniform was incongruous. I prefer to remember him as I knew him best: a soft-eyed, modest boy laughing with his friends as he walked down country lanes on his way back from a football match.

T. A. SCOTT

———

PRIVATE RICHARD ALEXANDER YULE

Killed at the Somme on July 1st, aged 19.
Although Richard came from an old army family and was known for his bravery, when the time came to enlist, he refused to accept a commission as an officer.

"It isn't in the spirit of democracy," he said. Anyone who had been to one of his late-night *salons* to discuss socialism and what he termed "the class problem" will not be surprised. In his eccentric political views, Richard was intensely serious, but he was not a grave person. He was quite the opposite—a delightfully merry, cheerful fellow, always making jokes and writing witty limericks. He had a knack for talking to anyone, and the scouts and groundsmen were particularly fond of him. He was bound for Cambridge when he enlisted, determined to fight "as the men did."

He took his mischievous playfulness with him to the front:

"We loathe our Corporal," he wrote, shortly before his death at the Somme. "We sneeze continuously whenever he appears until he edges nervously away."

He kept his good humour until the very end, and cheered on his men enormously. From an extract from his Captain:—"There was a man ten yards behind him who fell into a flooded trench, and your son turned around and said 'For God's sake, man, don't drink that water!' and as he turned his head forward again he was shot in the middle of the forehead. It was a gallant and glorious death."

P. W. G. McKAY

———

CAPTAIN AND ADJUTANT EDMUND HAMO ALDWORTH

Killed at the Somme on July 1st, aged 19.
Somehow I believed Edmund Aldworth would be one of the lucky ones. He had already been under fire (he was injured at Loos) and survived, and he always had an indelible feeling of self-assurance that made one feel, in his company, that there was nothing to worry about. Aldworth reminded me of nothing so much as a boy king, and indeed the boys of Hill House worshipped him as if he were their monarch. I was among the

admirers, but I was fortunate enough to see him when he was alone, when his guarded face would relax into a cheerful smile, and the real Aldworth could be spied. He was dutiful and gallant. I, and many others, longed to be like him—silent, brave, and kind. It brings me comfort to know that he was killed instantly—"shot through the head almost as soon as we had left the trenches." We all sympathise very much with his family and share their pride in his gallant death.

C. M. ROSEVEARE

_____

LIEUTENANT LAWRENCE ARCHIBALD LONG

Died of wounds from the Battle of the Somme on July 2nd, aged 20.
Few people knew the secret to Lawrence's optimism. He told me once: every evening, before bed, he wrote down three good things.

"I spend my day hunting for my nightly list," he wrote, a week before the Somme. "Here is today's: 1. The tea was still hot when it got to the men, 2. I received your letter (joy!) and 3. I saw a finch twirling rapturously at sunrise. It is impossible to be discouraged with three such things to think about, even if the coming offensive is as red as the men fear."

Not inherently a soldier-type, he nevertheless enlisted the moment he could, for he felt that war was a forge where men might be made strong. I know that, if he had survived, his theory would have proved true. His Captain writes:—"He got a bullet in his throat, and as he fell he shouted 'Go on, boys!' I had noticed him leading the men into a particularly rough patch, and the wonder was how any of them survived at all. As a matter of fact every officer in the regiment was hit. He lived for eighteen hours. I shall miss him personally very much." I am sure Lawrence should have found three good things in his own death. What is certain is that Pre-shute may well be proud of him, and of the way he gave up his life at his country's call.

J. M. ROPER

_____

SECOND LIEUTENANT LESLIE FREDERICK BLUMENFELD

Killed at the Somme on July 1st, aged 20.
He fell on July 1st, while leading his men to the attack. The only surviving officer of his company writes: "Your son was the first man to fall: I went and offered help, but he told me to go on with my men; then I saw him get up and struggle forward, but he was again wounded and fell. I could not find him again, evidently he was completely buried in one of the trenches or shell holes. He died gloriously leading his men, and he lies with many others of his Company, in the torn and shell-swept valley just *(cont. pg. 12)*

THIRTY-SIX

LIKE EVERYONE ELSE in his ward, Ellwood was plagued by nightmares. Unlike the others', however, his were quiet. He woke from them in awestruck silence, four or five times a night.

He was feverish with poetry. At night, he tore himself from his dreams to find his notebook, that he might inscribe the words pouring through his mind. He didn't need to edit. They landed just where they were supposed to on the paper. In the morning, when the light filtered in and the VADs came to dress his wound, he reread the pages and barely remembered writing them.

Maud came to visit. She brought a crossword puzzle and a copy of Charles Sorley's *Marlborough and Other Poems*.

"He was killed at Loos," she said.

Loos: the word conjured an instant vision of Gaunt's chest ripped open by lead.

"Like Kipling's son," said Ellwood.

Maud gave a surprised laugh. "Yes," she said. "And that completes the casualty list, I think."

Ellwood put the poems on the bedside table. He knew he would not read them.

He was conscious that he looked the hero, so long as his head remained bandaged. But Maud was not like the girls he had gone to balls with in the summer of 1914, who would have thought his wound glamorous. He could feel her eyes running over the dressing. She was too experienced not to recognise his injury for what it was: disfiguring.

He turned his face away from her.

"Would you like to see?" he asked her. "I can take off the bandages."

"I'm sure your doctor would rather you didn't," said Maud. *Coward*, he thought, and an image flashed before him of two Canadian privates he'd once found in No Man's Land, the skin on their hands coming off in slippery yellow peels, still clutching the white handkerchiefs with which they had tried to surrender.

"Have it your way," he said. "Why have you come, if not to ogle?"

"Ogle? Do you think I don't see enough at the hospital?"

Ellwood started to write in his notebook; mechanical, automatic words. The motion of pen on paper was soothing. *Loos*, he wrote. *Beaumont-Hamel. Ypres.* He wrote them often, until the words became so familiar that he was sure he misspelled them.

"I came because I was worried about you," said Maud.

"You came to see how bad the damage was," said Ellwood, his pen tearing through the paper, "but now that you're here, you can't bear to see it. Some marriage *we'll* have, if you can't even look at me."

There was a long pause. *Ypres*, he wrote, varying the height and length of each letter.

"I'm not marrying you," said Maud.

Ellwood laughed. "Of course not." The bandages on his face were slightly rough under his fingers. "I know perfectly well why you liked me, and that's all gone now."

"Yes," said Maud, coldly. "I rather think it is."

"Thanks for the poems," said Ellwood. "Perhaps they'll make up for my lost eye. I wonder where it went? Do you think it popped?"

"Stop it," said Maud. Her unhappiness twisted in Ellwood's heart, making an agreeable change from numb, piercing anger.

He had felt protective of Maud, once. That chivalry appeared to have bled out somewhere in France. He was unable to feel the old affection for her, however much he longed to.

"I wonder what happened to Henry's body," he said. *Ypres*, his pen wrote. *Loos. Beaumont-Hamel.* "Do you ever think about it? If it was buried—or left to rot?"

"You are not the only one grieving him," said Maud, quietly. "He was my *brother*."

Ellwood laughed, letting all his scorn ride free in the sound. Maud was silent for such a long time that Ellwood thought he had succeeded—that she had left. But when he turned his head, he saw that she was still seated beside him. Her hand rested on the book of Sorley poems.

"You always made me feel as if I was not quite clever enough," she said, when she noticed him looking at her. "Both of you. I *am*, you know. There's a place waiting for me at a university in Berlin, when all this is over."

"Ber*lin*?"

"I've a right to be interested in my mother's country. It's a very good university," said Maud, her voice rising defensively, as if she had expected his disapproval.

"I'm sure it is," said Ellwood. He swallowed. "Congratulations."

Maud frowned.

"Thank you," she said. She fiddled with the cloth cover of the poetry book. "I just . . . I don't understand why you've been so . . . so unwilling to be friends."

"Marry me," said Ellwood. He was too hot. He wished she would leave, so that he could kick off the covers.

"Sidney," said Maud. She was seated on his right. If he turned away, she could not see the half of his face that had been lost.

"I'm rich," he said. "You can be a politician, I don't care. I'll hide my face in all the pictures. I was quite good-looking, before. I still am, on this side." He touched the stubble on his right cheek. "Marry me."

"You don't want to marry me," said Maud.

"I've planned on marrying you since I was fifteen years old. *Something* ought to happen as I planned."

Maud took the book of Sorley poems, opened it at a random page, closed it.

"You're a poet," she said. "Who's my favourite poet?"

"Tennyson," said Ellwood.

She made a strange, aborted sound.

"No," she said. "Masefield. You're thinking of Henry."

"Henry hated Tennyson."

"He can't have done," said Maud. "It's all he read in the holidays."

Ellwood stared at the writing in his notebook, his thoughts catching on each other until there was nothing to think at all.

"Marry me," he said again.

"No," said Maud.

His fist clenched around the paper, ripping it from the binding.

"Then leave me alone," he said.

He did not look at her as she stood and collected her things.

"I'll come back on my next day off."

"Don't bother," said Ellwood.

She didn't.

He pretended to sleep whenever his mother visited. She cried too much. Her tears made him unspeakably angry.

Arthur Loring came to visit him once. He was the only friend of Ellwood's who had survived the Somme unscathed. He sat at Ellwood's bedside, his handsome eyes raking Ellwood's bandaged face. He was so thoroughly whole and undamaged that Ellwood alternated between wanting to fuck him and wanting to cut him to pieces. Perhaps his antipathy was apparent; Loring did not return.

"He's jealous," said the officer in the next bed, after Loring had left. His name was Cornish. A shell had erupted in a crump hole full of water where he had been nursing a wounded friend, near Mametz Wood. The water had boiled, scalding his friend to death, but leaving Cornish with only a few patches of waxy third-degree burns.

"Jealous?" repeated Ellwood. Cornish nodded his chin at the door Loring had just left through.

"Your friend. He has to go back," said Cornish.

Ellwood's lip curled in disdain. "Some of us aren't shirkers, cowering in shell holes," he said.

Cornish left him alone after that.

Sometimes Ellwood went to the window and watched women ride by on bicycles. *Isn't that nice,* he thought, wishing them crashes and miscarriages.

London was lazy and warm, as if it were on holiday.

The ghosts were worse here. It wasn't just Gaunt any more. Pritchard and West reproached him as he tipped into sleep, and the men from his platoon held out beseeching, bleeding hands.

He never, ever thought of the men he had bayonetted. There was a chasm where that memory was, and he skirted far away from it, hoping it would grow over with something less red.

"When can I go back?" he asked the doctor. The doctor only laughed. He was in his fifties, and had never been to France. Ellwood regarded him with deepest contempt.

Ellwood had been awarded a Military Cross. The ribbon was sewn onto his pyjamas. It seemed ironic that the part of him that would once have been overjoyed at the sight of the medal was precisely what had been blighted in obtaining it.

His poems were published in newspapers. People gobbled them up, glutting themselves with horror. They wrote glowing reviews, as if the War were a deliciously grim new play on the West End. Ellwood wondered who the reviewers were: Men too old to enlist? Women? Men whose journalistic pursuits had been deemed integral to the war effort? How could they live with themselves?

He didn't care about the poems, one way or another. He merely cut away the blackened, gangrenous bits of his soul and sold them.

He woke up one bright afternoon to find Gaunt watching him. He sighed. When Gaunt appeared in the daytime, his nightmares were always worse.

Gaunt wore a pale suit he had never seen him in before, and his expression was more guarded than wistful. He looked dreadfully thin. Ellwood frowned. He reached out and touched the soft fabric of Gaunt's sleeve. It felt like a wool-and-cotton blend. He pulled away as if he had been burnt and rang the bell for the VAD. She came rushing in (Ellwood never rang, to avoid distracting the staff from patients with wounds more severe than his).

"Is everything all right, Captain Ellwood?"

Ellwood did not remove his eye from Gaunt, whose eyebrows knotted together in concern.

"No. This ward is haunted. I'd like to be moved, please."

"I'm not a ghost, Elly," said Gaunt, softly.

"It's unacceptable to have ghosts parading about like this. I'd like a new room this instant."

"You don't mean Captain Gaunt, sir?"

Ellwood stared at her, then back at Gaunt, who was smiling.

"Can . . . can you see him, too?"

"Of course," said the VAD. She tried to feel his forehead, but Ellwood shrugged her off and pressed back into his pillows, feeling rather faint.

"I think that's all, thank you," said Gaunt to the VAD. She left. Gaunt turned to him with an expression that seemed to hold a thousand things at once.

"Hullo, Elly," he said. "How've you been?"

THIRTY-SEVEN

ELLWOOD STARED AT HIM. Gaunt stared back. Ellwood couldn't think. He couldn't *think*. He could only see, over and over, the dark blood that had bloomed across Gaunt's chest; hear Gaunt's last, treacherously *German* words.

To look at Maud and feel nothing was one thing; for it to happen with Gaunt was unbearable.

"I saw the bullet hit you," said Ellwood. He felt, somehow, as if Gaunt were trying to trick him. "Your whole chest caved in."

"I had a spot of good luck. Do you remember my cousin Ernst?"

Ellwood gritted his teeth so that the hysterical laughter brewing in his throat would not break free.

"Yes," he said. He didn't tell Gaunt what had happened to his precious German cousin. Let Gaunt find out for himself, since he was impervious to death.

"I thought I saw him in the trench before I was shot," said Gaunt. "It wasn't him, but the fellow I spoke to was struck with a pang of sympathy and got me to a German hospital in time. I'm sure I should have died if it weren't for him."

"Good old Ernst," said Ellwood, reaching for his notebook. He opened it to a new page, but could not form words. He scraped his pen viciously back and forth, creating a dark gash of ink across the page.

"Then I was sent to a prisoner-of-war camp," said Gaunt.

Maybe it was a new kind of nightmare. Or maybe Ellwood was dead. Some people believed that one's body went to Heaven in whatever condition it had been in at death. Ellwood studiously avoided imagining what Pritchard would look like, in that ghastly charnel house of an afterlife.

"You'll never guess who was in my dormitory there: Gideon Devi!" said Gaunt.

Ellwood glanced up sharply. Gaunt watched him as if he had been waiting for Ellwood's attention—as if he had mentioned Devi in order to attract it.

Ellwood dropped his gaze back to the page.

"It must have been a comfort, to have someone there with whom you are so close," he said, keeping his voice carefully expressionless.

"It was," said Gaunt, then paused. "He was shot as we escaped. I haven't been able to find out . . ." He trailed off. Ellwood would not look at him. "Anyway," said Gaunt, clearing his throat. "I'm sure he's fine."

Ellwood scoffed. "War's made an optimist of you, has it?"

He could feel Gaunt's eyes on him.

"I was never as close to him as I was to you, you know," said Gaunt.

Gaunt had never said anything like that before.

"Please tell me if this is just a dream," said Ellwood.

Gaunt pinched him. Ellwood did not react, beyond staring at his arm where Gaunt had touched him. It struck him, for the first time, that it might be *real*. That Gaunt might truly be sitting, unharmed, next to his hospital bed.

It was a possibility that spun out a million ways.

Hayes floated into his mind. Ellwood had avoided thinking about him, because it was not certain yet that he would live. Thorburn had told him so, in a short, businesslike letter:

Saturday 8th July
Somewhere in France

Ellwood,
    We've had a rough go of it here, not allowed to give you
numbers, obviously. Hayes is in critical condition; pulverised

hip. Don't know if you heard that Lantham was shot by firing squad. Anyone could see he had neurasthenia; it's a scandal, but he didn't go over the top on July 1st, so General Haig signed off. All the men shot wide, of course. I finished him with my pistol and told his family he was killed in action. If they ask you how he died, make something up, will you? Shot in the head will do; it's truthful enough.

Hope you're well.

Sincerely,
Capt. Thorburn

Ellwood had balled the letter up and thrust it under his mattress. When Mrs. Lantham came to visit him in the hospital, he described to her, in terse, imagined detail, how Maurice had died bravely in action.

"Hayes got smashed up," he told Gaunt, now. Gaunt felt in his pocket for his cigarette case, his expression unreadable. He offered one to Ellwood, shrugged when Ellwood shook his head, and lit his cigarette. Instantly, he gagged on the smoke. Ellwood sat up, alarmed, but Gaunt waved him off.

"Doctor's orders," he rasped. "To expand my lung capacity."

After a few drags, he stopped coughing, and looked once more at Ellwood.

"I heard about Hayes. Will he live?"

"I don't know," said Ellwood.

Gaunt nodded, then laughed. It sounded bitter. It was that bitterness, more than anything else, that convinced Ellwood it was true, that Gaunt was really there. Ellwood wanted to love him, but his heart seemed to be made up of edges; and instead of affection, a choking anger built beneath his ribs. He didn't know why, or how to stop it. His hands trembled with how badly he wanted to break something.

"Any other news to tell me?" asked Gaunt. "I understand you rather insistently asked my sister to marry you. I'm very glad to have made it back in time for the wedding."

"She said no. And you were *dead*," said Ellwood. The pen shook in his hand. The idea of Gaunt resenting him for seeking to fill the void that had ripped through him, that night in Loos . . . ! His mind hunted for words to write, but there was nothing, only paralysing rage. He could not express it. It was trapped in him.

Gaunt reached out and touched the Military Cross ribbon sewn to the front of his pyjamas. Ellwood stiffened, relaxing only when Gaunt withdrew his hand.

"Are you a hero, Elly?" asked Gaunt, softly.

"They're giving these out to anyone who sneezes at the Germans now," said Ellwood. "Doesn't mean a thing."

"You were mentioned in dispatches, I heard. Saved six people's lives."

Ellwood gave an exasperated sigh. "Half of them died at the clearing station."

"Caught a bullet for your trouble, I gather?"

"Bit of shrapnel," said Ellwood.

"I was never too keen on the left side of your face, anyway."

"I've lost an eye," said Ellwood, sticking out his chin.

Gaunt did not answer, taking a long drag of his cigarette. People had different ways of masking horror, Ellwood had learnt. Loring had chattered uneasily about a show he'd seen on the West End, his eyes ceaselessly examining the bandages, as if he thought he could peel them off by staring at them. Gaunt, apparently, hid his incipient disgust with cigarettes.

"Want to see?" asked Ellwood, feeling as he used to in No Man's Land, when he led his platoon closer to enemy lines than was safe or sane.

"Only if . . ."

"It's quite hideous," said Ellwood. It was extraordinary how light his voice sounded, how easy, when his heart was hammering its way out of his rib cage. "They've been hiding mirrors from me, but I wheedled one of the VADs into giving me one." He scrabbled at the bandages with his blunt fingernails. "I only caught a glimpse before they took it away. It's quite something, Gaunt, really."

"Elly," said Gaunt, but Ellwood wasn't going to let him pretend nothing had changed. He pulled the gauze away from his sticking skin.

"Oh, I'm sure you've seen worse," he told Gaunt, who had averted his eyes, the coward, *the coward,* "only it's always strange when it's someone you *know* who's been mangled, isn't it? *Look at me.*"

Gaunt looked up and stared at Ellwood, transfixed with horror. His gaze traced along the festering mass of wounds.

Ellwood had no illusions about how he looked. He dreamt about it, in fact, about the misshapen, molten lump of skin where his eye used to be, about the place where his left cheekbone had shattered, and the surgeon had tried to fold his face back together. He knew he looked like a wax doll that had been left out in the sun. What he hated most was the short strip of eyelashes that ran almost vertically down the scar tissue, like spider legs sticking out of a crevice. They were infected, because he kept taking off the bandages at night and trying to pluck them out with his fingers.

"There," said Ellwood. Something that might once have been misery swelled in his throat. At the very back of his mind, he clawed feebly for the fragments of a Rupert Brooke poem, but found nothing. He wished he were dead.

Gaunt stared in terrible silence.

"Well?" said Ellwood. "What do you think? Don't I look handsome? Have I taken your breath away?"

"I failed my medical," said Gaunt, still staring.

Ellwood's stomach dropped.

"What?"

"Seems the German surgeon who put me back together bungled the job." Gaunt paused, finally lowering his eyes from the horror of Ellwood's face. "Although I suppose I ought to take some responsibility. He told me to rest up for a year, and I can't say that I followed his advice to the letter."

"You aren't going back?" asked Ellwood.

Gaunt shook his head.

Ellwood gingerly pinned the bandages back in place. With a painful squeeze in his chest, he noticed that Gaunt seemed to relax as he covered himself up. On Divisional Rest, Gaunt had once stroked his eyebrow—the one that no longer existed—and called him "handsomer than ever." Gaunt had always loved beauty.

A sudden, horrible thought occurred to Ellwood.

"Are you dying? Is that why you failed your medical?" he asked, flattening the last piece of snowy gauze over his forehead.

"No," said Gaunt.

Ellwood breathed out.

"That's good," he said. "That's very good. You look all right. A bit thin, maybe."

Gaunt laughed. "You should see Archie Pritchard."

Ellwood seized his pen and dragged it back and forth, back and forth, forcing himself to focus on the widening stain of ink on paper.

"I was sorry to hear about Bertie," said Gaunt, which was a selfish thing to say, Ellwood thought. *I'm sorry,* people said, and then they had cleared their conscience, and Ellwood was left with the memories.

"Who?" said Ellwood, with a nasty laugh.

"It sounded like a pretty bad show," said Gaunt.

The pen spilled ink like a bayonet blade. It was not a comparison Ellwood had made before, and he grieved that his mind had stumbled on it.

"There wasn't enough of him left to be buried," he found himself saying, although he hadn't intended to say anything at all. "I went back and looked. I found something that might have been a bit of his face, but I couldn't be sure."

Gaunt was silent.

"They say I have shell shock," said Ellwood. "Absolute tosh. I can't *stand* being here, when Lonsdale and Thorburn and Ramsay and—and all the rest of them—oh, Jesus—"

The swelling in his throat cut off his words, but it did not rise any further. He shut his mouth and stopped his pen. His anger cooled, sinking back into his blood.

"I feel such a bounder, lying up in luxury like this," he said. He wished Gaunt would speak, or go, or promise never to leave. "But at the same time, I'm unspeakably glad to be away from it all. I'm disgusted with myself, but it's true. Have you ever heard of anything so cowardly?"

"I know just what you mean," said Gaunt. Did he? The words fell on Ellwood's heart like a balm. "I feel the same. I'm ashamed of myself, but when they told me my chest hadn't healed right, I was giddy with joy. And don't forget that *I* spent nine months safe and sound in a prisoner-of-war camp, reading *Adam Bede.*"

"Not her best work," said Ellwood, faintly. "Didn't they have *Middlemarch*?"

"*Adam Bede* is a very fine novel," said Gaunt. "I've read it four times."

Ellwood was surprised into laughter.

"Good grief," he said.

Gaunt laughed too, his eyes soft and searching.

"It's good to see you, Elly," he said.

Ellwood had to turn away, because it was painful to look at something so lovely without knowing if he would be allowed to keep it.

"I'm going home in a few days," he said. "To Thornycroft." He stared intently at his notebook and kept his tone casual. "My mother would like to see you."

Out of the corner of his eye, Ellwood saw Gaunt smile.

"I'd better visit her, then," said Gaunt.

Pain twinged deep inside Ellwood's head, as if someone was wringing out a fistful of his optic nerves.

"Christ. My head . . ."

"Don't talk any more," said Gaunt.

"All right," said Ellwood. A profound weariness washed over him, and to his embarrassment, he spoke without thinking. "Don't go."

"I won't," said Gaunt. "I'm not going anywhere."

THIRTY-EIGHT

ELLWOOD FELL ASLEEP. His dark hair was stringy with sweat. His right eyebrow curved gracefully at the arch, just as Gaunt remembered.

He hadn't let himself imagine his reunion with Ellwood, because he had been so convinced that it would never happen. It hadn't once occurred to him that Ellwood wouldn't be pleased to see him, if it did.

He did not fool himself into believing Ellwood's wound was the extent of the damage. More frightening than the bandages was the blankness in his remaining eye. The sense that Gaunt was looking at a stranger, one who did not love him and never would.

On the hospital bed, Ellwood stirred slightly, alive, vivid, lovelier than ever. Gaunt closed his eyes.

"Henry," came Ellwood's voice. Softer than before. Gaunt opened his eyes, and saw that Ellwood was watching him. "You look—are you all right?"

"Fine," answered Gaunt automatically.

"I know you're fine," said Ellwood, frowning. "But are you all right?"

Gaunt smiled through a long exhale of smoke, hope coursing through him.

"Yes," he said.

. . .

"But you only just got back," said Maud. She rose out of her chair and stood with her hand on the back of it.

"I want to get out of the city," said Gaunt.

"You can't go to Thornycroft. Mother will be distraught."

"You and Mother were all too happy to send me off in the first place," said Gaunt.

Maud blanched. "We didn't know," she said. "No one knew then how bad it was. I'm sorry."

Gaunt went to the bookcase and started pulling out the books he would take with him. The library at Thornycroft was well stocked with novels and poetry, but it was Classics Gaunt wanted: Plutarch and Xenophon and Thucydides, men who proved that Gaunt's own troubles were ancient and survivable. They were clear-eyed, the Greeks. They did not dress up the world with romance and chivalry, did not lure poetry-hearted fools into evil.

"You do know I'm sorry?" said Maud. And Gaunt had known, or, at least, had known that it was inevitable that both of them would put everything into the war effort, once it had begun. Anything to speed it on.

"I would have signed up anyway," he said.

"That's what Sidney said." There was a pause, and when Maud next spoke she sounded near tears. "Aren't you glad to see me?"

Gaunt put down his copy of Herodotus and turned towards her. "Maud . . . !"

"Well? Are you? Do you know that the very first thing you said to me was 'How's Elly?' All these months I've mourned you, and you . . ."

"I had to know if he was alive."

"Henry . . ." Maud tilted her head up to the ceiling, trying not to cry. "I've been reading Edward Carpenter."

Gaunt grew still. He had heard of Edward Carpenter, of course, although he had never dared to read any of his works, books like *The Intermediate Sex,* which argued that homosexual love was, if anything, purer and more noble than heterosexual romance.

"Some sort of pansy philosopher, isn't he?" he said.

"I'm not going to marry Sidney," said Maud. "You can stop *hating* me."

"Don't be ridiculous," said Gaunt. "Why should I hate you?"

"I didn't understand, at first," said Maud, blinking rapidly and still looking up at the ceiling. "I'm not sure I do now. And you've both been very cruel."

"I haven't a clue what you're talking about, Maud. Perhaps you need to get some rest."

"I'm not going to marry him," she said again, moving her head to look Gaunt in the eye.

"Do as you like," said Gaunt. "I've never tried to control you. I don't go in for that sort of thing."

"I don't *care*, Henry," said Maud. "I don't care that you're—"

She cut herself off, blushing. Gaunt's entire body was numb and tingling. He knew his mother was somewhere in the house, perhaps within earshot. They only had one servant now, but she was far away, in the kitchen.

"I don't care," said Maud again.

Gaunt took a deep, shuddering breath, and thought of Devi and Pritchard.

"Perhaps things might be clearer if you said what you meant," he said.

"You're . . . you're in love with Sidney."

Gaunt laughed a little shakily. Maud looked as if she had been expecting him to deny it. When he didn't, she took a step closer.

"It's true, isn't it?"

Gaunt nodded. A tear rolled down Maud's cheek and splashed onto the carpet.

"You might have told me," she said.

"How could I?"

"It was cruel of Sidney. It's humiliating, to feel as if you have a place with someone when you haven't," said Maud.

Gaunt turned back to the bookshelf.

"Don't you? He proposed."

He felt her arms wrap around him. She rested her head in between his shoulder blades.

"Are you . . . careful?" she asked.

"Yes," he said.

"And you're sure it's not just—just school, and the army?"

Gaunt stared unseeingly at the little pile of Classical texts he had made. The spines were old and worn. Maud moved her face gently against the fabric of his suit. Slowly, Gaunt covered her hands with his.

"I'm sure," he said.

"It makes me frightened for you," said Maud. She broke away and went to stand by the chair. "It isn't fair, or right."

How empty his limbs felt. He pressed his fingertips against the clothbound edition of Herodotus.

"Yes, it's an abomination," he said, lightly, although he knew it wasn't. Knew it couldn't be. It was the cleanest, purest part of him.

Maud reeled around.

"That's not what I meant," she said. Gaunt turned to look at her.

"No?"

"No," she said. "No."

They watched each other for a moment.

"No," she said, again.

"I wish I could have told you," said Gaunt.

"You mustn't keep things from me any more."

"I won't," said Gaunt, a feeling of weightlessness stealing over him like daybreak.

"I'm not going to marry him," said Maud. "He doesn't want me any more than I want him. I doubt he ever did."

Gaunt pulled his mouth into an unsuccessful smile. He was painfully aware that he was willing to throw over his life for Ellwood, but that Ellwood might already have finished with his phosphorus-bright, phosphorus-quick love for Gaunt.

"Oh, I think he did. Perhaps he still does, I don't know." He paused, not meeting her eye. "It would kill me if you married him."

"I know," said Maud. "I won't."

"I'm afraid I've been a terrible brother."

"Persuade Father to let me go to Berlin after the War, and you'll have made up for it."

Gaunt went to her and pulled her close, kissing the top of her head.

"Μεγαλοψυχίη το φέρειν πραέως πλημμέλειαν," he said. *It is magnanimous to bear offence calmly.*

"Συγγνώμη τιμωρίας κρείσσων," said Maud. *Forgiveness is better than revenge.*

"You belong in Oxford, not Berlin," said Gaunt. "Was that Thales?"

"Pittacus."

"Ah. I should brush up on my sixth-century sages."

"You're really going to Thornycroft now?" asked Maud. "Couldn't you stay until Monday?"

Gaunt thought of Ellwood, scribbling madly in his notebook. Maud looked rather small, as though she already knew what his answer would be.

"All right," he said. "I'll send Elly a telegram and let him know I've changed plans."

"Thank you," said Maud.

Gaunt paused at the door.

"I . . ." he started, but he didn't know how to begin.

Maud waited.

"I should never have told you, if you hadn't asked," he said, finally. "So. Thank you. For asking."

Maud smiled.

"Go send your telegram," she said.

———

Thornycroft Manor looked three hundred years old, but in fact Ellwood's father had copied it from a house he had taken in the Lake District in 1885. It was decorated in the Arts and Crafts style, with finely carved dark wood mouldings, William Morris wallpaper, and stained-glass windows. Gaunt had always loved it there. It was graceful and elegant, and seemed frozen in some dreamlike state of calm, no matter how many guests filled the rooms.

Gaunt's weekend with Maud had largely consisted of him trying not to notice how heavily his mother was drinking, how absent his already distant father had become. He understood, now, why Maud had wanted him to stay.

"They want me to leave my work at the hospital," she told him. "To stay home and help with housekeeping."

"You'd be terrible at housekeeping."

"Yes, but so is the maid," said Maud. "It's been impossible to find decent servants."

So Gaunt had a stern talk with his parents, with all the importance of one who has returned from the dead, telling them that Maud must on no account be prevented from serving her important role in the war effort.

He didn't know if they would listen. They both seemed utterly broken. His father worked such long hours at the bank that Maud said they did not see him for days on end, and his mother was vague and bleary-eyed from drink, even in the mornings.

On Monday, Maud went with him to the train station. She was returning to her hospital living quarters. He was glad not to be leaving her alone with their disintegrating parents.

"Say hello to Sidney for me," she said, on the platform.

Gaunt tried to smile. Maud kissed him on the cheek and said goodbye.

Ellwood's mother welcomed Gaunt warmly, but Ellwood wouldn't look at him, and did not say a word. Mrs. Ellwood filled the silence as best she could, and Gaunt tried to be courteous. It was hard to concentrate when Ellwood looked so sour.

They sat at the varnished wood table in the dining room. Gaunt reminded himself not to inhale his shepherd's pie (he was still always, always hungry), and Mrs. Ellwood smiled at him.

"It's so kind of you to visit Sidney. I do think it's hard for our boys when they're back from the front; they grow so used to companionship in France!"

There was a sudden sound of smashing crystal. Red wine trickled down the papered walls in rivulets where Ellwood had thrown his glass. Ellwood stood, alight with hatred, his mouth tightly shut. His hands shook at his sides.

"Sidney!"

"Companionship," he spat. "How jolly!"

"Sidney, please sit down!" cried his mother.

"I need some air," said Ellwood. He stormed out.

Mrs. Ellwood tried not to cry as the maid swept away the shards of crystal.

"It's the shell shock," said Gaunt. "He isn't cross with you, really."

Mrs. Ellwood shook her head. "He looks at me as if he hates me. I think he hates everyone who hasn't been to the front."

"It's . . . difficult for civilians to understand."

"I can't bear it!"

Gaunt found his handkerchief. It was clean. He gave it to Mrs. Ellwood, who smiled weakly at him and dabbed her eyes.

"I'm sorry," she said.

"That's quite all right. I sometimes think the War is hardest on the parents."

"You can't imagine how helpless I feel. I've read his poems."

"It's not so bad as all that," lied Gaunt. "It can be rather fun, when you're in billets. And you're only in the front line for a day or two before you're back in the reserve, and then it's all quite dull."

Mrs. Ellwood reached across the table for his hand and pressed it. He suspected she knew *something* about Ellwood, although he doubted she really understood; but she treated Gaunt as a privileged friend, and he and Ellwood always had rooms next to each other when he came to stay.

"You're very kind, Henry," she said. "I don't mean to make a fuss."

"I'd better go check on him."

"Thank you. I'm very glad you've come," said Mrs. Ellwood.

THIRTY-NINE

ELLWOOD WALKED ALONG the edge of the lily pond. The evening light was pale and cool, and he put one foot carefully in front of the other, testing his balance along the rim of the water.

He heard footsteps on gravel and looked up to see Gaunt, hands in pockets, strolling towards him.

He had seen Gaunt so often, at the front. He hadn't realised until the real Gaunt materialised how far his memories had strayed from the original. His mind had emphasised the crookedness of his features, the broken-mirror quality of his face. He had forgotten how intimidating he was, towering and strong-shouldered, with those purposeful eyes, that firm mouth. Only he was different now. Softer. There was something more open in his expression.

He came to stand next to Ellwood on the lip of the pool.

"Sorry about that," said Ellwood. He wasn't really sorry. Embarrassed, maybe. But *companionship*, to talk about the front as if it were a country-house party . . .

"It's hard for parents. They know something is being done to us, and they can't stop it."

"The heart bleeds," said Ellwood dryly. "Truly, what is my suffering, next to the struggles of middle-aged British ladies?"

Gaunt was silent.

"You think I'm being unfair," said Ellwood.

"Yes."

Ellwood didn't have the energy to argue his case, or even to feel it.

"The sky is bland," he said.

"Yes, I've noticed that, too. Not like in Belgium."

"I can't stand it here."

"I know," said Gaunt. But he did not look the way Ellwood felt: pent up and vengeful. Gaunt looked relaxed. Happy.

"You seem awfully steady."

"Some things are simpler than I thought. You're alive, after all."

Ellwood nudged at a lily pad with his toe, watching how the water rolled up into little balls against the leather of his shoe.

"Is there a Tennyson poem for us now, Elly?"

Ellwood hopped down from the edge of the pond.

"Tennyson," he scoffed. "What did *he* know? Imagining shipwrecks from his sofa, or battles in his bed. Stupid old fool."

"Keats, then," said Gaunt, after a pause.

"You returned from the dead to talk about Grecian urns, did you?"

"No, that's not it," said Gaunt. He did not elaborate. They waited, rather than watched, as the sun set.

Ellwood's bedroom was in an isolated wing of the house. Gaunt stayed next door. He did not go to his own room, however. He followed Ellwood into his bedroom and shut the door. Ellwood stood, still as stone. Gaunt tentatively put his hands on his waist and pulled him close.

"Elly," he said, as if he were urging him to look at something. Ellwood could not answer.

Gaunt kissed him, carefully avoiding the bandages. Ellwood kissed back, but the part of him that would once have felt euphoria was sleeping, or dead.

Gaunt undressed him with a look of intense concentration on his face. He kissed Ellwood's shoulders. He traced Ellwood's ribs and the muscles of his stomach. Once Ellwood was naked, Gaunt laughed, a joyful, spilling sort of laughter, like a cup overflowing.

"This feels rather uneven," said Ellwood, because Gaunt was still fully dressed. Gaunt's hands flew self-consciously to his chest.

"I got a bit banged up at Loos," he mumbled.

"I don't care."

Gaunt trailed his hand over Ellwood's torso.

"You're perfect," he said wistfully.

Ellwood snorted.

"Oh, yes, perfect," he said, and began to fumble with Gaunt's buttons. Gaunt stopped him.

"Let's—here, get into bed."

They climbed into bed, and Ellwood leant to turn off the lamp, thinking that might assuage Gaunt's fears about undressing. But Gaunt stopped him there, too.

"I want to look at you," he said.

"Good grief, *why*?"

Gaunt didn't answer. He pushed Ellwood onto his back and propped himself onto one elbow, staring at Ellwood as if he were an exhibit at a museum.

Ellwood knew there was a quotation for this particular, painful speechlessness, but it did not come to him. All his words were gone. There was something surging gloriously in his chest, and he had no way to express it. He slowly unbuttoned Gaunt's shirt. Gaunt held very still, and cast nervous glances at him as the shirt fell open, revealing a mass of thick red scars. Ellwood forced himself not to balk at the sight. Gaunt's once strong, powerful chest was now warped and fragile. Only one nipple remained, and the bones stuck out strangely. They hadn't healed well, and Gaunt was so thin that it was all the more noticeable.

Ellwood pressed his palm to the star-shaped centre of the wound.

Gaunt made a small, peculiar sound.

"Does it hurt?" asked Ellwood.

"No-o." He paused. "My lungs ache a bit when I go up the stairs too fast."

There was a quotation for scars, too. Ellwood groped blindly for it in his mind, but found nothing.

Since his mouth was useless, he pressed it to Gaunt's mangled skin in long, hopeless kisses.

"Do you mind them?" asked Gaunt.

"That would be hypocritical."

"Yes, but . . ."

"I hate them," said Ellwood. "But I don't mind."

Gaunt seemed to understand. He put a hand on Ellwood's head and made soft sounds as Ellwood worked his way down.

Our bodies were used to stop bullets, thought Ellwood. He could think of nothing else. His mouth was busy, and it hurt with a stinging pain on the left side of his cheek. He thought of a torn-off leg he had once found in the woods while on reserve. Blood so clotted it was nearly black.

"Elly," said Gaunt.

Ellwood tried to focus. It didn't work. He thought of Grimsey's groin, ripped out by shrapnel.

"Elly," said Gaunt again. "Stop."

Ellwood sat up, lifting his head. Gaunt had propped himself up on his elbows, and his eyes dropped to between Ellwood's legs.

"You're not . . ." he said.

Ellwood was bowled over by ravenous anger, at himself for having broken, at Gaunt for having noticed.

"Why should that matter? Lie down."

"Elly."

"Lie down," said Ellwood. "And *be quiet.*"

Gaunt looked at him for a moment longer. Thin lines across his forehead, jaw tight and wide. Ellwood glared back.

Gaunt had never been able to stand up to him in bed. He collapsed backwards with a sigh, and Ellwood bent over him once more.

Afterwards, Gaunt took him by the arms and tugged him up to lie beside him.

"Can I do anything for you?" he asked.

Ellwood stared at the ceiling. His hair had flopped into his face, he could feel it on the right half of his forehead, but not the left, still covered in bandages.

Gaunt stroked the strands out of his face.

"Elly?"

"No," said Ellwood. "Nothing."

Gaunt nodded. His fingers continued to run through Ellwood's hair. It made Ellwood feel as if his head were melting.

"I love you," said Gaunt, his eyes moving restlessly, enquiringly, over Ellwood's face.

Ellwood did not answer. Gaunt waited for a few seconds, his expression growing less and less open, until he drew his lips together in a tight smile and murmured, "Well. Good night."

Ellwood said nothing. He couldn't. Gaunt turned over, away from him. After a long while, Gaunt's breath became steady and even.

In the dark, Ellwood's anger grew, until he felt helpless paralysis in his chest, and had to leave the bedroom. He wandered the corridors, thoughts stuttering through his head, biting at each other's heels, until he couldn't think at all.

Gaunt was cautious around him the next day, and this prudence made Ellwood want to punch him.

At breakfast, his mother smiled.

"How did you sleep, dear?" she asked. What on earth did she expect him to say? She wanted him to pretend nothing had changed; wanted nothing more than for her comfortable Edwardian life to continue indefinitely, although it was the cracks in that life that had yawned open and swallowed him up.

Ellwood did not answer.

"Fine weather today," said Gaunt.

"Very," said Ellwood's mother. "You two ought to take luncheon out on the lake."

"I'm going riding," said Ellwood, because he knew Gaunt wouldn't join him. He was right. Gaunt sequestered himself in the library to work on his translation of Thucydides instead.

The hunting stallions had long ago been commandeered by the army, so Ellwood saddled up their only remaining horse, a useless creature named Conker, who was more suited to pulling carriages than galloping across fields. He was bad-tempered and unresponsive, but then, so was Ellwood. They cantered to the local pub, where Ellwood spent the day becoming thoroughly drunk. Not drunk enough, however, to avoid overhearing people's conversations about the War— Lloyd George, and General Haig, and peace terms, and cowardice, and putting Prussians in their place.

Neither Gaunt nor his mother said anything when he returned, dizzy and slurring, and fell asleep at the dinner table. He awoke late that night, alone in his bed.

Gaunt followed him to the stables the next morning.

"If you'd told me you were going to the pub, I'd have come with you," he said.

"I'm not going to the pub," said Ellwood. He had a hip flask of rum in his pocket. He didn't need the pub.

"I'm sorry if what I said the other day angered you," said Gaunt.

"No wonder you've never had any friends, Gaunt," said Ellwood, hating every inch of him, from his huge feet to his sandy hair. "You don't know how to behave."

Gaunt stiffened. "I have friends."

Ellwood laughed. "Don't fool yourself. Sandys just wanted to fuck you."

Gaunt turned and walked out of the stables, just as Ellwood had known he would, and yet it wasn't enough. Ellwood followed him out.

"Devi, I suppose you count Devi, although he was just some upstart Indian boy who weaselled his way into Eton," said Ellwood.

"Shut up."

"And then, me. Three friends in total, and one of them is *dead*."

Gaunt stopped in his tracks. He did not turn around, and Ellwood didn't dare touch him.

"Do you want to compare dead friends, Ellwood?" asked Gaunt, quietly, and Ellwood felt as if the lid of his brain had blown off.

"*There is no comparison!*" he shouted. "You never fucking loved anyone, so there was no one for you to *lose!*"

Gaunt turned slowly to look at Ellwood. To Ellwood's astonishment, his face was not angry, but gentle.

"That's not true, Elly," he said, and walked away.

Ellwood couldn't go riding, after that. He hid his face in Conker's neck and tried to cry, but couldn't. He could only heave, shuddering with powerlessness.

He ended up getting drunk, fully clothed, in his bathtub. By the time Gaunt found him, Ellwood had unwound his bandages and was plucking at the sick eyelashes with clumsy fingers, whistling "The Blue Danube."

Gaunt paused in the doorway, a peculiar, fond smile on his lips. The same expression he used to get in school when Ellwood recited poetry to people who wished he wouldn't; the same expression he had had on Divisional Rest in Loos, when Ellwood touched him more than was appropriate. It hadn't ever changed. Gaunt had always looked at him like that, as if Ellwood's flaws were qualities.

Ellwood turned away and tried to stick the bandages back in place.

"Feeling nostalgic, are we?" asked Gaunt.

When Ellwood didn't answer, Gaunt kicked off his shoes and stepped into the bathtub.

"What are you doing?" asked Ellwood.

"Budge over," said Gaunt, settling himself between Ellwood's legs, and resting his back against Ellwood's chest.

Ellwood wanted him so badly—or did he only want to want him?

"It's like in Hundreds," said Gaunt.

Only in Hundreds it had been Ellwood who had leant against Gaunt. That wouldn't work now. Gaunt's chest was too fragile, and anyway, Ellwood didn't want Gaunt to see his face.

Ellwood passed him the rum. Gaunt took a swig and leant his head into Ellwood's neck.

"Do you remember?" he asked. Ellwood laughed, slightly manically.

"Yes."

"I almost kissed you," said Gaunt. Ellwood took a deep breath of Gaunt's clean-smelling hair. He used to stare at the back of Gaunt's head in Chapel, and wonder how it was that such an ordinary person could have trapped him so completely.

"Why didn't you?" he asked. Gaunt turned his head on Ellwood's shoulder to look at him. The room spun.

"Well, there were people there," said Gaunt.

"In Munich, then."

Gaunt reached out, slowly, and peeled the bandages away from Ellwood's face. Ellwood held still and let him.

"You shouldn't pick at it," said Gaunt. He ran one finger delicately over the raw skin.

Ellwood tried to laugh. "Why? Because it might scar?"

Gaunt shifted so that he could turn around more. Ellwood drove his head back into the cool enamel of the bathtub and watched as Gaunt leant closer.

"Don't," said Ellwood, but Gaunt ignored him. He pressed his mouth against Ellwood's shattered cheekbone.

They were still for a moment before Ellwood broke away.

"I don't want your pity," he said.

Gaunt laughed. "Good, because you haven't got it." He laughed again as he settled himself against Ellwood's chest.

They were silent for several long minutes.

"I shouldn't have said that, earlier," said Ellwood, eventually. "About Sandys."

"And Gideon," said Gaunt.

"Yes," said Ellwood, trying not to bristle at the notion of Gaunt defending Devi, and calling him by his first name. "I'm sorry."

Gaunt drank from the hip flask and handed it back to Ellwood. Ellwood brought it to his lips, but when he tasted the rum on his tongue he suddenly wished he were sober, and lowered it.

"I've decided it doesn't matter whether you love me back," said Gaunt.

Some long-dead poet must have written the lines with which to answer, but Ellwood no longer knew them.

FORTY

ELLWOOD'S MOOD VARIED so wildly that sometimes Gaunt avoided him for days at a time. He was cruel to his mother and the servants. He made sneering remarks to Gaunt about the safety of the prison camps.

He apologised afterwards, stiffly. When he was not angry, he was stiff, even in the brief moments when he and Gaunt came together. After the day in the bathtub, Gaunt followed Ellwood to bed every night, and Ellwood didn't tell him to stop. He crushed his mouth to Gaunt's in a hollow, rageful imitation of affection.

As he lay in bed, Ellwood rigid and pretending to sleep beside him, Gaunt reflected that it did not feel like loving Ellwood. It felt like loving a brittle impostor, one who had stolen Ellwood and would not return him. And yet, Gaunt was powerless: he loved every part of Ellwood, changed or not. If there was a lonelier feeling, Gaunt could not imagine it.

In the hospital, Gaunt had spoken to Ellwood's doctor.

"Will he recover?" he asked, in the corridor outside Ellwood's ward.

"Oh, if it weren't for that eye, we'd send him straight back," said the doctor, looking at a clipboard.

"From the shell shock, I mean."

"Shell shock like that never harmed a soldier," said the doctor cheerfully. "It's a shame we can't pass him for active duty. The man's a machine."

As shell shock went, it wasn't so bad. Ellwood did not stutter, or scream, or refuse to eat. He did not have long lapses of memory, or strange physical pains. But Gaunt wondered whether a mechanical man could become human once more, or whether, like the battlefields in France, the landscape of Ellwood's character had been irrevocably marred by the War.

All Gaunt could do was be patient, and wait, and hope that the traces of tenderness Ellwood sometimes showed him were signs that he would one day love Gaunt again.

Some days, Ellwood was monosyllabic. Others, he spoke like a speeding train.

"I've written twelve poems this week," he announced at breakfast. "Only ten are any good but it doesn't matter because they're all gory and horrible, not a scrap of beauty in them, so they'll be published, all right—isn't it funny how that has changed, how two years ago we wanted nothing more than Rupert Brooke and—" he stumbled, he had clearly been about to quote from "The Soldier," but he never quoted poetry any more. "—and, and, all that sort of heroic stuff about dying for glory, but now all you've got to do is describe just how much blood spills out of a chap when his stomach's been torn out by shrapnel and people lap it up, *delicious, how horrid, those poor boys, can someone pass the eggs, I'm ravenous—*"

"Do be quiet, Elly," said Gaunt, because Mrs. Ellwood was peering tearily at her scrambled eggs.

"Oh, I don't mean to be unpleasant, I wouldn't want that, not to be *unpleasant*, how awful, only I do think it's peculiar, how much more drawn people are to disaster than to beauty, how curious we are about the things that can be done to a body, don't you find that interesting, Gaunt?"

"No," said Gaunt.

Mrs. Ellwood blinked several times, fast. A fat tear dropped onto her plate.

"I find it terribly interesting," said Ellwood. "Terribly! I say, do you remember the sound it makes when a man tries to speak after he's been shot in the throat?"

"Yes," said Gaunt. "I do."

Ellwood put his hands flat on the table.

"Of course," he said, quietly. "I'm sorry. Of course you remember."

Gaunt gave a slow nod, and Ellwood sheepishly took a bite of toast. They ate on in silence.

When she had finished her breakfast, Mrs. Ellwood hoisted a smile onto her face.

"What would you like to do for your birthday tomorrow?" she asked Ellwood.

Ellwood made a mean-spirited giggling sound. "Shall we go to the zoo and eat ice cream? Will there be cake? *Do* say there will be cake. At nineteen, I'm sure I will become a real man at last and perhaps you could finally explain to me the finer points of procreation."

Gaunt smashed his cutlery down onto his plate.

"If you're going to be a cad, Ellwood, do it elsewhere. No one has any interest in witnessing your humiliation."

Ellwood's malicious smile disappeared.

"You're an awful prig, Gaunt. I'm going riding."

That night, Ellwood crept into Gaunt's bed, trailing light, sorrowful kisses all over his face and hair. He was hard for once, and considerate. Gaunt's thoughts went quiet as Ellwood took over, touching him, pressing himself slowly into Gaunt with quiet reverence; a physical apology. Gaunt tried to pretend it was Ellwood, the real Ellwood, the gleaming, hopeful, true one. Neither of them spoke. Ellwood closed his eyes and buried his face in Gaunt's neck as he moved, would not look at him. Gaunt's chest twisted as he remembered all the times he had done that to Ellwood, before. Only once had he been brave enough to look Ellwood in the face all the way through. Ellwood had stayed giddy with happiness for a whole day, a happiness that Gaunt realised now had been relief.

Afterwards, Ellwood was solicitous and kind.

"Did I hurt you? It's been a while—at least—"

He went red and looked away.

"No, it has," said Gaunt. "But I'm fine."

Ellwood went to the washbasin and wet a facecloth. He brought it back and wiped Gaunt down, frequently dropping his head to kiss him, his thighs, his hips, his battered chest. When he was done, he lay beside Gaunt, slipping his head into the crook of Gaunt's shoulder as if it belonged there.

"It's not me you ought to apologise to," said Gaunt. He knew he had guessed right, because Ellwood went still in his arms.

"I can't stand to look at her," he said.

Gaunt bent his head and touched Ellwood's remaining eyebrow with his lips.

"It's not her fault that Austria declared war on Serbia," he said.

"I never said it was."

Gaunt didn't answer.

Ellwood sighed. "I wish I was back at the front," he said. "I feel filthy."

"I know," said Gaunt. "Me, too."

FORTY-ONE

I N AUGUST, the doctor told Ellwood he no longer needed to wear
the bandages on his face. Ellwood went home and locked himself
in his room. He took off the bandages, looked in the mirror and put
them back on.

———

Tuesday 15th August, 1916
Kingswood Court, Surrey

Dear Sidney,

Good to hear your head's all right. My shoulder's healed
up nicely and I just passed my medical. I'll be heading back
to France by the end of the month. I was thinking of visiting
Preshute on Saturday. Why don't you and Gaunt join? I was
astounded to hear he had survived. He'll be dining out on that
tale for a long time yet.

Let me know—it would be fine to see you.

Your friend,
Cyril Roseveare

———

The following Saturday, Gaunt and Ellwood put on their uniforms and boarded the train to Wiltshire. They bought first-class tickets and settled into an empty carriage.

The moment the train rattled into motion, Ellwood's heart began to beat urgently in his throat. Trains crashed, didn't they, why, just the year before, there was the Quintinshill crash, over two hundred men killed, soldiers—one didn't need to be at the front to die—

"Elly?" said Gaunt.

Ellwood glanced at the luggage rack. There was a lady's hatbox crammed into it. It wouldn't take much for the box to come tumbling over the rails and hit him in the face, and his wounds would burst open again—or perhaps he might lose his other eye—

"Elly," said Gaunt again. "Breathe."

"I want to get off," said Ellwood.

"All right."

"Pull the cord, I want to get off."

"Can you wait until the next station?" asked Gaunt.

If the train crashed, the glass windows would break into long, piercing shards. They would rip holes into Gaunt's body. Ellwood had a sudden image of blood pouring down the train carriage, the way it had flooded down the trench when one of his men had had his insides scooped out by shrapnel from a trench mortar.

Gaunt put his arm around Ellwood and held him close. It was at once comforting and terrifying. Ellwood was keenly conscious of the people making their way down the corridor.

"Gaunt," said Ellwood, straining to be calm. "I don't think . . ."

Gaunt leant into Ellwood's ear.

"We're both captains with Military Crosses and wound stripes. You could probably fuck me right now and they'd call it front-line camaraderie."

Ellwood was shocked into laughter, which continued and grew until he was no longer in control of the strange, hiccoughing sounds he made. Gaunt held him tight, muttering quietly in Greek.

"You do . . . realise . . ." Ellwood gasped, "that I have . . . no clue . . . what you're saying?"

"Probably for the best," said Gaunt. "Thucydides isn't actually very comforting. Menander might have been better, but I haven't committed much of him to memory."

"Say it again," said Ellwood. His body still throbbed with fear, but he could breathe.

"Ο δε πόλεμος . . . βίαιος διδάσκαλος," said Gaunt.

Ellwood closed his eyes and focused, not on splintered bones sticking out of stumps, but on his school Greek.

"War is . . . a violent teacher?" he said, eventually.

Gaunt smiled at him. "That's right."

The countryside streamed greenly past the windows.

"It didn't teach *me* anything," said Ellwood.

Gaunt looked thoughtful, but was silent.

When the train stopped, Gaunt asked if he still wanted to get off, and Ellwood shook his head. Gaunt tucked Ellwood back under his arm and read the cricket scores in the paper.

At Reading, two women got on the train and sat opposite them. One stared for a long time, misty-eyed, then whispered in carrying tones to her companion: "They make such good friends at the front . . . !"

FORTY-TWO

PRESHUTE WAS EMPTY for the summer. Gaunt was grateful for that. He didn't think he could have borne the admiring looks of fifteen-year-olds, nor the apprehensive, questioning stares of the Sixth Form boys. Ellwood was still pale and shivery after his funny turn on the train. He stuck close to Gaunt's side, their arms in constant contact.

Roseveare waited for them by the gates of the cemetery. He had filled out since school, and he was handsome in his officer's uniform. He had been promoted to lieutenant after the Somme.

"Sidney!" he cried, throwing his arms around Ellwood. His eyes were firmly fixed on the undamaged side of Ellwood's face, as if he had determined beforehand never to glance at the bandages.

He extended Gaunt a handshake. "You're supposed to be dead," he said.

"Yes, so I've been told."

"My father said it was a ripping yarn," said Roseveare.

"He was awfully good to us in Amsterdam. He was so worried about you."

Roseveare looked surprised. "Was he? Aren't fathers funny. All he said when I got home was that I'd better go back to France and try for the VC."

They wandered up and down the overgrown graveyard, relishing the quiet birdsong, the lush, undamaged grass, the ancient headstones, which had so long ago shed any trace of tragedy.

"I suppose we ought to say hello to Mr. Hammick," said Roseveare, sounding resigned.

Ellwood groaned. "You know perfectly well he's going to say he wishes he were twenty years younger so that he didn't have to miss out on the fun."

"It does seem rather exhausting," said Gaunt.

"Oh, all right, let's go to the Tea Room on High Street," said Roseveare. "Although we must see him afterwards. It's our duty."

Gaunt and Ellwood readily agreed. They had long ago learnt, in much more trying circumstances, how much easier it was to do one's duty after tea than before.

The Tea Room was usually packed with rowdy schoolboys slathering clotted cream on scones, but today it was quiet. They were shown to a corner table by the window, and Gaunt was silent as Roseveare and Ellwood exchanged news.

"Grimsey's healing up all right in London," said Roseveare. "He had a spot of gangrene, but they caught it in time."

"Is he still angry with me for saving his life?"

"Furious."

"Well, he's impossible to please," said Ellwood.

The waitress came with tea and a platter of cakes and sandwiches. Gaunt ate without much enthusiasm. Food shortages had taken their toll, and the cake was bland and mealy.

"We wouldn't like Grimsey so much if he weren't so very unpleasant," said Roseveare. "That's part of his charm. Like you, Gaunt."

"Thanks," said Gaunt.

"Anytime," said Roseveare. "Say, did you hear about that Indian boy from Eton?"

Gaunt's hand stilled on his teacup.

"Gideon," said Ellwood, and Gaunt looked up, surprised. Ellwood never used Devi's first name.

"Something like that," said Roseveare. "Do you know him?"

"What about him?" asked Gaunt, impatiently.

"Apparently he made it all the way to the Swiss border, pretending to be a Turk! He was caught at the last moment by a Berlin diplomat who was in South Germany on holiday. Questioned your friend in Turkish and discovered he couldn't speak a word."

"But—" said Gaunt, trying to form a sentence. He looked to Ellwood for help.

"So he's alive?" asked Ellwood. "Last we knew of him, he had been shot."

"Oh, very much alive," said Roseveare. "All the Etonians are talking about him. It's his tenth escape attempt. You know him?"

Gaunt nodded, then started to laugh.

"Yes," he said. "He's really all right?"

"Back in some German prisoner-of-war camp," said Roseveare. "I think he hurt his leg; he won't be able to try again for a few months."

Gaunt shook with laughter for so long that Ellwood and Roseveare began to exchange looks.

"Sorry," he said, finally. "Sorry, it's just—good news."

"Yes," said Roseveare. There was something complicated about his expression. "It's a wonderful thing, when your friends live."

Gaunt had read Roseveare's letters to Ellwood. He knew how casually Roseveare mentioned all the people he had lost: his two brothers, Harry Straker, Finch, Aldworth, Pritchard, West. He had been one of the most popular boys in school, yet he no longer had many friends.

"But I hear it's unlikely you'll be sent back?" said Roseveare to Gaunt.

"My doctor says he'll kill me himself if he finds out I've been to France," said Gaunt. "He's a little dramatic. I'm sure I could manage."

"What will you do until the end of the War, then?"

"I'll go where I'm told. Probably train junior officers in the countryside somewhere."

Roseveare pensively raised his teacup to his lips.

"What about after the War?" he asked.

"Oxford, surely," said Ellwood.

"I don't know," said Gaunt. "It would feel odd to be a student again."

Roseveare glanced quickly between them.

"Hmm," he said. "My uncle is always looking for clever young men to work in the British Embassy. In Brazil."

Gaunt choked on his cucumber sandwich. Roseveare thumped him on the back.

"Are you all right, Henry?" asked Ellwood.

"Brazil?" repeated Gaunt.

"Yes," said Roseveare. "I should think he'd want to hire both of you, if you were willing."

Gaunt could tell Ellwood had not understood yet.

"Aldworth wanted to go to Brazil," Gaunt told him. Ellwood's eye widened.

"Yes," said Roseveare, "he did." He frowned at his scone. They had been close, Roseveare and Aldworth. Gaunt remembered the way they used to stand together at Assembly, heads bent, talking in whispers. Both of them had had that air of holding something back that made people desperate to impress them.

"Cyril," said Ellwood weakly, "Cyril, you can't mean . . . for Gaunt and me to go . . . *together*."

"Sidney, old friend, you know I've always got your back. If you can't be happy in England, you jolly well ought to go be happy in Brazil."

"But England is magic," said Gaunt softly.

"What?" asked Roseveare.

"Nothing," said Gaunt. Ellwood stared at him.

"You don't have to give me your answer now, of course," said Roseveare. "I've already written to my uncle about you, just in case—"

He didn't finish. They both knew what he meant: *in case I'm killed before I can help you.*

Ellwood's hand went to his bandages.

"Cyril . . . did you tell him, about my . . . ?"

"Oh, yes," said Roseveare. His eyes flicked almost unwillingly to the bandages. "How bad is it, by the by?"

"Gaunt'll tell you," said Ellwood grimly. "He's seen it."

"No one will be able to accuse him of cowardice," said Gaunt. "He's fought in a war, all right."

"Ah," said Roseveare. "Well, you could always wear a mask."

"He doesn't need a mask," said Gaunt.

There was an awkward pause, in which Ellwood stared determinedly into his teacup, and Gaunt glowered at Roseveare.

"No, of course not," said Roseveare.

Ellwood looked up and placed a grateful hand on Roseveare's arm. "You're a good friend, Cyril."

"Nonsense. Now, both of you have been extremely rude. Aren't you going to ask if I have any news?"

"Well, have you?"

Roseveare grinned and waved his left hand in the air, revealing a shining gold ring.

"Cyril!" cried Ellwood. "You old devil! Who's the unfortunate victim?"

Roseveare grinned.

"Her name is Lillian. We've been friends since we were children. Here, I have a photograph." He showed them a pretty young woman with masses of thick blond hair.

"She's beautiful," said Ellwood. "What's she doing with you?"

"I'm a dashing officer in the British Army. Haven't you heard?"

"Those are a dime a dozen," said Ellwood.

"It's probably my good looks and charm, then."

"Doubt it," said Ellwood. "I say, Cyril, congratulations."

"Yes, congratulations," said Gaunt. "She looks marvellous."

"She is," said Roseveare. He started to put the photograph away, but was distracted by it, and paused to stare fondly at the picture. "Truth be told, I never thought I had a chance with her."

"I think you'll be very happy together," said Ellwood.

"Thanks," said Roseveare. He smirked at them. "I think you will be, too."

Gaunt busied himself with pouring more tea so that he wouldn't have to meet Roseveare's eyes. Next to him, Ellwood reached out and grabbed Roseveare's arm again.

"You've made me feel almost human, Cyril. Really, you have."

"Glad to be of service. I know *I've* been a bit out of sorts since the Somme. How did your friend David Hayes fare?"

"Pulverised hip," said Ellwood. "He's not answered any of my letters." He smiled, although it was too angry. "Writes to Gaunt, though."

"We ought to visit him," said Gaunt.

"Hip wounds are tricky," said Roseveare.

"He won't walk again," said Ellwood.

"It's my hands I'm most worried about," said Roseveare. "I think I could manage anything but that."

"Sight," said Gaunt. "I'm terrified of blindness."

Ellwood's profile was caught in light. From this angle, he looked whole, angelic.

"My face," he said.

There was a long silence.

"Well, you always were a vain bugger," said Roseveare. "Glad to see nothing's changed."

Gaunt waited for Ellwood to laugh before he let himself join in.

After tea, they visited Mr. Hammick.

"What wouldn't I give to be twenty years younger!" he exclaimed. "I would have been out there, fighting with the best of them."

FORTY-THREE

ON HIS WORST DAYS, Ellwood hated England. He hacked
through the countryside on Conker and saw nothing but
midges and stinging nettles. He hated the old men in the pub
who looked down on the French, on the Germans, who felt that the
colonies must be grateful for the chance to give something back to
Britain for a change. He hated the watery sunshine and the clouded,
milk-white sky. He hated Fagin and Shylock and Marlowe's Barabas.
They were a small-minded people, the English, and their greatest art
form, writing, was small-minded also, it was provincial; it did not
translate like music and painting, it was only for the English-speakers.
That Charlie and Bertie Pritchard, and Martin and Clarence Roseveare, and the Straker brothers, and West, and Finch, and Lantham,
and Gosset, should all have to die so that England could continue in
its smug small-mindedness seemed worse than a tragedy, for it was not
beautiful. No, it was only stupid, and Ellwood hated the muddy fields
and the dreary sheep and the clumsy, prehistoric rock formations that
they had all been asked to die for.

So he arranged to be sent back to France.

The morning he was due at the depot, he dressed carefully in his
uniform in front of the mirror. He slanted his head to one side and
wondered if he had really taken advantage of the fact that he had once
been handsome. He felt obscurely certain that he had squandered his

years of good looks, although he was not sure what else he could have done with them.

He took off the bandages and threw them in the wastepaper basket. In France it would be useful to be scarred. He would be doing bayonet training, and it would make his students listen more carefully. But that was not why he had decided to show his face. He had thrown the bandages away because there was something ruthless in his heart that burnt like acid and said he must make himself hate England more and more before he left it forever—for he did not intend to come back. He *wanted* people to stare at him in the train station. For children to cry. He wanted to hate them all so thoroughly he would never think of them again.

He went downstairs, his shoulders stiff and his expression fixed woodenly in place. His mother leapt to her feet, but Gaunt remained seated and did not look up.

"Oh, darling," said his mother. She took his shoulders and kissed him on both cheeks, without the slightest hesitation. "You look so handsome. Doesn't he, Henry?"

Gaunt glanced up, but looked down just as quickly. Coward, thought Ellwood, *coward.*

"Don't compliment him," said Gaunt. "You know it just goes to his head."

All of Ellwood's anger disappeared at once, as if it had been blown away by a north wind.

"Oh, come now, Gaunt, don't I deserve a little encouragement?" he asked.

"You're conceited enough as it is," said Gaunt. "Are you ready? We'll miss the train to London."

Ellwood smiled, more grateful than Gaunt would ever know.

On the train, Gaunt noticed the moment Ellwood started to panic, and began talking about Pericles' theories on maritime empires.

"You're ... the most boring ... person I know," said Ellwood, through gasps.

"What's interesting to note is that Pericles does not argue in favour of empire from a moral perspective, merely from a practical one. That is to say, that once an empire has been created—it's sort of a Faustian deal—it quickly accrues so many embittered enemies that to dismantle it becomes a frightening prospect."

"I don't *care* about Pericles."

"Feel free to change the subject," said Gaunt, grinning, because Ellwood could still scarcely breathe. "In the meantime: Pericles."

The people on the train snatched glimpses of Ellwood, pretending not to look. One woman caught his eye and gave him a pitying smile. Ellwood glared at her until she turned away. He was furious with her, just as he had been furious with the civilians on the train when he was given a white feather on his leave.

No one would ever give him a white feather again, at least. Not now that war had been written on his face.

———

Gaunt wished he could have spent a night with Ellwood's bare face, so that he might have had a chance to grow used to it. He wanted to stare at it until it made sense, until his brain stopped trying to fill it in and fix it. He didn't know how to look at Ellwood without hurting him.

Ellwood, with his keen sense of what *looked* right, was impeccable in his uniform. It was a testimony to his innate understanding of appearances. At the start of the War, it had been fashionable for soldiers to wear shabby uniforms, to prove they had really been in the trenches. Now that there was conscription, however, men who had been at the front wore their uniforms so neatly and sharply that they might have just walked out of a tailor's. Gaunt had not noticed this until Ellwood remarked on it.

As they neared London, and Ellwood seemed to grow calmer, Gaunt stopped talking about the Peloponnesian War. Ellwood stared out of the window, and Gaunt stared at Ellwood.

Gaunt was tempted to think, *Even with his injury, he is handsome,* but that wasn't quite right. Ellwood wasn't handsome *despite* his disfigurement. The loss of his eye had been what guaranteed his life, and so, to Gaunt, it was beautiful. He was grateful to that wound. He would not change a single, scarred inch of it.

When Ellwood turned away from the window, Gaunt hastily closed his eyes and pretended he had been napping.

They had lunch near the station. Everyone stared at Ellwood. Ellwood stared right back, an ugly, belligerent expression twisting his features. Gaunt was silent, not wanting to provoke him into an argument.

At noon, it was time for Ellwood to catch his train to Dover.

Gaunt shook his hand. "Good luck," he said.

"I'll be well out of it," said Ellwood.

"Yes, and stay there. Don't go . . . *visiting* the front."

"I'm not a *tourist.*"

"No, you're not."

The station was packed with young men and their tearful families. Everyone knew where they were going, although they were not permitted to say. The Battle of the Somme raged on, and the British Army poured soldiers into it as if it had a limitless supply.

Ellwood glanced down at the scrap of paper Gaunt had slipped him when they shook hands.

"It's nothing," said Gaunt. "Only Keats."

Ellwood tightened his grip around the piece of paper.

"Elly," said Gaunt, fear making him brave. "I'm not playing. I'm not just passing the time."

Ellwood looked at him as if he was trying to figure out some puzzle in Gaunt's face.

"Come to Brazil with me," said Ellwood. "After the War."

Gaunt thought of the darkling plain, of skating in the winter, of crunching over frosted grass early in the morning, of bluebell meadows in spring. There was nothing he wanted more than to spend the rest of his life on Wiltshire country lanes, Ellwood at his side. It was what he had fought for, what his friends had died for.

"I . . ."

"I used to feel rapture when I stood on the roof at Thornycroft and looked at the countryside," said Ellwood. "I went up this morning and tried to feel it."

Gaunt wished he could tell him he loved him, but they were in public, and it was illegal.

"I didn't feel a thing," said Ellwood. His gaze was hard and furious. "Brazil. Promise me."

Gaunt wondered whether Ellwood would ever feel anything but anger again.

"Yes," he said. "I promise."

FORTY-FOUR

HAYES WAS in a pleasant, sunny ward, propped up on clean white cushions. He thanked Gaunt for the grapes and chocolates he had brought, and laid them on his bedside table.

"You're supposed to be dead," he told Gaunt.

"People keep saying that."

"I used to see you moving out of the corner of my eye when I was tired," said Hayes. "You were bleeding and angry with me."

"I'm not angry with you. Or bleeding."

"No," said Hayes. He shifted uncomfortably in his bed. The covers were pulled up to his waist, but they were eerily flat over one hip. He was also missing the other leg, which had been amputated at the top of the thigh. He kept startling at small noises, and he blinked too often.

"Ellwood wanted to come, but he didn't have a chance," lied Gaunt. The truth was that Hayes had answered Gaunt's letters, but not Ellwood's, and Ellwood had pretended to be angry rather than admit he was hurt.

"Back to France already. He mentioned, in his letters. Shame about his eye," said Hayes.

"You ought to have written to him."

Hayes snorted. "He would have corrected my spelling."

"He wouldn't," said Gaunt.

"Ellwood and I aren't going to be real-world *chums*."

"I don't see why not," said Gaunt.

"He's too . . . he's too . . ." Hayes moved his hands, as if looking for the right word. Finally he sighed. "Rich."

"I'm rich," said Gaunt, wondering if this was code for something. Gaunt had come to realise that it often was, when people spoke of Ellwood. It wasn't his money that troubled people, but his heritage, his dark good looks, his confidence.

Hayes made a dismissive hand gesture. "He looks down on me," he said.

"I don't think he does," said Gaunt. Hayes scrunched up his face, and Gaunt decided to move on. "Listen, I didn't come here to argue about Ellwood. I've come to offer you a job."

Hayes tried to sit up. "What?"

"I talked to my father," said Gaunt. "When the army releases you, you can come work at the bank, if you like."

"I can't walk."

"There's a ground-floor office waiting for you."

Hayes scowled. "What about my accent?"

"Don't be an ass, David."

"Do you know what Ellwood said to me once? He said it was quite respectable. Like a shopkeeper's."

Gaunt laughed. "What an idiot," he said.

"You want to make a proper gentleman of me," said Hayes. "Give me a cushy bank job, so I can send my children to Preshute and teach them to be ashamed of where they came from."

"I don't have a better solution for you, David. I'm not saying it's fair."

Hayes sighed. "I don't mean to be ungrateful."

"England is changing," said Gaunt. "It's long overdue, but it's happening now."

"Not fast enough," said Hayes.

"He'll correct my spelling," said Hayes again, as Gaunt got up to leave at the end of an hour. But he said it differently this time, as if he was hoping Gaunt would argue with him.

"Ellwood respects you very much, David."

Hayes nodded, looking at the flat space where his legs should have been.

"All right," he said. "I know that. I'll write to him."

Mrs. Ellwood had told Gaunt he was welcome to return to Thornycroft until he went to Yorkshire to train junior officers, but he could not face the thought of the long, empty nights there. He went to his house in London, and tried not to think of Ellwood.

"Brazil?" repeated Maud. They were holed up in their old nursery, surrounded by the toys of their childhood. It was at the top of the house, so they couldn't be overheard.

"We're unlikely to go through with it," said Gaunt. "You know Elly, he's fickle."

"Not about you," said Maud.

Gaunt picked up a train set he had received for his tenth birthday.

"For all I know, he's playing the same games he always did," he said.

"Won't you miss Europe if you leave?"

"I doubt it will come to that," he said. "I imagine both Brazil and I will have lost our charms for Ellwood by the time the War is over."

Maud leant her head against the roof of her old dollhouse.

"Maybe not," she said.

Gaunt crashed his train into her dollhouse drawing room. They were both occupied for a few minutes, making the dolls run away in terror amid a cacophony of crashing noises.

Laughing, Gaunt set the train down. Maud rearranged the doll furniture that he had scattered across the floor.

"I think," said Gaunt, watching her set the dollhouse to rights, "that if he gave me the smallest hope—I should wait forever."

Two days later, he received a letter from Ellwood.

Saturday 2nd September, 1916
Somewhere in France

Dear Henry,
    I'm not playing, either.

Yours, always,
Sidney

Evening Standard

No. 29,428.   LONDON, MONDAY NOVEMBER 11TH, 1918.   ONE PENNY.

END OF THE WAR

GERMANY SIGNS OUR TERMS & FIGHTING STOPPED AT 11 O'CLOCK TO-DAY.

ALLIES TRIUMPHANT.

FOCH AND LLOYD GEORGE TELL NEWS THAT SENT THE WORLD REJOICING.

The following historic announcement, which means that the world war has come to an end at last, was issued by Mr Lloyd George to the nation at 10.20 this morning:—
"THE ARMISTICE WAS SIGNED AT 5 a.m. THIS MORNING, AND ALL HOSTILITIES ARE TO CEASE ON ALL FRONTS AT 11 a.m. TO-DAY."

FULL ARMISTICE TERMS

EVACUATION TO THE RHINE AND BRIDGEHEADS FOR ALLIES.

U-BOATS TO SURRENDER.

GUNS HANDED OVER AND BATTLE SHIPS DISARMED.

REPATRIATING PRISONERS.

FORTY-FIVE

DECEMBER 1918—RIO DE JANEIRO, BRAZIL

ROSEVEARE'S UNCLE William Meyrick helped them find a house near the embassy. It was enormous, with marble floors and a verandah. Marmoset monkeys played in the garden by the swimming pool.

"You'll find your staff are very discreet," Meyrick told Ellwood. Ellwood felt his face flush under his mask, and wondered just how much Roseveare had told his uncle.

The mask was made of black silk and whalebone. It covered the left half of his face. He had had it made in London, when he returned briefly after the Armistice. With it, he felt charming again, new. People still looked at him, but he could choose to imagine they were thinking he was mysterious, rather than—whatever he was. He hated words like "deformed" or "disfigured," words that made him feel damaged.

Their positions at the embassy consisted largely of paperwork, long lunches, and cocktail parties. Gaunt was good at the paperwork, and Ellwood was good at the parties. Even here, people had read his poetry. It was gratifying to be praised for work he barely remembered doing. He had not written in over a year, but after the third or fourth party in which an ex-officer told him he had put words to his thoughts, Ellwood tentatively picked up a pen and began to write again.

They had been in Brazil for a little under three weeks when Ellwood received the telegram telling him of his mother's death.

They were on the verandah, drinking gin-and-tonics before heading out to an event at the U.S. Embassy. Ellwood read the telegram quickly, then threw it on the table and drained his drink.

Gaunt took the telegram.

They had been cautious around each other since they had been reunited. More than two years apart had made Ellwood question whether Gaunt still meant what he had said that day in St. Pancras Station. Yet here they were, sleeping together in the same bed every night. They did not make eye contact during sex, or talk about important things.

Gaunt read the telegram and put it back on the rosewood table.

"I'm sorry, Elly," he said. He and Maud had both caught the Spanish flu back in England. Gaunt hadn't told Ellwood he was sick until after he'd recovered, which would once have made Ellwood furious. But his anger was less predictable, now.

Ellwood watched the late-afternoon sunlight play on the surface of the pool.

"Will you ever call me Sidney, do you think?" he asked.

Gaunt checked to see if their butler, Luís, was near, which was ridiculous, because Luís brought them breakfast in bed every morning.

"I promised myself long ago that I should never call you that unless I was sure I could keep you," said Gaunt.

Everything felt rather fuzzy, as if Ellwood's brain needed to be cleaned.

"You can never keep anyone," he said.

"You know what I mean," said Gaunt.

Ellwood nodded.

"We ought to change for dinner," he said, rising from his chair.

"We don't have to go to that beastly dinner," said Gaunt. "Your mother . . ."

"Don't use my mother's death to get out of social obligations," spat Ellwood, fury swelling in him with the flickering speed of fire.

Gaunt stood, holding his hands out appealingly.

"I wasn't. Elly."

Ellwood had been unkind to his mother when he last saw her. Cold and standoffish. He had counted on having decades in which to learn how to love her again.

Gaunt stepped closer, took him by the waist, drew him near.

"Call me Sidney," said Ellwood.

"Sidney," said Gaunt, so quickly, as if he had been waiting years to say it. His hands went to Ellwood's face, the fingers creeping under the edge of Ellwood's mask. He pressed their foreheads together. "This means I'm keeping you," he added, his voice fierce with warning. As if it wasn't exactly what Ellwood wanted to hear.

Ellwood wished he could cry. He had an indistinct feeling of drought in his chest, as if nothing would grow inside him until he managed to spill tears. But his eyes remained dry.

"You can have me," he told Gaunt, and suddenly he couldn't breathe. He could only think of the awful remoteness with which he had said goodbye to his mother. Gaunt was saying something; he held Ellwood's head close and said the same word over and over, and it took Ellwood quite a while to realise it was just his name.

FORTY-SIX

APRIL 1919—RIO DE JANEIRO, BRAZIL

ELLWOOD WAS STILL SLEEPING, the scarred half of his face pressed into his pillow. His long eyelashes curled darkly against his cheek. Gaunt liked waking up before him, because it meant he could look at him freely, loving each constituent part.

Things had improved between them since the day Ellwood had asked him to call him Sidney. Before, Ellwood had been aggressively charming in public and simply aggressive in private. Now he occasionally fell into the old enchanted moods, when he was enraptured and poetic, even if he still never quoted anything. Each time, it was like a veil lifting, and Gaunt could scarcely breathe for the teeth-grinding fear that it would not last, that it was only the ghostly echo of who Ellwood used to be.

Ellwood loved Brazil. On weekends, he dragged Gaunt through the blazing streets, gasping and exclaiming. Within a month, he knew the names of all the trees.

"Skyflower," he said, one afternoon, as they strolled down a lush, shaded street. He plucked a purple flower and tucked it into Gaunt's buttonhole. Graceful, nimble, long-fingered, the same hands Gaunt had wanted on him since he was thirteen.

"Reminds me of foxglove," said Gaunt. He used to put foxgloves on the tips of all his fingers and run after Maud to scare her. Foxglove, clover, chestnuts. Conkers in autumn, and daffodils in spring. He dreamt of them, sometimes. He woke from these dreams in anguish, with nothing but the garish bougainvillea that crushed into their stifling-hot bedroom to comfort him.

And Ellwood, of course. Ellwood, who slept lightly, and always woke when Gaunt did, who pressed his nose into Gaunt's ear and murmured, "Just a dream, Henry."

Gaunt knew it was a dream. All England, filtering away like a lost memory.

"Skyflower's much nicer than foxglove," said Ellwood. "There. How handsome you are!"

Gaunt flicked Ellwood's remaining eyebrow.

"Gone blind in both eyes, have you?"

"No," said Ellwood, steadily. "I haven't."

Their most recurrent fight was about the War, which Ellwood claimed Gaunt had enjoyed.

"It *improved* you," he said one night, after a party at which Gaunt had managed not to be taciturn, and Ellwood had fluttered from one group of admirers to another, talking about poetry and England and foreign relations as if it were 1910.

"That's dangerous even to speak of," said Gaunt.

"It's true. It made a man out of you," said Ellwood.

"So what if it did?" said Gaunt. "It might have improved a million men. That wouldn't change the fact that it was a crime against humanity."

"Well, at least you had your chance to play at being Thucydides," said Ellwood. "Tell me, was that the highlight of your existence? Or was it lounging around a prison camp, in bed with Gideon Devi?"

"You're drunk, Elly."

"Call me Sidney."

"Sidney."

Their fights never lasted long. Ellwood always apologised, and Gaunt always forgave him.

. . .

Gaunt ran his fingers through Ellwood's hair, and Ellwood stirred slightly.

"Is it morning?" he mumbled.

"Mhm," said Gaunt.

"Appalling development," said Ellwood into his pillow.

There was a knock at the door.

"Come in," said Gaunt. Luís entered with breakfast on a tray. Ellwood sat up at the smell of coffee. "Thank you, Luís," said Gaunt.

"There was some post, sir," said Luís.

Ellwood groaned as he stretched.

"Don't read the papers on weekends, Henry, they're always so ghastly," he said.

Gaunt raised his eyebrows at Luís, whose lips turned up in what was almost a smile, although he would never have indulged in it fully. Luís was as professional as he was discreet.

"Put them on the bedside, please, Luís."

"Yes, sir," said Luís. He put the papers and a letter from Maud on the bedside and left with a small bow.

"Look, there's an issue of *The Preshutian*," said Gaunt.

"Does it have an Honour Roll, still?"

Although the War had ended almost six months ago, news of the dead continued to trickle through the school paper. Gaunt glanced at the front page without reading it.

"Yes."

"Don't let's look now, it's too depressing."

"After breakfast, then," said Gaunt, taking the silver letter-opener and ripping open the letter from Maud. "Have some bacon."

"I can't," said Ellwood. "I'm getting fat."

"You are *not* getting fat."

"Oh, well, I might some day. May as well start on the grapefruit now. Pass that coffee, won't you?"

Gaunt poured him some from the silver coffee pot and unfolded his letter.

Friday 28th March, 1919
Berlin

Dear Henry,

Thank you for the lovely book of Brazilian postcards. It looks like heaven.

You asked about Berlin. I won't lie to you, the situation here is bleak, and people are poorer than you can imagine. Winifred keeps asking me to come home—but the British government is desperate for women to leave! There are constant articles in the papers about how we all ought to move to the colonies and marry the men there, since there are too many of us "Surplus Women" in Britain. Winifred broke off her engagement, did I mention? Charles only sits on the sofa and drinks. It doesn't feel as if he came home from the War at all.

I've made my mind up not to marry. There isn't time; there's too much work to be done.

I have met the most interesting people through the Scientific-Humanitarian Committee. Our principal aim is to abolish Paragraph 175, a piece of imperial legislation criminalising homosexuality, and Dr Magnus Hirschfeld does the most marvellous research at the Institut für Sexualwissenschaft.

I tell you all this, although I know how uncomfortable it will make you, to show you that things are changing in Germany. The Weimar Republic is more open to progress than the governments of England and France. I know you miss Europe. I hope you miss me. I cannot say whether Paragraph 175 will be revoked this year, or this decade, but I can tell you that there is a world for you and Sidney here. There has never been a movement like this before.

Come <u>home</u>—you are wanted.

Love,
Maud

"Well? How is she?" asked Ellwood. "You look awfully serious." Gaunt lowered the letter.

"She's well," he said blankly.

Ellwood loved Brazil, but Gaunt couldn't. He thought it beautiful—he admired it—but it filled him with yearning. He continually reminded himself that Thucydides, too, had been exiled, but nothing could lessen the grief he felt in the strangest places: in the shops, when they did not sell the tea he liked; or when it rained, and the rain was nothing like the cold, thin drizzle he knew and loved. He missed England as if it were a *person*. Germany was not England, but it was *closer*, and if Maud was right—if changes were happening in Germany—might the wave of progress not reach England, too? Could he help to spread it?

Ellwood wrapped his hands around his cup and sighed happily.

"You were watching me sleep again," he said.

"Do you mind?"

"No, I like it," said Ellwood.

Gaunt kissed him gently on the lips.

"Maud says things are changing in Germany."

Ellwood stilled.

"Oh? Pass me my mask, would you?"

"I like you without it," said Gaunt, handing it to him. Ellwood gave a small laugh and wrapped the mask's ribbon around his fingers without putting it on.

"What kind of change?" he asked. Gaunt showed him the letter. Ellwood read it slowly.

"Well," he said, folding it without looking at Gaunt. "Perhaps you'd better go, then."

They had fought terribly about Ellwood's mother's funeral. Ellwood had refused to return to England, no matter how much Gaunt told him he would regret it.

"Don't be absurd," said Gaunt, reaching for Maud's letter. "I wouldn't go without you."

Ellwood nodded to himself.

"Yes," he said. "And you know that I always do what you tell me to. But would you do the same for me? What if I asked you to stay here?"

He looked so small. He would not meet Gaunt's eye. Gaunt took Ellwood's chin in his hand and made him look at him.

"Then I'd stay," said Gaunt. "Are you asking me to stay?"

"Are you asking me to go?"

Gaunt traced Ellwood's right eyebrow with his thumb.

"I don't know," he said, honestly.

"You would really stay here if I asked?" said Ellwood.

"Yes," said Gaunt.

Ellwood frowned at the mask in his hands.

"Then . . ." he said. "Then I'm asking. Will you stay here. With me."

It would be cool, now, in England. In Munich, too. It would be cool; that pale season when the earth woke slowly from the dead.

There was no spring in Brazil.

Ellwood tipped his face out of Gaunt's hand.

"It's all right," said Ellwood. "I shouldn't have asked."

Hayes had remarried. Gaunt and Ellwood had gone to the wedding. He didn't write to them often. Gideon Devi and Archie Pritchard both lived in London. They wrote Gaunt letters about the strange parties they went to, about the recklessness of the eighteen-year-olds who had just missed the War—untarnished, youthful revellers, intolerant of those who had been foolish enough to fight.

But there was almost no one left to write Ellwood letters.

"Yes," said Gaunt. Ellwood had been in the process of tying his mask on. His hands paused when Gaunt spoke.

"What do you mean, yes?" he asked.

"Yes, I'll stay. As long as you like. Forever, if you want."

Ellwood stared at him, his remaining eye stretched wide in disbelief. Then his face broke out into a smile that was so simple and happy it made him look his age—only twenty-one.

"You mean it," he said. Gaunt reached out and took off the mask. He kissed the scar where Ellwood's eye used to be.

"I love you," he said.

Self-reproach clouded Ellwood's lovely face.

"Henry, I . . . you know that I . . . I . . ."

Gaunt knew Ellwood would probably never love him again. He had accepted it long ago.

"It's fine, Elly," he said. "I understand."

Ellwood grimaced and shook his head, clearly frustrated.

"No, Henry, I," he said, "I—'I cannot heave my heart into my mouth.'"

Gaunt stared at him. Ellwood looked just as shocked as he was.

"Shakespeare," said Ellwood. *"King Lear."*

Gaunt put his arm around Ellwood's shoulders and drew him close, his chest swelling greedily with joy, with *hope*. He kissed the top of Ellwood's head.

"There," he said. "It's a start."

THE PRESHUTIAN

VOL. LIV.—No. 795.   MARCH 31ST, 1919.   Price 6d.

⁀ROLL OF HONOUR⁀

Hughes, Lieutenant Henry Philip, Lancashire Fusiliers,
of pneumonia, following influenza, contracted on active service, aged 29.

Rhys-Pryce, Lieutenant Peter Francis, London Regiment,
of pneumonia, following influenza, contracted on active service, aged 22.

In Memoriam.

CAPTAIN CYRIL MILTON ROSEVEARE

Killed in action around November 10th, 1918, aged 20.
So passes the last of the three Roseveare brothers, all Head Boys, all dead for their Country. How can I explain Cyril to those who had the misfortune not to know him? He was a brave soldier, mentioned twice in dispatches, a fearless commander, a noble British officer. But I am not thinking of Captain Roseveare. I am thinking of Cyril, who was quiet and kind and steady. Cyril, whose loyalty to his friends knew no bounds, who was thorough and conscientious. He did not express his feelings often, but they were strong. I know the desperate grief he felt when first his brother Clarence, and then his brother Martin, fell in battle. The three Roseveare boys were very close, and each blow was felt intensely by the family. I cannot imagine the sorrow and pride that must be felt by his stricken parents, and by his young widow, Lillian Roseveare, only 20 years old. Despite his popularity, his memorial service was but poorly attended, for his friends have all gone before him.

It is a tragedy to lose Cyril, but it is especially bitter to know that he was most likely killed the day before the Armistice. Had he lived but one day more, I might have had my friend at my side again.

Only one thought can comfort, and that is that he died, not for war, but for peace. After the calamity of the past four years, we look to the future with hope, determined to make Cyril's sacrifice, and that of a thousand others, count towards a lasting harmony in Europe. Let us, like the soldiers of Waterloo, have our century of peace and prosperity, for we have paid for it in blood.

—L. M. GRIMSEY

ACKNOWLEDGEMENTS

I am forever grateful to Anna Stein for being the kind of agent every writer dreams of. Thank you to her assistant, Julie Flanagan, to my U.K. agent, Sophie Lambert, and to Claire Nozieres and Grace Robinson, who were in charge of foreign rights. All of them have improved my life immeasurably. I am also so lucky to have had Will Watkins to guide me through selling the film rights.

I would never have known any of these wonderful people if it weren't for John Burnham, who plucked me out of obscurity with the most exciting phone call of my life.

I am indebted to my U.S. and U.K. editors, Diana Tejerina Miller and Isabel Wall. I thought the book was done—I was wrong! Their careful, methodical edits made a profound difference to the book. I'm grateful to have worked with the kinds of editors who not only improve the book, but also how you write. Thank you also to Chloe Davies at Viking for her unwavering support, Vanessa Haughton for all her help and the teams at Knopf and Viking for being so good at their jobs. A special thanks to Maggie Hinders and the design team—the newspapers were a logistical nightmare from start to finish, but they are such an integral part of the book and it has been incredible seeing them come to life.

My writing has been shaped and crafted by my brilliant, rigorous friends, most of whom read not only this book but the three unpublished novels before it: Sylvia Bishop, Lizzy Christman, Mik Clements,

Chesca Forristal, Clara Mamet, Adam Mastroianni, Nicola Phillips, Ed Scrivens, Zander Sharp, Julia Wald, Melisa Wallack and Yael van der Wouden. Without their faith and hard work, I would never have been capable of writing a book about something as huge as World War I. I am similarly grateful to my readers online, who encouraged me and taught me so much, so painlessly. Thank you also to Julie Oh, Laurie Christman, Nita Krevans, Ellie Darkins and Aimee Liu for their kind words and encouragement; to Greg Berlanti, Mike McGrath, Robbie Rogers and Sarah Schechter for their belief in me; and to Theo Hodson, Archie Cornish and Zander Sharp for lengthy interviews about boarding school.

Throughout writing, I was constantly grateful to Marlborough College for putting so much amazing archive material online. Anyone who knows Marlborough will see how it impacted the writing of this novel. I hope my old housemaster, Tim Marvin, and people who were at Preshute with me will forgive the use of the name.

I have been fortunate enough to have a long list of wonderful English teachers, but two come to mind when I think of this book. James Taylor introduced me to *Journey's End* when I was thirteen. It remains one of my favourite plays to this day because of how vividly he taught it. Dr. Simon McKeown was a wonderful English teacher at Marlborough, and helped me get in touch with the college archivist, Gráinne Lenehan, who sent me everything I needed to map out Siegfried Sassoon's time at Marlborough. This was an early inspiration for the book.

I had help with the German and Greek: my sister-in-law Franzi Winn kindly went over my German one hectic Christmas, and the Greek was checked by both Dr. Alicia Ejsmond-Müller and Dr. Brook Manville. Thank you also to Patrick Stérin, Jean-Paul Deshayes and Laurence and Alain Kergall for checking my French. Any mistakes are my own!

Thanks to my siblings and in-laws, who tolerated my many tiresome monologues about the War, the Great War, the War of 1914.

My father has supported me in my writing with a tenacious belief that is as touching as it is irrational. But what a kindness to believe in a child unconditionally!

When I was a child, my mother used to take me to war cemeteries and cry. She read me Edwardian children's books and would pause midsentence to tell me that all the boys would inevitably be killed in the trenches. She taught me Greek mythology, Chinese history, the lives of the English kings; she read me poetry and guided me through her enormous library of classic literature. She was, and remains, my first and most important teacher.

Finally, my husband, Chris: without whom I would probably still be telling people at parties that One Day I'd Like To Write A Novel. He listened to my ambitions and forced me to realise them. He listened (unwillingly) to my lengthy, mournful speeches about horrible war literature. He read the first draft of the first chapter and said, "I think this will be good." He built our life so that I would have time to read and write, even though I thought this was an indulgence. Thank you so much.

HISTORICAL NOTE

In Memoriam is indebted to dozens of primary accounts of the war.

The Preshutian is based on the Marlborough College newspaper from 1913 to 1919. I tried to get across the atmosphere of the paper, but I also lifted directly in places, especially when detailing front-line deaths.

The first paper features elements of different editions of the *Marlburian*. The debate, "This House declines to believe in the existence of ghosts", was taken from the April 1914 edition. Ellwood's poem is a close paraphrase of "Evening at Marlborough College" by W. P., in the March 1914 edition.

Cuthbert-Smith's "In Memoriam" was a combination of a few different "In Memoriams". T. G. Meautys, in the November 1914 edition, who was shot in the stomach and died in a cave that was being used in a hospital: "He died a soldier's death on the field of honour. He was a very gallant fellow . . . They had never seen such bravery—it was marvellous!" Captain E. K. Bradbury's "In Memoriam" in the October 1914 edition: "He first had a hip and one leg shot away, and still managed to fire off a round or two more, until the other leg was taken off just above the knee. The doctor who told me about it afterwards said that all he asked for was heaps of morphia, so that the men should not hear him screaming, and that he might be taken quickly to the rear. The whole story is that 'Brad' died as one felt he would do." Harold Roseveare's

"In Memoriam" from the November 1914 edition: "Marlborough has suffered many blows since the outbreak of the war, but perhaps the hardest is the news of the death of one who left us only at the close of last term, who but two months before had been an essential part of the College . . . In all our sorrow, we cannot but envy him. All too short though it was, his life, if any can, can truthfully be said to have touched perfection . . . A happier boy one cannot imagine—happier still in realising his ambition, in dying as he did a true soldier's death."

Clarence Roseveare's "In Memoriam" was a combination of a few different "In Memoriams". H. G. Morris' "In Memoriam" in the May 1915 edition: "He came past me with a very cheerful face, and laughing, under a very hearty cross-fire from machine guns, and sang out to me, 'Shall I push on?' and I answered, 'Go on, laddie, as hard as you can.' Poor lad, I did not see him again, but heard he was shot in the head, but he would not let anyone stay with him. He was such a good boy, always cheerful and always ready to do anything that was wanted. He was very popular with everyone—officers and men." Bryant McClenaghan's "In Memoriam" in the July 1915 edition: "I regret to say that Bryant was killed yesterday in an attack we made on the German trenches . . . he was rallying some men at the time, when he was shot through the heart. I placed him in a trench, hoping that the wound would not be fatal. The only words to me were, 'Don't mind me'. . . When I saw him a quarter of an hour later he had died a very gallant death at the head of his Company, and the men are very sad to have lost him, as he was extremely popular among the men. I need hardly say how sorry the officers are. He was the cheeriest and most popular subaltern among us and he was my best friend in the regiment."

Ellwood, Gaunt and Maud were partly inspired by certain characteristics in Siegfried Sassoon, Robert Graves and Vera Brittain respectively, although they are wholly fictional, and quite different in personality from the historical figures mentioned.

While I named Cyril and his brothers the Roseveares, they are in fact based on the Woodroffe brothers (Sidney, Leslie and Kenneth) who were all three Marlborough Senior Prefects, and all three killed in the war, one by one. (Sidney Woodroffe won a VC) Harold Roseveare ("In Memoriam" seen above) was a contemporary and friend of the three Woodroffe brothers, and their names appear constantly in the papers while they were at school, for example in cricket matches.

I lowered the ages of the dead in the newspapers. I wanted to get across the sensation evoked by writers like Robert Graves and Vera Brittain of a whole generation of young men wiped out. In the *Marlburian*, while most of the dead are in their twenties, there are also plenty in their thirties and a few in their forties.

Almost all names of Preshute boys in the novel were taken from editions of the *Marlburian*, although I tended to avoid using lists of the dead and chose instead from, for example, cricket teams.

Lists of the dead in the *Preshutian* are scrambled versions of lists of the dead from the *Marlburian*. This is particularly notable in the newspaper following the Battle of the Somme. For this, I went through four editions and counted up every man who died on July 1st, 1916. In reality, the news of the dead was spread across several months as reports trickled in; I put them all into one edition for effect.

In the novel, I give the impression that the school newspaper is how most boys find out about the dead. In reality, those close to the deceased would likely receive a telegram, and *The Times* would report casualties faster than a school newspaper.

In one of Ellwood's letters, he quotes the glorious "In Memoriam" of Lieut. Dods. This was lifted from a letter from the front in the October 1914 edition of the *Marlburian*, recounting the deeds of M. J. W. O'Donovan, who survived the war—although his younger brother was killed in 1916, at the age of twenty.

To ensure that the "In Memoriams" of previously unintroduced characters after the Battle of the Somme felt real and poignant, I wrote them about my friends. I had planned to write as many "In Memoriams" as there were dead but found the exercise too disturbing to continue.

Lawrence Archibald Long's "In Memoriam" included a quotation from the November 2nd, 1915 edition of the *Marlburian*, from the "In Memoriam" of Norman Douglas Stewart Bruce Lockhart: "'He died instantaneously; he got a bullet in his throat, and as he fell he shouted, "Go on boys." He was one of the best subalterns I ever had' . . . 'I particularly noticed him leading his men in what was really a storm of shot and shell, and the wonder was how any of them came out of it alive.' As a matter of fact, every officer in the regiment was hit."

Richard Alexander Yule's "In Memoriam" included a quotation from the November 24th, 1915 edition of the *Marlburian*, from the "In

Memoriam" of C. W. M. White: "There was a man ten yards behind him, wounded in the stomach, and your son turned round and shouted, 'For God's sake, man, don't drink that water!' and, as he turned his head forward again, he was shot in the middle of the forehead. He lived for eighteen hours and was never conscious again."

The war announcement on p. ix of the novel is a reformatted version of the real announcement as it was made in the *London Gazette*, Tuesday 4th August, 1914.

In one of Ellwood's letters he mentions a teacher saying Britain will be galvanised into a twentieth-century Renaissance by the war. This is an allusion to the moment in Alec Waugh's *The Loom of Youth* (1917) when war is declared, and the protagonist's teacher exclaims:

> "Glorious! Glorious!" said Ferrers, as they staggered out into the cool night air. "A war is what we want. It will wake us up from sleeping; stir us into life; inflame our literature. There's a real chance now of sweeping away the old outworn traditions. In a great fire they will all be burnt. Then we can build afresh. I wish I could go and fight . . . This war is going to save England and everything! Glorious!"

The plotline of Caruthers and Sandys was inspired by two sources: Alec Waugh's *The Loom of Youth* (1917) and the death of Vera Brittain's brother, Edward.

The tone of the section in which Ellwood first joins Gaunt at the front, as well as the scene in which Gaunt and Ellwood are sent to capture a German after the Battle of Loos, are both indebted to R. C. Sherriff's *Journey's End* (1929).

The men fishing with explosives comes from Ernst Jünger's invaluable *Storm of Steel* (1920). Jünger also provided the bulk of the deaths and injuries of the novel.

In the section in which countless officers are killed or injured in Ellwood's company, I reference the writer Saki's infamous last words in 1916, which allegedly were "Put that bloody cigarette out!" moments before he was killed by a German sniper.

Crawley's death by suicide drew on Siegfried Sassoon's poem "Suicide in the Trenches" (1918).

The conversation between Ellwood and the bloodthirsty Lansing is a paraphrase of one of Sassoon's most savage poems in its prepublished form (it was defanged in publication), "Atrocities" (1919).

The tunnelling affair is heavily based on the Holzminden prison escape (a detailed account of which can be found in H. G. Durnford's *The Tunnellers of Holzminden*, 1920), but general life in the prison, other escape attempts, and the train escape are all based on A. J. Evans' wonderful *The Escaping Club* (1921). This book was such a huge influence on the prisoner-of-war section that I named a character after the author—Evans. Almost all specifics are lifted directly from or inspired by the account Evans gives in this fantastic book. (To temper this recommendation I will also note that Evans is racist towards the Turks, and generally xenophobic.)

Gideon Devi was inspired by Erroll Chunder Sen, a key figure in the Holzminden prison escape. He was an Indian RFC pilot and was in the Holzminden tunnel when it collapsed.

Maud's headmistress's speech is taken from a speech given by the senior mistress of Bournemouth High School for Girls in 1917. It is something of an anachronism to insert this before the Battle of the Somme, which is when people began to understand the scale of the attrition. The war left over a million "Surplus Women" who never married. Virginia Nicholson explores this phenomenon in her fascinating book *Singled Out: How Two Million British Women Survived Without Men After the First World War* (2008).

A company of the East Surrey Regiment was given several footballs to kick across No Man's Land on July 1st, 1916, at the Battle of the Somme by their captain, Wilfred Nevill. Nevill was killed, but one football did reach the German trench. The story became so famous that it was perhaps a bit much to use the anecdote for Ellwood and the fictional Royal Kennet Fusiliers.

Archie Pritchard's reaction to his brother's death alludes to Sassoon's "To Any Dead Officer" (1918).

The conversation Gaunt and Ellwood have at the end of the novel about the war having improved Gaunt stems from Robert Nichols' introduction to Sassoon's *Counter-Attack and Other Poems* (1918).

He just wanted a decent book to read ...

Not too much to ask, is it? It was in 1935 when Allen Lane, Managing
Director of Bodley Head Publishers, stood on a platform at Exeter railway
station looking for something good to read on his journey back to London.
His choice was limited to popular magazines and poor-quality paperbacks –
the same choice faced every day by the vast majority of readers, few of
whom could afford hardbacks. Lane's disappointment and subsequent anger
at the range of books generally available led him to found a company – and
change the world.

*'We believed in the existence in this country of a vast reading public for intelligent
books at a low price, and staked everything on it'*
Sir Allen Lane, 1902–1970, founder of Penguin Books

The quality paperback had arrived – and not just in bookshops. Lane was
adamant that his Penguins should appear in chain stores and tobacconists,
and should cost no more than a packet of cigarettes.

Reading habits (and cigarette prices) have changed since 1935, but
Penguin still believes in publishing the best books for everybody to
enjoy. We still believe that good design costs no more than bad design,
and we still believe that quality books published passionately and responsibly
make the world a better place.

So wherever you see the little bird – whether it's on a piece of
prize-winning literary fiction or a celebrity autobiography, political tour
de force or historical masterpiece, a serial-killer thriller, reference book,
world classic or a piece of pure escapism – you can bet that it represents
the very best that the genre has to offer.

Whatever you like to read – trust Penguin.